Serendipity

Lisa Clark O'Neill

Copyright 2012

WITHDRAWN

CHAPTER ONE

AVA Martinez tried everything short of setting the unconscious man's pants on fire to get him to wake up.

It was a damn shame she didn't have a match.

Shaking him hadn't worked. Nor had slapping, poking, hair-yanking, begging or kissing him on his very fine mouth. Fighting panic, she looked at the cup in her hand with desperation. The frigid water from the bottom of the ice machine appeared to be her last hope.

She knew he wasn't dead – yet – because his broad chest rose and fell beneath his torn oxford-cloth shirt. But dishabille was the least of his problems. When she'd pulled the hair-yanking thing out of her bag of tricks, she'd felt the sticky, golf ball-sized lump erupting from his disordered mop of dark curls.

At least the bleeding appeared to have stopped, which meant he probably wasn't in danger of dying before she got him out of the stupid trunk.

If she got him out. With all the luck she was having, the sucker's chances weren't looking too good.

Frustrated, Ava wiped her damp palm on her linen pants before remembering it was covered in blood.

"Buddy." She glared at the inert form stuffed like a sausage into the Impala's casing. "No offense, but I'm starting to wish I'd stayed home tonight."

She shuddered to think of why she hadn't. Summoned to her uncle's club – a dressed-up titty bar that called itself a "gentleman's club," though judging from what went on in those back rooms, she figured it was anything but – Ava had been reaching for the back door handle when she overheard the club's manager, Ricardo, cursing out a pair of Uncle Carlos's goons. His voice rose over the nocturnal din of frogs and the cheesy music pulsing through the blackened window, explaining how the goons were idiots because they'd somehow kidnapped the wrong man.

Ava couldn't say she blamed him. U.S. attorney Stephen Finch – the man they were apparently supposed to have shanghaied – was about five-eight, one hundred and fifty pounds, and the color of an espresso bean.

The man bleeding all over the trunk of the goons' car was a six feet plus Caucasian, and pushing two hundred pounds if he was an ounce. Ava had the backache to prove it. But wrong man or not, she knew for a fact what was going to happen if she didn't get him moving.

Her uncle's men were going to kill him anyway.

It was difficult to believe Carlos had attempted to kidnap the prosecutor in charge of her father's case. The sonofabitch thought he was untouchable, but this was ballsy, even for him.

But then what was a little kidnapping and murder when you already operated one of the biggest crime syndicates in the South?

Shoving aside her angry thoughts, Ava glanced back at the unconscious stranger. Regardless of who he was, he was dead if she didn't move him. So she picked up the cup, tossed the icy water in his face, mentally saying a prayer as she held her breath.

Relief jellied her legs when his wet lashes fluttered. He squinted against the light and certain pain – not to mention the freezing water – before shifting his gaze toward her.

And Ava felt like she was the one who'd been doused. Even in the dim light, the guy's eyes were stunning. The color of those blue flowers – what the hell were they called? – that grew alongside the road in summer.

She found herself staring, fascinated, until common sense kicked in.

The frogs had grown louder.

The frogs had grown louder, because the angry voices from inside the club had quieted down. Figuring it was only a matter of time before the goons spilled back out like deranged monkeys from a barrel, Ava forgot about his eyes, wrapping her hands around his arms to urge the bulk of him up.

"Come on, buddy." Frustration gave way to urgency. "You've got to help me out a little. I can't move you all by myself. Believe me, I've tried."

He sat up, hit his head, and fell flat on his back.

"Oh no, you don't." Ava jerked his arm. "You've already ruined my best pair of pants and just about put me in traction. The least you can do is haul your butt out of this damn trunk."

She threw a worried glance over her shoulder. "Sit up, and watch your head. If you knock yourself out again, I'm leaving you on your own."

"Sure. Fine," he slurred. "Do you think you could stop clawing me now?"

He moved like wet cement, but Ava lessened her hold. "Now how about trying to stand? You can lean on me if you have to." Though if he stumbled, they were both going down. Seeing as how he was built like a water buffalo, gravity wasn't working in their favor.

"Your nails are too long."

"What?"

"I said your nails are too long. You scratched my arm." He hefted his limb to show her three red gouges beneath his rolled sleeve.

"Yeah well, that's the least of your worries. If you don't get yourself out of that trunk soon, something a hell of a lot sharper is going to be scratching you. The goons in there have a penchant for blades, and you've got plenty of square footage to carve on. This is the last time I'm going to tell you. You need to haul ass."

"Where's my shoe?"

"What?"

"My shoe," he repeated, pointing toward the huge sock-clad foot dangling against the license plate's chain holder.

Ava didn't waste the time to tell him it wasn't important. She simply looked through the fat curls of fog creeping like fingers over the asphalt, finally spotting it lying drunkenly against the vintage Chevy's back tire. "Here." She scooped it up. "It must have come off when I tried to drag you out of there."

"You tried to drag me out of here?"

Her patience with his lack of comprehension was all used up. "What do you think I've been doing for the past ten minutes? Now pay attention." She clapped her hands, hating the fact that they'd started to shake. "Either you get out of that trunk and into my car, or the men who hit you over the head and roughed you up are going to come back here and finish the job. And believe me, you'll wish they hit you hard enough to kill you the first time. So please." She swallowed, hard. "Hurry."

Ava wedged herself under his shoulder to help ease him to his feet, and he draped himself around her. They wobbled, Ava cursing the vanity that consistently provoked her into wearing three-inch heels, but managed to shamble forward.

Until he touched the knot on his head, drawing them both to a stop. "I'm bleeding."

"No kidding." She used her hip to shove him forward, not unlike a large and unwieldy chest of drawers. He half climbed, half fell through the open passenger door, and she crammed his right leg in.

"Ouch!" He shot her some irritation when she slid quickly into the driver's seat. "What's going on?"

Ava didn't bother answering him. She was entirely too focused on putting as much distance between them and that parking lot as humanly possible. Luckily, the music coming from inside the club was loud, so Ricardo and the goons probably hadn't heard her peal out.

Probably.

"Was there an accident?"

"You could say that." Ava flicked a glance at her rearview mirror to make sure they weren't being followed. No goons running out of the building, no Impala on her tail. When she caught the guy staring at her she shook her dark hair to form a curtain, not wanting him to get a good look at her face. Temporarily stymied, he leaned back and closed his eyes.

And proceeded to bleed all over the headrest.

"Did you see what happened to my car?"

Resigned to spending the next day cleaning the evidence from her passenger seat, Ava shook her head. She had no idea where his car was, or what condition it might be in, so she kept her gaze focused on the climb over the bridge. The lights of Savannah shimmered through the veil of mist shrouding the river, the gold dome of City Hall the shining crown of the Hostess City.

Her city. And she'd be damned if she let her uncle ruin this one for her, too.

"Is it totaled?" Her passenger managed to stir himself to ask. "Damn it, the thing's brand new."

He sounded miserable, but Ava wasn't about to correct his misinterpretation. The less he knew, the better. She detoured off the interstate, taking a circuitous route to the hospital. If they were caught it would spell a heap of trouble for her, and certain death for him.

Ava slid a glance his direction. It appeared he'd passed out again, which truth be told was fine by her. Better if he didn't remember one thing about the night's misadventure.

In a quick blink, he opened his truly amazing eyes. Remembering that she didn't want him to get a good look at her face, she turned her attention back to the road.

"You're not injured, are you?"

"What?"

"In the accident," he explained. "You weren't injured, were you? Did I hit your car?"

She wanted to point out that they were driving her car, but the poor guy obviously wasn't firing on all cylinders. "I'm fine."

"That's good."

Since he was no longer looking at her, Ava snuck another glance. The man was damn easy on the eyes. His wife would certainly be happy that she'd saved him. She took a hasty peek at his ring finger. No wedding band. Well, his girlfriend would be happy. Or boyfriend, for that matter.

"Where are we going?"

Jerking her eyes away from his hand, Ava returned her focus to the darkened street. Gas flame streetlights pushed back the worst of the fog to boil in the shadows of time-worn buildings, and Spanish moss dripped like loose skin from the gnarled limbs of ancient oaks.

A pair of headlights appeared in her rearview mirror, making her nerves jump like Mexican beans.

Controlling a shiver, she cast another quick glance at her passenger. "I'm taking you to the hospital. Someone needs to take a look at your head." Given his slurred speech, the way he'd moved like he was walking through molasses, she was fairly certain he had a concussion.

"I think I might get sick."

Concussion symptom three. "Not in my car, you won't." She reached into the back seat, grabbing the paper sack of fruit she'd bought from a roadside stand. "Here."

He peered at a melon. "I'm not really hungry."

"Use the bag." And her tone added *moron* before she had a chance to think how unfair that was. "If you feel like you're going to be sick, dump the fruit out and use the bag."

He clutched it between his large hands, then subsided against the headrest. The car behind her turned off, and Ava's jittering nerves flashed back to anger. It wasn't like her uncle hadn't done similar shit before. But she'd made it pretty clear to her father that she wanted no part of that life.

He'd understood completely, which was why she was so surprised when she heeded Ricardo's call, inadvertently stumbling into her current mess. Either her father had lied to her, or he didn't know what his brother was up to. Both thoughts infuriated her. How was she supposed to lead a normal life, when her family conspired against her? But this was it, Ava assured herself. No more.

Once she got this man out of her car, she was through playing her uncle's games.

The emergency room appeared like a glowing beehive through the fog, buzzing with people and activity, and relief crumpled her shoulders. She turned to her passenger and nudged him. "Okay, Blue Eyes. Ride's over."

She pulled as close as possible without being seen – God help her if someone identified her to the police – and then leaned across his lap to release the handle. She didn't dare get out of the car. There was bound to be an investigation, and she wanted no part of that. As her uncle once coldly informed her, "The only good witness is a dead one." It wouldn't matter that she happened to be his niece.

He'd never had much use for her or her mother anyway.

"You need to move." Ava pushed the door open, and when he didn't go fast enough to suit her, put her heels to his hip and shoved. A couple of peaches tumbled out right along with him, but she couldn't worry about that now. She needed to get out of there, swing by her place and change, and then hightail it back to the club. Ricardo would be waiting. Even though he was her father's friend, he still worked for her uncle, and that was a relationship not to be trusted.

One last conversation to cover her butt, and then she was through with her uncle for good.

Noticing the man's shoe sitting forlornly on the passenger seat, she tossed it from the car.

"Sorry," she barked when it smacked him in the chest, and he lifted his head to glare.

Well, she'd done what she could. And really, did it matter if he thought her a crazy bitch? It wasn't like she'd ever see the man again.

CHAPTER TWO

AFTERNOON sun poured into the room, brightening the institutional green walls to an almost tolerable shade of mint. Jordan Wellington squinted, watching dust motes stirred to life by the AC unit humming beneath the window.

"He lives."

Jordan turned toward the familiar voice. Wiping the haze of drug-induced sleep from his eyes, he located his brother's long form sprawled in a bedside chair. Jesse's bark brown hair stuck up at random intervals where he'd been running his fingers through it, and summer blue eyes – their mother's eyes – peered over horn-rimmed glasses.

Jesse tossed aside an old issue of Newsweek. "How's your head?"

Jordan raised a hand to his scalp. The shaved, raised lump wasn't nearly as off-putting as the stitches. The thought of a needle flashing through his skin made his stomach do a short, hard roll. "Just super."

"And that hairdo sure is pretty. Adds just the right touch to your backless gown."

"Makes it easier for you to kiss my ass."

"Now, now. That's no way to talk to the sibling who spared you the Wrath of Mom."

"Oh, hell." Jordan's queasy stomach sank straight to his toes. "Tell me they didn't call her cell phone."

"Well, at least that bump didn't ruin your deductive reasoning." Jesse sat up, stretched, and brushed his knuckles against the Savannah Sand Gnats logo on his T-shirt. "You can thank my incomparable negotiation skills for the fact that she's still in Florida."

Their parents were visiting Disney with their brother Jack and his family, and that's where Jordan wanted them to stay. The accident, the hospital, the damn backless gown – all of that was bad enough without ruining his family's vacation. He might not remember much of what happened, but he knew it wasn't pretty. "Was anyone else injured last night?"

Jesse's brow shot up. "Not that I know of."

"Thank God for that." Jordan let out the breath he hadn't realized he'd been holding. "What about my car?"

"What about it?"

"Is it totaled?"

"No." The dark brows crept lower until they gathered just above his glasses. "Your car's fine, Jordan. What exactly do you think happened?"

"Honest to God, Jesse, I don't know. I don't even remember getting behind the wheel. I just… what do you mean, my car's fine?"

"You think you were in an accident?"

Jordan hesitated. "Maybe you should tell me."

Jesse took a moment to study his hands, and when they bunched Jordan's stomach churned again. He hid it well, but his brother was angry. "Well, from what the police have been able to gather, someone used your head for a whipping post, took you for a little joy ride, then dropped you off for a visit. A couple of EMTs found you lying outside the ER."

"What?"

"Just telling you what I heard. I know you ADAs have regular fan clubs, but you piss off any particular defendants recently? Maybe prosecute a gang member?"

"I…" Jordan scrubbed a hand over his face and tried to think. "Hell, Jesse. I piss off defendants every day. And besides, you know I've been wrapped up in the Fuller case for the past couple months. A media shitstorm like that is bound to bring out the crazies."

Elijah Fuller was the man indicted for the brutal murders of three Savannah women. When the lead prosecutor had been forced to step down due to health concerns, Jordan was tapped to take over. Professionally, his career went into overdrive, but on a personal level Jordan seemed to be stuck in neutral. Not only did he hate the limelight, but he'd grown uncomfortable with the whole case. The evidence, though more circumstantial than concrete, seemed to prove they'd indicted the right man, but as Jordan delved deeper into trial preparations, he unearthed more doubt than assurance.

However, this wasn't the time or the place to get into that with his brother. He had more immediate concerns.

"Do you remember anything from last night at all?" Jesse asked.

Jordan tried to clear his head. Bits and fragments of memories floated around like flotsam from a shipwreck. "Only pieces," he admitted. Absently scratching at the tape holding his IV – he tried not to think of the needle – Jordan looked down when he felt the welts.

He remembered the rake of long nails, a flash of dark hair. "I… hell. I think there was a woman."

"There usually is."

"Ha. I mean during the… if I say assault now I'm going to feel like a douche. But yeah, I think a woman was involved. See? She scratched my arm with her nails."

"When was this?" Jesse examined the marks with a frown. "Before you were hit?"

"I…" Man, he wasn't quite sure. "I don't think so. Seems to me it was after. She was pulling at me, and her nails dug into my arms. Everything was… sort of surreal. But I know she wanted me to get in her car. My head felt like a bowling pin, and when I grabbed it my hand came away bloody. Had to have been after."

"Do you remember anything about her car?"

Jordan closed his eyes, tried to drum up a mental image. His head throbbed, but he knew his brother – and FBI agent – as well as whatever detectives might be assigned his case would want as many details as they could get. "Uh… red. I think. Small. A coupe, maybe." He pressed his fingers to the bridge of his nose. "I couldn't even hazard a guess as to make or model."

"I'm guessing a license plate number is too much to ask."

Jordan's half-lidded gaze said: get real. But there was something... "I think there was a chain around it. The plate." Though something still wasn't right. "Except, I don't think the chain was on her car. It –"

"Wait, wait." Jesse held up a hand, eyes sharpening like blue razors. "You're saying there was a second car involved?"

"I think so. Seems to me I must have been in the trunk of the second car. I felt the chain with my heel, and it made me wonder how I lost my shoe. The woman threw it at me when she kicked me out of her car. I thought it was damn rude."

"Kidnappers these days. They just don't have any manners."

"Yeah, yeah." Noticing the tray of food next to the bed, Jordan lifted the silver cover. "Did you eat my breakfast?"

"Believe me, I did you a favor. What were you doing at the Marriott on River Street? That's where they found your car."

"Ah, that." Jordan grimaced, pushing the remnants of something egg-like off to the side. "I got roped into giving a speech. Steve Finch phoned me a couple of days ago and called in a favor. He was scheduled to give a lecture to a group of bureaucrats about that joint task force we were on last year. Something came up last minute, so I was the stand in."

"So you were leaving that conference when you were attacked?"

"Sounds like. But honestly, I don't remember."

"Pretty common with an injury like yours. It might come back to you, it might not." Voices sounded in the hall, and Jesse climbed to his feet, ambling to the door to peer through the crack. "Looks like the detectives are back. Get ready to go through everything again." He turned, and his jaw was set. "I'll hold my tongue, because it's their jurisdiction. But make no mistake, little bro. From this point on, I've got your back."

CHAPTER THREE

THERE was a goon in Ava's parking lot. Heaven help her, she got so angry every time she looked through the window that she nearly howled like the dogs in her kennel.

Protection, her ass. Her uncle just wanted to intimidate her.

"Staring isn't going to make him go away, Dr. Martinez. Believe me, I've already tried."

Hands on hips, Ava turned toward her assistant. Auburn hair spilled from beneath a blue bandana as Katie's head popped up from behind the computer monitor, putting Ava in mind of a colorful jack in the box.

"What are you going to do?"

"I have no idea."

Abandoning her hunting-and-pecking, Katie came around the reception counter to join Ava at the window. "That guy's facial craters might warrant a visit from NASA."

Ava couldn't help but laugh. "I knew there was a reason I hired you, Katie."

"You mean other than the fact that I blew you away with my extensive knowledge of everything that walks on four legs, not to mention my outstanding public relations prowess and exceptional secretarial skills?"

"You barely knew how to turn on the computer."

"I'm getting better, aren't I?"

"Well you certainly couldn't have gotten any worse. But just for the record, One-Eyed Jack convinced me. Anyone who can give him a bath without losing their own eye deserves your meager salary."

"Nah, Jack's a sweetie." As if on cue, the aptly-named gray feline rubbed against Katie's long, long legs. He circled around her in a figure eight, giving Ava a wide berth. "I think he's still mad at you for that rabies shot."

"He'll get over it." Ava watched the cat jump onto the counter, where he flicked his tail to show how wrong she was.

"Homemade Sin out there is going to scare off all your business."

Ava turned back toward the window. The man *was* exceptionally ugly, all oily dark hair and pockmarked skin encased in a dirty wife beater. Chains of gold dripped like gilded sweat.

But more disturbing was the fact that she knew, without question, that he was also exceptionally ruthless. And she had no doubt as to why he'd been posted. Her uncle was giving her a warning. Talk to anyone, about anything, and I'll know it.

When she'd finally made it back to the club last night, the goons were gone – no doubt scrambling around trying to find the man who'd disappeared from their trunk – and Ricardo had been distracted. But he'd let her know that her loving uncle, worried about his only niece's safety during her father's upcoming trial, had ordered a security detail to see to her protection. Carlos was concerned about the associates of the man her father murdered seeking out Ava for reprisal.

Which was bullshit.

Her uncle just wanted to ensure that she stayed quiet during her father's trial. Unlike her father, Ava had no loyalty to Carlos, and the bastard knew it. Which was why he'd sicced his ugly dog.

"Bastard."

"Language," Katie said. "Do you really think he'll keep a tail on you twenty-four hours a day for the duration?"

"I don't know. Hopefully, once he realizes I'm not inclined to play footsies with the prosecution, he'll leave me alone. If it was his neck on the chopping block, I'd be standing over him with the axe, but I'm not about to do anything to hurt my father."

"Why don't you tell him that?"

"That would mean speaking directly to the man, which I haven't done in over a year and a half." Since her mother had disappeared.

Ava pressed her fingers to the pain that had begun to bang against her head like a nasty neighbor at the door. "I'm sorry, Katie. I never should have dumped this on you in the first place, but I felt it only fair you understood who you worked for. The severance package I offered still stands. I understand if you want to quit."

"You keep saying that, Dr. Martinez, and I'm afraid you and I will have words."

"Well I certainly wouldn't want to be subjected to this if I had a choice." Ava threw her hand away from her aching head.

"And for the last time, will you please stop calling me Dr. Martinez?"

"Not between nine a.m. to five p.m. Outside business hours: Ava."

Ava's eyes rolled. "Lord save me from propriety."

"You've just uttered a blasphemy against the Southern Ladies' Sacred Code of Conduct. I'm covering my ears. "Uh-oh." Her fingers flew to her lips instead. "Looks like Mrs. Phillips and her poodles just pulled in. The goon got out. He's leaning against his car."

Shit. Ava ducked out of sight. "Quick, tell me what's happening."

"Is the black or the white poodle Muffin?"

"Uh, the black one, I think."

"Well, Muffin is currently trying to choke herself off her leash. She looks like she wants to take a bite out of the goon's leg."

"Tell me he didn't pull a knife."

"No, but he looks pissed." Katie glared at Ava. "Now look what you've made me say."

"Oh, hush it, Katie. Update."

"Mrs. Phillips is trying to control Muffin, and the white one – what's its name? Biscuit? Well, the white one just had an accident all over the front of her dress. That dog always has been nervous. Oh, the goon looked directly at Mrs. Phillips. That should be enough to scare that awful perm right out of her hair." Katie allowed a moment of contemplation. "Maybe not such a bad thing."

She reached out a hand toward Ava. "Get up. She's coming, and she looks upset. You might want to go into the back. My people skills are better than yours."

"Don't you mean your ass-kissing skills?"

"There's that language again. Run along now, before I'm forced to get out my soap."

Ava couldn't make it in time. She'd only gotten as far as the counter when the spectacle at the front door stopped her. Despite Mrs. Phillips' considerable bulk, the woman could haul ass. Slap a saddle on her and she could have taken the Derby. The door flew open and she shot in, one poodle clutched to her breast, the other snapping and yanking against the tangle of hot pink leash around the woman's feet.

Eyes wide and white as a nervous mare's flew up to meet Ava's. "Dr. Martinez, I'm sure you weren't aware of it, but there's an unsavory character lurking around in your parking lot."

Unsavory was apparently Southern Lady lingo for scary-looking sonofabitch.

"Oh, bless your heart. Here, let me help you with that leash." Katie rushed over to assist.

"Thank you, Katie." Mrs. Phillips patted her hair back into the style Ava thought of as a drain clog.

"As I was saying, there's a criminal element loitering outside. And to think, you pretty young ladies here alone. The police need to chase that riff-raff off. I'll just dial 911 from my cellular."

She started to reach for her purse and Ava shouted "No!"

The poodle at her breast let out a yip when the woman's hand leapt to her heart instead. "Oh, Biscuit. My poor baby. Mommy didn't mean to strike you."

"I'm sorry, Mrs. Phillips. It's just that –"

"That's Dr. Martinez's brother."

"Oh, my dear." Mrs. Phillips looked out the window in dismay, and Ava what the hell'd at Katie. She didn't have a brother. "I... well. Brother, you say?"

"Yes. He's in the private security business."

Ava hip-checked her assistant on her way to take Mrs. Phillips' arm. "Well, that's enough about me. Let's get Muffin and Biscuit vaccinated, shall we?"

"Oh. Yes, yes. Of course." Mrs. Phillips patted her drain clog while Katie took charge of Muffin, blithely ignoring her employer's glare.

With one last look toward the parking lot, Ava followed them toward the back.

CHAPTER FOUR

JORDAN'S lungs burned, his stitches itched, and sweat rolled down his back. His head beat like a drum with every slap of his feet on pavement.

It was heaven.

Ever since his mother had blown back into town in an overprotective maternal maelstrom, he'd been confined to his parents' sofa. Never mind the fact that he was past thirty. As all five of Addison Wellington's sons could attest, life went along easier once you learned to say: yes ma'am. Not a one of them under six-foot tall, but their petite mother snapped her fingers and, to a man, they fell in line.

But Jordan had pulled a fast one today. He'd cited some paperwork that needed attending as his excuse for escaping the house. If he neglected to mention the run he intended to indulge in afterward – well, he figured what she didn't know wouldn't hurt her.

Though his own body was starting to protest.

But hell, he was used to running five miles at least three days a week, so the confinement was making him crazy. And running helped clear his mind. Now, more than ever, Jordan needed to think clearly.

Longtime family friend Clay Copeland was flying in today to help Jordan prepare the prosecution for the Fuller trial. A member of the FBI's Investigative Support Unit, Clay was an expert on serial killers, and his offender profiles and expert testimony had helped put a number of them behind bars. Given the circumstantial nature of their evidence – not to mention the fact that Jordan had been second choice for heading up this trial, even before his little medical mishap – the Chatham County DA's office wasn't taking any chances.

Jordan could have been mildly offended, but truth was, he wanted Clay's input. He'd be the first to admit he'd been distracted the past week, but he still couldn't see how he could argue, beyond a reasonable doubt, that Fuller was their man. In fact – and this was the point that was really sticking in his craw – he was even starting to have some doubts.

And if he couldn't make the case for it, there was little chance a jury would believe it either.

Not what Jordan's boss wanted to hear. No city wanted a serial killer on their hands, but for one that courted tourist dollars the way others pimped major league athletics, a knife-happy lunatic running amok wasn't exactly good for business.

Pulling his ball cap lower, Jordan ran past a hedge of azaleas splashed with pink and white flowers. He was all for wrapping up the case, he mused as a few spent blooms fell beneath his feet. As long as he made damn sure he was sending the right man to prison.

Confederate jasmine sweetened the air, fresh and lovely as a pretty woman still warm from the bath. He loved spring, its riot of color and scent. The way nature just seemed to burst like a happy balloon, spreading bright confetti everywhere. Riding on the headiness of the exercise, the fresh air, Jordan crossed a small wooden footbridge before realizing he wasn't alone.

And angling his head, caught the flash of blond on his right.

He'd been worried the dog wouldn't be here.

Jordan first spotted the stray a few weeks back, following him from a distance, scuttling under the nearest bush whenever Jordan stopped, or stuck out a hand. It made him sick to think about what kind of abuse must have turned the dog skittish. You could tell from his big, goofy retriever face that he was meant for a family. For chasing balls in the backyard and sneaking scraps under the dinner table. The kind of dog he'd grown up with as a kid.

So Jordan courted the animal, patient, until he'd licked Jordan's outstretched hand. He'd almost gotten close enough to slip the leash he carried from his pocket.

That was the Friday before his abduction. He hadn't been by in nearly a week, and Jordan had worried about Animal Control.

But here the animal was. Faithful as a shadow.

The throb in his head began to churn in his stomach, and Jordan figured he'd better pack it in before his breakfast decided to pay a call. Collapsing onto a park bench, he dropped his head between his knees.

Warm fur brushed his leg.

Jordan opened an eye. The dog's tongue lulled to the side, and Jordan had a chance to think the animal's teeth looked pretty good. Though Christ, his breath could fell a rhino from twenty paces. Carefully extending his hand, he stroked it down the blond head, and was rewarded by the happy thump of a matted tail.

Dappled sunlight warmed their backs, shifting like liquid gold across the fur ruffled by Jordan's fingers. He nearly swore when his cell phone rang, frightening the dog away.

And did curse when he checked the readout. "Hey, Mom." If he cleared his throat, he'd sound guilty. "I was just finishing up. I'll be on my way home in a minute."

"Well, take your time, sweetheart. No need to rush. Though it's such a fine day, I hate to think of you stuck behind a desk. You could do with some fresh air."

"Yes, ma'am. I'll be sure to, uh, sit in the garden after lunch."

"Speaking of, how does a nice barbeque sound?"

"Like a little slice of heaven."

"Some slaw, potato salad, sweet cornbread?"

"My mouth is already watering."

"Good. I called in an order at McCready's. Since you're already there at the park, swing next door and pick it up."

"MRS. Wellington, you make a mean chocolate chip cookie." Clay Copeland grabbed a cookie the size of a saucer fresh off the cooling rack. He broke off a piece, popped it into his mouth, chewing happily while she patted his cheek.

"I'm glad you like them, Clay."

Leaning an elbow on the counter, Clay flashed the grin that had been known to charm lesser women right out of their shirts. "Run away with me to Antigua. We'll drink rum in the moonlight and you can ply me with your decadent confections."

"Clay, stop flirting with my mother and haul your butt over here," Jordan said from his seat at the kitchen table.

"And bring that plate of cookies," Jesse added.

Neither of them seemed overly concerned about the fact that he'd just attempted to seduce their mother. But then, they'd heard it all before. Ever since Clay had gone through Quantico with Jesse – and gotten a taste of Addison Wellington's cooking – he'd been making similar propositions.

So far, Clay thought ruefully, she'd managed to resist.

Blue eyes twinkling, Addison handed Clay the plate. "One of these days, you handsome devil, I'm going to take you up on that offer."

Clay rubbed a hand over his heart. "Don't tease me that way, Mrs. W. You build up my hopes then dash them cruelly, time and again. It's a wonder I keep coming back."

"You come back for the food."

"Beautiful, talented and wise." With a wink he headed toward the enormous pine table that dominated the sunny kitchen. Flipped a ladder-back chair and straddled it. And pilfered two more cookies before relinquishing the plate.

"Greedy bastard." Jesse tugged the cookies closer and snagged a couple for himself before reluctantly passing them to his brother.

"Ah, no thanks," Jordan said absently. He pulled a legal pad and pen out of his briefcase.

Jesse tipped down his glasses to peer at him with suspicion. "Mom let you eat the dough before Clay and I got here, didn't she?"

Jordan's grin was fast, and wicked. "She likes me better than you."

"I heard that, Jordan," Addison called from the sink.

"Because you have ears like a bat."

"And eyes in the back of my head. Don't any of you ever forget it." Folding the dish towel she'd been using into a neat rectangle that mystified Clay, she hung it on a clever little silver hook before heading toward the French doors. "Now. I have some rose bushes that need pruning. I'll be in the garden, so if you want something, get it yourselves."

"Hell of a woman," Clay sighed, watching her tug a huge straw hat over blonde hair just a shade darker than his own.

"Dad seems to think so." Jesse rose, slapped Jordan's shoulder and tucked three more cookies into a napkin. "I guess I'll head out, too. I have my own work to do."

"Thanks for fetching me from the airport."

"Not a problem." Clay's shoulder got its own slap. "I'll see you at my place later tonight. Dinner's set for seven. Jillian will hogtie you if you're late."

"Woman has him whipped," Jordan muttered when Jesse'd cleared the room, and Clay took a moment to study him. He'd lost a little weight. And dark circles hollowed eyes the same bright shade as his mother's. "You look like shit."

"Always good to see you, too."

"I get paid to notice stress when I see it, son. And I'd wager it's more than just that whuppin' you took. I've taken a look at the files you sent me. That sleep you're losing is over this case."

Jordan tossed the pen he'd been fiddling with onto his yellow notepad. "Three women. Different ages. Different occupations. Different appearances, social statuses, religions. Three women, Clay, raped, violated, their tongues cut out, and left to drown in their own blood."

"It's frustrating, sickening, for you more than some. You're a care-taker by nature. It's why you're one of the few men – few straight men – I know who has houseplants. Why you teach that self-defense class down at the Y. Three women. But the man charged with their deaths is behind bars. You worried your skill in the courtroom isn't enough to keep him there?"

"I'm worried," Jordan said grimly "that he isn't behind bars at all."

"Ah," Clay said, and thought: of course. The double whammy. A killer on the loose and an innocent man on his way to prison. No wonder his friend couldn't sleep.

"You're the behavioral expert, Clay, but something about this guy just doesn't play for me. It took a cool head and a… huge sense of entitlement to do what was done to those women. He couldn't have had any empathy, any feeling for them as human beings. Fuller… hell, he cried when they showed him the crime scene photos of the last victim. I wasn't there – this wasn't my case yet – but I watched the video. And he bawled like a damn baby. They were neighbors, but more, I think to his mind they were in love. If the detectives hadn't found the little shrine he'd made to her in his closet and some of her blood on the floorboard of his car… Maybe he's just a damn good actor, but I can't reconcile the manner of these women's deaths with the nervous – and to all appearances heartbroken – kid we have locked up."

"You've expressed these doubts to your boss?"

"Why do you think you're sitting here, eating my mom's cookies?"

Reminded, Clay snagged the plate. "I'll just bet," he pointed a cookie at Jordan "that went over well."

"Like a lead balloon." Rocking back in his chair, Jordan rubbed at his stomach. "I'm hoping you can convince me of the error of my ways. If you think Elijah Fuller's personality fits these crimes – super. Then I'll eat crow and turn him into a blubbering pulp on the stand. If not… I hope your reputation is good enough to convince everyone we've made a mistake."

Clay took a bite of cookie. "No pressure or anything."

The sound of the doorbell interrupted Jordan's half-laugh.

"I guess I need to get that."

THE cookie dough turned to lead in Jordan's stomach when he opened the door. Chip Coleman, one of the detectives investigating his assault, stood on his parents' front porch.

"Chip, this is a surprise. Something I can do for you?"

The man eased the sunglasses from his freckled face. He might look like Opie Taylor, but Jordan knew him to be shrewd as hell. "If it's not a bad time, I have a few questions."

"Of course." Jordan stepped back, gestured him into the front parlor. "Can I offer you something to drink? There's, ah, lemonade. Fresh-squeezed."

"Nothing for me. Thanks." Coleman perched on the edge of the toile settee that Jordan had spilled Kool-Aid on as a child, and Jordan gratefully took the wing chair across from him. That damn settee still made him nervous. "You seem to be recovering well."

"Hard head." Jordan smiled.

"Are you acquainted with City Councilwoman Leslie Fitzsimmons?"

The smile dissolved in surprise. "Um. Sure. I know Leslie."

"Intimately?"

Irritation followed surprise.

Leslie Fitzsimmons was the fly in the ointment of Jordan's romantic past. He'd dated the gorgeous redhead here and there over the period of several months, making the mistake of assuming that they were on the same, very casual, relationship page. Until she'd started dragging him past jewelry stores on their after-dinner walks, and thumbing through Modern Bride while they sat on the beach. Jordan had no qualms about the concept of marriage in general, but a strong objection to marrying Leslie. They'd just never gotten that serious.

Though Leslie hadn't seen it that way.

"We dated. But if you're asking if we had sex, Chip, I'm afraid that's none of your business."

Coleman boosted his hip to pull a notebook from his pants. "You were seen… speaking heatedly with her in the hallway of the River Street Marriott, on the night of April second. Just after the speech you delivered."

Jordan opened his mouth. Closed it. He'd been unhappy to see Leslie's glaring visage in the crowd that night, and even less pleased by the tearful scene afterward. A scorned, southern, red-headed woman was apparently the temper trifecta.

But then the date, the location, struck him.

"You don't think Leslie had something to do with my head injury."

The gray eyes above the aw shucks freckles went hard and sharp as a blade.

"I'd like to ask Miz Fitzsimmons that very question, if I could run her to ground. But friends, relatives, neighbors – nobody has seen her. Funny thing, Jordan. It seems she's been missing since that night."

CHAPTER FIVE

JORDAN lay in the bed where his childhood self had slept, dreamed, and discovered the wonders of his own anatomy. The bed he'd snuck Shelley Eberhart into when he was a nervous and horny seventeen.

He'd washed the sheets himself – twice – shaking with fear at the thought of his mother discovering what he'd done with the pastor's daughter.

He smiled, remembering Shelley fondly. She'd known things, Shelley. And had been happy to spread the wealth.

But his mother had found out, anyway.

That storm had eventually passed, along with countless others from his childhood. Amazing, when he looked back on it, to realize how completely, if benevolently, his mother had ruled the house.

Which was why he stayed in bed until he heard her car pull out of the garage. Judging it safe, he yanked on running shorts and a T-shirt before heading downstairs to breakfast.

His father sprawled at the table with the morning paper.

And some suspicious looking white powder around his mouth.

Tom smiled when he saw his middle son. "You slept in this morning. Feeling better today?"

"Good as new." Jordan popped a whole wheat bagel in the toaster, poured coffee into the #1 Dad mug that he'd given his father a million years ago. "But I didn't sleep in. I hid out."

The lines at the corners of Tom Wellington's dark eyes gave way to deeper creases. "You always were the sneakiest of the bunch." He sat the sports section aside. "But clever with it. So damn polite and well behaved that it even took your mother a moment to figure out she'd been hornswaggled."

Jordan sighed, remembering it fondly. "Half the time, Jesse or Jack caught the blame." He took a bite of bagel, gestured toward his father. "I learned it all from watching you."

Tom pretended ignorance. "Why son, I'm not sure what you mean."

"Do you still hide your stash of powdered doughnuts behind the volumes on tax law?"

"How the hell do you know about my stash?"

"I have my ways." Jordan took a drink of coffee. "But you're slipping a little in your dotage. You never used to leave the evidence all over your face."

"I'll be damned." Tom frowned at the powder he'd wiped off with his hand.

"Undoubtedly. Especially if Mom finds out that you've been cheating on your heart healthy diet." He cleared his dishes from the table, stacked them with the others in the sink. He studied them, considered. "If you take care of these, I should be able to forget that we had this conversation."

Tom shook his head. "I'll tell you what, son. I'll take care of the dishes, because that's just the kind of guy I am. And I won't tell your mother that, against doctor's orders to take it easy, you've gone running again."

Jordan dropped a loving hand on his father's shoulder before heading out. "It's a comfort to me that we understand each other so well."

THE park was alive.

Tourists, with their maps, their digital cameras, strolled in pairs or less orderly groups. Teenagers roamed, sneering from their skateboards at lovers embracing in quiet shade, while parents pushed plump babies in colorful strollers.

Frisbees were tossed, blankets napped on. Students from the Savannah College of Art and Design conducted an impromptu show with buckets of sidewalk chalk.

Jordan ran. Sweated out some of his frustration. What the hell did it mean that Leslie had seemingly vanished into thin air?

She'd been angry with him, certainly. But furious – and foolish enough – to attempt to hurt him?

And how did that explain the other woman from that night?

Engrossed in thought, Jordan almost didn't register the bark of greeting.

"Well, good morning to you, too." He pulled the tennis ball from his pocket, grinned when the dog shifted into a crouch. Then lobbed it with the sureness of arm that had helped his high school baseball team clench the state title.

Matted fur flew as the dog shot off like a rocket.

When he brought it back, dropped it at Jordan's feet, Jordan decided that today was the day. They'd tiptoed around each other long enough, and it was time to make things official.

A short while later he looked in the rearview mirror and saw a furry grin looking back.

And wasn't it going to be fun to show his mother what he'd brought home?

It was surely one way to convince her he should head back to his own place.

"Okay." He turned around to have a little man to man talk with his dog. "Don't get too excited over the fancy digs, or the size of the garden, because this is not where we're going to live. The truth is we have a renovated loft over what is currently a florist's shop."

Jordan held up a hand. "Yeah, yeah, I know. Trust me – my brothers have already covered all that manhood impugning ground before. But we're going to stop in here, horrify my mother just enough so that she kicks us both out, and then we'll head home."

Waltzing in the kitchen door had some obvious advantages, but he decided to ring the front doorbell.

A large copper pot filled with lilies had materialized on the verandah, reminding him that tomorrow was Easter. There'd been lilies on his parents' doorstep this time of year for as long as he could remember.

He depressed the quietly lit button, grinning at the ragged looking animal at his feet.

As if on cue, the dog thumped his tail when his mother appeared, aiming his snout right for her crotch.

Perfect.

"Can I keep him, Mom, can I, can I?"

Addison nudged the snout aside. "Where on earth did you find this... creature?"

"At the park," Jordan explained, looking down at the dog with affection. "We've been seeing each other on the sly."

Addison studied the animal, then her son. "I imagine you think you're pretty clever, don't you?"

"I have no idea what you mean."

She bent down then and rubbed a hand between the animal's ears. "Well, the boy looks better after his run today, doesn't he?" Jordan winced, realizing he'd forgotten to change his clothes. "I guess he'll survive if I allow you to take him home."

She held out a hand, and was rewarded with a paw.

"Oh, he's a keeper," Addison laughed as she shook. "Does he have a name yet?"

"We tossed around a few possibilities on the way here. Finn seems to have stuck."

"Well, if you're set on this, you should get him checked out by a vet. Let me give Joyce Phillips a call."

"Ah, jeez, Mom. Not the poodle lady."

"Don't be rude, Jordan. I'm sure she has an excellent veterinarian."

A smile twitched at his lips. "Does she still have that yippy little tan one – what was its name? Cupcake? Do you remember the time that Jesse took the electric razor and …" his voice died off as he caught his mother's mutinous expression.

"Sorry. Tell Mrs. Phillips that I would appreciate her vet's number."

CHAPTER SIX

AFTER double checking the address, Jordan pulled his car into the parking lot of the small brick-faced building. The place was... homey, Jordan guessed. Not merely functional and utilitarian, as so many commercial buildings were.

He thought the whiskey barrels spilling over with pansies a nice touch.

But on closer inspection Jordan noted that the pansies weren't so much spilling as they were drooping. His gardener's heart, which he secretly – very secretly – had inherited from his mother, cringed.

"Let's just hope she takes better care of her patients," Jordan murmured as he unhooked his seat belt. Grabbing his cap off the dash, he turned toward the backseat. "Well, I'm not going to lie to you. We're at the vet's."

Finn dropped his head onto his paws.

"Look, I hate going to the doctor as much as the next guy, but at the risk of sounding like a cliché, this is for your own good. You need a bath and a haircut. And in the interest of full disclosure, there might be a few shots involved." Jordan clipped the new leash in place and wrapped the other end around his hand. "Sorry pal. Sometimes it just doesn't pay to be man's best friend."

The front door jangled as Jordan walked into an empty reception room. Empty, he thought with a small degree of panic, except for the bored-looking gray cat lounging on the counter.

He tightened his grip on the leash, just in case Finn developed notions, but thankfully his dog was too busy balking in the doorway to worry about the cat.

"Come on," he muttered, giving another aggressive tug on the leash. "Let's try to make a good first impression, shall we?"

When he'd basically pulled the animal over the threshold, Jordan took a look around the room. Bags of animal food and supplies lined sturdy wire shelves along the back wall, and full color posters depicting the life cycle of the flea, the ravages of heartworms, and – to his mild horror and utter disgust – actual photographs of people who'd been infected by their animal's untreated tapeworms decorated the walls.

Apparently, Doctor Ava Martinez had never heard of Monet's Water Lilies.

"Well, let's get this over with." He depressed the service bell on the front desk.

AVA cursed when she heard the little ding that let her know there was someone in the waiting room. It always made her feel like a cheap motel clerk being summoned to rent a room by the hour. But when Katie was out of the office, she'd yet to come up with a better solution.

Distracted, she stole a glance at her watch to realize it was time for her next appointment, and was rewarded by a swipe from one very large, very angry cat.

"Now, now. That wasn't very nice, Lambchop." The horribly misnamed feline glared back, docile as a hyena. She gripped him by the scruff of the neck, careful now to keep her other hand out of reach, and depressed the syringe into his hindquarters.

"There. All finished." She quickly and efficiently scooped the yowling animal under her arm before he could flay the skin from her bones. "Let's just get you back –"

The ring of the bell had her shifting Lambchop to avoid a wicked display of teeth. She called out, hoping she managed to keep the irritation from her voice. "Be right there!"

If there was one aspect of her job that she hated, it was handling the owners of her patients with diplomacy. Animals, at least, conformed to some fairly basic rules of behavior. It was the humans you had to watch out for.

But if she wanted to grow her practice, she needed to polish up her ass kissing.

When the bell rang again, she gritted her teeth, and wrangled the feline AntiChrist into his cage. Just because the idiot in her waiting room lacked both patience and manners didn't mean she was entitled to tell him off.

No matter how badly she wanted to.

Burying her annoyance beneath a false smile, she stalked toward reception, coming up short at the sight of a tall man holding onto a blond dog while goggling at Jack's eye patch. Her lips twitched with genuine amusement until the man swung around.

"I'm sorry. I didn't mean to rush you. I was just so surprised to see the, uh, eye patch that I accidentally..." His apology lost steam as he noticed Ava's horrified expression. "Hey, are you alright?"

Icy needles of panic pricked Ava's skin. How the hell had he managed to track her down?

Her car. He must have recognized her car. Why had she parked it out front today?

Because she'd almost been late opening up. She'd entertained herself by leading one of the goons in a big circle around the city, because their very existence was still pissing her off.

And now her little show of temper had come back to bite her in the ass.

"Uh, I didn't mean to startle you. My name's Jordan Wellington. I called and arranged for a twelve o'clock appointment? My mom is a friend of one of your clients. Mrs. Phillips. You came highly recommended."

Despite the ringing in her ears, some of what he was saying got through.

He'd made an appointment. She remembered now that he'd called about an hour ago to see if she could squeeze him and his dog in.

A stray. He'd found a stray in the park.

And wasn't that just an unfortunate coincidence?

Gauging his wary expression, Ava realized how inappropriate her reaction had been. She snapped out of deer-in-the-headlight mode, hoping she hadn't given anything away.

"Of course. I'm sorry." And cursed herself for the nervous laugh. "I just had a bit of an altercation with a demon masquerading as a housecat, and I'm afraid I forgot about your call." Better he attribute her behavior to being a jumpy female with a faulty memory than a guilty female with a memory she'd rather forget. "But I recall now that you said you found a stray."

With reclaimed poise she moved around the counter. "Is this the lucky guy?" She bent down, let the dog lick her hand, utterly relieved that it didn't tremble.

"YEAH, this is Finn." Whom Jordan eyed with envy. Now that the woman's dark eyes weren't swallowing her lovely face, he had a chance to appreciate the rest of the package. And a tidy little package it was. Delicate. Curvy. The exotic coloring that brought to mind warm breezes, hot blood, painted women in red dancing like living flames.

Licking her didn't seem like such a bad idea.

"I'm Jordan," he repeated as he offered his hand.

"AVA. Ava Martinez." No point lying about that, she thought, when her name was printed in bold black letters on the front door.

With her mask of composure fully in place, she returned his handshake, gestured with the other. "Why don't we head back toward one of the exam rooms and we'll get Finn all checked out." She would keep the small talk to a minimum, make short work of what needed to be done. And get this guy the hell out of there.

"I appreciate you seeing us on such short notice," he said as he followed her down the narrow, vinyl-floored corridor that smelled of the bleach solution she'd used to clean. "I've had my eye on this guy for a few weeks now, waiting to see if he belonged to somebody. It doesn't seem that anyone's come around to claim him, and I couldn't stand the idea of him ending up at the pound, or splattered by a car on the street. My mom suggested that I have him checked out right away, since he's obviously been on his own for a while."

"Sound advice," Ava agreed. And damn if she didn't feel a little tug in her belly because the guy was clearly a softie. It made her feel a strange mix of guilt and pleasure that she'd pulled the big fool out of the car. Stealing a quick glance at his cap, she wondered how his head was faring.

The guy – Jordan – noted the direction of her glance. "You'll have to forgive me for not removing my hat indoors. I had a bit of an accident last week, and the cap reminds me not to scratch the stitches. I'm afraid I'm not an ideal patient."

"Ah, well," Ava managed, surprised she hadn't swallowed her tongue. "Stitches can be uncomfortable."

She opened the door to the small room, gesturing toward the metal table in the center. "Let's get Finn settled up here." As she went to one of the cabinets to pull out a pair of latex gloves,

Jordan tugged the leash to urge his reluctant dog inside. "Remember our pep talk," he murmured. "You just need to come in here and take it like a man."

Ava smothered a smile as she snapped on the gloves.

When he'd hefted the fifty or so pounds of struggling canine into position, Ava tried to keep her mannerisms, her tone, even her thoughts strictly professional. She checked the dog's ears and skin for signs of parasites, clucked over the condition of his coat, and nodded approval that his teeth seemed to be strong and healthy.

Jordan winced as she took a stool sample with ruthless efficiency.

She led Finn onto a scale, noted he was underweight for his size, and mentally calculated the amount of food he should be given, in decreasing amounts, until he'd rebounded. She readied the necessary shots, stroked and murmured to soothe the animal's occasional tremors, and held onto her own nerves with rigid control. She managed to tamp down the little licks of panic by focusing all of her attention on the animal.

The animal's owner she largely ignored.

JORDAN attempted small talk while Finn underwent his examination, but the pale, shaken woman he'd first seen had morphed into a cool-eyed professional. She answered all of his questions pertaining to Finn with straightforward, helpful answers.

And deflected personal inquiries like blows.

Curious and intrigued, Jordan pulled a few weapons out of his not inconsiderable arsenal. He was a reasonably attractive guy. Knew how to hold a decent conversation. And charm, like blue eyes, was just part of his DNA.

He was shot down like a lame duck.

"You're lucky," Ava commented as she rolled Finn over on his back to palpate her fingers along his belly. "This guy's already been neutered."

"Lucky and neutered are two words that should never be used together."

Her hands stilled, and when her lips twitched, Jordan thought: aha!

But the moment was gone when she headed toward the trashcan, putting the better part of the room between them. "Well, other than the grooming, Finn's good to go." She pulled off her gloves, tossed them in. "My assistant usually handles that, but since she's not here at the moment, I'll take care of it myself."

"So you're here alone?"

"Not entirely alone. There are clients in and out, and of course One-Eyed Jack."

"One-eyed… Oh, the cat out front. I guess that explains the eye-patch."

"Mmm. Well, I'll just take Finn to the grooming area and make him good as new. It shouldn't take more than twenty minutes. If you'd like to wait out front –"

She wasn't brushing him off that easy. "I'll tag along. Just in case you need a hand."

"I can assure you I'm perfectly capable of dealing with this by myself."

"Then you can instruct me on the proper way to do it. I'm a dog grooming novice." He wrapped his hand around Finn's leash, laid the other on Ava's shoulder.

IRRITATION began to edge out the panic Ava felt when she'd first seen him in her waiting room. Who did this guy think he was? She simply wasn't used to being… maneuvered.

A few choice words, Ava thought as they headed down the hall, his hand burning into her shoulder. And she could have the presumptuous idiot back in his place.

But this was one man with whom she couldn't afford to lose her temper. So in the interest of self- preservation, she thought it was best to hold her tongue.

When he deliberately brushed his knuckles across the nape of her neck before releasing Finn from his leash, she had to hold back that tongue with both hands.

The look she sent him could have cut glass, but he countered with a mild-mannered grin.

She guessed the dimples were supposed to be charming.

Too bad they damn well were.

Reigning in frustration, she selected a shampoo and clippers for Finn and then focused on the task at hand. Allowing Jordan Wellington to get to her was a very bad idea.

JORDAN watched the little bursts of irritation shoot out from her like angry darts. Had he actually thought this woman was delicate? Aroused and amused, he reconsidered his initial impression. It wasn't like him to have been so off base. But her reaction in the waiting room had thrown him for a loop.

Maybe it was his imagination, but she'd seemed a good bit more than startled.

Of course, that may have had nothing to do with him. Perhaps, like she'd said, she was reeling from a run-in with a vicious cat.

But she certainly didn't seem to be having any trouble handling Finn. Even when he bared his teeth and snarled a warning as she zoomed clippers over his matted fur. She simply looked him in the eye, laid a finger on his nose, and told him sternly to behave.

The kick-your-ass tone had vague visions of velvet handcuffs dancing in Jordan's head.

Huh. The woman was a puzzle. He loved puzzles. It gave him a great deal of satisfaction to mess with all of the pieces until they fit.

He had a feeling he'd get a great deal of satisfaction from messing with Ava Martinez.

"So, Doctor Martinez, is there a mister Doctor Martinez waiting for you at home?" He'd already checked out the ring finger, found it bare, but figured it best to test the water before he dove in.

AVA ignored the second little tug in her belly and kept her eyes on Finn's coat. "No." Don't elaborate, don't encourage. Don't say another word.

"Any lovers, boyfriends, older brothers with strong protective instincts that need to be hurdled over or knocked out of the way?"

Dammit, dammit, she was not going to smile. Okay, dammit, yes she was. "There's no need for any hurdling, Mr. Wellington. I have no interest in… track and field events."

Jordan's lips quirked. He hooked his thumbs in the front pockets of his jeans and rocked back on his heels. "Yeah, me neither. Baseball's my sport. I never saw the appeal of jumping over obstacles when it's so much more fun to just round all the bases and slide yourself into home."

As far as sexual repartee went, Ava decided that it wasn't half bad. And she decided that Jordan's grin should be considered a lethal weapon. Top it off with those drop-dead eyes, a killer body, and just enough cocky charm to make him dangerous, and Ava figured she should be a corpse by now. Her blood began to hum under her skin.

All the more reason to get him the hell out of her clinic.

After the dog's hair had been clipped free of mats, she lathered him up with a shampoo designed to kill the adult fleas which had infested him, and explained that Jordan would have to give Finn a monthly pill to keep any of their larvae from hatching. She scrubbed, rinsed, and turned on a massive blow dryer which made the dogs jowls fly back as if he were riding with his face stuck out the window of a car.

She finished him off by tying a red bandana around his neck. Jordan's dimples flashed as he bent down and let Finn lick his face. "Look at you, big guy. All duded up and totally unavailable to the ladies. Well, we'll just let them ogle your fine self and weep." He stuck his nose in Finn's neck. "Man, you even smell good." He looked up at Ava as he scrubbed his hand between the dog's ears. "Thanks, Doc. He looks great. So what do I owe you?"

"Come on up front and we'll get settled."

After Ava loaded him down with heartworm preventative, flea medication, dog food, grooming supplies and a plaid bed with little appliqué bones, she helped him pile it all into his car and sent him on his way.

Then, locking the front door behind her, sank bonelessly into her chair. Thank God he hadn't recognized her. Thank God the goon in the parking lot hadn't recognized him.

That possibility had given her a few bad moments. But maybe the goons who were stalking her weren't the same ones who'd kidnapped him. Or maybe they were just stupid. Or maybe… she stopped herself before she drove herself crazy.

But really, of all the vets in the city, what were the chances he'd walk in her door? And the hell of it was, after the flood of relief washed through her that she'd managed to shoo him out without a proposition or an altercation, it left her with a residue of disappointment.

She wondered why Jordan Wellington hadn't asked her out.

Deciding that her rush of nerves must have killed off a few brain cells, Ava pushed out of the chair and went to unlock the front door. Who cared why he hadn't, when she should simply celebrate the fact that he was gone.

The crisis had been averted and her secret remained intact.

CHAPTER SEVEN

IT was nearly twilight by the time Ava got home. The jolt of finding the man whose life she'd saved standing in her reception area, coupled with a busy afternoon, left her feeling abnormally drained and edgy.

Not to mention the fact that she was sick and tired of having her uncle's men follow her around. She hated the fact that she had no choice but to play his little game. Move, countermove. Maneuver and feint. They forever circled one another, wary and distrustful, unwilling or unable to take that final step which would take the other down. They shared blood, and they shared her father.

And if not, she was certain that they would have gone after each other like hungry wolves.

Ava pulled her Mustang into the drive beside the carriage house, raising the top as she freed One-eyed Jack from his carrier. She looked at the little home she'd made for herself. The sturdy, painted brick dripping with whimsical gingerbread lace. Solid, yet feminine. Not, Ava thought as she looked toward the enormous Victorian in whose shadow she sat, unlike her landlord.

Calhoun House stretched toward the treetops like a pretty woman, all graceful curves and ornate trimmings. Narrow windows winked like heavy-lidded eyes in the remnants of early evening sun. The bold yellow paint had worn a bit, softening as it aged. Wisteria clung like a colorful accessory, and the bright punch of rioting azaleas suggested that she might be old, but she wasn't tame. Underneath all the ornamentation, the house was sturdy to the core.

It fitted its owner perfectly.

Lou Ellen Calhoun was gracious as a Sunday luncheon, solid as stone, and in the manner of any southerner worthy of the confederate flag, crazy as a loon.

Ava absolutely adored her.

As the feeling was mutual, Lou Ellen rented Ava the charming apartment over her detached garage for a song.

Well, for a song, and as many home cooked meals as Lou Ellen could squeeze out of her.

Ava's spirits lifted the minute she saw the older woman on one of the twin gazebos of the front porch. Paintbrush in one hand, a mimosa in the other, and what was certain to be a godawful creation on the easel behind which she stood.

"Is it happy hour yet?"

"Honey, around here, every hour's happy." She handed Ava the drink she'd just poured into vintage green Depression glass. Oblivious to the paint on her fingers, she ran them through her short cap of dark hair. "Sit."

Ava obliged her by sinking into a garishly cushioned wicker chair. Of course, the fabric was tame compared to what Ava'd glimpsed on the latest unfortunate canvas. But she knew better than to comment, or it would end up adorning her wall.

Recognizing the mood, Lou Ellen leaned against the rail. "Looks to me like you had yourself an unpleasant day."

Ava drank deeply. Other than Katie, Lou Ellen was the only person she trusted to unload on. She'd told them each different bits and pieces, so that neither of them ever had the full story. That kind of knowledge could be a burden. God knew it was a burden to her.

But Lou Ellen had seen the blood on Ava's car seat.

"The man I pulled out of that trunk last week came into the clinic today."

"Well." Lou Ellen tossed back her own drink, refilled both their glasses. "Bet that made for an interesting conversation."

Ava managed a withering stare across the rim of her glass. "As luck would have it, he wasn't there to accuse, harangue or persecute me. Turns out he found a stray dog at the park. A friend of his mother's recommended me. Please," Ava said, while the sound of the other woman's laughter rolled over her. "Feel free to enjoy yourself at my expense."

"Darling, you have to admit, there's a great deal of irony at work here."

"The friend of his mother's is Joyce Phillips."

"Ugh." Lou Ellen's amusement fled. "Detestable woman. What sane person matches her pets to her hair?"

Ava couldn't help but laugh. "Surely you're not still holding a grudge because she stole your high school sweetheart."

"Have you seen Bucky Phillips lately? Looks like a potbellied stove with hair. Being married to that is punishment enough. But that's neither here nor there. What are you going to do about trunk boy?"

Trunk boy, Ava thought as the champagne fizzed in her throat, who in no way resembled anything potbellied. "I believe I've done enough." The breeze picked up, sliding the sweetness of confederate jasmine through the air, but it turned Ava's stomach sour. "I saved his life and took care of his dog. No harm, no foul. Everybody's happy."

"Funny. You don't look happy."

"He flirted with me." Ava frowned into her glass. "And he's pretty good at it."

"Oh." Lou Ellen tucked her tongue into her cheek. "What tangled webs we weave."

"Not so amusing, seeing as my uncle's doing the weaving. I'm just the damn fly caught in the web."

"I'm not laughing at you, darling." Lou Ellen stroked Ava's hand, and the clatter of her bracelets was somehow soothing. "I'm simply appreciating the whims of fate. If I'm not mistaken, and I rarely am, you're attracted to this young man."

Ava pictured the wink of dimples against stubbled cheeks. "I could eat him up in one greedy bite. Well, make that two. He's awfully big."

"And it sounds like this big, delicious man is attracted to you, as well. How… ironic is it that you were in the wrong place, at the right time, to save his life?"

"Exactly what are you getting at, Lou Ellen?"

"Destiny." Her green eyes sparkled bright as her glass. "What if he's yours?"

"You've been hitting the mimosas too hard. Seeing him again is completely out of the question."

"So says you, my doubting Thomas." Lou Ellen's penciled eyebrows wiggled. "That cool scientific brain makes you cynical."

"I'm not cynical, Lou Ellen. I'm realistic." As Ava could feel a headache coming on, she decided to leave the remainder of her mimosa and moved to rise. "And anyway, the point's moot because he didn't ask me out. Now unfortunately, I have a sink full of dirty dishes and some paperwork that can't be ignored. I appreciate the drinks. I'll make you Easter dinner tomorrow night."

Ava unlocked her front door, One-eyed Jack streaking past her legs to sulk near his empty food bowl.

Sighing, she dropped her purse on the bench of the hall tree that served as her catch-all, and followed him toward the kitchen. The orange and green checkerboard tiles never ceased to come as a shock. Lou Ellen was color blind as the day was long. It amazed Ava that her friend had found someone able to install it all without suffering some sort of breakdown.

She filled Jack's dish, rolling her eyes at the greedy, proprietary noises he tended to make while he ate. "I guess you can take the cat out of the alley, but you can't take the alley out of the cat."

The alcohol she'd downed intensified the ache that had begun to throb behind her eyes, so she snagged some ibuprofen and dropped into one of the chairs from her bistro set. Maybe after they'd kicked in, the mountain of dishes in the old cast iron sink wouldn't seem so daunting.

Ava tended to let things go little by little throughout the week, until they reached a saturation point that resulted in a weekend cleaning blitz. Unfortunately, today was D-Day.

As the kitchen was ground zero for the worst of the disaster and she wasn't feeling particularly motivated, she decided to start in her bedroom and work her way back around.

She made a pass at the bathroom, scrubbing the old claw foot tub but turning a blind eye to the floor's less than sparkling grout. Dustbunnies were chased from under her cherished brass bed. The sheets probably needed to be laundered, but she wasn't feeling ambitious enough to mess with her temperamental washing machine.

When she pulled out the furniture polish to hit her mission style coffee table, the unexpected rush of tears had the dust cloth dropping from her hand.

"To hell with it." She dropped onto the sofa, admired the simple lines of the Spanish antique. It had been in her family for generations, coming to Ava through her mother.

She missed her mother so much.

And worse, so much worse, was not knowing what had happened to her.

Unwilling, unable to think about either of her parents right now, Ava swiped angrily at her cheeks. Then plumped the pillows on the sofa, cursing loudly when she saw the claw marks.

"I'm reconsidering my position on de-clawing you," she called toward the kitchen in frustration.

Full dark had fallen by the time she made it to the dishes.

The pan she'd used to cook paella for Lou Ellen sat beneath coffee mugs, cereal bowls, and various assorted utensils. A wine glass perched dangerously on top.

Her single greatest wish was for a dishwasher.

But as all of the profits from her practice were being funneled right back into the business, such luxuries would have to wait.

Resigned, Ava started scrubbing with a vengeance.

Vengeance, she considered, was what her uncle's life was all about. Vengeance against those who crossed him. Vengeance against life for the miserable childhood he'd been dealt. The oldest son of a day laborer who'd died too early, and died too hard, Carlos sold his way out of abject poverty one chemical high at a time. He'd expanded from selling drugs to selling sex and whatever vice he could capitalize on. Ava couldn't really hold that against him, or at least not much. She knew that survival wasn't always pretty.

But she could resent the carelessness that had led him to draw her father into that life. A life of greed and violence. Of building an empire on others' pain. A life that demanded loyalty to Carlos, above all else.

And God help anyone who threatened that life he'd created.

Jack leaped onto the counter and growled.

"Shit. Just hell." Ava looked at the broken glass in her hand. Blood oozed sullenly from a shallow slice. "Well, Jack, you got your revenge for those shots. And I'm jumpy as a damn rabbit."

Wrapping her hand in a clean dish towel, Ava stretched to open the cabinet that held her household medical supplies. She shoved aside the ibuprofen, flipped the latch on the small first aid case.

Screamed when she saw the eyeball.

The bistro chair clattered to the floor as Ava slammed against it, sending Jack streaking from the room on a hiss. The case toppled, spilling its contents, and Ava's frozen heart began knocking like her old washing machine.

The eyeball bounced, and rolled toward her.

"Sonofabitch." The damn thing was rubber. Ava pushed herself to her feet.

She peered out the window above the kitchen sink, saw the shadow of a car parked on the street. Light flared, just one brief burst from a match, and she caught the goon's smile as he lit his cigarette.

It burned her ass that he'd obviously heard her scream.

Shoving her good hand through her hair, Ava considered that he'd been in her home. Left a little reminder that her uncle was watching.

She wanted to scrub everything again, and with bleach.

She looked toward Calhoun House, saw Lou Ellen's bedroom light on. And felt the cold breath of fear against her neck. Her very presence put her friend in danger. She was, and always had been, very careful about whom she allowed herself to get close to. And wouldn't have confided in either Lou or Katie but for the fact that they needed to be aware of the situation, for their own safety.

And, damn it, she was entitled to a few real friends.

Hadn't Carlos already cost her the only man she'd ever really cared for? Not to mention both of her parents?

Furious again, Ava refused to draw the blinds at the kitchen window. Let the goon outside watch.

Slowly, methodically, she bandaged her hand, then finished washing and stowing her dishes.

And left the light burning as she got ready for bed.

CHAPTER EIGHT

EASTER Sunday dawned bright and beautiful, but Ava's mood was anything but sunny. Exhausted, angry, and anguished by last night's dreams of her mother, she brooded into her morning coffee.

Her mother had always loved Easter. The concept of hope. Of rebirth. No matter how many times Ava's father had disappointed her by falling back in with his brother, Lorena Martinez hadn't lost faith. Not in her God. Nor in her marriage.

Ava was forced to admit that she herself had lapsed. But in honor of the woman who'd done so much more than give her life, Ava dressed for mass.

A light, raspberry colored sweater, she decided, to compliment the dress of shell pink linen. The wedged mules added just the right touch. Long, willowy women like Lou Ellen and Katie might be able to get away with flats, but as Ava's particular gene pool ran toward short and well packed, she suffered the necessity of heels.

Tottering down the steps in those heels, she flicked a disgruntled glance toward the black T-Bird. Bastard had good taste in cars, she'd give him that. When she fired up her Mustang, the T-Bird's engine roared to life as well. She wondered if he'd follow her into church.

The cathedral was packed with the faithful, and those who were simply there out of habit. Ava watched with some amusement as more than one chiffon-clad child suffered the inevitable candy-induced meltdown. But as she fanned herself with her bulletin, listened with one ear to the homily, Ava felt herself settle.

When the service was finished, she bucked the flow of people and angled her way up the aisle. The goon would undoubtedly be waiting for her out front, so she decided to sneak out the back.

Forsyth Park was just a block over, and it was a beautiful day for a stroll.

The warm breeze slid over her skin, fragrant with fresh grass, the light perfume of spring. Of life renewing itself. Ava could almost feel her mother's touch in the whisper of air. Lighter now, she tossed her sweater over her shoulder and walked with satisfaction.

Despite the long shadow her uncle cast, she decided her life was fulfilling. She had a satisfying career, good friends, and a comfortable home. She worried for her father, loved him terribly, but had come to realize that the choices he'd made were his own. There was nothing she could do about the bed he'd made, and it wasn't her responsibility to lie in it. At this point all she could do was try to make her own.

Ava passed families spread beneath the oaks with their picnics, fat ham sandwiches and deviled eggs, and jellybeans by the bagful. Some children engaged in an egg hunt. They carried handled baskets, ground dirt into the knees of their good pants, and darted about like pastel fireflies, brightening the air.

A young girl in a lavender dress tucked a number of her brother's eggs into her own basket when he dared to turn his back.

Grinning, Ava didn't notice the dog until he brushed against her leg.

"Finn!" She stroked his well-groomed head. "What are you doing here?"

But even as she asked the question, she knew. And looked up, toward the stretch of field several yards in the distance, to meet a pair of familiar blue eyes.

About a half second later, those eyes, and their owner, were knocked to the ground by a couple hundred pounds of leaping male.

"HEY dumbass!" Jordan heard Jesse call out in exasperation. "You're supposed to run when you catch the ball. Not stand there like an idiot." Jesse turned toward their brother Justin, the MD. "I think you should check him out. Maybe he suffered some brain damage after all."

Justin grinned, but Jordan paid no attention to his brothers. When he'd spotted Ava, his mind emptied faster than a classroom after the final bell. Several seconds elapsed before he even realized he'd hit the ground.

"Get off me, James." He bucked the heavy bulk of his youngest brother to the side, tossed the football toward the still grinning Justin. Like he cared about a little touch and tackle after he'd gotten a look at Ava Martinez's bare legs.

Ignoring the various catcalls coming from the field behind him, he made a beeline toward the good doctor. It was beyond him why he'd left her office yesterday without figuring a way to get his hands on her in the none-too-distant future. He wouldn't make that mistake again.

As Jordan watched, Finn licked the back of her knee.

Once again, his dog had the right idea.

"WELL shit," Ava muttered to herself as the man approached. Out of the frying pan and into the fire.

"Down boy," he said mildly, reaching to grasp Finn's collar. But his gaze never left Ava's. "Hey, Doc."

He was slightly winded, glistening with sweat, and smelled pleasantly of soap and male. The hair sticking out from under his cap had dampened into sable curls.

His eyes were blue headlights, pinning her.

"Mr. Wellington." Because her legs felt weak, she kept her tone cool.

"Okay, if you keep saying that I'm going to feel like my father. Call me Jordan."

"Okay. Jordan." She slid a glance over his shoulder toward the field. "It looks like I've interrupted your game."

"What? Oh. No big deal. Just killing some time with my brothers before dinner."

She blinked once, and then gave the field another look. "All of them?"

"All of what?" He offered a friendly smile.

"Are they all your brothers?"

"Oh. Yeah." He spared a quick glance. "Well, all of them except for the blond." The blond, Ava noted, who was making a rather rude gesture at Jordan's back. "We keep him around for entertainment purposes. Anyway, enough about them. You look fantastic." He reached out and slid a finger along the wide strap of her dress.

Ava took what she considered a prudent step back.

Jordan's smile edged into a grin. "So listen, I was wondering if I could take you to dinner."

"I... I..." Shit. Was she stuttering? "I have plans."

"Not tonight," he clarified. "I've got the whole family thing going on. But another night this week. How about tomorrow?"

"It's a workday."

"You eat on workdays, don't you?"

"No. I mean yes, but..." What the hell was the matter with her? "But the answer is no. I'm not interested in having dinner with you tomorrow." There. She'd finally located her brain.

"Friday, then. Wait." He held up a hand before she could answer. "Saturday. I forgot that you work half the weekend."

"I don't think so."

Jordan chewed on the inside of his cheek while he squinted at her. "Why not?"

"What do you mean, why not? You've made a proposition, I've declined. Simple as that." Finn licked her leg again and she jumped.

The reaction didn't go unnoticed.

"Do I make you nervous, Ava?" His murmur was low.

"Don't flatter yourself."

"So you find me unattractive?"

"What? No. You're…" Gorgeous? Mouth watering? "Attractive enough."

"Hmm. Then you must prefer having dinner with ugly men."

Ava's lips twitched against her will. "Look, Jordan, I appreciate the offer but –"

"Do you have a policy against dating clients?"

Oh, that would make this so easy if it were only true. But it was Easter Sunday, and she wasn't going to lie. "No."

"THEN have dinner with me." If Jordan hadn't seen the interest, felt the heat coming off of her in little riffs, and if he didn't want her so badly, he wouldn't have persisted. But since he had and he did, he wasn't going to back down.

Bottom line, he didn't want to.

"You're very aggressive," Ava informed him.

"Not so much aggressive," Jordan mused. "That's my brother Jack. He's a barracuda. Or what my parents politely refer to as driven. Me? I'm what you might call persistent."

"There's a difference?"

"Sure there is. Aggressive is obviously overbearing. Persistent is more… quietly determined. Subtle, if you will."

AND why, Ava asked herself, was she standing here discussing semantics with this man, when she should be getting the hell out of Dodge?

"You think you're being subtle?" she asked instead.

"You would understand the difference if you met my brother."

"Well, then." She looked toward the other men again. They'd formed a large pile and seemed bound and determined to pound one another into the ground. The blond launched himself on top of the others with a bloody cry of glee. "I'll have to make it a point to stay away from your brother."

"His wife would appreciate that. Have dinner with me."

It was like being ever-so-slowly pummeled by a velvet fist. "You just don't give up, do you?"

"Like a dog after a bone. No pun intended."

"Okay." She drew a deep breath, slapped a palm against his chest before he could pummel her again. "Despite the fact that you're… attractive, you have great taste in dogs, and you're unbelievably persistent, I'm afraid this just isn't going to happen. My reasons are my own, and if you're half the gentleman you appear to be, you'll respect that and leave me alone. Now," she removed her hand, unsure whether the sheen of sweat on her palm was Jordan's or her own. "If you'll excuse me, I have someplace I need to be."

STYMIED, and not a little bit worked up, Jordan watched her walk away.

He had enough complications in his life right now without factoring in a challenging and by all appearances difficult woman.

Her hips swayed, and he was riveted.

Since when had he backed down from a challenge?

Tipping his cap back to better appreciate the view, he decided he might just be aggressive after all.

AVA slammed her hand against her steering wheel as she merged into the traffic in the square. Jordan Wellington was a complication that she couldn't afford and didn't need. And it was just her bad luck that he seemed to keep popping up whenever she least expected.

Did the man have to be so damn cute?

Why couldn't she have yanked a buck-toothed, mullet-sporting redneck out of that trunk? Or maybe a basement dweller with an obsession for computer games and an unnatural aversion to the sun?

Damn it, it just wasn't fair.

She thought of Lou Ellen, and what she would have to say about fate. Well, if you asked Ava, fate was a real bitch. Dangling a man like that in front of her when she was powerless to take the bait.

A growl of frustration clawed its way out of her throat, and when she checked her rearview mirror and caught sight of the T-Bird riding her ass, the infamous Martinez temper snapped its leash. She lowered the convertible's top, flipped an unseemly finger high into the air, and smiled grimly as she punched the gas.

Blowing through a red light, Ava watched in amusement as the goon narrowly avoided the business end of a pick-up truck.

Nothing better to ease her frustration than a nice Sunday drive.

CHAPTER NINE

WHENEVER their five sons, two daughters-in-law, infant grandson and toddler granddaughter gathered with him and Addison, Tom Wellington felt like the ringmaster in a very busy circus. And now there was the addition of a large, playful grand-dog to add confusion to the melee.

He grumbled about hiding the breakables, groused over the fact that he was going to have to work well into his dotage because they'd eat him out of house and home. Generally bluffed and blustered.

No one took him seriously.

It could have had something to do with the fact that he let his granddaughter play with his autographed baseball from when the Braves won the World Series. Might be because he snarled at anyone who tried to take his grandson off of his hip. Or was possibly due to his tendency to sneak bits of ham to Finn when no one was looking.

He was a man who adored his family.

And he was a man who knew his family well. It always amazed him that the five rambunctious boys he and Addison had produced had turned into five very fine – yet very different – men.

But of all his sons, he shared the closest connection with Jordan.

It wasn't preference, or favoritism. He loved each of his children as a father should. It was simply a matter of like understanding like.

And despite the fact that Jordan smiled and laughed, traded insults with his brothers and Clay, and chatted amicably with his sisters-in-law over dinner, Tom could sense the shadow of trouble in his son's eyes. So while the others were involved with the tail end of an egg hunt in the backyard, Tom carved out a few moments alone by asking Jordan to help him bring out more beverages to stock the cooler.

Normally he would have enjoyed wheedling out the problem with clever discourse and quiet cunning, but as time was an issue he decided to cut to the chase.

"You want to talk about it?" Tom stacked a couple of six packs of Blue Moon in his son's arms. He rooted around in the back of the fridge, found the juice boxes that his granddaughter liked best, and balanced a couple of them on top of Jordan's load.

"Not particularly." Jordan watched as Tom continued his search of the refrigerator. "If you're looking for that container of plain, non-fat yogurt that you use to hide your Girl Scout cookies, Mom threw it out."

Tom froze. Then stared at his son with horror. "She threw it out?"

"Mmm-hmm. The date was expired."

"So you knew what was in there, and that she was going to toss it, and you just... let her?"

Jordan looked at him with amusement. "What was I supposed to say? You can't throw that expired dairy product away because Dad uses it to stow the sugar and saturated fat he's not supposed to have?"

"You're a clever boy. You could have come up with something."

"What's it worth to you?" Jordan's grin was evil.

"Damn, son." Tom closed the refrigerator door. "I believe I've underestimated you. You took the container out of the trash and hid it, didn't you?"

"Leave me the autographed ball in your will and I just might tell you where the cookies are."

"Are you anxious to kill me off?"

"No, you're doing a fine job of that with doughnuts and cookies."

"Hmm. Funny that you've never bothered to lecture me before. It's also funny that you've neatly turned the tide of conversation away from your problems and toward my own. You think I wouldn't notice?"

Jordan shifted the weight of the drinks into one hand so that he could pat Tom's shoulder with the other. "I just wanted to be sure all that bran and oatmeal Mom's been feeding you hadn't muddled your brain." He jerked his chin toward the pantry. "I hid the Thin Mints in the bottom of the box of Wheaties."

"The breakfast of champions."

"Exactly." His son's grin mirrored his own. "And now that we have that settled, let me answer your question. The Fuller case is weighing on me like a ton of bricks," he admitted as the smile disappeared. "A woman I once cared about seems to be missing and may have tried to maim me. And I have the worst case of sexual frustration that I've experienced since high school. Other than that, I'm dandy."

"Well." Tom stroked his chin as he considered his son's troubles. Jordan was, always had been, the family crusader. And carried responsibility like a shield. "The only thing I can say about the first problem is that you're a brilliant attorney. But sometimes even brilliant attorneys can only practice the law to the best of their abilities, and leave the trickier issue of justice in the hands of a higher power."

"I know. I know. It's just… easier said than done."

"Number two." Tom shoved another six-pack of Coke at his son. "Never piss off a redhead. But when, and if, you get proof she had something to do with that, you throw the damn book. And as to the third…" He put his arm around Jordan and steered him toward the door. "If you can't figure out a way to fix that, then you're no son of mine."

JORDAN considered how to do just that while he bounced his nephew on his knee and fought off the well-meaning intentions of the child's mother. Jack's wife was a romance novelist, and tended to take the whole matchmaking thing a step or ten too far.

"Caitlin, I know you have my best interests at heart, but I have no interest in being set up with any more of your friends."

The baby gurgled and spit up, and Caitlin wiped a cloth across her son's mouth before turning deceptively innocent eyes on Jordan. The angelic look was a crock. She was an out of control cupid, and there was a bulls-eye on his ass.

"It's not a set up, Jordan. Simply an introduction. Katie's a wonderful young woman, very lovely, and I thought that you might enjoy her company."

"Uh-huh. And while I'm enjoying her company, would I be expected to provide a meal, a movie or sexual favors?"

"Honestly, Jordan. I was only going to suggest that you meet her for a couple of drinks."

His nephew made a fumbling attempt to wrap his pudgy fingers around Jordan's nose. "Don't listen to her, Caleb. Today it's drinks, tomorrow you're trading your Oshkosh B'Gosh for a rented tux." The baby laughed, drool running from a crooked grin. God, the poor little sucker looked exactly like his father.

Caitlin's pretty mouth twisted into a pout.

"Is this guy giving you trouble, sugar?" Clay strolled over, liquored up and mellow, and swung a companionable arm over Caitlin's shoulder.

"I simply wanted to introduce my favorite brother-in-law to a woman I know," she told Clay, "and he's accusing me of all manner of vile things."

Jordan rolled his eyes. They were all her favorite brother-in-law, depending on whose love life she'd decided to meddle in. "Let me tell you about the last time she talked me into one of these introductions." He stood and handed the baby off to Caitlin so that he could shift his attention to Clay.

"About four months ago, I made the mistake of letting Caitlin set me up with one of her friends. Now don't look at me like that, Caitlin – it was a mistake, and you know it. Anyway," he turned back at Clay. "This girl was a cute little redhead from Caitlin's book club. We met for dinner, had a nice time, took in a movie about a week later. Things were going along fine, and after a fairly interesting make-out session on her couch I began to entertain possibilities. Apparently, she began to entertain some possibilities of her own. So she decided to pay me a visit one day, wearing a raincoat and nothing else."

Caitlin bit her lip, but Clay looked at him like he'd sprouted another head. "Let me get this straight." He tilted his beer toward Jordan. "Your sister-in-law hooks you up with an attractive female who acts out one of every man's fantasies, and you're… complaining?"

"I was in the middle of a trial when she decided to act it out. Literally. She showed up in the courtroom."

"Look, you made him choke." Caitlin pounded Clay on the back.

"Yeah, give me another three or four decades and I'm sure I'll find the whole thing funny, too."

"I'm sorry, Jordan. And I know it was all my fault." Merriment danced in Caitlin's eyes when she turned to Clay to explain. "You see, there's a scene very similar to what Jordan just described in one of my novels. I'm afraid Miranda read it and, well, got some ideas." Laughter bubbled out before she could stop it. "But I swear, Jordan. Katie's not the raincoat type."

An ant crawled up the back of Jordan's leg, and he reached down to swat it. "Did you meet her through your book club?"

"Well, yes."

"Does she read romance novels?"

"Of course."

"I've heard enough." He threw his arms to his sides, an umpire declaring the runner out. "Thanks, but no thanks."

"Just because she enjoys a good love story and has auburn hair doesn't make her a stalker."

"Well, you just clinched it. I can't have drinks with her because I'm through with redheads." Thoughts of Leslie Fitzsimmons – yet another redhead – brought an uncomfortable little twist in his gut. "Case closed."

Grace, Jesse's two-year-old, toddled over, and Jordan picked her up and tossed her into the air amid peals of laughter. Her pink dress was covered in juice, there was something dark and sticky in her tumble of blonde curls, and her chin bore the melted remains of a chocolate Easter bunny. When Jordan set her down Finn charged after her to lick her face.

"Oh, come on Jordan. It's just drinks."

"Yeah, come on Jordan."

Jordan looked at Clay with irritation. "If you're so game, Clay, why don't you go?"

"That's a great idea!" Caitlin lit up so brightly that Jordan and Clay both blinked. "You guys can double up. I'm sure Katie has a friend she could bring along. That way there's no pressure."

"Okay." Clay was clearly much more wasted than Jordan thought.

"Clay, you're here to help me with a case, not play matchmaker. If I want a date, I can get my own."

"You weren't having too much luck at the park today."

Jordan sent him a fulminating look. "A temporary setback, and none of your damn business."

"Now, Jordan." Clay sat his empty bottle on the step and rested both hands on Jordan's shoulders. "That thing about all work and no play isn't just a cliché. Trust me when I tell you that sometimes it helps to step away from the situation so that you can gain a little perspective. We can start as early as you like tomorrow, and by, oh... let's say seven o'clock we should be ready for a break. A couple of drinks, some conversation. Clears the mind, son."

Jordan scrubbed his hand across his face. "I can't believe this. What happened to male solidarity?"

"One word: raincoat." The traitor winked at Caitlin. "You think your friend would be interested in getting together tomorrow?"

"Wild horses wouldn't keep her away."

"Well then. It sounds like we have ourselves an introduction."

THE bright light of Easter Sunday had softened toward dusk by the time Ava pulled into her drive. Dinner was going to be late, but Lou Ellen wasn't one to mind the clock. Besides, Ava'd had too much damn fun to allow guilt to ruin it.

She'd driven halfway to Florida and back, passing every police station she could find along the way. Then she'd stumbled on a roadside festival, disappearing into the crowd.

The cotton candy had been nearly as tasty as the goon's frustration.

Though she had to give this one credit. He'd stuck like a bloodthirsty tick on a plump hound. And by the deep red flush that had crept up his neck whenever she waved at him, she didn't think he was too happy with his assignment.

Good. That made two of them.

Running her fingers through her tangled hair, Ava smiled at herself in the rearview mirror. Nothing like making one of her uncle's trained dogs jump through hoops to brighten the day.

Her smile turned to a grimace as she stepped from the car and noticed the state of her dress. The wrinkles would come out when she had it dry cleaned, but she wasn't so sure about the grease stain from the carrousel. If she ruined one more garment due to dealing with her uncle's shenanigans she was going to be seriously pissed.

Gravel crunched behind her, and she turned.

The switchblade flashed, and Ava felt the bite of it under her chin.

"Hola." The word was no less menacing for its pleasant tone, the goon's face no less threatening because it smiled handsomely. His skin was dark and clear, and a leather band restrained hair that was thick, black, and long. But his eyes told the real story. They were flat, desolately cold.

"What the hell do you think you're doing?" Ava wasn't afraid, not yet. But she was cautious, and that kept her from flicking the knife away with an angry hand.

"I might ask you the same thing. You take foolish chances, querida, when you play your little games with me. You tried my patience today." He moved closer, until her back was against her car. Her thighs pressed intimately against his. He wasn't that much taller than she, but his presence was disproportionately huge. His breath floated warm and almost sweet against her skin.

Despite herself, Ava shuddered. This man was unlike the others in her uncle's employ – smooth, well spoken.

And somehow, that made him worse.

"You don't scare me."

"No?" The blade pressed, just short of penetration. "Then you're a fool. I could kill you with a flick of my wrist."

"You wouldn't dare." Ava was determined to hold her ground despite the curl of unease in her belly. "My father…" if either of them moved, just the slightest bit, it would be her blood that spilled. "My father would skin you like an animal."

"Your father is in jail."

"And you think my uncle would reward you for killing his only niece?" She regretted it the minute she said it. And she cursed herself as pathetic for using her uncle as a defense.

The goon chuckled. And stepping back, just a little bit, used the blade to groom his nails. "What makes you think your uncle didn't give the order?"

The question, asked so casually, had a chill snaking down her back.

"Ah, I see the cat has taken hold of your sharp tongue. But you're correct, senorita, your uncle doesn't wish to see you harmed." The goon patiently trimmed his thumbnail, discarded the remnants near his booted foot. "Your uncle is a passionate man. A man, you could say, who's ruled by his blood. And his blood flows in your veins. But you and me…" He pointed at her with the blade and then angled it back toward himself. "We share no blood. So don't believe I would suffer your uncle's compunction about spilling yours."

The blade flashed again as he ran the flat of it down her cheek. For the first time in longer than she remembered, Ava truly tasted her own fear.

"You think about that next time you decide to play your little games with me."

The sound of a shotgun being pumped caused Ava's racing heart to stutter.

"And you think about this, senor." Lou Ellen stepped off the porch, her whiskey voice iced with cold fury. "The next time you threaten my tenant, the next time you set foot on my property, the next time you so much as breathe within a five block radius of either one of us, I'll shoot your balls off. And believe me, I'll suffer no compunction about eliminating you from the gene pool." She held the shotgun steady and gestured with her chin. "Now get the hell out of here before my finger gets itchy."

With a careless movement of his wrist, the man looming over Ava closed the switchblade, then rapped it lightly against her nose.

Ignoring Lou Ellen, he whistled I'll Be Seeing You as he strolled away.

"Oh my God." With an uncharacteristic loss of composure, Ava threw her arms around Lou Ellen's neck. "Oh my God. You didn't have to do that. You shouldn't have done that. I'm sorry, I'm so sorry Lou."

LOU ELLEN held the shotgun aside and wrapped Ava in a tight embrace. "Stop your babbling, child." Her heart, which had all but stopped when she'd looked out the window, began to pulse an erratic beat. Ava was the closest thing she had to a daughter. And despite the fact that Ava told her little, and complained even less, she knew the girl was under a tremendous strain.

The men she'd seen at all hours of the day and night weren't lurking on the street because they needed veterinary services.

Knowing that Ava would talk about it only if and when she needed to, Lou Ellen tucked a lock of tousled hair behind the younger woman's ear. Her smile was bland as she shouldered the shotgun. "So. What are we having for dinner?"

Because it was exactly what she needed to hear, Ava laughed.

CHAPTER TEN

AVA had passed a perfectly pleasant evening with Lou Ellen over dinner and a bottle of wine. She'd inoculated a litter of kittens, treated a rabbit with sore hocks and removed a benign lump from a Labrador before noon. Lunch was spent at her desk, catching up on paperwork. Her life was too busy to waste time with worry.

But whenever she had reason to be out front, Ava found herself looking for the black Thunderbird.

God knew why she'd had to provoke the man yesterday. Galling as it was, she had to admit she'd behaved foolishly.

And the worst part of it was that she'd inadvertently drawn Lou Ellen into the fray.

Since that was bad enough, she'd held her tongue when Katie asked about her weekend. Keeping it to herself – and keeping herself in line – was the best way she knew to protect the people she cared for.

Her thoughts wandered back to the task at hand as she finished a neat line of stitches on the abdomen of the pampered cocker spaniel she'd just spayed. The little minx had gone looking for adventure, digging under the backyard fence while her mistress planted gladiolas.

She'd found that adventure with the lab-terrier mix next door.

The puppies had been given away and the fence repaired, but the purebred's reputation was damaged beyond repair. She'd retired from the dog show circuit in shame.

Ava rolled weary eyes while she considered the ridiculous things people worried about.

"Okay, Katie. Let's get this little tramp into post-op."

Katie smiled as she finished cleaning up the implements Ava'd used during the surgery. "Don't let Mrs. Harris hear you say that. By the way that woman was carrying on you'd think it was Queen Elizabeth that got knocked up." She helped Ava shift the unconscious dog into the room they used for recovery.

Ava grabbed a paper towel to dab at the Betadine she'd gotten on her sleeve. "Now why is it that you can make comments like that," she asked Katie, "but when I do you mutter about sarcasm and customer relations."

"First of all, I never mutter. You mutter. I enunciate clearly and concisely. The mode of delivery makes all the difference."

"Kiss. My. Ass. You're right. That sounds much better," Ava said as she headed toward her office.

"You've got fifteen minutes to consider why curse words are a crutch of the unimaginative," Katie called after her. "There's a guinea pig with an infected war wound due in at four. Suspected hamster uprising."

"I'll be sure to bring along a little purple heart."

Ava pushed a lock of hair from her face as she plopped into her seat. The stack of files on her desk from her weekend patients threatened to topple over, so she grabbed one off the top. And took the punch to the gut when she saw Finn/ Wellington scrawled by her own hand.

The man was insanely appealing, but that surely didn't warrant this dragging sense of disappointment. It wasn't like he was the first attractive man to ever express an interest. And he wasn't likely to be the last.

Was she feeling so peevish because her uncle had inadvertently made Jordan something akin to a forbidden fruit?

How long had it been since she'd felt this way? All tingly and excited and nauseous. Probably not since... Michael.

Almost two years. Almost two years since her mother had gone missing, her father had gone out of his head, and her engagement had gone the way of the dinosaurs. Michael had taken his ring back in a fiery explosion of anger and fear, leaving her to choke on the cloud of their relationship's dust. He'd loved her, but he hadn't loved her enough to take on her family.

And God, how could she really blame him? The Brady Bunch, they were not.

She told herself that things were better this way. Better that the only man who'd caught her interest since then was for all intents and purposes unavailable. Given her situation, she needed to view the opposite sex as... meringue. Tasty enough for a moment or two, but basically lacking substance.

Dating was fine, but dating sexy, persistent men with cute dogs and cuter dimples was completely out of the question. To do so, she risked wanting more.

And more was something she wasn't sure she could have.

Especially not with Jordan Wellington.

Sighing, Ava picked up her pen and began to transcribe some notations on Finn's file. She'd no sooner written her first letter when Katie burst through her office door.

"Cole Nash's Bernese was hit by a car. He's out there bleeding all over the waiting room."

"Get him back to surgery," Ava said hurriedly. "And grab the lead apron out of the closet. I'll need to take some X-rays."

She dropped the pen on top of the folder and rushed out the door.

IT was past six by the time Ava finally locked the clinic's front door. She'd spent the better part of two hours repairing the extensive trauma caused when a ninety pound canine takes on a car. Muscle and tendon damage, slivers of shattered bone. Two delicate steel rods had been inserted to give the dog the chance of independent mobility. Due to his size, and his breed's tendency toward hip dysplasia, she knew that he and his owner had a long, difficult road ahead.

But at least she'd managed to save his leg.

Sighing, Ava flexed her fingers, trying to work out some of the cramping brought on by hours of delicate work. Then sliding her keys into the pocket of her lab coat, started toward post-op. She now had two patients recovering from surgery, so it looked like she would be spending the night. There was a well-used folding cot in her office, and a full bath off the small kitchenette in the back. She wasn't in the type of profession where you could count on leaving your work at the office at five o'clock and heading home.

Yet she wouldn't have it any other way.

"Ava?"

"Hmm?" Ava blinked twice and brought Katie into focus. She noticed that the other woman – who'd switched into friendship mode as it was past five o'clock – was holding a bottle of shampoo, a bar of soap, and a clean, folded towel in her hands.

"You're a mess," Katie said mildly. "Why don't you go hit the shower and wake yourself up? I'll keep an eye on the dogs for you."

"Oh." She blinked again. "Thanks, Katie. But you don't have to stay. The cocker spaniel's already perking up, and I imagine our big guy will sleep for several hours. He came out of the anesthesia fine, but the pain meds are going to keep him down."

"Nevertheless." Katie thrust the shower accouterments into Ava's arms. "I think I'll stick around, just in case. Run along, now."

She hustled Ava toward the back.

AS soon as her boss was out of the room, Katie rushed over to the desk to grab her purse. She touched up her makeup, swept her shoulder-length hair into a casually elegant twist, and exchanged her jeans and sneakers for a short, floaty skirt and a pair of sandals. She'd debated the issue of heels, but wasn't entirely sure of the size of the men she'd agreed to meet.

And besides, she didn't want to look like a stick figure next to Ava's petite package of curves.

She was bent over, fastening the strap around her left ankle when she heard the knock on the front door. Perfect. Lou Ellen was right on time. The woman might be flighty, but she could be counted on in a pinch.

Katie waved at the older woman before hurrying over to let her in.

"Thank you so much for coming."

"You think I'd miss this?" Lou Ellen drifted in, smelling faintly of rosewater and the peppermints she favored. "Girl hasn't so much as sniffed at a man in going on two years. Doesn't start using what the good Lord gave her it's likely to weld shut. Here." She handed Katie a figure hugging red dress and a pair of open-toed pumps.

"Perfect." Katie gave the outfit an once-over, decided that she couldn't have done better herself. The dress was sensational. Casual, tasteful, but brief enough to make it hot. Ava would look like a siren.

Lou Ellen glanced around, taking in the neatly organized supplies, the tidy reception area, the scrubbed floors. The mingling scents of animal and antiseptic in the air. "So this is it, huh?" She wrinkled her nose. Katie knew that work, let alone work that involved the tending of animals and their bodily functions, left an unpleasant taste in the other woman's mouth.

It was why, despite her and Ava's close relationship, this was the first she'd stepped foot in the clinic.

"And the... dogs I'm supposed to keep my eye on are where?"

"In the back." Katie knew it spoke of the depth of Lou Ellen's affection for Ava that she would be willing to lend a hand. She had no great love for man's best friend. "One has been moved into the kennel and should be no trouble. The other is still sedated. You'll just need to monitor him for any signs of trouble."

"And what am I supposed to do if there's trouble? Restrain the beast?"

Katie laughed. "He's drugged and he has a broken leg. He's not going anywhere. But if he becomes agitated when he wakes up, or looks like he's going into distress, just call Ava. Chances are good that he won't even wake up until after we get back. We should only be out a couple of hours."

"Well, then." Lou Ellen pursed her lips in an expression that hovered between distaste and resignation.

"You're a good sport, Lou Ellen. With everything that Ava's had to deal with lately I think that a couple of drinks with a pair of attractive men might be just what she needs."

"After tonight, that might be just what I need as well."

Katie swung an arm around the older woman's shoulders. "I'm afraid I don't have any adult beverages to offer, but if you'll come to the back with me, I can introduce you to a big, prostrate male."

"When you put it that way, darling, how's a lady to refuse?"

AVA washed the day's work, if not the day's worries out of her hair. The metallic odor of blood, the chemical tang of disinfectant, slid away in a sudsy froth that hinted of coconut.

She had to admit the shower helped her transform herself into something remotely human.

When she stepped out and began toweling off, she noticed that Katie had taken her soiled clothes. Always efficient, that was Katie. Well, mostly efficient, Ava considered as she looked around. She'd neglected to bring Ava the spare sweat suit she kept in her office. But no matter. Ava simply wrapped up in the towel and padded across the hall herself.

When she opened the drawer, she found a note instead of her sweat suit: *Don't Argue*

Perplexed, mostly naked, she wandered back into the hall. She found her assistant in the process of closing the door to post-op behind her. When Katie turned, smiled, Ava waved the paper. "Would you like to tell me what this is about?"

"We're going out for drinks."

Ava noted how Katie was dressed, the short skirt, the makeup. "It's a nice thought, Katie, but I'm afraid it's not the best time." Pushing the still dripping hair out of her eyes, she nodded meaningfully toward post-op.

"It's the perfect time." Katie grabbed Ava by the elbow, and steered her across the hall. "Wait right here."

When she reappeared, Ava blinked in recognition at the red dress. "How did you get that?"

"Your landlord." Katie pushed her toward the bathroom.

"Lou Ellen? Lou Ellen brought you this? So what, she just… let herself into my apartment and rummaged through my things?"

"Pretty much."

Why Ava was surprised, she didn't know. Lou Ellen would think no more of violating Ava's privacy than she did of drinking whiskey with breakfast. Other people's mores had never been her concern.

"You've had a bad time of it lately and we decided that you need a distraction. So we're going to go drown your concerns in a nice bottle of wine."

"Katie, I appreciate the thought, but you can't expect me to leave when I have two patients to tend."

Katie waved that away like a gnat. "Lou Ellen's sitting with them as we speak."

"What?" Ava felt, literally felt, her heart skip a beat. She dug her heels in and looked toward post-op in panic. "Lou Ellen doesn't know a thing about –"

Katie wouldn't let her finish. "I've given her instructions, and she has both of our cell phone numbers. Give the lady some credit." She gave Ava another unceremonious shove into the bathroom and all but tossed the dress in after. "Oh and Ava? Put on some makeup. We're going to be meeting a couple of men."

"I can't believe I let you talk me into this," Jordan complained as he nursed his beer.

They'd arrived early, at Clay's insistence, because he wanted to loosen his friend up. Jordan was almost always good company, but after he'd had a few drinks he was downright entertaining. Despite his size, he had the tolerance of a ninety pound co–ed. Needless to say, Clay considered it his duty to get his friend stinking drunk at least once a year. It was always good for an evening of laughs, not to mention the fodder for the harassment mill.

Clay figured Jordan could use a few laughs right now, but the man didn't seem inclined to cooperate. "Would you like me to put a nipple on that thing?"

"I'm driving. And anyway, don't think I don't know what you're up to." Jordan narrowed his eyes at Clay. "Pump a few beers in me, diminish my faculties, throw in a couple of desperate females and see what happens. You're a pot-stirrer, Clay. A six foot wooden spoon."

"It's what I do," Clay agreed.

"Well, I'm onto you, so stir things up elsewhere. And just so you know, you've got an hour." He glanced at his watch, noted the time. As a concession to good manners he'd left the ball cap in the car, but he hadn't exactly put bells on. "Eight o'clock rolls around, and we're out of here."

"What if I'm having fun, Dad?"

"Ha ha. If you're not ready by eight, you'll just have to get one of the romance groupies to give you a ride. No pun intended. I'm going to go home and take another look at those files."

Clay examined the dregs of his beer and decided he was ready for another. "Jordan, we've just spent a whole day with crime scene photos, autopsy reports and enough interview transcripts to sink a boat. It's gone a long way toward giving me some ideas about your killer's personality, but son, it's time for a break. Just let it go for an hour or two."

Jordan picked at the label on his bottle. "If we don't have the right man, I may still have to go to trial against the man we do have. What if I win? How can I, in good conscience, live with that on my hands? And worse, so much worse, is what if all this dicking around leaves the real killer free to do it again?

Some innocent woman could die." He frowned at his beer. "I just can't help feeling... responsible."

"That kind of responsibility will kill you, friend." As Clay well knew. The stress inherent in what he did caused many to burn out faster than a match head. "Don't forget you're part of a team that's part of a system. Sometimes the system works, sometimes the system fails. You can only work within its confines to the best of your abilities, and do what you believe is right. After that, it's up to fate."

"That's almost identical to the advice I received from my father."

"Your father's a wise man." Sitting aside his empty glass, he signaled the bartender for another. "Now listen to the advice of another wise man, and try to have yourself a little fun. I meant what I said about all work and no play. You don't find a way to strike a balance, the next hospital you wind up in is likely to have padded walls."

"I can't believe I let you talk me into this."

Ava grimaced at the old plaster façade of Moon River Brewery. Gas flame lanterns spurted and danced, burning off the deepening shadows of dusk, while music and voices spilled through the open doors like bright candies from a box. The Savannah landmark might be known for its ghost, but there were plenty of live patrons tonight.

She glanced down at the red dress. They were about to go in there and meet up with a couple of strange men, and she looked like a walking come on. "Shit."

"Language," Katie sing-songed as she nudged Ava down the sidewalk. "And look at it this way – if nothing else, you've escaped from your spy detail for a couple of hours. The goon wasn't paying any attention to the fact that I made off with you in my car. He'll be sitting in the parking lot guarding your Mustang, and you'll be frolicking with attractive men."

"No offense, Katie. But you only have your friend's word that these men are attractive. They could be trolls. They probably are trolls. Trolls with bad breath." The thought cheered her vaguely. "Trolls with bad breath who stalk women's book clubs."

"Oh, hush. This is Caitlin Cavanaugh we're talking about. She's just released her third bestseller, so I'm pretty sure she knows attractive when she sees it."

"Ah, yes. The bodice rippers you like to read when you're pretending to be studying the computer manual."

Katie blinked, then quickly recovered. "They're not bodice rippers," she said indignantly. "They're very well-written, critically acclaimed romance novels." She pulled up short as they reached the door. "And I can all but guarantee that these men aren't trolls. I've seen photos of her husband, and if his brother looks anything like him, well, all I can say is: wow. We should be safe."

Safe, Ava thought grimly as she looked around, wasn't exactly what she was feeling. There was more of a crowd than she'd expected for a Monday, most of them baby-faced and sunburned on top of it. Spring-breakers, Ava decided when one of them looked over, then elbowed his pal. And here she was dressed like a little red sports car, just begging to be pulled over.

In defense, Ava turned away, studied the old black and white photographs that lined the brick walls. But the shot of the fountain in Forsythe Park did little to improve her mood.

"Okay," Katie drew her attention. "We're looking for a blond and a brunette... Oh. I see them up at the bar. Holy... check them out." Katie sucked in a breath. "To the left, ten o'clock. The blond is definitely hot. And the one in the blue shirt is –"

"Jordan Wellington." Ava's own breath clogged in her throat as the men turned from the bar. Warning bells echoed shrilly inside her head while her stomach did the gastric rumba. "Christ in a sidecar, Katie, you've dragged me along on a date with Jordan Wellington."

"You know him?" Katie blinked.

"New client. Long story." Ava scrubbed her hand across her face and laughed. Fate was a sneaky sonofabitch. "Look, Katie, I have to get out of here before he sees me."

"What? Don't be ridiculous." Katie grabbed Ava's arm as she tried to pull away. "And anyway, it's too late. Mr. tall, dark, and... oh, lethal smile, has apparently spotted you. Whoa.

Dimples. And while I would like to point out that he was supposed to be my date, it's obvious there's something going on here of which I was unaware."

She spared Ava a reproachful look. "Now buck up, sister. They're on their way over."

JORDAN could hardly believe his eyes. He'd been told to watch out for a tall redhead, but Caitlin's details had been sketchy on the friend.

He decided that the completed picture had turned out better than he could have hoped.

"What?" Clay followed Jordan's gaze toward the door. "Man. Check out the pins on the redhead. And hey, isn't that –"

"Ava Martinez," Jordan concurred, and followed the statement with a wolfish grin. "And now I understand why they use red to stop traffic." He rubbed a hand over his heart. "Clay, I take back every irritable word I said. Thanks to you, it looks like I'm going to get my date with the good doctor after all."

CHAPTER ELEVEN

THE man was deadly. After twenty minutes in his company, Ava felt like she'd plunged bodily into quicksand. How was anyone supposed to be able to breathe when they were being drowned by all that charm? Where was her foothold? Couldn't someone toss her a damn line?

"Would you like another glass of wine?"

Ava looked down at her glass in surprise. She had no idea how it had come to be empty. And the worst part of it was that she'd inadvertently consumed a glass of her uncle's label. The small vineyard which produced it was one of the "legitimate" businesses that Carlos used to launder his money. She'd been too flustered when she ordered the house white to bother to check.

She was not a woman accustomed to being flustered.

She returned Jordan's gaze, got pinned by that piercing blue, and then realized he was waiting for an answer. "Actually, I think I'd like a mojito."

"Is the wine not to your liking?"

She thought of the money that she'd just put in her uncle's pocket. "Let's just say it leaves a bad taste in my mouth."

"Well, we can't have that." Jordan signaled the waitress, ordered her drink. When it came she took a greedy gulp. She figured if she just kept drinking this whole situation might not seem so absurd.

Jordan smiled, and she funneled more alcohol.

Sweet Jesus, did he have to smell so good?

Off balance, Ava shot an imploring look at Katie, only to realize she'd get no help from that quarter. For a woman who prided herself on manners, her employee was being awfully damn rude. Sidled up against Jordan's friend, with whom she flirted outrageously, she'd left Ava to flounder like a landed trout.

Not that she normally had trouble talking to men. But what the hell was she supposed to say to this one?

We need to stop meeting like this? You seem a lot more intelligent when you're fully conscious? By the way, you owe me a hundred bucks because the blood from your gaping head-wound ruined my favorite pants?

She directed the pointed toe of her shoe toward Katie's shin.

"Ow. Oh, hey." Katie gauged Ava's desperate expression and finally deigned to toss out a conversational gambit. "So, Jordan. Caitlin tells me you're a lawyer."

Ava's shoulders relaxed, and she took another swig of her drink. If she could just keep Katie talking, she might be able to get through the next forty-five minutes without accidentally incriminating herself.

"That's right. I'm an assistant district attorney."

Rum sprayed out of Ava's mouth, covering the table in effervescent droplets.

"Are you okay?" Jordan rubbed her back as Ava continued to choke. Tears swam into her eyes when the rub turned into a pat.

"I'm fine. Wrong pipe." She waved a hand to ward him off. Shit. Holy shit. Consorting with a prosecutor.

That just about topped the list of Things One Shouldn't Do When One's Uncle's a Known Criminal.

She turned doe in the headlight eyes on Katie.

But Katie was too busy smiling at the blue-eyed can of worms she'd opened. "Really? That must be interesting."

"It has its moments."

His friend – Clay – snorted, which of course drew Katie's attention right back to him. "Are you an attorney, too?"

"God, no."

This time Jordan was the one to snort. "Worse. He's a psychologist."

"Private practice?" Ava asked, because if it hadn't been for her love of animals, that may have been the path she'd have chosen. She'd always been fascinated by what made people tick.

"Ah, no, actually. I'm a behavioral specialist with the FBI."

To her credit, Ava managed to keep herself from choking a second time. Good thing, since the *behavioral specialist* was watching her like a hawk.

Looking around the table, she decided this little gathering was starting to resemble a den of lions. And she was the sacrificial Christian. If it weren't for the fact that Katie had brought her, she would have suspected some kind of sting.

Not that she herself had ever done anything illegal – or nothing major, anyway. But when one's relatives were players in one of the biggest crime rings in the southeast, one acquired a "person of interest" status by default.

And then there was the little matter of her pulling Mr. Assistant District Attorney here– *Jesus* – out of that stupid trunk. Try explaining that without ending up in jail.

"Oh hey. Look at the time." Ava glanced down and was relieved to find that she was, indeed, wearing a watch. Otherwise her ruse could have been a little awkward. "It's been nice, and I hate to cut the fun short, but I'm afraid I have to be going. Katie, don't worry about the ride. I'll take a cab."

Hell, she'd walk, run, or sprout wings and fly if that's what it took to get out of there.

A prosecutor and an FBI agent.

Mother of God.

"What's the rush?" Jordan reached for her hand as Ava stood. When she attempted to pull away he manacled her wrist like a human handcuff.

And okay, that image wasn't helping. "Professional crisis." She smiled, much like a canary trying to dissuade a hungry cat.

"Ava saved a life today," Katie explained. "A client's dog was hit by a car."

"Wow." Jordan maintained his death grip on her wrist and leaned his chin casually on his free hand. "That's fantastic. Not the car-hitting part, but the life-saving part. What did you have to do?"

"Well, it was more of a leg that we were in danger of losing. Basically I repaired the damage as best I could and set the leg with a couple of steel rods." She gave what she hoped was another inconspicuous tug of her hand. "He's recovering from the surgery now. That's why I have to get back. I really hadn't planned on staying long."

"What a coincidence. Neither had I." Jordan changed his grip so that her fingers had no choice but to interlock with his, then pulled his wallet out of his back pocket. Opening it one-handed, he tossed Clay a couple of bills. "Here. Drinks are on me." He turned his attention to Katie. "I'll take Ava back to the clinic if you don't mind giving Clay a ride home."

Ignoring the warning look in Ava's eyes, the traitor continued to smile at Jordan. "I'm sure that won't be a problem."

"Excellent." Jordan let go of Ava's hand long enough to slip a key off his ring. "Don't wait up." He passed the key to his friend, who only winked when Ava's mouth fell open.

For the second time since she'd met him, Ava realized that Jordan Wellington had completely maneuvered her.

When they reached the sidewalk – where the cool, damp air did little to relieve her temper – she finally shook off Jordan's arm and whirled on him.

"What the hell do you think you're doing?"

Jordan halted his stride long enough to give her a considering look. "I think I'm giving you a ride. What do you think you're doing?"

"Don't be cute, Wellington."

"Ah. So you do prefer dating ugly men." He stuck his hands in his pockets and rocked back on his heels.

"Look." Ava scrubbed a hand across her eyes as irritation and amusement waged a quick and bloody battle. "I thought I made myself clear before, but apparently you're a bit thickheaded. This whole you and me thing? It is so not going to happen."

"Uh-huh. You keep right on thinking that."

Amusement went down like a lamb. "Okay, just so you know, there's a very fine line between persistent and downright annoying. After annoying comes creepy, and then we venture off into the murky waters of stalker territory. Being a prosecutor…" Damn it. "I would think you would realize that."

Jordan hit a button on the remote to unlock his car. Then he opened the passenger door for Ava and waited for her to get in.

When she just stood there he let out a little sigh. "Last time I checked, offering a woman a ride wasn't a criminal offense.

Call a cab if you want, but it seems silly when I have my car right here."

Ava shook her head, disgusted with herself for any number of reasons, and disgusted with him for putting her in the position of either acting like a shrew or capitulating to his inconsiderate use of logic. "Fine." She stalked forward, shook off his solicitous grasp on her elbow, and plopped into the seat with little grace.

When he joined her in the car, she clicked her seatbelt into place. "But just so you know, my accepting a ride from you doesn't give you the right to expect anything else."

Jordan backed out of the parking space and cast a glance at her over his shoulder. "Are you this prickly with everyone or is it just me?"

"I'm prickly, rude and short tempered by nature. I can't imagine why you would want to bother with me."

"You mean aside from the fact that you're intelligent, interesting and my head does a full three hundred and sixty degree turn whenever I get within thirty feet of you?" Dimples flashed, a vortex of charm, and Ava felt herself being sucked in. "I guess I enjoy a challenge. And my dog seems to like you."

"Trust me," she said, hating herself, hating the situation. "You don't want to get involved." There, at least, was some truth. If he knew who and what she was, he'd either attempt to indict her or run screaming in the opposite direction.

"I'm going to have to disagree with you. Because I apparently have a thing for prickly, rude, short tempered women. You should wear red every day." He reached out, ran the backs of his fingers down her cheek. "It suits you. All fire and heat."

Ava cursed the tight little ball of lust which rolled into her belly. "You're like a damn Sheltie," she muttered.

"A Sheltie?" Jordan asked with amusement. "How, exactly, do I remind you of a Sheltie?"

"You're all cute and playful, and though you look pretty easygoing, you're really not. You just nudge, nose, circle around and herd your quarry until you've got them boxed into whatever corner you've chosen. The damn sheep doesn't even realize what's happening until it's all over and done with."

Jordan laughed out loud. "I'm not sure which one of us should be more insulted by that analogy, but I guess you're right. Herding is one of my more impressive but lesser known skills. I tend to work with, through or around things until I get my way."

Ava was about to offer her opinion on what he could do with his way when a flash of black caught her eye. A quick glance at the side-view mirror had the blood draining from her face. The T-Bird was behind them.

Nausea rolled like oil over the alcohol in her belly.

Noting the direction of her gaze, Jordan glanced in the rearview mirror. "Is something wrong?"

"What? Oh, no. Nothing's wrong." She forced her voice to sound normal. She'd learned a long time ago to control outward manifestations of fear. "Nice car, by the way." She cast her gaze around, remembering that he'd been worried about his new vehicle after she'd pulled him out of the trunk. "Charger, right? One of your classic American muscle cars. She accelerates like a dream." Ava ran her fingertips down the black leather seat in appreciation. "This the Hemi?"

"Right." He looked surprised. "You obviously know your way around cars."

"Uh-huh. One of my more impressive yet lesser known skills. So how does it corner?"

"What? It, uh, it corners… great."

"Good. Why don't you show me?" At the next intersection, Ava grabbed the wheel and yanked it to the right.

"Are you crazy?" Jordan slapped her hand off the steering wheel, correcting the angle of the turn so that they didn't plow into the sidewalk. A group of wide-eyed tourists goggled as they careened past.

"Yep. Crazy." Ava looked over her shoulder, and saw that the T-Bird continued to go straight. Her breath whooshed out with relief. Maybe it had simply been a coincidence. Maybe it had been a different T-Bird.

Maybe pigs would fly.

She flicked a glance at Jordan, who was looking less than amused. Good. Let him think she was nuts. "Like I told you. You don't want to get involved."

JORDAN narrowed his eyes as she settled more comfortably into the seat. Wild and exotic in that red dress, dark hair rioting against her shoulders, she did indeed look like the sort of woman that could cause considerable trouble. The type of woman, he thought grimly, who'd nearly caused him to crash his new car. Under normal circumstances, that was enough to have him running the other way.

Hadn't he ditched the attractive redhead when she'd walked into court in a raincoat? Hadn't he fought off Leslie Fitzsimmons when she was on him like white on rice?

Hell, what was it with him and crazy women?

But he'd seen the look on Ava's face when that black Ford had come up behind them. She'd been spooked. And the flighty routine simply didn't mesh with the competent professional who'd taken care of his dog.

Instead of scaring him off, she'd only piqued his curiosity.

"I'm not that easily discouraged, sweetheart." They pulled onto the street where her clinic was located, and he noticed that she took another glance around.

Something, or someone, clearly had her worried.

After she'd thoroughly scanned the parking lot, she offered a sheepish smile. "Thanks for the ride. Really. And I'm sorry about the theatrics earlier." She paused, took a breath. "You seem like a really nice guy."

"Thanks." Jordan all but bolted out of the car and went around to open her door. Being called a "nice guy" was part one of How to Let a Man Down in Two Easy Steps, and despite the fact that Ava Martinez may or may not be crazy, he wasn't about to let her get to part two: the ego-shredding "but..."

But I really just want to be friends. But I'm not looking for a relationship at the moment.

Both were just variations of "kiss off."

Whatever she was about to say, he didn't want to hear it.

He offered his hand, and as she stepped from the car into the swirl of evening mist that danced about their ankles, he thought of a siren rising from the sea. Dazzled, he almost forgot his game plan until she awkwardly said "Goodnight."

"Do you have any water?"

"What?"

"Water," Jordan repeated. "Do you have any inside?"

"Is that some kind of variation of aren't you going to invite me in for a drink?"

Jordan's smile was all innocence. "Clever, but no. I really just need to get some water." He cast her wilted pansies a sympathetic glance. The purple and yellow blossoms hung listlessly from drooping stems.

"Um. Sure. There are some bottles in the fridge." She opened the front door, relocking it once they were inside. After another wary glance at the parking lot, she led Jordan toward the back.

"Ava, darling, is that you?"

Ava halted mid-stride, then cursed under her breath. "Yeah, it's me, Lou Ellen." She hesitated, then with a bright, bright smile, turned back toward Jordan. "Um… Give me just a minute, would you?"

"Sure," Jordan replied easily. And wondered who she thought she was kidding.

AVA walked off toward post-op, leaving Jordan loitering in the hall, and the sight which greeted her as she strode into the room would have caused a lesser woman's jaw to drop. Lou Ellen sat on the table with the semi-conscious dog's head on her lap, a shotgun propped near her feet and a suspicious looking flask at her lips. Having known Lou Ellen long enough that nothing she did surprised her, Ava took it all in with good natured resignation. "Were you expecting him to give you trouble, Lou Ellen?"

"Honey, this big fella's a pushover." She let the dog's silky black ear, which she'd been stroking, slide out of her fingers. "I've almost reconsidered my position on the species. The trouble I expect is from an entirely different source… Oh. Hello." She stopped her explanation as her gaze drifted over Ava's shoulder.

Ava didn't have to turn around to know that Jordan hadn't stayed where she'd put him. He ambled forward, plastered himself against her back and peered over her shoulder.

"Wow. That dog's big, but the shotgun looks like it could take down an elephant. Is that how you subdue all your patients?"

Ava sighed. As if this night weren't bad enough. "Lou Ellen, this is Jordan Wellington." Her eyes met Lou Ellen's in a silent plea for her to behave herself. "Jordan, this is my landlord, Lou Ellen Calhoun."

Jordan skirted around Ava. "Landlord, huh? My last landlord was an eighty year old man with a bad toupee and a penchant for polka. Where did I go wrong?" He lifted Lou Ellen's fingers to his lips. "It's a pleasure to meet you."

"Well aren't you a smooth one?" Lou Ellen slid an approving glance from head to well-shod toe. "And good-looking, too. Women must stick to you like flies in ointment."

"They land." Jordan grinned. "But they don't stick."

"Slippery, are you?"

"Only when I'm wet."

Ava rolled her eyes amidst Lou Ellen's delighted laughter. This was so not what she needed. "Did you still want some water?" she asked Jordan, hoping to hurry him along before Lou Ellen decided to keep him. "The fridge is that way." She pointed out the door.

"Actually, I need a bucket."

"A bucket. You need a bucket of water."

"Umm-hmm." He walked toward her again, stood closer than was strictly necessary. "Do you have one?"

"A bucket."

"Small, roughly cylindrical. Holds fluids."

"In the hall closet, wise guy. The question is why do you need it?"

"It's for your flowers."

"My flowers."

"Sweetheart, you might save dogs," he tapped her nose "but you're murder on pansies."

Bemused, Ava watched him saunter away, then turned to meet Lou Ellen's knowing look.

"Hubba hubba."

"Oh, stop it," she hissed, quietly closing the door behind her. "There is no hubba hubba allowed. I've implemented a moratorium. Lou, that's the man from the trunk."

"Well that's interesting." Lou Ellen took another sip from her flask. "I thought you turned him down."

"I did turn him down," she whispered. "But then Katie's friend is married to his brother, and tried to set them up, but it all got turned around when he saw me and … don't you dare say anything about fate." Ava pointed an accusatory finger when Lou Ellen turned smug. "Aside from the fact that I keep waiting for him to have a sudden epiphany and recall where he first made my acquaintance, I found out tonight that the man's an assistant district attorney. A prosecutor, for God's sake." She sent an anxious glance over her shoulder.

Lou Ellen burst out laughing. The dog opened glazed eyes, and Ava hushed her before soothing her charge.

"Sorry." The older woman gently extricated herself from the groggy canine, hopping from the table with the grace of a dancer. Then she unobtrusively slipped the flask into the pocket of her virulent purple dress. "I guess you're too close to the situation to appreciate fate's fine sense of humor."

"Okay, enough already. We don't have a lot of time, and right now I'm more interested in hearing why you felt the need to barricade yourself in here with a gun."

Lou Ellen's finely stenciled brows knit together as she picked up the Winchester. "Let's just say I'm not a fan of uninvited guests."

Ava had a sinking feeling that she knew what Lou Ellen was talking about. "The goon in the T-Bird?"

"That's the one."

"Shit," Ava said, abandoning all hope that seeing him tonight had been a coincidence. "What happened?"

"About ten minutes after you and Katie left, the little yapper you have out back in the kennel started to put up a real din. Naturally, being cognizant of my responsibilities, I went out to investigate the cause of the distress."

Ava interpreted that to mean that Lou Ellen went out to tell the cocker spaniel to shut up.

"At first I didn't notice any detectable problems, but after I'd... consoled the animal and decided to go back inside, I caught a movement out of the corner of my eye. When I turned, he was there, leaning against that oak at the back corner of your property. He had the blade out again, trimming his nails, casual as you please."

"Oh, Lou Ellen." Ava's hand flew to her mouth as any number of horrible scenarios played in her head. Just because the goon – most likely – would hesitate before slitting her throat, it didn't mean that he would think twice about doing a little carving on Lou Ellen. And the guilt that came with that knowledge gripped Ava's heart like a vise.

If anything happened to the older woman, she wouldn't be able to bear it.

"Why didn't you call me?"

"Because it was nothing I couldn't handle. I took the yapper inside with me and put her in one of the cages, then got my shotgun and my liquid fortitude out of my car. By the time I came around back again he was gone."

"I'm so sorry, Lou Ellen." Ava cursed the goon, her uncle, and herself for dragging her friend into this.

"No sugarplum, sorry is a grown man who gets his kicks out of threatening women with his big, scary knife." She sniffed her disdain. "Compensating, if you ask me."

Ava's laugh was weak, but admiration had taken the sharpest edge off her anger. "You're one hell of a woman, Lou Ellen Calhoun."

"Honey, tell me something I didn't know." She swung her free arm around Ava's shoulder. "You gonna be okay here tonight?"

"I'll be –" Ava broke off as the door handle began to rattle.

"Okay, your pansies should live to see another day," Jordan said as he came back into the room. He took in the women's positions and Ava's strained expression. "Is there a problem?"

"Nothing that a big strong man such as yourself shouldn't be able to handle," Lou Ellen proclaimed, to Jordan's amusement and Ava's dismay. "And since it seems to me that my continued presence here is superfluous, I'll bid you both good night." She hefted the shotgun over her shoulder. "Take care of yourself tonight, Ava. Jordan, I assure you, the pleasure's been mine."

"Well," Ava said when she and Jordan were uncomfortably alone. "Thanks again for the ride." She moved to show him toward the door but he grabbed her by the arm.

"Are you planning on staying here all night?"

Ava gave his restraining hand a pointed look before raising her eyes toward his. "Not that I see where it's any of your business, but yes. As a matter of fact, I am. I have two patients recovering from surgery, and I don't feel comfortable leaving them alone."

"I'll keep you company."

Her brow winged up. "Like hell you will." She started to move past him but he tightened his grip on her arm.

"Look, Ava, I'm aware of the fact that, for seemingly inscrutable reasons, you're uncomfortable having me around. But the fact of the matter is that something obviously has you spooked enough to try to wreck my car, and for your landlord to guard your clinic with a shotgun. For equally inscrutable reasons, that worries me. I don't like the idea of you being here all by yourself."

And the fact that he had sensed there was a problem worried Ava. It was in her best interest to keep that sort of thing as far off his radar as possible. With that goal in mind, she covered her irritation, and her nerves, with a smile. "As flattering as it is for you to go all white knight for my benefit, I can assure you there's no need to worry. Lou Ellen's merely... eccentric. And I can take care of myself."

JORDAN looked at the woman in front of him, all five feet three inches of her, and thought she might very well be capable, indeed. There was a toughness about Ava Martinez, despite all the soft feminine curves, that hinted of personal battles hard won. Regardless of that, Jordan had spent the day looking at evidence of what one depraved man could do to a woman. And being a slave to his protective nature, wasn't about to leave her alone.

"Humor me," he cajoled. "My chain mail gets rusty if I don't use it often enough."

Detecting that he may have put a chink in her own armor when her lips twitched, he pressed his advantage. "And you'd be doing me a favor. If I stay here, it won't put me in the awkward position of kicking Clay and your friend out of my bed."

The lip twitch turned into a frown. "And what makes you think that Katie's just going to fall into bed with a man she just met?"

"Well, no offense." He tugged innocently at his ear. He thought no such thing. "But she was sort of... rubbing against him for the best part of the last hour. Just making an educated guess."

She rolled her eyes. "Men are such pigs."

"First a knight, now a pig. I've really come down in the world. But since you're a veterinarian, the fact that I'm swine shouldn't pose too much of a problem."

When her smile threatened again, Jordan ran his hand down the arm he was still holding. "Can I stay? I promise not to wallow in the mud."

FOR the first time in her determination to be rid of him, Ava wavered. Despite the fact that she had what she considered a very strong backbone, she had to admit that the goon in the T-Bird was beginning to make her nervous.

Jordan Wellington spelled bad news for her in almost every possible way, but tonight she figured he just might be the lesser of two evils.

Plus, she had to admit. He was awfully damn cute.

"Okay, Porky. You can stick around." And when he grinned, dimples flashing, and Ava was tempted to just eat him up, she figured it was a damn good thing that she happened to be a vegetarian.

CHAPTER TWELVE

IT was stupid. Yes, it was stupid, and ill advised, and an all-around bad idea, and there was every probability it would blow up in her face. But it was hard to remember that fact when Ava was having so much fun.

There was no denying that aside from having a great personality, a keen mind, and a body that made her want to pull on her hiking gear and launch an expedition, Jordan Wellington was fun to be around. She looked at him over the stingy remains of the pizza – half loaded, half plain – that sat between them on the cot.

"I swear," Jordan commented as he tossed the crust from his final piece back into the open box. Ava closed the lid, stretching over to toss the box onto her desk because the cot had chewed up the tiny bit of floor space that wasn't stacked with product samples and files. "I don't know where you managed to put all that in your tiny little body."

"Give me a break," Ava shot back around her final mouthful of cheese. "I had a carton of yogurt and a banana for lunch today, and then the surgery took so long that I didn't have a chance to eat dinner. Do I look like the kind of woman who makes a habit of skipping meals?"

"I…" he closed his mouth. "You do realize there's no safe way for me to answer that."

"Tactful."

"Cautious. A man doesn't learn to step carefully around a question like that – or its close relatives, do these jeans make me look fat and do you think she's prettier than me – he's going to trip a landmine every time."

"Why do you think we ask?"

WHEN she smiled – landmine defused – Jordan tried to find more room for his long legs by crossing one bare foot over the other.

He'd ditched his shoes a couple of hours ago, and was working his way up to losing the pants. Not that he had any ulterior motive in mind. He simply could not be comfortable sleeping in his clothes.

He hoped to convince Ava that she wouldn't be comfortable in hers, either.

"So do you do this often?" he asked, as an alternative to moving forward with that portion of the night's program. If he didn't think about something other than Ava Martinez naked, his pants were bound to become even more uncomfortable.

"What? Sit in my office in the middle of the night and eat pizza with random guys?" She licked sauce off her fingers and nearly caused Jordan to break out in a sweat.

"First of all, I'm not random. I've seen you three times in as many days, so we practically have a relationship. But I meant do you often stay overnight to keep an eye on your patients?"

"Probably once a week." She brushed her hands together as the last piece of crust disappeared into her mouth. "I try to schedule most of my surgeries on a single day, so that I only have the one night to contend with. But there are emergencies, like today, so I can't always plan."

"It's so cool, what you do." Jordan thought of the dog she'd operated on today, which he'd helped Ava move into a cage after the animal had woken up. Then he thought about Finn and hoped that Clay would remember to let him out. "I guess I never really considered the fact that veterinarians are actually doctors."

Ava snorted, and pulled her legs up onto the cot beside her. Pretty legs. Really, really pretty legs. "Let me guess. You thought I spent my time vaccinating cats and tying little bows in poodles' topknots."

"Something like that," Jordan admitted uncomfortably.

"Typical. Sort of like saying that lawyers only chase ambulances."

"A practice I've sworn off. It was hell on the feet."

Ava cast him a sideways glance. "So tell me, Mr. Assistant District Attorney. Are you any good?"

"I've been told that I'm spectacular. But I'll be happy to demonstrate if you'd like to find out for yourself."

Jordan chuckled at her bland stare. "Oh. I take it you were referring to my professional skills."

"I believe that was the topic."

"Right. Well, yeah. I'm damn good, if I do say so myself."

"You know, you're a very cocky man."

Jordan flicked a crumb off his thigh. "I believe a more appropriate term would be self-assured."

"That's the third time you've nitpicked my word choice. What are you, a damn thesaurus?"

"As we've already discussed, I'm a damn lawyer. Playing with words is what I do."

"I see." Ava shifted so that she was facing him, legs tucked to the side. The cot frame creaked ominously, and a metal brace popped out of nowhere to stab Jordan's butt. The thing clearly hadn't been intended to hold two. Glancing over, he considered that a gentleman might point out that he could see straight up Ava's dress and into the Promised Land, currently covered by a very sexy pair of black lace panties.

"And here this whole time I've been under the impression that you presented the evidence brought forth against a defendant in a criminal investigation."

"What?"

"Being a prosecutor? Hello?"

"Oh. Right." Jordan guessed he wasn't a gentleman, after all. He struggled, with a questionable degree of success, to keep his attention on the conversation. Flicking one last appreciative gaze toward her legs, he forced himself to look into her eyes.

"You're correct on the most basic level. But as my brother Jack, who's a defense attorney by the way, always says: there are two sides to every crime. Evidence, however concrete it may be, is often open to interpretation based on circumstance. As a prosecutor, I choose my words very carefully when I present the evidence, so that it is most likely to be interpreted in a manner which falls into accordance with the current law."

"That's an interesting way to put it."

"Laws change," Jordan explained. "Societal mores are fluid, and laws generally reflect their times. Eighty odd years ago, hemp was poised to become the country's first billion dollar crop, and twenty years before that we could have been arrested for the consumption of the alcohol we imbibed tonight. Now there's a war on drugs, and liquor is perfectly legal. Several hundred years ago you could have been jailed, banished, or maybe even stoned for spending the night with me without the benefit of marriage, regardless of the fact that we may or may not have had sex."

"It seems the law doesn't necessarily have anything to do with justice."

"Sometimes it doesn't," Jordan admitted. "Especially when it's used to support some questionable government or corporate agenda. But a very wise man told me just yesterday that I can do no more than practice the law to the best of my ability, and leave justice in the hands of a higher authority."

"Interesting advice."

"Yeah. My dad's full of it. Advice, that is." He looked at Ava thoughtfully. "You know, I've told you quite a bit about my family over the past couple of hours, but you've yet to tell me one thing about yours."

AVA did her best to swallow past the lump in her throat. And berated herself for allowing him to stay, for starting this conversation. "What do you want to know?"

"Anything. Everything." He waved a hand in the air. "Brothers and sisters?"

"Nope. It's just me. There were some complications when my mother had me, and she ended up having a hysterectomy. Otherwise, I probably would have been the first of many. Big families run in the blood. My mother's sister has ten children."

"Yikes. And I thought five was a lot. Are you close to your cousins?"

Ava recalled the way her nervous aunt had all but shunned her during childhood, worried about the effect a Martinez might have on her children. "Not really."

"That makes you sad."

When she merely stared at him he touched a finger beneath her eye. "You got a sort of wistfulness here, when you said it. My father's an only child also." He took his finger away. "So I don't have any cousins stateside. But the Australian branch of my family, my mother's – my dad met her during a semester abroad, fell like a stone, but that's a story for another time. Anyway, they breed like rabbits. You know, I seem to be using an awful lot of animal similes tonight."

Ava grinned. "Well, you know what they say about being in Rome."

"Yeah." He ran his gaze around the room. "So did you always know this was what you wanted? Being a vet, I mean."

"For as long as I can remember. I was forever bringing home an orphaned this or a wounded that. It horrified my poor, long-suffering mother to realize that all of those pink frilly dresses she'd bought were being wasted on a tomboy. She had visions of tea parties and ballet lessons, and I was busy raising a family of frogs in the bathtub."

Jordan laughed. "That sounds like the stuff my brother Justin used to pull. But as he's an MD and not a veterinarian, he used us as his guinea pigs. Of course, that meant he was obliged to bloody one of us before patching us up. But anyway, despite the trials and tribulations, I'm sure your mother's proud of you now."

"She was," Ava admitted, and couldn't quite keep the thickness from her voice. "Very."

"I'm sorry." His tone gentled. "I didn't realize you'd lost her."

He had no idea how appropriate his word choice actually was. Her mother had disappeared from her church parking lot and hadn't been seen for almost two years.

"What about your father?"

"You know." She looked down her nose. "You're very nosy."

"Curious."

"There you go again, playing thesaurus." But she was relieved that the conversation had turned back to safer ground. "Let's hear the definitions, Lawyer Boy."

"WELL, nosy is a next door neighbor who buys a pair of binoculars and pretends to watch birds while in reality hoping to get a glimpse of what you're doing in your backyard. Trust me, I know whereof I speak." Jordan thought of the way Mrs. Phillips had hawked him and his brothers when they were growing up, waiting for a chance to tattle. Of course, her choice of veterinarians had redeemed the woman somewhat.

"Curiosity," he tilted his head toward Ava, "is what leads two people who are interested in one another to find out all they can about the other party. It's also known as getting to know each other and, more specifically, dating. Being a veterinarian – and an incredibly attractive woman – I would think that you would know a thing or two about mating rituals."

Her brow shot up. "That's what you think this is? A… mating ritual?"

"Doc," he mirrored her expression. "We're sitting on a bed. And despite the fact that it feels like at any moment it's going to collapse under our combined weight and is adorned with Mickey Mouse sheets – it's still a bed, and as such is a traditional forum for the whole mating thing. It's…" He checked his watch "nearly one o'clock in the morning, neither one of us has made any sort of overture indicating we're interested in sleep, and since the first moment I laid eyes on you I've been… Well, let's put it in some terminology you'll understand: I've been quivering like a stallion anxious to mount a ready mare."

He didn't want to rush her, but the leash he'd kept on his libido was definitely ready to snap. "Cut me some slack here, Ava. If I don't touch you soon I'm going to break down and weep."

"Jordan, it's not you. What I mean to say," she continued when he winced "is that it's just… it's that I..." He met her eyes, watched her bite back the refusal that trembled on her lips. "Oh, what the hell. I've never liked to see a grown man cry."

With a noise of thanksgiving, Jordan pulled her into his arms.

HE wasn't gentle.

And why, Ava wondered as his lips molded to hers, had she assumed that he would be? This was a man who knew what he wanted. And knowing, took.

Hadn't he ended up here, with his mouth on hers, despite all her efforts to the contrary?

Hadn't he herded her like a damn sheep?

Pride pricked, Ava raised a hand to his chest, considered bringing him to heel after she'd gotten a taste, just a taste of him.

But when she parted her lips, Jordan charged like a warrior into battle.

Open-mouthed and hot, his lips plundered hers, tongue dancing inside to pillage with light, teasing strokes. The fingers of one hand tangled in her hair, and forming a fist at the base of her skull, tugged it like a rope. With her neck exposed, he traded lips for teeth.

White knight? More like a damn Viking.

He pulled her in close, heart pumping so that she felt it like her own. A shudder coursed through her, vibrated through him. And when his hand closed over her breast, Ava heard herself moan.

"Probably," she sucked in air, felt it burn her lungs like flame. "Probably we should slow down. Try to get a grip."

"I like the grip I have." Ava's eyes nearly crossed when his thumb found her nipple. He rolled it to a hard peak, then shifted his hand, cupped her. "All those meals you haven't been skipping? Definitely keep that up. Your body is…" he let his eyes roam. "Sorry. I think my brain just fried."

"You do have a way with words."

He lowered his mouth to hers in greedy little nibbles, and Ava threaded her fingers into the curls at his nape. The hair there was soft, and sifted through her fingers even as the power to reason slipped from her mind. She knew she needed to stop, needed to consider, but it was all she could do to breathe.

One more kiss, she thought vaguely. And then got lost in the taste of him again.

It was like drowning. In heat. In pleasure.

When he nipped her by the hips, she flowed like liquid onto his lap. The protesting squeak of the cot was no more than an echo through the waves.

"Ava." He breathed her name, the murmur hot against her neck. His fingers skimmed her collarbone, slid down her arms to squeeze her hip. When he eased her dress up the length of her thighs, she sank her teeth into his bottom lip.

"Jesus. Ava, let me see you."

Aggressively now, he pushed at the clingy fabric. Tried to pull it with hands that weren't quite gentle over her dampened skin.

"It's just cruel," he said between gritted teeth "to make a dress like this out of glue."

"I… it's… oh, hell." Ava gave up the protest, and added her efforts to his.

The dress was halfway over her head when the cot collapsed.

"Shit." Ava was swamped by a sea of red. As Jordan had muttered the same curse, though, she was pretty sure the second thunk she'd heard was his head hitting her office wall.

Discarding the dress in a heap, she saw that she was correct. Hand pressed against his stitches, the unmistakable look of pain glazed Jordan's eyes.

"Oh, poor baby. Let me see." She lifted his hand away and saw the telltale streak of blood. "You opened up your stitches."

And her own blood cooled, degree by degree, as she studied the wound.

And studying the wound – the wound her uncle's men had inflicted – reminded herself of exactly why she shouldn't be sitting here, half naked, on the verge of having what no doubt would have been incredible sex with Jordan Wellington.

"NO biggie," Jordan hissed, although it hurt more than a little.

But the headache was nothing compared to the pain in the part of his anatomy currently doing the thinking. Her bra was pink. Pink satin sort of... cut out here and there to reveal pieces of black lace. Eyes burning, Jordan made an effort not to swallow his tongue. "Where were we?"

He reached for her, but Ava evaded his hands. "We were just about to go back to an exam room so that I can stitch you back up."

"What? Wait. What?" Had she just said something about stitching his head? "My stitches are coming out tomorrow."

"Not anymore, they're not." She stood up and made a grab for her dress. "The skin on the head's delicate. It splits relatively easily, and tends to bleed a lot. You've broken at least two sutures. I'll patch you up, and you can call your doctor tomorrow and tell him what happened." She pulled her dress over her head and held out a hand to help him up.

"But... but..." Jordan sputtered, unsure which horrified him more, the fact that the pink satin – and all it barely covered – had disappeared, or the idea that Ava actually thought she was going to stick a needle through his scalp.

"Can't we just skip that part and go back to the underwear?"

"You're bleeding on my wall."

"So give me a band-aid." When he saw that was getting him nowhere, Jordan took a different tack. "Ava, you're a vet," he pointed out.

"No kidding." She made an impatient gesture with her hand. "Come on, big guy. I promise I'll be gentle."

"But, you can't stitch my head."

"Why not?"

Jordan blinked, having a hard time understanding why she needed to ask that question. Being a sane, rational person, he thought the answer should be perfectly clear. "Because you're a *vet*."

Storm clouds gathered behind her eyes, sending out small, angry bolts of lightening. "Yes, well you're a horse's ass, so I think that makes me qualified." Turning on her heel, she and her underwear sailed out the door.

"Wait a minute!" Jordan struggled to gain his feet. Exactly how, he asked himself, had the situation deteriorated from the fulfillment of three days' worth of lustful dreams into him defending himself from a needle?

She was a veterinarian, for God's sake.

"Ava!" His voice echoed off the cinderblock walls as he hobbled off to find her, his body protesting the fact that the other half of the mating ritual had flown the coop. Cursing, he staggered down the hall until he located her in the room where she'd examined Finn.

Her back might have been toward him, but the wave of ill will that slammed into him when he approached made it clear she knew he was there.

"Ava, I appreciate that you want to help but…" His voice died on a strangled sound as she turned, suspicious looking hypodermic in her hand.

"Look. You can't be serious." Could she? "I mean surely there's some… code or ordinance or something that prevents you from working on humans." He shifted his bare feet, damp flesh sticking to the linoleum. He would have wiped his sweaty palms on his pants, but was mortified enough as it stood.

"You're the lawyer," she said after a beat. "Why don't you tell me?" Giving the hypo an almost infinitesimal push, she sent a small stream of liquid from the tip.

"Ah-ah." That sucking noise was the sound of his testosterone drying up. "Well, off the top of my head I guess… no, no – I'm certain that your license limits your practice strictly to veterinary medicine. Unless you have some secret M.D. lurking around that I don't know about." He did a quick scan of the walls, half afraid that he might find one.

Shit. He hated stitches.

"Jordan." Ava tilted her head to the side. "Are you afraid of letting me stitch you up. Or are you afraid of stitches in general?"

It was a trick question. Just like the thing about her weight. Because either way he answered, he was going to come out looking bad. The first way he insulted her, the other he looked like a wuss.

And when it came to doctors and needles, his wuss quotient was pretty high.

Damn that cot to hell and back.

"Uh. A little of both." Given a multiple choice question, he figured it best to pick all of the above.

Ava seemed to relent. She laid the hypo back on the metal tray behind her. Thank God. "Okay. If you don't want me to do it, that's fine. Your other choice would be to go to the emergency room. If you'll get your shoes on, I can drop you off."

"I don't need the ER for a couple stitches."

"Well, you're probably right. We'll just leave that wound open, hope it doesn't attract bacteria. What's a little staph infection, anyway?"

Oh, the woman was good. "I know what you're trying to do."

"Do?" She batted her eyes. "I'm just a lowly veterinarian. Why would I be trying to do anything to your thick head?"

Jordan eyed her. Her dress was inside-out, her hair mussed from his own hands and her lips swollen from his kisses. And despite the fact that his mind screamed "Sex!" whenever he looked at her, there was no question she was an intelligent, capable professional. And had presented a logical argument that he would be stupid to ignore.

Sort of like when he'd given her the choice earlier over accepting a ride from him or calling a cab.

"Hell," he said out loud, and meant it. He, the resident king of herding, had somehow allowed himself to be fenced in. "That syringe," he eyed it warily "it's not filled with some kind of horse tranquilizer, is it? What with me being one of their asses, and all."

With only the slightest quirk of her lips, Ava picked it up. "Much as I've enjoyed your little bout of trypanophobia – that's the fear of needles, by the way – I'll set your mind at ease. This is your basic lidocaine, used by human healthcare professionals everywhere. I keep it on hand, and have been trained in its proper usage, because animals are unpredictable creatures. A beak here, a tooth there. I've had to stitch my own skin more times than I can count."

And yes, that was his stomach, doing that long, slow roll. "Okay." He fought down the nausea, the panic that wanted to rise like bile. "Okay. If you take a solemn oath to forget the whole… girly nerves thing ever happened."

"Promise." But when she started toward him, Jordan held up a warning hand.

"One more thing."

"WHAT'S that?" Ava tried not to smile. It was so damn cute that he was afraid of a little needle.

Jordan eased closer. Then drew her closer still. He drew his finger down her nose and brought it to rest on her lips. "After you're finished, you have to kiss it and make it better."

Despite the firm talk she'd just had with herself about not going there with Jordan, Ava's heart fluttered. How could anyone, anyone not dead and buried resist those incredible eyes? "All part of the service."

He dropped his lips to hers, softly this time, and the sweetness of it flowed through her like honey. This kiss, so different from before, stirred something in her beyond lust.

It occurred to her that Jordan Wellington was the kind of man women fell in love with.

Luckily, he distracted her from that thought. "Does that mean you make a habit of kissing your patients?"

"Only the ones who whine about getting stitches. Now buck up, Blue Eyes." She patted her hand on the seat of the folding chair beside her. "This will only take a minute."

Jordan didn't move. "What did you just call me?"

"I called you Blue Eyes. Why? They happen to be quite striking. In fact, I'm sure it's not the first time someone has commented on that particular feature."

"Yeah, I get that. It's just…" The sentence trailed off.

"It's just what?"

"NOTHING." He shook his head, and dropped into the chair. And because he was trying to recall why that sounded so familiar, he didn't even feel the needle.

CHAPTER THIRTEEN

WHEN her internal alarm told her that morning had come, Ava was mildly embarrassed to find herself wrapped around Jordan like a human bow. Head pillowed on his shoulder, legs tangled with his, and damn if her fingers weren't clutching a handful of his shirt.

His shirt. She gave the article in question a little pat of relief. At least they both had on their clothes.

Had their clothes on, she mused, because the tenor of the evening had changed after she'd pulled the last suture through his scalp. The work had cleared her own head, reminding her that a sensible, intelligent woman, a woman with a healthy instinct for self-preservation, didn't just fall into bed with the enemy. Or let him into hers. Well, technically, he was in her bed at the moment. But the point was they hadn't had sex.

She'd half expected him to leave when it became clear that that possibility was no longer on the table.

But he'd stuck.

And part of her – the part she tried to keep buried under a thick layer of self-sufficiency – couldn't help but be grateful. Couldn't help but wallow a bit, she admitted, sliding her hand across his warm chest. Couldn't help but feel foolishly female, safe and protected in his arms.

Jordan was a good man. The first man in as long as she could remember that made her feel... delicate.

Ava cursed that notion as soon as she had it. She wasn't some damsel in distress.

Okay. So maybe she was a damsel, and her life situation at the moment might fit anyone's definition of distressing, but that was beside the point.

She had always been able to take care of herself.

She didn't need a man to look after her. And more importantly, Jordan, by nature of whom and what he was, was no safe port for her storm.

If anything, he was an iceberg waiting to take her down.

But despite all that, she couldn't help but appreciate how nice it felt simply to be held. Of course, it had felt pretty nice to be kissed and groped and fondled as well. And as her brain climbed out of the thick muck of slumber, she began to wonder how it would feel to be kissed and groped and fondled again.

Pretty damn good, she decided.

Squinting against the stream of daylight intruding through her cracked office door, Ava tried to stop that thought from developing. No point in going there, being as she was a sensible, intelligent woman.

But she could hear Jordan's steady breathing, feel the rise and fall of his chest under her hand. And considered how easy it would be to slide that hand just a few inches lower.

To see exactly how the good and luscious counselor felt about the case she could make for morning sex.

She doubted it would take him more than a minute or two to agree to cross-examination.

Ava stretched her fingers, and the front door chimed.

"What? What happened?" Jordan shot up, dragging Ava with him. His arm tightened around her as he blinked like a bat rousted from the cave.

"At ease, soldier." Ava sighed against his chest, unsure whether to be grateful to or annoyed with her assistant. "Katie came in, that's all. She's early. Or I'm late. Either way, I have to get up." She started to throw the sheet off, but Jordan grabbed her arm.

"Not yet." He pulled her toward him, heavy-lidded eyes warm on hers. His cheek was creased from the wrinkled sheets, his hair standing up at odd angles. The smell of the antibiotic ointment she'd used over his sutures tickled the back of her nose.

She'd never seen anything so sexy.

He kissed her forehead, a gentle press of lips. "Good morning."

The sweetness of it made her smile. "Good morning to you, too. Sleep well?"

"Are you kidding? This mattress has the approximate density of a piece of cardboard. On top of that, I have two new stitches that are already starting to itch."

"Whiner."

"Yeah?" He splayed his hand over her back and inched her closer. "Well you remember what your policy is regarding patients who whine." He settled his mouth against hers.

"Oh. Wow. Sorry." Katie leaned oh-so casually against the doorframe. "And to think I came in early to check on you. Guess I should have slept in. Good morning, Jordan."

"Ah… Back at you. Katie." He ran a hand through his hair. "Is it just me, or is anyone else feeling awkward?"

"It's just you," Katie assured him. "I feel absolutely divine. I have doughnuts." She gave the white bag in her hand a little shake, releasing the scent of cinnamon and spice.

"From Sugarplum's?" Jordan eyed the bag with interest.

"Uh-huh. Just made. They're still warm."

He let out a helpless groan. "If you give me one, I'll be your slave."

"Come on." She jerked her head to indicate that he should follow her to the break room. "I'll make some coffee and you can tell me how you talked Ava into letting you spend the night."

"Coffee? Doughnuts? Forget Ava, and let's talk about you, instead." Dumping Ava off his lap, he stepped over the mattress. "I was thinking that we'd keep the wedding simple, and how do you feel about two kids and a dog?"

"I'm sitting right here," Ava reminded him, as Jordan threw his arm around her laughing assistant.

"Yes," Jordan cast a pitying look over his shoulder. "But let's face it, Doc. You don't have doughnuts."

"SO." Clay sipped his coffee as Jordan stood at the kitchen counter, checking his tie in the mirrored backsplash. "Have you been fitted for your collar yet?"

"I was wondering how long it would take you to work that into the conversation." Jordan tugged the ice-blue knot into place, turned. "Shower, breakfast, and two cups of coffee. Your restraint's to be commended."

"A man who's getting cozy with a vet has to expect a few leash and neuter jokes. Not to mention the obvious doggy-style innuendos. No offense, Finn." He tossed a piece of cold bacon to the dog sitting hopefully at his feet. "Did Doctor Red Dress make you wear one of those cone things last night?"

"Don't be an ass."

"But I do it so well. I'm just glad you pulled your head out of your ass long enough to notice that little number she was almost wearing. Bet she looked even better out of it."

Jordan, who'd never had a problem with a little harmless locker room talk in his life, found that he just wasn't interested in doling out any details about his night with Ava. Jokingly or not. "She's an amazing woman."

"Uh-oh."

Jordan fixed Clay with a stare. "What do you mean, uh-oh?"

"Well now." Clay took another sip from his mug. "You respond to my prerequisite masculine post-game commentary by telling me she's an amazing woman. That's what I like to call

'Non-specific Answer Evasion Syndrome.' It's a favorite of politicians. You answered my implied question, but didn't tell me a thing."

"You're making that up."

"The syndrome? Sure, I coined the name, but that doesn't mean it doesn't exist. In layman's terms it's known as giving the runaround."

"I'm not giving you the runaround, Clay. I told you, she's an amazing woman."

"Uh-huh," Clay drawled lazily. "You did. But you left out a few things between the 'amazing' and the 'woman.' Like, she's an amazingly agile woman. Or, she's an amazingly insatiable woman. So either you didn't have the opportunity to find out, and still think she's amazing rather than frustrating, or you found out and don't want to share the details. Either way, that's an uh-oh."

Jordan snapped his briefcase shut. "What the hell are you talking about?"

Clay chuckled, clearly enjoying himself. "I sense the beginning of the end, my friend. You seem to have early stage infatuation inamorata, likely to become terminal."

"You see," Jordan pointed to his head, made a little circling motion with his finger. "This is why you shrink types shouldn't be allowed among the general populace. Too much psychobabble. Especially at eight-thirty in the morning."

Clay's chuckle turned into a laugh. "Well now you're just being bitchy." At Jordan's warning snarl, he relented. "Okay, okay." He held up his palms in a gesture of peace. "The subject is officially dropped."

Jordan stuffed his hands into his pockets. "I wish I'd been wrong."

Clay sat his mug on the table, knowing they were no longer discussing Ava. "Jordan. You know that the profile I built is just a guideline. And really, it's just an opinion. An educated opinion based on the evidence at hand, but you know that doesn't frequently hold much water in court."

Clay had used Jordan's absence last night to finish the profile of the type of individual who was not only capable but likely to do what had been done to those three women. Some of the points fit. But more, far more, suggested that Elijah Fuller wasn't even close.

Jordan looked out the bank of windows behind the kitchen table. The sky was a pure cerulean, softened, as if by an artist's brush, with thin strokes of wispy clouds. Tulips stuck up like lollipops from the big pots the florist had positioned on the sidewalk. Cars blurred past, people strolled out of the coffee shop carrying fat pastries and skinny lattes, a little girl skipped, hand-in-hand with her mother, toward the preschool on the corner.

A beautiful spring day in a beautiful city.

And somewhere, among the cobblestones and horse drawn carriages, the haze of history and specters of the past, lurked a modern day monster.

A man who cut out women's tongues so that no one could hear their screams.

"So," Jordan looked back at his friend. "I'll just have to convince the rest of the team that an educated opinion is sometimes more watertight than circumstantial facts."

"WHAT the hell is this?

A visibly annoyed Jeff Simpson – SCMPD detective and all-around pain in Jordan's ass – glanced up from the printout Jordan had passed to him. Cocky in his mud-colored suit, he looked at the others gathered at the conference table – members of the team who'd investigated, arrested and/or indicted Elijah Fuller – inviting them to join in his sneer.

"This," Jordan handed the final paper to Simpson's partner before reclaiming his seat at the end of the table "is an offender profile of the person who murdered Tracy Buckler, Sonya Kousman and Mackenzie Wright."

Four pairs of eyes dropped to their printouts.

"White male." Simpson skimmed, his bulldog face set in a frown. "Likely between the ages of eighteen and twenty-five. Solid knowledge of forensic evidence and police procedures. Organized, control motivated, history of childhood abuse…" He flicked the paper with his hand. "This is all just great, Wellington, but in case you forgot, we already caught the guy."

"I'm not so sure about that." Oh yeah, that got everyone's attention.

"People, people." Barry Feinstein, Jordan's boss, raised his voice over the din. Then turned his own ire on Jordan. "Way to handle that diplomatically." He looked down the considerable length of his nose.

"It needed to be said."

"What is this?" Simpson repeated, angrily this time.

"Exactly what it looks like," Jordan said. He'd worked with Simpson, butted heads with Simpson, on several trials already. And though the man was thought to be a solid cop, Jordan had found that solidity to be unbending. "Based on the victimology, the manner of death, the method and locations of the body disposals, Agent Copeland –"

"Agent Copeland? You called in the fucking feds?"

"I agreed to it," Feinstein interjected. "We're talking serial murder, here. A behavioral profile and testimony to that effect is pretty standard procedure in a trial like this. Of course, one would hope that our expert's testimony would actually work in our favor." He frowned at Jordan again.

"As I was saying," Jordan carried on. "A few of the characteristics jibe. Elijah Fuller is a white male. He's young, mobile, intelligent, we know he was abused as a child. But Fuller was also obsessed with – stalked – Sonya Kuosman. He followed her, photographed her, constructed an elaborate relationship in his mind based on her being friendly to him in their apartment building's laundry room. It was creepy, and probably criminal, but the point is he saw her as a specific person. If you'll read further, you'll note that Agent Copeland believes the killer dehumanized the three victims – didn't know much about them, really, didn't care. They simply met some basic criteria that, he believed, entitled him to dominate and destroy them for his own gratification. And probably from the need to affirm his own self- worth."

"Don't stalkers sometimes kill the, uh, object of their affection?" Simpson's partner, Carrie Dawson, commented. "Maybe the other women were just substitutes until he worked up the nerve, or got the opportunity, to go after Kuosman."

"Doesn't play." Jordan had wondered the same thing, initially. But didn't believe that now. "There are almost no similarities among the women – physical, background, or otherwise – to conclude that the first two were somehow substitutes for the real deal. I –"

"How does your damn expert explain the victim's blood in Fuller's car?"

"He doesn't." Jordan gazed steadily at Simpson. "He's giving us the benefit of his experience and considerable knowledge, not attempting to investigate every aspect of the crime. That's your job, Jeff."

"You son of a –"

"People," Feinstein raised his hands. "Let's take a minute to cool off here."

"You're going to let him do this?" Simpson pushed away from the table, stood. Vibrated with enough outrage that his hands shook. "You're going to let him, what, torpedo the trial? Drop the damn charges? Let this asshole go free?"

"What I'm doing," Feinstein's gray eyes turned to smoke "is giving this some consideration. The evidence we have to work with is mostly circumstantial –"

"Your office, your prosecutor – the first one, the one who could tell the difference between good, solid police work and psycho bullshit – is the one who said we had enough to indict. The one who got the indictment."

"And so we did." Feinstein laid a restraining hand on Jordan's arm. "But if our expert witness is raising these questions, you can be damned sure the defense will be, too. We want a conviction, we might just need something more solid."

"But that's not the point," Jordan objected. "There were other discrepancies –"

"More shrink mumbo jumbo."

"This particular shrink's mumbo jumbo," Jordan aimed a lowering glare at Simpson "has helped put away more killers than some of us have brain cells."

"Shut up, Jordan."

Reminding himself that Feinstein was his boss, Jordan shut up while Simpson smirked.

"We'll work on it," his boss said to the detectives. "We'll work on it, you'll work on it, and for now, we keep this under wraps. Understood?" He fired that smoke at Jordan.

"Understood." Though he didn't have to like it. He didn't have to agree.

"Okay, then." Feinstein nodded, and released Jordan's gaze. "Meeting adjourned."

AVA thought she'd never been so glad to see the stroke of five o'clock.

Both of yesterday's surgery patients had recovered sufficiently that their owners were able to trundle them off home, and aside from her own temperamental feline, the office was one hundred percent animal-free.

She was exhausted. Right down to the bone. The small of her back ached from scrubbing the floors of the kennel, and her feet in their ancient sneakers had given up aching and now quietly wept.

She wanted nothing more than a quick dinner, a quicker shower, and a long, long stretch of reacquainting herself with her bed.

Actually, in the grand scheme of things, dinner and the shower didn't seem all that important.

Taking the file from her last patient of the day – an African Gray parrot with an attitude problem and a bad case of nasal discharge – she tossed it onto the desk in front of Katie.

"Long day?"

"Long life." Resting her head on the reception counter, Ava's eyelids dropped like stones. Hearing a purr near her ear, she automatically extended her hand to stroke it over One-eyed Jack. "But the day, at least, is over."

"Or not."

Ava groaned as the bells on the door jangled behind her. "Whoever it is, tell them I'm not here," she murmured to Katie. "Or better yet, that I've died."

"Oh, I don't know." Ava opened her eyes, and Katie's smile shone like sunlight across a meadow. "You may want to resurrect yourself for this one."

Ava turned.

Jordan stood, looking annoyingly well-rested and pleasant in his tan slacks and crisp white dress shirt – a far cry from her worn jeans and dog-bone scrub top – brown paper sack curled into one arm and a potted plant balanced in the other.

And damn if her exhausted body didn't rev back into action.

"Shit," she muttered, just loud enough to reach Katie.

"Language," Katie sang without dimming the smile a watt.

"Hey," Jordan drawled, in a general kind of greeting for both women.

"Hey yourself." Ava was relieved that her voice sounded normal. "What –"

But before she could ask what he was doing there, what was in the bag, what was up with the greenery, his breath fluttered across her cheek, and his lips pressed to hers.

As if he had every right to do so.

As if it was the most natural thing in the world.

As if she would want him – big, pushy, hot-looking, needle fearing man that he was – to just waltz into her clinic, her personal space, and kiss her like they had some kind of relationship.

And wouldn't you know? That irritated her so much that she kissed him back.

If it hadn't been for Katie looking on with obvious interest, she was pretty sure she would have done so with even more enthusiasm.

"Hey," he repeated, softly. Drawing back, Jordan deposited the plant on the counter so that he could brush a thumb over her bruised eyes. "You look tired."

"A little," she minimized. And because it was a bad idea altogether to encourage this sort of thing, put another solid step between them. "So. You've abandoned the law and have taken up selling foliage door-to-door?" She nodded her head toward the counter.

I brought you a cactus."

"A cactus."

"Mmm-hmm." He beamed at the little plant, complete with terra cotta pot and red cellophane wrapper.

"Okay. Why?"

"It won't die if you don't water it."

Oh, you adorable man. How could a woman not be charmed? Especially considering Ava had been nearly as prickly to him as that cactus. "And the bag?" she couldn't help asking.

Jordan shifted the bag so that she could see into it. "Since you kept turning me down when I asked you out to dinner, I thought I might have more success if I brought dinner to you."

Behind her, Katie made a noise that sounded suspiciously like a coo. And damn if Ava didn't feel like billing, also. Curious, she pushed her ponytail behind her shoulder and took a peek into the bag. And pulled out a raw bell pepper.

"You shouldn't have."

Jordan laughed, grabbing the vegetable out of her hand and dropping it back into the bag. "It's an ingredient, Ava. I'm making you vegetarian lasagna."

Another approving noise emitted from the direction of her employee.

Ava cut her eyes toward Katie, who smiled like a loon. When she returned her attention to Jordan he'd shifted the bag again, and had closed the distance between them. She tilted her head back to frown. "You cook?"

"I've been known to." He took advantage of her tipped up face to drop a quick kiss on her lips. "I would have invited you over to my place," and here he spared a quick glance for the still enrapt Katie, "but Clay's currently camped out in my living room. So I left him to his own devices," – another, more pointed look – "and picked up everything we'd need to do dinner at your place."

"Well." Katie, no fool, picked up the hint that Jordan had just quite obviously dropped. Grabbing her purse, she pushed her chair away from the desk. "Seeing as how it's after five o'clock and there's no real reason for either of us to stick around here any longer, I think I'll be going." She scooted around the counter with a deftness born of practice, long legs eating up the space to the door in a few quick strides. "It was nice to see you again, Jordan. Ava, I'll catch you tomorrow. Enjoy your dinner."

As bells jangled, Ava turned her scowl on Jordan. "Subtle."

"I try."

"So let me get this straight," she motioned toward the bag. "You're inviting yourself to dinner at my place?"

"No." Alone now, he anchored an arm around her waist and pulled her against him. He sat the bag of groceries on the counter next to the cactus so that he could run his other hand along her spine. "I'm inviting you to dinner. I'm making it, remember? Your place is simply the venue."

And a recipe for disaster. Because the desire to lean on him, both physically and emotionally, was so strong, Ava forced herself to push back. "That's very sweet of you, Jordan, but I'm afraid that's not a good idea. I'm..." she searched around for a reasonable excuse that involved at least a kernel of truth. "I'm really tired. Like you said."

Jordan danced his fingers up until they wiggled her ponytail. "All the more reason for me to cook, so that you don't have to. You can kick back and relax with a nice glass of wine, while I dazzle you with my culinary prowess. And besides," his face went straight. "I get the feeling Katie may be headed over to keep Clay company, so I really have no place to go."

Ava rolled her eyes. "You don't seriously think I'm going to fall for that again, do you?"

"Hope springs. Find something that works, might as well stick with it."

"Well aside from the fact that you're pathetically transparent, I appreciate the offer." She couldn't help but grin at the plant. "And the cactus. A creative alternative to roses and a candlelit dinner."

"Wait." Rummaging in the bag, he drew out a pair of votives. "Who said we weren't going to dine by candlelight?"

Looking at the candles, Ava was struck by a sudden epiphany. Here – standing right here in front of her – might possibly be the perfect man.

Or at least as close to perfect as any woman not completely masochistic might hope to expect. Hell, maybe Lou Ellen wasn't crazy. Maybe fate had put her at the right place at the right time to save him.

Not that fate intended him for her, of course. But a glowing example of natural selection at its finest like this wasn't meant to be cut down in his prime.

That kind of thing would have been a crime against womankind.

And since she'd done such a good thing, a worthy thing, a purely selfless thing by preventing that genetic loss, she figured she was entitled to at least one lousy dinner.

"You're a smooth one, Jordan Wellington." Lou Ellen had been right about that. "And since you are, and you've gone to the trouble, and I probably would have eaten cold cereal otherwise, I'll allow you to make me dinner. Just let me grab Jack and lock up."

After seeing that everything was as it should be for the night, she followed Jordan outside. The spring air was like a first kiss, tentative and full of promise. Though hers and Jordan's first kiss, Ava considered wryly, had been anything but light.

Jordan pointed to his car, parked under the bud-heavy magnolia shading her lot, and approval hummed through her again. It looked like a fat, silver bullet.

"I'll follow you," he suggested, stowing the groceries on the back seat.

"That's fine." She tossed him an easy smile. "I'll just…"

Whatever she'd been about to say was forgotten as she caught her first real glimpse of her car.

It sat alone.

No black T-Bird, no beat up blue Chevy nearby. Nary a goon in sight. Her heartbeat picked up as she realized she'd blithely walked into plain view, accompanied by Jordan. ADA Jordan. Upholder of law and order. The man who still bore the evidence of her uncle's assault on his head.

Had one of the men seen him going in? Had they recognized him?

Or, alternately, had Uncle Carlos finally called off his dogs?

Frozen by a surge of nerves, Ava noticed that there was something a little off about her car. The back end sat considerably lower.

Nerves fled, fury nipping at the heels.

"Son of a bitch," she muttered, and had Jordan straightening from his car.

"Problem?"

"My tire," Ava answered noncommittally. Sitting One-eyed Jack's carrier down, she knelt on the ground to examine the damage. Sure enough, the high-performance Pirelli, not two months old, had a six-inch gash running across it.

"Son of a bitch," she growled it loudly this time, and then shot to her feet and spun around. Nothing popped up, no sneering jackasses with their stupid knives poking their heads out of the shrubbery. Just the hush of old brick walls, that whisper of a breeze. The quiet hum of the occasional car passing. But she knew the goon had to be watching. She could all but feel the bastard's eyes on her.

JORDAN walked over, brow raised as she turned the air around her blue. But when he saw the slashed tire, any sense of amusement fled.

"Any idea as to who might have done this?"

"What?" When she jumped, darted another nervous look around, he feigned a casualness he didn't feel.

"Slash like that," he gestured to the tire, "doesn't get there because you ran over a nail."

He watched the denial creep into her eyes.

And knew she was going to lie to him.

HERE it was, Ava thought dismally. The first of many lies to be told. And the fact that she did have to lie, for his sake as well as her own, was a bare-knuckled punch to the gut. She hated to lie, hated for people to not know exactly why they might not want to hang around her. It was the reason she'd confided in both Lou Ellen and Katie. They deserved to know what they were getting into.

Jordan deserved no less.

If he were just a man – the first man in a long, long while that she felt the almost irresistible urge to confide in – she knew, instinctively, that he was also the kind of man you could trust.

But she couldn't trust him with this.

To do so would mean explaining exactly how he'd ended up at the hospital that night. And who had put him in that trunk to begin with.

"Probably just some kids pulling pranks." And because she wanted him to forget about her car – there were still traces of his blood on the headrest, for pity's sake – she realized she had to put him off. "Um, listen, Jordan," she glanced back toward her clinic because she couldn't look him in the eye. "I'm afraid I might have to take a rain check on dinner. I need to get this taken care of."

"Do you want to call the police? File a report for your insurance?"

"No. No, I really don't."

"Okay. Do you –"

"You're not obligated to help. Really, I can handle this. We'll do dinner another time."

"Uh-huh. Do you have a spare?"

"No." She shook her head, thinking it was like trying to stop a steamroller with her bare hands. "I popped a tire a few weeks ago when I was visiting a client's farm. I haven't gotten around to buying a replacement. But –"

"I'LL tell you what." Jordan slung an arm around her shoulders and started steering her toward his car. Kids, hell. It might be spring break, but he knew – from personal experience – that kids up to no good usually waited until after dark to sneak out of the house and wreak their havoc. As it was only a little after five, he really didn't think they could pin this on marauding teens.

The note of disquiet he'd felt last night struck another chord.

Factor in the tail when they left the bar, her landlord's shotgun, Ava's jumpy demeanor… Jordan was starting to think along the lines of a dangerous ex.

He'd get to the bottom of it, eventually. Right now he just wanted to remove her from the scene. She'd be more likely to confide in him over an intimate dinner than hanging around the parking lot. "I'll give you a ride home, and then we can stop and pick up a new tire before I bring you back in the morning. I'd be happy to change it for you."

"Jordan, I don't think –"

"Exactly." He squeezed her shoulder. "You're tired, and you're not thinking clearly. So why don't you just let me take you home and make you dinner."

When they reached his car, he tucked her into the passenger seat, ignored her various protests. Then he scooped up the carrier filled with yowling cat, depositing it on the back seat. He climbed in with hurried grace, threw the car in reverse, and got the hell out of there before Ava could realize she'd been herded.

This was one sheep he wasn't going to let slip away.

DOWN the street, a black car started.

CHAPTER FOURTEEN

"WHY don't you go take a shower and get comfortable, and I'll get started on this." Jordan took a carton of portabella mushrooms out of the bag, sat them next to the ricotta cheese. A package of green lasagna noodles – spinach, Ava gathered – followed a colorful array of peppers and tomatoes on the vine. Garlic, fresh parsley and basil. She guessed he really did know how to cook.

"Ava."

Her head snapped up, and he pressed a smiling kiss to her lips. "You. Shower. Go."

"Are you sure you don't need any help?"

JORDAN set aside the fresh mozzarella. She was hovering. She was hovering, and he could tell that she wasn't used to having someone else in her kitchen. The well-thumbed cookbooks, neatly organized collection of stainless steel cookware, the pots of herbs on the windowsill – guess he'd jumped the gun, there – amidst an otherwise, well, ugly-ass kitchen suggested she was a woman who liked to cook.

And a woman, apparently, who was suspicious of a man who could.

Locating a wine glass in one of the glass-fronted cabinets above the counter, he poured her a glass of the Bardolino he'd brought along.

"Here, drink this in the shower. It will help you relax."

Ava accepted the wine and frowned. "What makes you think I'm uptight?"

"Honey, you're so stiff I could nail you to the wall and use you for shelving." He poured his own glass half full and leaned back against the sink. "Just do me a favor, would you, and set the oven to broil on your way out."

"Broil? You're planning to broil the lasagna? Oh, ha ha," she said in response to his grin.

"If it will ease your mind, I'll tell you a little story. I'm one of five boys, as you know, and my mother, bless her heart, had to put up with an awful lot while we were growing up. One night, after she'd put in a long, crazy-making day of child rearing and had just put dinner on the table, one of my brothers – who will currently go unnamed as we're all still a little angry with him – told her that he didn't like her tuna casserole and wasn't going to eat that slop."

The corners of her mouth turned up. "Bet that went over well."

Jordan lifted his glass at the understatement. "You have to know my mother to appreciate the full effect that had. But nevertheless, some good did come of it." He sat his wine down, grabbed a trio of peppers and carelessly juggled them. "She made us learn to cook. A couple of us took to it, a few of us didn't, but the point is, we all know how. Now," he set the peppers back on the counter. "Will you go take your shower and leave me to this?"

"Only if you're one of the ones who took to it."

"You're a tough customer, Doc. But lucky for you, it just so happens that I am."

AVA went, still baffled by the fact that there was a gorgeous man – a gorgeous prosecutor, for God's sake – currently making dinner in her kitchen. Her life over the past couple of weeks had been one long, strange ride.

But, she mused, dropping her soiled clothes on the bathroom tile, taking another sip of a surprisingly nice Italian red. As much as she hated her uncle's manipulations, and what for her was an uncustomary lack of control, she realized that she couldn't count the past week as a total loss.

She'd saved a man's life.

And while it pretty much sucked that she couldn't play finders keepers with this particular man, it was still nice to know that he was around.

Setting the water to parboil, Ava climbed into the shower and let the heat ease some of her tension.

The goon had slashed the tire on her car. Petty, she admitted, slicking the heavy mass of her hair back from her face.

Petty, and pretty damn effective at keeping her on edge. Her clinic, her car – the two material possessions she gave a damn about – so points to the goon for hitting her where she would hurt. But a business, a vehicle, hardly mattered compared to the people for whom she cared.

Lou Ellen had been threatened last night. So far Katie'd been left alone, but Ava couldn't count on that lasting. And now, now despite every effort on her part to discourage him, Jordan had joined the mix.

The big idiot.

After tonight, whatever she had to do – be it rudeness, lies, or actual physical violence – she had to make it clear to him that this dinner was a one shot deal. No more wavering back and forth, getting plowed under by his will. It was time to be that sensible, intelligent woman and stick to her damn decisions.

Leaning her hands against the wall, Ava watched the red and white tiles blur as shampoo stung her eyes. Not shampoo, she realized. She had yet to wash her hair. To her horror, she felt her throat swell up, and realized those were tears.

Maybe she wasn't handling the whole thing quite as well as she thought.

It sucked being caught in a web that wasn't of your own spinning. And it sucked finding a man you really liked, only to have to cut him loose lest he get caught up in the web with you.

Blinking hard, Ava grabbed a bottle, squeezed the fruity shower gel onto a sponge. Worked up some anger with the lather, because it sat easier than tears. Damn Carlos. Damn him for so thoroughly screwing with her life.

She didn't need this right now. She had enough trouble, as it stood – nearly six and a half feet of which was currently standing in her kitchen.

Making something that was starting to smell awfully good.

Shutting off the water, Ava grabbed a towel, headed into her bedroom. She picked out a sturdy bra, a pair of simple white cotton panties. And then hesitated when she noticed the bright red silk lying next to them.

It was stupid, she told herself, as she gently refolded the cotton. Ran her fingers over the silk. She was a sensible, intelligent woman. There was no point in entertaining even the briefest of lascivious fantasies.

But she pulled the sexy lingerie out of her drawer, anyway. It would make her feel better to know she had it on under her clothes. She might have to get rid of the man, but it didn't mean she wasn't one hundred percent woman.

She threw on an innocuous looking red T-shirt – trying to pretend that neither the shirt nor the underwear had anything to do with the fact that Jordan told her it was her color – a comfortable pair of jeans, and decided to forgo footwear. She was in her own home, after all. And she hadn't invited him here, damn it.

Leaving her hair loose and damp, she slicked some gloss over her lips. That was it as far as makeup. If he didn't like it, well he could leave. Big, pushy man. She padded through the living room, and heard him talking to One-eyed Jack.

"Yeah, I see you over there pretending not to like me. You've got that whole beady-eyed thing going on, just like your mama. She pretends not to like me, too. Well guess what, I'm

onto you – both of you – so you can save yourself the effort."
There was a short pause, during which Jordan obviously bribed
Jack with some kind of food, because she could hear the cat's
usual growls. Followed by his purr. "Uh-huh, just as I thought.
I feed you, and you're all over me. Now let's see if that works
with her."

The mad Ava had managed to work up dissolved faster than
lather.

The man talked to cats. He offered to make vegetarian
lasagna – and damn it, actually seemed to know how. He had a
weak spot for stray dogs. He willingly spent the night on a
rickety old cot and was terrified of needles – but let her sew him
up anyway.

He'd brought her a cactus.

Jordan Wellington wasn't just the kind of man women fell in
love with. He was the kind of man she could fall in love with.

"Shit," she whispered, for what felt like the thousandth time.
That was exactly what she was stepping into. A deep, deep pile
of it.

With the knowledge that she was perched on the edge of a
very big cliff – and that despite all the back peddling and arm-
windmilling and localized panic, was very likely to lose her
balance – she walked into the kitchen and straight into Jordan's
arms.

Pleased, clearly surprised, he smiled when she tilted her head
back. "See, I told you the wine would relax you."

"It's good wine." She moved out of his arms to pour another glass. "You have excellent taste."

"I do indeed." Jordan lifted his own glass toward her. "Especially in women."

Ava felt the warmth of that all the way down to her toes. "That smells wonderful," she gestured toward where the lasagna bubbled and baked in the oven. She glanced around, noting the candles burning on her small wrought iron table, the tossed salad and basket of warm bread already in place. The white cloth napkins which he'd apparently brought with him.

The man was nothing if not thorough.

"Why don't we get started on the salad?" Jordan gestured her toward the table, pulled out her chair. "The lasagna should be ready in about twenty minutes. In the meantime, you can tell me about your day."

She did. And while she enjoyed what she had to admit was a very skillfully prepared portion of lasagna, found herself telling him a whole lot more. She edited, occasionally fudged, but otherwise shared things she hadn't even considered. Maybe it was the wine going to her head, the candlelight, the excellent meal. But he was incredibly easy to talk to. Actually, Ava was forced to admit, it had little to do with the trappings, and more because they just seemed to click. That subtle, internal connection that allowed you to hear someone and think: yeah. I get that.

They talked about everything from religion to literature – with him shuddering only mildly when she admitted a fondness for medical thrillers. Childhood idols, sports teams followed. Relationships. While he could claim nothing more serious than a six month stint in law school, Ava found herself describing her narrowly missed trip to the altar.

"So this Michael," Jordan referred to her ex-fiancé as he gestured with his water glass. Since her tiny dining set hadn't been designed with someone of his size in mind, he stretched his yard of leg out to the side. "Is he still hanging around?"

"What do you mean?"

"I mean, has he been giving you any trouble, wanting to get back together, anything like that?"

Ava folded her napkin and laid it next to her empty plate. "I haven't seen or spoken with Michael in over a year now. Closer to two." She angled her head. "And besides, he's the one who dumped me. Why would he want to hang around?"

"Maybe he realized he was a complete idiot."

Ava smiled a little ruefully. "Well, as flattering as that is to hear, I can assure you that as far as Michael is concerned, it was more like good riddance. But anyway. Why do you ask?"

JORDAN considered how best to address the question. He'd noticed Ava's reticence after they'd been followed the previous night. Her nerves when they'd discovered her flat tire. All the other strange occurrences that indicated someone had her running scared.

Although scared wasn't really the word he'd use to describe Ava. She seemed nervous. More than a little ticked off. Edgy, certainly, but cautious.

And maybe it was his ego talking, but he also thought her situation had a lot to do with why she kept pushing him away.

"I'm not blind Ava." Straightforward. Straightforward was the way to handle this, since he knew damn well she'd already lied when he'd asked her about the tire. "Nor am I stupid. Someone's giving you trouble. Why, and what kind, I'm not sure, but the fact is that people who follow other people around, slash their tires, and God knows what else has happened that I'm not aware of, are dangerous. It's called stalking – and as you nearly accused me of it last night, I know you're familiar with it – and there are laws against it. If you're having trouble, I'd like to help. It would be no problem for me to get a restraining order put through, if you'll tell me who's doing this."

Ava went still.

"Well." She sat her wineglass down, narrowed those big brown eyes on his. "Aren't you the perceptive one."

"Ava –"

She held up a hand. "Don't. Don't run right over me like you do. You've said your piece; give me a chance to say mine. I won't insult your intelligence by insinuating you've imagined the problem."

"Good."

Her chin came up in defense. "First of all, I want you to know that I appreciate your concern, and the spirit in which it's given. You're a good man."

"Why don't I like the sound of that?"

"You're a good man," she continued "who obviously tries to do the right thing. And while I admit that there have been some... issues I've been dealing with lately, I can assure you that it's nothing I can't handle."

"Ava. Do you know how many women say just that? Before their loved one takes it too far one night, blackens their eye, breaks their ribs. Maybe decides that he just won't take no for an answer, and pulls out a gun."

"Well, that's mildly sexist –"

"It's not sexist, it's reality. I'm a prosecutor, Ava. I see it almost every day."

She dipped her head in acknowledgement. "I'm sure you do. But that isn't the case here. Just trust me on this one, and leave well enough alone. I like you, Jordan. I really do. And I understand that, being the good man that you are, you're used to taking charge, looking for a solution, because that's the only way you know to help. But I'm pretty good at taking care of myself. If I run into anything I think I can't handle, I promise you'll be the first person I call. But unless I do, I'm going to have to ask you to step back. If you can't handle that, then there's no point in this going any farther."

Jordan assessed the cool-eyed woman staring back at him. And thought of all the other women he'd known of who – yes – thought they could handle themselves. Women whose murders he'd prosecuted because they just didn't think that their husband, or ex-boyfriend, or the guy in apartment 2-D was really anything for them to be overly concerned about. Sure the guy might hit them when he was drunk, or follow them around while they ran errands, or look in their windows at night.

But it wasn't something they couldn't handle.

And admitting that they couldn't handle it, asking for help, telling others that they were frightened or had been abused, was something those women had been either too ashamed to do, or something they'd viewed as weakness.

And inevitably, they'd ended up a case file on his desk.

"I teach self-defense."

"What?"

"I don't know if I've ever mentioned it, but I volunteer at the Y. Basic self-defense for women."

"That's… noble of you." She eyed him warily over her wineglass. "Is that supposed to be some kind of hint?"

"What would you do if a man – bigger than you, stronger – had you in a chokehold, for example?"

"Is this before or after I kick his ass for patronizing me?"

"I'm not being patronizing; I'm being serious. Come on." He eased the glass from her hand, sat it on the table and stood. "Just show me. What would you do?"

TORN between annoyance and amusement – oh, hell. Who was she kidding? She was thoroughly annoyed – Ava pushed her chair back from the table. "Jordan, this isn't necessary –"

"Humor me."

She nearly rolled her eyes. Until he grabbed her, spun her around. Locked his arms around her throat. "What do you do?" he repeated.

"I throw up vegetable lasagna all over his nice shoes."

"Ava." He tightened, just slightly. "What do you do?"

His body was big. His arm like warm steel. She grabbed it, pulled down hard. Stepped one foot to the side, swung her hip out. And throwing her weight into it, bent them both over.

"Very good," he said from behind and above her. "That's the right place to start. You've had some training."

"I told you, you were being patronizing."

"No, I'm being concerned. Hit my knee."

"What?" All this heat was confusing. She was supposed to be alarmed and afraid – or annoyed, at the very least. Certainly not aroused.

"With your elbow. Hit my knee with your elbow. Ouch. Okay, you got it. See how it makes me loosen my hold?"

She angled her head, met his gaze. Both of them upside down. "Satisfied?"

"Hardly. But," he grimaced when she shot her arm backward again. "Your elbow is sharp as hell."

"I took a course in college," she said as they both straightened, Jordan rubbing his abused knee. "I'm a little rusty, but I'm not going to just lie down if someone tries to grab me."

"Ava, I didn't mean –"

She held up a placating hand. "I know you didn't. I know it's your nature to want to protect. But I'd rather have your respect."

"You think I don't respect you?"

His mouth went thin, and she touched his arm. "As a person, of course I do. You wouldn't be here if I thought otherwise, no matter how tempting your little bag of vegetables. But as a woman capable of knowing when she needs help... you've got Sheltie tendencies, I'm afraid. You want me over here, where you think I should be, so you're doing your best to herd me."

Jordan stared at her, finally shrugged. "Okay. I apologize if I came off as patronizing."

It had been too pleasant an evening to let it end in discord. "No problem." She flashed a smile. "It gave me a chance to work off some of that lasagna. Which was wonderful, by the way. Kudos to your mother."

And moving toward the table, she started to clear their plates. "Since you cooked, I'll take care of the dishes."

"YOU wash, I'll dry." Jordan had no choice but to drop the subject. He'd just have to find a way to work around her, that was all. To hell with being straightforward. "Then I can get my hands on you again that much sooner. Though you can keep your elbows to yourself."

Ava met his bland smile. "Do you always expect that sort of payoff for a meal?"

"Absolutely." He stacked his dishes beside the ones she'd just placed in the sink. "But I believe in equal opportunity. Next time you can make dinner, and then expect me to put out."

Ava grabbed a sponge and dish soap from under the sink. "And that's your idea of equal opportunity?"

"Uh-huh." Jordan unbuttoned the cuffs on his dress shirt and rolled the sleeves to his elbows. "As the saying goes, you've come a long way, baby." He reached over, turned the knob of the art deco radio she kept near the sink. "You've never heard of an iPod?"

"Little do you know." She opened a drawer, pulled out the docking station, the wires. "It's retrofitted. There's just something about an old-fashioned radio in the kitchen. I like the nostalgia."

"Nostalgia," he said, as Elvis proclaimed in that velvet voice that he was All Shook Up. "Well. At least The King has the right idea."

When the last dish had been stowed away, Jordan hung the damp towel over the edge of the sink. Ava dropped the sponge into a dish to dry. Patsy Cline was Crying, and the air between them crackled.

AVA looked for something to do with her hands other than help him out of his clothes.

"Would you like to…"

She turned toward his voice, met his gaze, got lost in that shimmering blue.

"…dance?"

"Dance?" She blinked at the hand he extended.

"Mmm-hmm. Candlelight. Music. Seems to call for a little dancing."

"Here?" She looked around her tiny kitchen.

"It's where we happen to be." He snagged her hand, gently tugged. Enfolded her in arms that tightened. "You'll just have to hold on real tight so that I don't knock anything over with my gangly body."

Gangly, hell. He was all lean muscle, long lines. Smooth, smooth moves. While Fats Domino crooned about finding his thrill, Jordan maneuvered her so skillfully that the full twelve inches difference in their heights didn't make her feel like a midget.

Instead she felt relaxed, content. And very, very sexy.

He eased her into a dip.

"Jordan." She swallowed hard, met the flicker of heat in those striking eyes. It had been so long since she'd been with a man. And she so badly wanted to be with this one. "Do you want to…"

"If you're about to suggest anything other than me making love to you for the rest of the night, the answer's no."

"Well," she said after she'd managed to catch her breath. "I guess it's lucky for me that I wasn't."

He lowered. Simply sank against her lips. And when she opened, seeking, danced his tongue toward hers as skillfully as he'd glided her around the room. The kiss spun out, slow, slower, until Ava wasn't sure if they were still standing.

"Wow," she managed when they came up for breath. He slid his hand under the edge of her shirt, rubbed the small of her back in a gentle circle. "That was... nice."

He jerked them both to standing.

"Nice," he stretched his hand. Unhooked her bra with a twist of his fingers. "Isn't exactly what I'm after."

He... devoured. There was simply no other way to describe the press of his body, the crush of his lips. The clever hands that stroked, then kneaded.

That quick snap of lust that had her blood humming and wiped her mind clean.

Needs, so long unmet, tangled in her belly. And when he tipped her head back, closed teeth over her neck, Ava's mouth turned to dust.

"Well... Jesus," she gasped, looking for air like a landed fish.

"That's more like it." He palmed the seat of her jeans, lifted her to her toes. And when he brought her tight against him, laid any question she may have had about his own need effectively to rest.

The man was hard as stone.

One of the candles burned out on a sizzling hiss, and Gary Allan sang about the woman who ran.

Not this woman, Ava thought. At least, not this night. She was through with running scared. So wrapping her legs around his waist, thought it was time to join the tango.

LUST was a rough and ready jolt when Ava crushed her mouth to his. Jordan staggered into the counter, righted himself by throwing out a hand. Found his other arm overflowing with warm, willing woman. She clung to him like kudzu. Climbing legs. Wandering hands.

When one slipped beneath the edge of his shirt, found his flat nipple, his eyes nearly rolled in his head.

Pleasure slammed into him in a quick, crashing wave.

No longer trusting his legs to hold them both, Jordan boosted her onto the countertop. Her breasts, unencumbered by the bra he'd loosened, bounced against his chest.

"Ava." The wave broke, and his body shuddered. What was it about this woman that made him feel like a teen about to round first base for the very first time?

With a flashback to last night's pink satin, he yanked her T-shirt over her head.

"Good God." He wrapped his fingers around the edge of the counter, took a bracing breath. Red silk. It shimmered in the light of the remaining candle, liquid rubies against the honey of her skin.

Gliding his fingers along the red, the gold, he freed her from the straps.

When his mouth closed over her, hungry, hot, Ava felt something inside her tighten. It wound, a slippery coil of need that had her fisting a hand in his hair.

"Bedroom's that way."

Jordan lifted his head to her insistent tug, gave it a second's consideration. "Not gonna make it. Next time."

WITH that promise, he reached for the snap of her jeans, fingers slipping as he wrestled the zipper. Satisfaction twisted along with the need, satisfaction that she'd made this smooth man fumble.

And because she had, her own fingers steadied as they worked the buttons of his shirt. Impatient, he snatched them away, and yanked it off himself.

Buttons hit the floor like fat raindrops.

"Oh." Ava had to take a moment to simply appreciate. It was her duty as a red-blooded woman. Raking a nail down the line of hair below his navel, she watched gooseflesh pop out on his skin. "That's some body you've got there, Counselor."

"Same goes. Doc." Hooking his hands under her arms, he brought her to her feet. "Your jeans are in the way." And when they slid down her legs, simply lifted her again, and out of them.

When he stood back, stared at her, naked except for a scrap of red silk, Ava had never felt more desirable.

Winding her hands through the weight of her hair, she lifted it, watched his eyes watching her, then dropped it to her shoulders.

"I just lost the power of speech."

"Quite the casualty for a lawyer. But at least you still have your feet."

With a noise between a laugh and a groan he snatched her up, dropped her onto the counter. And shoving her legs apart, covered her with his mouth.

"Oh. God." The silk rasped, his tongue stroked. Ava fell back onto her elbows. The radio went skidding into the sink, cutting off the Flamingos and their famous eyes.

She hadn't expected the outright assault, but that was damn sure what she was getting.

When he used his teeth, the coil exploded with a thousand springs.

"God. God. Give me a minute to catch my breath." Head ringing, Ava sprawled on her counter. "I think I'm blind. Wait." She opened her eyes. "Damn, these tiles are ugly. Maybe I'll have them bronzed."

"You're recovered." Jordan pulled her up, and she fell against his chest.

"No. No, I'm really not. My head's still ringing. Or…
shit." Pushing him aside, she basically fell off the counter. And
hand to her head, staggered to where she'd stowed her purse.

"What?" Jordan asked, frustration lending the word edge.

"My pager." She dug through the lip gloss, receipts, gum
wrappers and dog treats which constituted the somewhat
irregular contents of her purse. And… whoops, the little pistol
she didn't want to explain to Jordan. Finally locating the pager,
her stomach sank as she studied the number. "Damn."

"No." That edge of frustration cut through to panic. "No
damn. Not now. Whatever it is, just pretend you didn't hear it."

"I can't." Ava's voice held true regret. "It's Sam Bailey out
at Long Branch Farm. He has a mare that's ready to foal, and
this page means she's gone into labor."

"So buy him a cigar tomorrow."

"Jordan…" She watched the knowledge that she was
expected to take part in the delivery sink in, and he stabbed both
hands into his hair.

"Are you telling me that I'm going to be the first ever
documented case of death by sexual frustration, because you
have to go deliver a baby horse?"

"A foal," she corrected, and scooped her discarded bra off
the kitchen floor. "And as sorry as I am about your condition –
and believe me, I'm really very sorry – I'm one of only a handful
of licensed equine vets in the area. And Sam's a friend." She
shrugged, a helpless gesture. "This is his first year of breeding,

his first mare to come to term. I promised I'd be on hand for the birth. Look," she ran a hand through her own hair before hooking her bra, gathering her jeans. And where the hell had she left her boots? "I'm afraid I'm going to have to ask you to give me a ride, since my car's still back at the clinic. You can just drop me off and then head on home. I'm not sure how long this will take – sometimes it's a finger snap, sometimes it's hours – but I can't promise we can pick this up again tonight." She glanced at the clock on her microwave, saw that it was already past eight. "I'll have to make it up to you another time."

Jordan dropped into a chair. "You're killing me here, Ava."

"I really am sorry." She dragged on her T-shirt, met his mournful scowl with a contrite smile. "If it's any consolation, that," she gestured to the counter "was… well. Wow."

A smile ghosted. "Glad to be of service."

"Okay." And wasn't this awkward? "If you'll excuse me for just a moment, I need to go grab my boots."

THERE was a special circle of hell, Jordan mused as he watched her walk out, reserved for horse breeders who lacked the common courtesy to wait for morning to conduct their reproducing.

With that uncharitable and certainly illogical thought, he pulled on his ruined shirt.

CHAPTER FIFTEEN

LONG Branch Farm sat almost thirty minutes outside the city, a pastoral area of old traditions and new money. Homes were large, stately and recently constructed, with carefully manicured grounds and shiny luxury cars sprinkled in the driveways like the colorful decorations on a pretentious cake.

Jordan's simmering annoyance heated another degree.

Between the hot water he'd found himself in after the meeting that morning and the way frustration – professional and personal – had salted the broth, he figured he'd worked up to a good stew.

The bucolic surroundings were just garnish.

Looking around, Jordan noted that Sam Bailey – late-thirties, former investment banker abandoning the rat race for the slower pace of country life, according to what he'd managed to pump out of Ava – was doing pretty well for himself.

Backed by the ever-changing natural wonder that was tidal marsh, the farm consisted of a lush twenty-five acres of fertile Lowcountry bottomland enclosed by four-board fence.

Live oaks crouched like oversized gargoyles along the twisting length of the drive, botanical guardians to Bailey's kingdom. In the gathering darkness, their Spanish moss fluttered and swayed in a ghostly gray dance. The whole fairy tale forest feel irritated him further as his car crunched over the oyster shell drive.

Damn horse farmer.

On a low cry, a Great Egret unfurled like a sail above a small pond alongside the drive. Jordan watched it cut through the beam of his headlights, until what he thought of as Tara came into view. All columned porticos and white painted brick, the house sat like an overindulged southern belle with the emerald jewel of marsh spread at her feet.

"Turn in here." Ava indicated a fork in the drive which veered off toward a long, metal-roofed stable.

Jordan pulled in beside a black Ford F-250, hitched to a silver horse trailer bearing the name of the farm in fancy script. A pool of golden light illuminated the stable's open door, a kamikaze formation of insects playing their deadly game with the overhanging lantern.

"Thanks." Ava grabbed her doctor bag and offered Jordan a distracted smile. "I appreciate the ride." She moved to buss his cheek but he cagily shifted. "Jordan –"

Ignoring the protest, he met her lips, took the kiss deep.

And deeper.

"Mmm." He pulled back, noting her dazed look with satisfaction. "I'll walk you in. I want to check out the horse that beat me out."

It smelled of hay, Jordan thought as they entered the barn. Hay, with a faint wash of leather. They passed empty stalls, a tack room neatly lined with shiny bridles and saddles of all kinds. And veered around the corner, to what Ava referred to as the foaling stall.

The mare, an elegant sorrel that Ava told him went by Josephine, was pacing erratically, and blew heavily when they approached. Two men leaned over the half wall watching the nervous creature– one grizzled, lined and so brown that he put Jordan in mind of a human walnut, the other tall, lean and what Jordan thought of as sun-gilded. Streaky blond hair. Perfect, golden tan.

The man basically glowed all over when he turned, caught sight of Ava.

Dimming, Jordan noted, when he saw that she wasn't alone.

"Ava." The warmth in the voice spoke of familiarity. "I'm so glad you came. We, uh wrapped her tail, like you said. Washed her udder, her hindquarters with mild soap. The stall's been scrubbed, disinfected, clean bedding installed. Hell, it's clean as my mama's kitchen."

"Your mother's obviously an admirable housekeeper." Ava slipped a band off her wrist, bundling her hair into a kind of knot before opening the door to the stall. Murmuring unintelligibly, she approached the wide-eyed, tail-switching creature with what Jordan thought of as one part caution and three parts balls. Laboring female or not, that horse was damn big. But Ava stood, boots firmly planted, and ran her hand over the animal's flank. "You've done everything right. Foaling rails in the stall should keep her off the walls, out of the corners, so that the foal has plenty of room to come out." She inspected the wrap, and the animal's… well, genitals, Jordan guessed. And felt oddly embarrassed to watch.

"Tailhead's become more prominent, pelvic girdle's relaxed, so we're moving right along. Josephine is clean, well-fed and cared for, and I've boosted her vaccines myself. She's healthy, and happy, as far as it goes." With that, she stroked the mare's head, gave Bailey a brilliant smile. "She'll give you a beautiful foal, Sam."

"After three hundred and forty days of anxiety on my part, I can tell you that'll be a pure relief." The warmth in his tone edged to nerves when the horse moaned. "Is there anything we need to do for her?"

"Not unless she suffers any complications," Ava said with another smile. "She's still in the first stage of labor, but even after that moves to visible contractions and the foal begins the final descent through the birth canal, we're pretty much here to offer moral support while nature takes its course. In fact, she'll probably progress more easily the less we try to interfere. No female really likes an audience when she's laboring."

The mare blew through her nose as Ava stepped out of the stall to join the men.

"I guess this is sort of what it feels like to be an expectant father," Sam said with a rueful grin. "Excited and helpless and… hell, almost guilty." At that, Josephine jerked her sweaty head. "I know girl. This is all my fault."

"That comment lends itself to some very interesting interpretations," Jordan remarked dryly.

Sam's gaze slid to where Jordan stood, and Ava said "Oh."

Realizing she'd all but forgotten him didn't make Jordan feel any more kindly toward the farmer.

"Sam, Carl, this is Jordan Wellington. He gave me a ride because my car's still at the clinic."

They exchanged pleasantries, Sam moving away from the stall to shake Jordan's hand, and more, take his measure. Keeping his eyes on Jordan, he called over his shoulder. "There a problem with your car, Ava?"

Jordan lifted a brow. If you were familiar with human nature – and Jordan was – there was a whole lot of subtext to that question.

Ava, caught up in conversation with Carl, didn't seem to notice. "Oh, uh, flat tire."

Sam stuffed his hands into the pockets of his jeans. Rocked back on the heels of well-worn cowboy boots.

Squinted like Dirty Harry.

"So. You a client of Ava's?"

Jordan stuffed his own hands into his pockets. He was enough of an angler himself to recognize a fishing expedition when he saw one.

And because he'd had a crappy day, and a frustrating, if exciting night, he figured it just might be interesting to tug this guy's line. "Among other things."

Sam glanced back at Ava, then tried to set the hook. "So have you been... using her services long?"

"A little less than a week, actually."

Sam nodded with satisfaction, as if he'd reeled in a keeper. "Not long, then. She's been treating my horses for the better part of a year." And it was abundantly clear to Jordan that the man had had his sights set on Ava for the same length of time.

Jordan eyed Sam levelly. Decided to break the line. "Is that so? Guess us city boys move a little faster."

Irritation spiked, but before the other man could offer a retort, the mare let out a soft whinny.

"You're doing fine," Ava soothed when the animal paced past the stall door.

Both men's eyes flicked toward the females, then just as quickly snapped back.

"You look familiar," Sam said after another moment of blatant scrutiny. "Have you been on TV recently?"

"Not unless it was As the Courtroom Turns," Ava called over her shoulder. "Jordan's an assistant district attorney."

"That's right." Sam snapped his fingers, memory kicking in. "I saw the press conference you gave a couple of weeks ago about that serial killer. What's his name?"

"Elijah Fuller," Jordan replied, and felt another hook in his mouth that had nothing to do with Ava.

"Are you prosecuting that case?" Ava's dark gaze swung back toward Jordan.

"I'm lead counsel, yes." It was true, but what he didn't say was that if it were up to him, there wouldn't be a case left to try.

"A terrible thing, that." Carl leaned against the stall, wizened face set in lines of disgust. "All those innocent women. I sure hope you're going to send that fella up the river."

Uncomfortably aware that all eyes in the barn aside from the horse's were focused in on him, Jordan firmed his jaw. "I'm going to do my best to see that justice is done."

Something about the way her gaze narrowed told Jordan that Ava hadn't forgotten what he'd said the night before. That despite the best intentions of the law, it didn't always go hand in hand with justice. But as the mare moaned again, she returned her focus to more immediate concerns. "There's no need for you to stay any longer, Jordan. Like I said, I'm not sure how long this is going to take. This first stage can last anywhere from two to twenty-four hours. I'm sure Sam or Carl wouldn't mind giving me a ride home."

Over his cold, lifeless body. "I'm sure you're right," he agreed. "But if it's all the same to you, I'm going to stick. It's not every day you get to witness the miracle of birth."

Obviously caught between manners and the desire to boot his competition out the door, Sam chewed the inside of his cheek. "Well." Graciousness – barely – winning out, he turned over an empty five gallon feed bucket and gestured unhappily toward Jordan. "You might as well have a seat. It's likely to be a while."

It took the better part of two hours. After the sac ruptured, which Jordan couldn't help but compare to the popping of a truly enormous, but far more disgusting, water balloon, the contractions became visible. You could literally see the animal's uterus tightening in an effort to push the baby inside of her out. All three men winced when Ava explained that Josephine had entered the active phase of the birth, and they should soon see the presentation of the foal's feet, easing the way for its head and shoulders to make their passage through the bony pelvis.

"Thank God I got a Y chromosome," Carl muttered, and had Jordan suppressing a grin.

"Shouldn't she be lying down?" Sam asked after a nerve-wracking ten minutes. He paced, ran his hands through his hair, and then stuffed them into his back pockets. "Everything I read indicates she's supposed to be lying down."

"Most mares do," Ava agreed, easing closer to the stall to check the mare's progress. "Some insist on standing. Seems Josephine's independent-minded, and is going to do this her own way. You'll need to hold her." She motioned Sam and Carl forward, and pulled some rubber gloves out of her bag. "So she doesn't move around. I'm going to catch the foal."

Catch the foal, Jordan thought with amazement.

And then he watched her do just that.

"Is it stuck?" Sam fretted after the spindly legs emerged and nothing followed for several minutes.

"It's okay. It's great. Josephine's just taking a minute to rest."

Jordan was overwhelmed by the fearless, competent way Ava helped the baby into the world. The blood that came with new life streaked her arms as first a head and finally a small brownish body emerged from its panting mother.

When the foal slithered free, sloppy and wet, Jordan's momentary disgust was replaced with sheer wonder. Here was life at its very start. New. Unsullied. Bursting with possibility.

The baby began to struggle as Ava lowered it gently to the hay. "You've got a fine looking colt here, Sam."

"Hot damn. It's a boy. You've got a son, Josephine."

Sam came around to get a look at the foal, and Ava explained that they needed to wait at least ten minutes before cutting the umbilical cord. Carl held the mare, who was actively trying to turn around and see her newborn, until Ava had made the cut, and dipped the stump in antibiotic.

"She's getting fractious," Carl warned.

"Mother's instinct. We should step back, let them get acquainted."

"Congratulations," Jordan said as they filed out, and caught up in the moment, Sam even shook Jordan's hand.

"Hell of a thing." The other man shook his head in wonder. When he looked back toward the stall, Jordan caught the sheen of tears, and resigned himself to tolerating the man. It was pretty hard to drum up an active dislike for someone who cried at his first horse birth.

Provided, of course, that man kept a safe, professional distance from Ava.

After the mare had a chance to clean the foal and Ava had dealt with the placenta, she made use of the tack room sink. "He should be trying to stand soon," she commented to Bailey as she lathered soap up to her elbows. "He doesn't show signs of it within four hours, you give me another call. But I think you've got a strong, healthy mother and foal. Shouldn't give you any problems."

Accepting the towel the man held out, she choked out a laugh as he caught her in a hug.

"Thank you." And casting Jordan a glance, he dropped a kiss on her surprised cheek. Were Jordan a betting man, he'd put money on that kiss landing on her lips if Jordan hadn't been in the room.

"My pleasure, Sam. Best part of the job."

Once they were on the road and she started to come down off of the inevitable high, Jordan could see the exhaustion pressing her into the seat. Tendrils of hair slipped out of the knot in messy, curling ribbons and Jordan could swear he heard her jaw crack from the force of her yawn.

"Thanks again." Weariness dragged at the words like tin cans tied behind a car. "You really didn't have to stay."

"It was amazing," he admitted. And then thought of the blood. The other stuff he didn't have a name for, and truthfully didn't care to. "A little gross at times, but amazing nonetheless."

"You handled it well." A thread of amusement tied up most of the cans, and had her words bouncing out like balls. "I was worried it was going to be a high price for you to pay just to assert your jurisdiction."

"My jurisdiction?"

"Uh-huh. You know, the whole marking your territory thing you were doing with Sam."

Jordan winced before he could stop himself. "You noticed that, huh?"

Ava's chest rumbled with a sleepy chuckle. "As you said earlier tonight, 'I'm not stupid, nor am I blind.' I was a little surprised you didn't come over and pee on me."

"I've been potty trained since I was three," Jordan said with a chastised laugh. "And besides, I'm pretty sure Mr. Bailey got the message without my resorting to urination."

"I suppose a liberated woman such as myself should take issue with you for that."

Ava's eyelids dropped to half mast, but she managed a mystified smile. "But for reasons that escape me, I thought it was kind of cute."

"Oh yeah?"

When she didn't immediately answer, Jordan glanced over and realized he'd already lost her. Her lids had completely lowered, lashes smudged like soot against her cheek, the spark of will that turned her eyes from an ordinary brown to something warm and brilliant quietly banked for the night.

She looked so much smaller, somehow.

Tenderness welled. And as lights began to wink here and there against the black sky until the outline of the city took shape, Jordan saw his own pattern emerging. While it may not have been what he'd expected – she may not have been what he expected – he had enough of an eye to discern the big picture.

He was falling in love with her.

He waited for the rush of nerves, the pure male panic that should come with such a revelation, but wasn't wholly surprised to find himself steady. Fact was, he was a steady man. A man who knew his mind, knew his heart, and had little difficulty trusting either.

In that respect, among others, he was very much his father's son.

When he pulled up at Ava's carriage house, he left the car running and simply watched her. *Mine*, was the singular thought that ran through his brain.

He'd known it somehow, the minute he'd seen her. Those wide, dark eyes making her look a little bit stunned herself. Like maybe she'd sensed it, instinctively, as he had.

Though she'd certainly given both of them a hard enough time.

Remembering the way she'd gone cool, gone professional had a smile tugging at his lips. Her whole attitude had bewitched him. Maybe partly because it presented a challenge, but more so because a woman who looked like she did had more backbone than three fully grown men.

Ava wasn't the kind of woman who could be pushed around.

Maneuvered, he mused. Very, very carefully maneuvered. So he guessed it was a damn good thing that he was like a farm dog, after all.

And when he put everything in just those terms, realization smacked him in the head.

"My God." He gaped at the woman curled against the seat. "No wonder I fell for you so hard. You're cut from the same cloth as my mother." And he, being like his father, hadn't stood a minute's chance.

Like the Titanic, he thought. One glancing blow, and down he went.

Laughing quietly now, Jordan reached out, stroked the bare skin of her arm. "And you, my darling, are now just as sunk as me. You just don't know it yet."

Settled, Jordan turned off the car and fished her house key out the front pocket of her medical bag.

Time to take his own little iceberg upstairs and tuck her into bed. It was a damn shame that he couldn't tuck himself in with her, but he knew that what she needed now was sleep. And if he told himself he could spend another night with her cuddled up next to him and do nothing about it, then he was an outright liar.

She mumbled something that sounded like "goon" when Jordan bundled her against his chest, but otherwise lay like an inanimate lump in his arms.

After carefully readjusting his hold so that he could unlock the door without dropping her, he nearly tripped over One-Eyed Jack.

"That wasn't funny," he whispered when he could have sworn the cat smirked. "I nearly dropped her on her head. And after I gave you table scraps."

Stepping carefully since he didn't trust the animal not to sabotage him again, he eased into her bedroom.

The bed was already unmade, so he simply laid her between tangled sheets blooming with yellow poppies. Her feet hung off the side, and he pulled off her boots before going to work on her jeans.

He'd had her out of them once already that night.

Knowing what he would find didn't make the sight of the red silk any easier, and he gritted his teeth to block the memory of how it had felt against his mouth.

Soft. Hot. Wet.

"Not helping, dumbass," he muttered. There was a piece of hay in her hair, so he leaned over to pluck it out.

Dusty from the barn, her red shirt was also smeared with some kind of nefarious substance. Deciding it best not to consider the source – another of those things he didn't want to know about – he wrinkled his nose and tugged it up.

"Ouch. Hey." He muffled a laugh as she grumbled and punched him. "Take it easy, slugger. It's just me."

"Jordan?"

"That's the one."

She looked at him from beneath lids that blinked like a motel's vacancy light. "Tired."

"I know." He pulled the shirt over arms that she held out like a child.

She rolled onto her side and went back to sleep.

And Jordan took a moment to marvel. Then going with impulse, ran a hand over her hip. She looked, he thought, like a pin-up girl from the nineteen forties. When women weren't afraid to have curves.

Certainly nothing like the current crop of rail-thin celebrities who sniffed at a carrot stick and called it lunch.

He imagined that occasionally bothered her. Women were forever looking at other women's thighs, and finding their own to be fat.

It was a mystery he couldn't hope to understand.

With a final squeeze for that curvy hip, he pulled the sheet up and kissed her goodnight.

"Sainthood," he mumbled as he made his way to the kitchen in search of pen and paper. "That level of restraint deserves canonization."

After dropping her dirty clothes in the basket on top of the dryer, he scrawled a note reminding her he'd be by in the morning. Propping it on her nightstand, he checked to make sure her alarm was set. Since it was nearly one a.m., it would be going off before she knew it.

As Jordan pulled away and headed down the street, he noted the dark car parked in front of Lou Ellen's house. And found himself slowing.

Deep blue domestic, out of town plates. Florida, judging from the orange depicted between the tag numbers. As Jordan drove away, a piece of memory raised itself like a crumpled red flag, though he was several blocks away before it smoothed out.

The tag had been secured in position with a shiny gold chain.

CHAPTER SIXTEEN

"DO you have any idea how many dark blue, midsize domestic sedans are registered in Florida?" Jesse asked as Jordan leaned over his shoulder to get a look at the computer.

"No, but I'm sure you're going to tell me."

"Too many." Though his brother had narrowed it down, Jordan noted, and had the plate numbers sorted into lists. Even as they spoke the printer spit one into Jesse's waiting hand. "At least you caught part of the tag this time."

"Being conscious tends to help. Here. Drink your coffee." Jordan exchanged the printout for the large – Jordan refused to call it venti – Caffé Americano he'd brought along to make up for having woken his brother in the middle of the night.

Jesse grunted, and picked up one of the scones Jordan had added to sweeten the deal.

Thank God Starbucks opened at five a.m.

Jordan took a drink from his own cup when the words he was reading blurred on the page. His brain cells might be moving with the lubrication of caffeine, but the rest of his body was quickly turning to lead. He was exhausted. When he'd realized the significance of the chain, he'd backtracked toward Ava's only to find the car gone.

But had sat there, watching, for hours.

Maybe it was paranoia on his part, but the chill that had danced over his skin when the memory kicked into place was enough to have him pick up the phone. He'd called his brother, told him what he'd seen. Jesse had started running tags, no questions.

"The ones on that list are registered to individuals who came up as having some form of criminal record. Mostly nickel and dime stuff – your petty thievery, drunken and disorderlies, simple assault – but we have at least ten convicted felons. From armed robbery all the way up to murder one. One or two have served their time, several others are out on parole. A few are still locked up, but the vehicles might be being used by relatives." Jesse slipped off his glasses to rub his eyes. "You'll want to look it over and see if any of these names jump out at you from one of your cases."

"Thanks." Jordan pulled out a chair and joined his brother at the desk. The computer hummed as Jordan scanned the names, probed his memory. Consulted his stored notes whenever memory failed. The house creaked occasionally, in the language of old buildings, and when morning streaked its first pink fingers across the sky Jordan heard the shower kick on above Jesse's home office.

"Clay's up."

Jesse just grunted. "Bastard took me for thirty dollars last night. Should have kicked him out of the house. Never play poker with a psychologist."

By the time the water pipes gave their final groan Jordan had cross-referenced most of the list.

"Anything?" Jesse asked.

"The only name that jumps out as even a possibility is Eileen Zeigler. Looks like she got busted for shoplifting back in eighty-five. Community service, no time served. But it's her son who came through Chatham County's system. Bodie Zeigler is doing the flip side of a dime for possession with intent."

"That's pretty stiff for a drug charge."

"Aggravated. He'd been slapped on the wrist a couple times before for simple possession, which – though you didn't hear it from me – is a waste of both manpower and taxpayer money. I've seen enough of these guys come through multiple times to know that people who want to get high are going to find a way to do it. But anyway, he went from being a danger mostly to himself to a predator when he decided to pedal smack to middle school kids." He circled the name even as he shook his head. "Mrs. Zeigler lives in a retirement community outside Orlando. Wore a Mickey Mouse sweater at the trial, and sat in the lobby knitting during recess. It was one of those things that hit home for me. Even degenerates have mothers."

Jesse eyed him over the rim of his cup. "And this particular mother has sticky fingers. Just because she knits, it doesn't mean she's a model citizen, Jordan."

"She's probably seventy years old by now. I can't see her bashing me over the head. I know," Jordan said when Jesse continued to stare. "She could have had help. Though after six years, why bother? Unless something happened to the son.

People can go batshit when they lose someone. But anyway. I'll pass this along to Detective Coleman."

"You sure you don't want me to check it out?"

"Let's do everything through the proper legal channels. This is Coleman's jurisdiction. I don't want to hang anything up on a technicality." He crossed the room to his briefcase.

"Speaking of Coleman's jurisdiction, still no word on that red-headed succubus you were dating?"

Jordan turned, cocked his head. "Does your wife realize you're an ape?"

Jesse stretched out his legs, covered in jeans he hadn't bothered to button, and propped his bare feet on the extra chair. "Jillian's the one who called her that. Woman would have sucked you dry within a year. No idea what you saw in that one, apart from an exceptional rack."

"Who has an exceptional rack?" Clay asked as he walked in, buttoning his shirt. "Damn, is that coffee?"

"All gone." Jesse shook his empty cup.

Spotting Jordan's cup on the edge of the desk, Clay walked over and popped off the lid.

"By all means. Help yourself."

Ignoring Jordan, Clay slapped Jesse's feet aside and sat. "About this rack. You talking about the veterinarian? What?" he said in surprise when Jordan bared his teeth.

"Do not. Say one word. About Ava's breasts."

Jesse's low whistle accompanied Clay's raised brow. "Well. Mostly I was yanking your chain again, but apparently I've roused the beast. You're serious."

"I'm going to marry her."

Clay bobbled the coffee, spilling some across his lap. "At least it wasn't hot. My God son, have you gone insane?"

But Jesse was grinning like a fool. "The Wellington Curse strikes again."

"What?" Clay looked over his shoulder as if expecting an attack from behind.

"Relax, Copeland. The only unattached female in this house is Grace, and I don't think she's considering marriage just yet."

"Not until she's forty," Jesse agreed. "Or I'm dead. Whichever comes first."

Jordan closed his briefcase, then dropped onto the leather sofa angled in the corner. And sank. It felt so damn comfortable that he knew it was a mistake. "Trade me spots, Clay. If I sit here, I'll fall asleep."

"Yeah, I want to hear about why you were skulking around before the crack of dawn," Clay said as he grabbed a napkin before heading to the couch. He dabbed it at his lap. "Right after you explain why I shouldn't suggest that your family have you committed."

"Our dad proposed the day after he and Mom met," Jesse explained, scooping up the last scone and breaking a piece off. "Took one look and basically handed his testicles over on a platter. Been her puppy ever since. It's the stuff of family legend."

"Hey." Jordan reached out and snatched the scone from his brother's hand. "Having the good sense to know what you want when you see it is in no way emasculating. And it's not like you're not married, Jesse."

"Yes, but —"

"Jesse?"

Jordan had the pleasure of seeing his brother jump. Then Jesse pressed the button for the intercom system he'd wired throughout the house. "Uh, yeah, honey," he responded to his wife's disembodied voice. "I'm here."

"Could you come help me deal with Grace? I need to pop in the shower, and she's refusing to get dressed unless I let her wear her Easter dress to school. They're finger painting today."

"Sure. Be up in a sec. Shut up," he said when Jordan picked up the plate from the scones and mimed handing it over.

"Excuse me?"

"Not you." Jesse said to his wife before grabbing the plate and smacking it on Jordan's hand. "I'm talking to the idiot who shares my parents. Though I suspect he was probably adopted."

"Oh." Jillian's smile came through. "Good morning, Jordan. And I'm assuming Clay's there, too."

After their chorus of responses, Jesse turned off the intercom and climbed to his feet.

"Woof," Clay said, and Jesse just stabbed a finger toward him.

"Jesse?" His brother turned, and Jordan nodded to the computer. "Thanks."

"I told you. I got your back."

"Well, that was fun." Clay popped up and grabbed the scone from Jordan. "Orange cranberry. My favorite. So what happened last night?" he asked around a mouthful.

Jordan filled him in on the car, and what he and Jesse had uncovered.

"Crazed septuagenarian mourns loss of son, assaults prosecutor. Full coverage at five."

"Sounds ridiculous, doesn't it?"

"Stranger things, and all that. But now you're worried because that car was parked in front of your woman's house. You're serious about the ball and chain? Okay." Clay held up a hand. "You are. And now you're worried."

"I see why you took Jesse for thirty dollars. Yes, I'm worried. More than I was before. I don't want any of my dirt smeared on Ava. I don't like the idea that maybe somebody followed me last night. I don't like that they know where she lives."

"Assuming," Clay popped the last piece of scone. "That this car actually means something. Could have been a random tourist."

"Could have been."

"But you're not taking any chances, now that Ava's potentially involved."

"You know, you should be a psychologist. And... hell, is that the time?" He squinted at the clock on the computer. "I've got to run home and let Finn out and change."

"I thought we were doing that witness interview today. That's not until ten."

"But I've got a flat tire to deal with before that."

Clay looked out the window, which faced the drive. And the four un-flat tires on Jordan's car. "Here." He snagged the plate from the desk. "Better take this along."

"Ha ha. I'll pick you up at nine-thirty."

THE pitiful howling woke her moments before someone pounded on her door.

Peering at the clock, Ava cursed with creative viciousness when she saw that it was blank. She checked the cord. Plugged in. So the damn power must have gone out.

"Perfect." She pushed the hair out of her eyes, spotted the scrap of paper next to the clock. "Well, at least that gives me an idea who's out there banging," she said to Jack as she read the message on the back of one of her order forms. "And a lot of good you are. Lying there at the foot of the bed, watching me sleep the day away."

The pounding started again.

"I'm coming, I'm coming. Dammit." Rolling to her feet, Ava looked on the floor for her shirt from last night. And saw... absolutely nothing but floor. Even her boots sat in the corner. Neatly.

"Hell. The man even picks up after himself. Time to start cloning."

When the knock sounded for the third time, Ava forewent the nicety of clothing and, snarling, stomped to the door.

"Hey. You're... not dressed." With a quick, panicked look over his shoulder, Jordan hustled her back inside. His own clothes smelled of fabric softener, his skin of a recent shower. "You can't answer the door like that. What if I'd been the UPS guy, for God's sake. That's grounds for a lawsuit. Inducing cardiac arrest."

"My UPS guy is gay."

"So he'd try to knock you down and steal your underwear. Why aren't you dressed?" he persisted as he trailed her into the kitchen.

She needed caffeine. Lots and lots of caffeine.

"First, I said he was gay, not a cross-dresser. Two separate things, that don't necessarily go hand-in-hand."

"I'd rather you not use that sort of expression when we're discussing men who like other men. Not that there's anything wrong with that."

"Second." She ignored that bit of nonsense, and scooped out the coffee, filled the pot. "What have you done to Finn? He sounds like the Hound of the Baskervilles."

"He doesn't like being left in the car. Ava, why aren't you dressed? I double checked your alarm. It was set for six-thirty."

He'd double checked her alarm, Ava thought in amazement. Helped her out of her dirty clothes. Put them away.

And then left.

She noted the bruised look of fatigue, the concern in those gorgeous eyes.

He'd given up half his night for her.

And had come to change her tire, first thing this morning. With his silly, howling dog in tow.

"You really are a gem, aren't you? A regular treasure."

"I don't know about all that, but I like the look in your eye. Push that coffee pot aside and we'll pick up where we left off last night. Except, uh, the pot doesn't actually seem to be doing anything."

"What? Shit. Shit."

"You plug it in?"

"Yes I plugged it in. I'm not an imbecile." She slapped a hand on the counter. "Or maybe I am. The power is out. That's why I answered the door in my underwear."

"Breaker box?"

"Behind you. In the closet with the washer and dryer."

While Jordan fiddled in the closet, Ava pulled her cell from her purse to check the time. "No time for coffee anyway. I'm just going to run and grab a shower. A cold one, I guess."

"Okay."

Her first appointment wasn't until eight fifteen. She could make it, Ava thought as she turned on the water, held her breath. "Damn, damn that's cold." Her spine stiffened like it had simply been frozen, but she toughed it out and grabbed the shampoo.

Barely make the eight fifteen, she acknowledged while she scrubbed. Stupid power outage. Probably a crew working on the lines, as they were forever fiddling with this or that. Like people didn't need their caffeine in the morning. Luckily the patient was just Big Lloyd, with a suspected UTI. Both the cat and his owner were sweeties, and she could call the woman if she had to make an emergency coffee stop. After all, no one wants a doctor making judgments with only partial brain function.

Ava braced herself, and stepped back under the spray.

It hit her in a thousand icy needles. "Okay. Okay, that's more than enough."

She jumped out, feeling like she'd just been dipped in liquid nitrogen. How did water get that cold in the south? In April, for pity's sake.

Snatching at a towel like it was a lifeline, Ava wrapped it around her middle, grabbed another for her face. Maybe she wouldn't need that coffee after all.

Something warm licked her leg.

"Oh. Hello, Finn." She looked down into brown pools of pure canine adoration. His tail thumped against the awful tile when she scratched under his bandana.

"Sorry." Ava glanced up as Jordan's voice sounded from the doorway. "I had to let him out before somebody called the cops."

And speaking of expressions better left unsaid...

Ava managed a smile despite the reminder. "He's fine. Let me just grab some clothes and I'll be good to go."

"I want to show you something first. Get dressed. I'll meet you in the kitchen."

"Well, isn't he a bossy britches this morning," she said to Finn. But the look on his face had sparked her concern, and it flamed in her empty stomach. She knew him well enough by now to understand he was pissed.

Ava threw on some scrubs, tied her hair into a damp tail. And pasting some bright-eyed and bushy-tailed on her face, followed the dog into the kitchen.

"What's up?" The chipper tone met his stony expression and clashed.

He opened the door that led to the garage below, gestured her down the stairs.

Finn bounded down in front of her, all happy barks and wagging tail.

"I never use this entrance," she told him, her voice echoing a little in the steep, narrow well. The bare bulb above them cast the sort of shadows that gave her the creeps, huge and menacing. "The outside door is easier, since I park my car in the drive."

And besides, it wasn't so damn claustrophobic.

"So I gathered. I could see my footprints in the dust. And watch your step there. The wood on that last tread has gone a little soft." She emerged into the dim garage, next to the enormous Cadillac that Lou Ellen had inherited from her father, and hadn't driven since. Her classic Karmann Ghia sat beside it, the SUV she drove parked outside.

"Your main breaker wasn't on the panel with the others," Jordan said as he hopped over the last step, snapped his fingers at Finn, who was sniffing the Cadillac's tire. "Finn. No. So anyway, I figured, hey, must be downstairs. Which is kind of odd, but whatever. The building is old, and they probably finished out the apartment later. I went down, let Finn out, circled around to the back door. Which was locked. But the window beside it was broken."

Glancing over, Ava could see the missing pane, the shards of glass.

Her heart began to gallop.

She knew the goon had been in her apartment once, but she'd changed the locks herself. Deadbolts. Solid. Lou Ellen had a spare key – which she'd already used, blast her – but Ava knew the hardware was good.

Apparently good enough that the goon had resorted to breaking windows.

"Well, damn. I'll have to tell Lou Ellen. Looks like the cars are both okay. I can't imagine she had anything valuable inside them, as they're really never driven. But still, it –"

"Ava."

She stopped babbling, swallowed.

"Ava, they broke in and tripped your breaker. You're right, the cars are both okay, from what I could tell. And my footprints were the only ones in that dust when I went up and tried the door. Which was locked, thank God. But if my footprints were the only ones in that dust, it means that someone broke in, ignored the vehicles, tripped your main breaker so that you'd lose power in the apartment, and then didn't even try to get inside."

"Maybe something scared them off."

"Could be," Jordan agreed, and something moved behind his eyes. Something just a little dangerous. "Could be a botched attempt at breaking and entering. And that's exactly what I would have thought if I hadn't noticed this."

He snagged her elbow, led her to the power box, and pointed out the smiley face scratched into the metal.

"Well, huh." Finn came over and sniffed, so Ava rubbed his head. "I guess Lou Ellen must have done that when she was a kid. Although her artwork hasn't improved, considering."

When the hand on her arm tightened, she reluctantly met his gaze. Oh, yeah, the guy was furious.

"It's fresh, Ava. There are shavings on the floor. So someone broke in, ignored the cars, tripped your breaker, decided to try their hand at a little carving instead of walking up your stairs, got spooked and fled the premises, thoughtfully taking the time to relock the door on their way out."

Something inside her trembled.

"When you put it that way, it doesn't make much sense."

"Gee, you think?"

Finn whined and bumped Jordan's leg, and Ava took the opportunity to step back. Physically. Emotionally. "I'll tell Lou Ellen about the window, so she can have it replaced."

"You need to call the police. Get this on record."

What trembled inside her cracked. "I'll leave that to Lou Ellen."

"Damn it, Ava. Don't try to tell me this was just a prank, or a coincidence. I've got a new tire in my trunk that suggests otherwise. Two incidents of a destructive and threatening nature in two days. That's what we lawyers like to call harassment."

Where was her mad? She needed to find her mad. She'd asked him to stay out of it, hadn't she? Told him it was none of his business. And yet here he was, scolding her like a child.

"Ava."

But the raw scrape of concern as her name tumbled from his lips made anger impossible. The crack turned into a fissure, and the fissure threatened to flood. "I'll tell Lou Ellen about the window."

"Baby –"

"Don't ask me to do more. I'm sorry. I can't. Now please. I have to get to work."

She turned and fled up the narrow stairs, and found the shadows deeper than ever.

CHAPTER SEVENTEEN

"IF you say one word about this to Jesse," Jordan threatened Clay as he pulled into the parking lot of Riverview Apartments. Which was completely misleading as a name, since the view was more decaying warehouse and fast food dumpster. Maybe if you stood on top of the building...

"One word," Jordan continued as Clay checked out the roof, "and I'll stake you to a fire ant mound and pour honey on your naked, bleeding body."

"Sounds like Jesse's bachelor party. Though I think the stripper was naked, I was covered in beer, and it was more of a bean bag than an ant mound." He scratched his chin. "Could have been a futon."

"Shut up."

"Shutting."

Jordan whipped out his phone. Clay rolled down the window to release some of the steam pouring from his buddy's ears. Eu de dumpster wafted in, but Clay had certainly smelled worse. Instead he admired a seedling palmetto tree growing right up from a crack in the pavement. Determined little sucker. Life did find a way, he mused, even when the conditions sucked.

It hadn't been the best of mornings. Aside from the sleepless night, Jordan had been late picking Clay up – and from the look on the man's face, the vet's tire wasn't the only thing causing him trouble – then when they'd finally made it to the DA's office, their witness decided not to show up.

Since Jordan had managed to track the man down and they were even now preparing to visit his residence, Clay concluded that this particular phone call was of a more personal nature.

He sat back, prepared to hear his friend grovel.

"Hey Jack, it's Jordan." The use of the eldest Wellington brother's name had Clay's eyebrow sliding upward. Not the vet, after all.

"Wow, is that Caleb I hear? I take it you're still at home. Oh, that's too bad. Tell Caitlin I hope she feels better. Hey, the reason I called is –"

There was an ear-splitting cry from the phone.

"Man, the little dude is mad. Well, I can't say that I blame him. I'd rather have a breast than a bottle, myself. Anyway, I was wondering if I could get the number for Evan's cell."

"Evan Hardwick? As in Hardwick Investigations?" Clay'd played poker with the man last night.

Jordan glared at Clay's interruption. "Don't you have anything better to do than eavesdrop?"

"Not at this precise moment."

"What? Sorry, Jack. No, I was talking to Clay. And no, the DA's office isn't trying to horn in on your best PI. This is personal."

Jordan laughed, but it was brittle as glass. "Well, if I told you that, it wouldn't be personal anymore, would it? Come on, Jack." The chatty tone died. "It's important. Yes, I'll owe you. Firstborn son, and all that. Okay." He snagged a pen from one of the cup holders, scratched a number on the back of a business card. "Got it. And Jack? Thanks."

He flipped his phone shut and opened his door. "Ready?"

Clay tugged his ear. Stretched. Rolled his left shoulder.

Jordan leaned his head back against the seat and sighed. "You are such a woman. What happened to the manly aversion to talking about anything other than sports?"

"Psychology doctorate. Comes with a fancy piece of paper and a pretty skirt."

"Because I'm in a hurry, and I want the full power of your concentration focused on the man we're about to speak with once we get inside, I'll forgo the pleasure of telling you to mind your own damn business. So here's the deal. I replaced a tire for Ava today because the old one got slashed. Someone broke into the garage beneath her apartment and shut off her power, carving a smiley face on the breaker box as a happy little parting gift, and when I took her back to her clinic the other night – and we were followed, by the way. But when we got inside, I found her landlord guarding the place with a shotgun."

"Okay." A boat horn split the air like an axe, and Clay figured he'd do the same with his usual bullshit. Jordan apparently needed an ear, just this once, and not a smart mouth. "I'm assuming, since you're looking to hire Hardwick – and if the man's investigative skills live up to his poker game, I'd say you made the right call, there – that you're not counting on the police to do their job."

Jordan's eyes moved behind his closed lids. "She wouldn't call them. Tried to pass it off as kids, an eccentric landlord. Hijinks. Blah, blah."

Uh-oh. "Well, I've met the woman and she didn't strike me as dumb. So I'm guessing, just from what you've said, that it's one of two things. She knows or at least suspects who's responsible, and is embarrassed. Maybe it's a crazy relative, a former associate who's turned nasty, the neighborhood delinquent, a disgruntled ex. Someone she thinks she can handle, for whatever reason. She just doesn't want to do it in front of you."

"I'm leaning toward the ex. Broken engagement about a year and a half ago. She says it was his call." He opened his eyes, turned. "I don't know if I believe her."

And the pain Clay saw there told him that was the sticking point. "Jordan. You've known her, what, a week? You may be on the fast track, son, but most of us prefer not to dash into things like a crazed rabbit. She's well within her rights not to feel comfortable letting you rifle through her life like it's your sock drawer."

"That was the worst analogy in the history of pep talks. What's the second thing?"

"Well, my second guess would be that she knows or at least suspects who it is. But that more than embarrassed, she's afraid. Of the responsible party, or of what might happen should the authorities get involved."

Jordan scrubbed a hand across his face. The bruises of fatigue showed deeper now that they'd been painted with the shadow of worry.

"Everything I've seen tells me she's not the kind of woman to avoid a confrontation. But either way, it amounts to the fact that she knows something and she won't tell me."

"Which is why you're hiring a PI behind her back."

"I ran a quick check on the ex. Lives locally, no criminal record. I would have done more, but I was running late as it stood. I don't have time, just now, to dig as deeply as I would like, and the police can't do much of anything without her cooperation. So I'm hiring Evan. You think it's a wrong move."

"Knowing you, I think you need to do what you can to ease your mind. Maybe you'll find out her ex has been harassing her, and you can prosecute him to the fullest extent of the law, after you beat him to a bloody pulp. Maybe you'll find out a whole lot more than you bargained, which is what you risk when you rifle through other people's sock drawers. I think that analogy's pretty good. But whatever the end result, you have to be prepared for the fact that she will likely not take kindly to the means."

"I know that. I do. It's... well, presumptuous, to say the least. Hell, let's face it. It would piss me off if she dug up my past. And if I wasn't half crazy already – worrying about her, my happy little hospital stay, and this political short stick of a trial – I'd probably have enough sense to sit back and see how things play out. But I am half crazy, so sense isn't really an option."

"Admitting to insanity is the first step."

Jordan managed a half laugh. "Can we just go talk to my witness now? Whether I like it or not, I have a prosecution to prepare."

"Sure."

Clay stepped around the palmetto as he climbed from the car, wishing both it and his friend the best of luck.

They were surely going to need it.

"I convinced her to move in here. Insisted, really. Did I tell you that?"

Daniel Hatcher peered at Jordan out of bleary brown eyes. The sunny kitchen stank of last night's whiskey, of garbage just gone over. Of despair.

Jordan looked at the man who'd been three weeks away from vowing to love, honor and cherish Sonya Kuosman. Before a killer took her away.

"Mr. Hatcher –"

"Insisted." The man slapped the butcher block table with the flat of his hand. "Why pay rent on two places? Didn't make much sense. Not when we had the wedding, the honeymoon to pay for. Her parents, they don't have a lot, what with her father being on disability and all, so we didn't feel right asking. Besides, I make pretty good money, and Sonya, she was almost finished with her degree. Four credit hours, the certification deal, and she would have been a high school teacher. History. Knew everything about every invention, war, skirmish, plague and land purchase there ever was. Could talk your ear right off. But she wouldn't have bored them. Not my girl. She made that shit interesting. Because she talked about it on an everyday level, know what I mean? Kids could relate. Sonya, she had a, I guess you could call it a gift for spinning a yarn. Real colorful. And man, could she curse up a storm when she was on a tear. But... I'm sorry. That's not what you were asking. We were saving to buy a house. That's why I insisted she move in here."

Jordan waited a beat, unsure if the man was going to hold or simply break into pieces at the kitchen table. Not that he blamed him. The woman Hatcher loved had been brutally murdered. Scrape away the rage, the purpose that had bled from him like a wound after Sonya's death, scabbing over after Fuller's indictment, and what festered there was guilt.

Because he'd talked his fiancé into sharing his home. And it was here that she'd met Elijah Fuller.

Recognizing a man sliding into the black hole of depression, a man who needed something worth fighting for to help him climb back out, Jordan figured it was time to rally. He may have doubts – was in fact riddled with them – but he owed it to the city, to the victims, to the loved ones they'd left behind, to carry out his duties.

And he needed this man's testimony to do that.

The coffee pot sputtered on the counter behind him. "I'll get it," Clay said, and slapped a hand on Jordan's shoulder as he rose. "Uh, mugs?"

"In the cabinet next to the fridge." Hatcher ran a hand through his disordered black hair, gestured vaguely. "And… there might be milk in the fridge. Sugar's… uh, I haven't gotten around to buying any, I guess. Sonya was on a diet before the wedding. But I think there are some packets of that artificial deal. Somewhere."

Before he lost him again, Jordan took charge of the conversation. "Mr. Hatcher… Daniel. I won't say that I know what you're feeling, because I can only imagine. But I need you to pull it together. It was your insistence that had police looking Elijah Fuller's way, your testimony before the grand jury that helped bring down the indictment. I've got the transcripts, I've seen the tapes of your interviews, and I know you held up. Did what was needed, when it needed to be done. But this is the first time you and I have met, face to face, and I have to say that I'm a little concerned."

Clay sat filled mugs on the table, but Jordan ignored his and continued to push. "You didn't show up today, Daniel. You didn't show up, and when I track you down, make it easier on you by agreeing to come by your residence, I find you not just hung over, but still drunk. It's ten-thirty in the morning, Daniel. And you smell like the barroom floor. You do this at trial, and you might as well hand Elijah Fuller the acquittal yourself."

"You son of a bitch." The mugs pitched, one of them crashing to the floor as Fuller erupted from the table. Coffee splashed and ran, some of it onto Jordan's lap. Fuller's bathrobe fell open to reveal the heaving chest of an angry bull. "You sit there, in your damn suit, and run your two-hundred-dollar-an-hour mouth. Look down your fucking nose because a few shots made the thought of going through this again a little more bearable. Because you don't know. You say you can imagine, but you can't. No one can, until it happens to you."

"That's right." Jordan nodded his head, ignored the heat burning through his pants. He figured the pain was small change, in comparison. "I don't know. I don't know until you take me back through it, step by awful step. And neither will the jury. It's horrible, and it's harsh, and it's unfair that you have to relive it. But I need you, Daniel. Sonya needs you."

"I want her back."

Daniel sank into his chair, and there was misery in his voice as well as anger. The man needed both to make it through, so Jordan didn't mind deliberately baiting him if that's what it took to get there.

"I know you do. So bring her back for me, Daniel. Tell me about Sonya, and what you witnessed happening between her and Elijah Fuller."

"Okay."

Clay handed the man a dish towel to mop himself up, and grabbed another one for Jordan.

"I'm… I'm sorry about the coffee."

"Those pants of his are ugly anyway." Clay patted the man's shoulder, winked at Jordan. "Two hundred an hour, you'd think he could buy something a little better. I'll make more coffee."

Two hundred an hour for a public servant. What a joke.

Clay brewed another pot, and Jordan listened to Hatcher's story. How his fiancé, who talked to everyone, started chatting up Fuller in the building's laundry. How Fuller started hanging around, catching Sonya in the parking lot, even showing up where she took classes. "Just happened to be passing by," Daniel said. "Which was bullshit, but Sonya was too nice to call it."

The escalating tension between Daniel and Sonya, because Daniel had had enough of Fuller. "'He's harmless,' Sonya would say. Until I caught him with that camera."

Jordan knew the story, but consulted his notes. "You and Mr. Fuller had an altercation on the seventeenth of March, last year."

"Saint Paddy's Day." Hatcher agreed, and sipped his coffee. Clay'd made it strong enough to peel the skin from the roof of your mouth, but it seemed to be doing the job. "You know how crazy the city is. People everywhere, most of 'em drunk."

"Had you been drinking, Mr. Hatcher?"

"Not a drop. I had to work, missed the parades and whatnot. But Sonya, she'd been out with friends. Was going to meet me here, have a little dinner, then we'd head out together for round two. You know we've got this ground floor unit, and when I park and get out of my car, I can hear her singing. She's got the window open, like she likes to do. And she's in there just belting out some Irish song. Danny Boy, I think. Woman carried a tune about as well as a buffalo can do the two-step, but she's singing anyway. So I think, hey, I'll just sneak around to the window. Throw a rock or something. Maybe scare her a little so she'll get fired up."

"That's when you noticed Fuller."

"The bastard." Hatcher's face tightened with rage. "Hiding in the damn bushes, taking... taking pictures of Sonya through the window. I'm sorry." He grabbed the discarded dishtowel, rubbed it against his watery eyes.

"You're doing fine."

"So, I, uh, confront the little prick. Pop him one in the jaw, and he squeals like a girl and goes down. Sonya comes over to the window and starts asking what the hell is going on, and Fuller is blubbering and there's just this... red haze in front of my eyes. So I pick him up by the shirt – I don't really even remember doing it – and just... slam him into the window."

Jordan had sworn to uphold the law, to conduct himself in a manner befitting a representative of the court, but part of him pumped its fist. Even if Jordan couldn't be sure that Elijah Fuller had caused three deaths, his behavior had been reprehensible. "Fuller was later treated at the hospital for lacerations to the back of his head."

"Yeah. Uh, some of the glass flew in and hit Sonya, too. She got five stitches right about here." Hatcher made a slicing motion across the top of his foot.

"You spent that night in jail."

"Some of the neighbors called the cops. I was... I guess I was still working him over, and just got caught up in it and took a swing at one of the officers. Sonya, uh, she finally agreed there might be a problem and was talking about getting a restraining order. The cops had Fuller's camera, the memory stick pretty well filled with pictures of Sonya. Here. At school. Walking through the damn park. We figured we'd move, get away. Get the glass replaced and break the lease, who cares? But a little over a week later she's dead.

"The same day the stitches came out of her foot."

CHAPTER EIGHTEEN

AVA stared at the tub of pansies with helpless rage.

They were dead. Not just withered. Dead.

She knew – even before Jordan had so thoughtfully pointed it out – that she had a tendency to neglect them. They always looked so cheerful, their happy purple faces bobbing in the barrel as she breezed in and out the door, and then – whoops! They'd be drooping. Forgot to water them, again.

But Jordan had watered them, hadn't he. Not four – or was it three? – nights ago. And now they lay lifeless, leaves shriveled, faces dark.

The bastard had poisoned her flowers.

Ava looked around, noted with little surprise that the lot was empty. She hadn't actually seen the goon since he'd confronted her with the knife. And the thought that he'd been sneaking around her clinic with a can of poison had her furious blood running cold.

What if it had been one of her patients?

What if it had been one of her friends?

"Okay." Ava pulled her keys from her purse with shaking fingers. "Okay, asshole. You want to make me uncomfortable, that's one thing. But enough is enough."

Riding on nerves, on anger, Ava twisted the key in the lock before stomping toward her car. She'd parked it directly in front of the door to discourage any more creative tire carving. Recalling the way Jordan had changed the flat that morning, despite the fact he'd been quietly furious with her, had her own temper snarling and snapping like a nasty little dog.

She guessed that was pretty well over, considering he hadn't bothered to say goodbye before he'd left.

And while she would have liked to say good riddance – she hadn't wanted to get involved, had she? Hadn't she told him to leave her be? – Ava was too honest with herself not to recognize the little bump to her heart.

Just a bruise, she told herself, and checked her rearview as she slid her Mustang into the line of traffic in Calhoun Square.

Better to take the hit now, get them both out of the line of fire before someone got seriously hurt.

And it wasn't like she hadn't been bruised before. Her uncle had seen to that, and Michael... well, Michael had been all too eager to abandon the field.

All but righteous now with the rage that threatened to blister anyone who got too close, Ava whipped into Lou Ellen's drive. So many of her corpuscles had boiled away that she went lightheaded as she slammed into park.

Jack streaked out from under a camellia bush, and Ava's heart shot up to her throat.

"Dammit. Jack, how did you get out?" Fingers tingling from the heat of her rage, from the scare, Ava reached down to scoop him up. In her hurry to get to work that morning, she'd decided to leave him at home. Inside, she recalled irritably, where he couldn't be run over by a stupid car.

Annoyed by the tightness of her grip, Jack dug his claws into her arm.

"Stop it. Just stop it right now, you ingrate. I almost hit you."

His warning growl let her know he was pissed. "Yeah, well, get in line, buddy. I've got plenty of damn fool men angry with me already."

"Problem, Ava?"

Ava glanced up to see Lou Ellen, glass in hand, cropped orange pants and bright green shirt making her look unfortunately like a skinny pumpkin, standing on the veranda with a uniformed young man.

"No, not at all. Everything's just peachy. Ouch. Ouch, you little shit." With the mark from his teeth burning her arm, Ava dropped the cat to the ground. He crawled under an oleander to glare, eyes narrowed, tail twitching.

Lou Ellen cleared her throat. "Seems the peach crop is rotten this year."

"You have no idea," Ava muttered.

"Um, if that's going to be all, Ms. Calhoun?"

Ava looked at the man who'd spoken, noted the Glass Doctor logo on the cap pulled low over short, light hair. There was a name embroidered on his shirt, but she was too far away to see it. If she hadn't been so angry that she was all but deaf, dumb and blind with it, she would have noticed his van parked along the street.

"Yes, I'm sorry. You need me to sign something, baby doll?"

"Yes ma'am." He turned red to the tips of his ears. "Here and… here." He avoided looking at Ava as Lou Ellen took the clipboard.

Probably a good call, as he'd likely suffer corneal flash burn.

When he'd trotted down the steps and hurried away, Ava sighed and walked toward Lou Ellen.

"I'm sorry about the window."

"I do believe you frightened that young man." Lou Ellen offered her a drink, which despite the brownish color and slice of lemon bore little resemblance to iced tea. But Ava shook her head. She was volatile enough without adding alcohol. "And it's glass, Ava. Old glass. Probably needed to be replaced, anyway."

Ava dropped, simply dropped, onto the rosy brick steps. And lowered her head to her knees.

The tinkling of ice let her know that Lou Ellen had joined her a moment before she felt the hand stroke down her back.

"Lou Ellen. I'm —"

"Don't you tell me you're sorry again, child, or you're just gonna piss me off. One of us in a temper is about all I can take."

Disgusted, Ava felt tears swim into her eyes. She couldn't let it make her cry. She just couldn't. "I hate," she sucked in a breath, let it shudder out instead of tears "that any of this is touching you."

"Seems to me that if something isn't touching you in this life – good, bad, what have you – you must not be living right. Me? I prefer to take a chance of things getting messy rather than inhabit a sterile box. Might as well live in one of those damn snow globes that litter Joyce Phillips' parlor. The ones with those little Precious Moments creatures inside? And her a grown woman. She ought to be ashamed."

A laugh tickling her throat now, Ava lifted her face to the evening breeze. "Those things always creeped me out. Their eyes look like black teardrops, and their heads are entirely too large for their bodies."

"There you go." Lou toasted her with the glass. "It's little wonder those poodles are so nervous."

Because she felt better, marginally, Ava took a swig since it was there. "Jesus." Her eyes watered. "I think you forgot the mixer."

"Why ruin a good drink? I saw your handsome prosecutor drop by this morning."

Ava watched Jack slide out from the oleander and dart after the first butterfly she'd seen that spring. "Yeah, well, I'm pretty sure that won't be happening again anytime soon. He's sufficiently annoyed because I wouldn't call his good friends, the police. I think he's ready to wash his hands of me."

When Lou Ellen didn't immediately respond, Ava turned to glance at her friend.

"What?" She knew that look.

"Well Ava, it seems that you've managed to piss me off anyway." The anger frosting those dark eyes was cool where Ava's was hot. "Not everyone is willing to cut and run quite as easily as that pansy-assed Michael. I'm not sure who you're doing the bigger disservice, that young man or yourself. And since I am pissed off, I think I'll leave you to your sulk and go paint. I find I'm more creative when I'm annoyed."

If that was the case, Ava thought as Lou Ellen glided away, the woman must have been happy as ten clams every other time she'd picked up a brush.

"Aren't I just the bitch tonight?" Ava watched the butterfly outmaneuver Jack. Big, hungry predator. Little, clever invertebrate.

"And you don't even have a spine."

Ava decided to wrap up the pity party and find hers. "Let's go, Jack." She needed to hit the shower, change clothes.

Just what did one wear to visit their father in jail these days?

Ava figured it was time to find out.

"YOU think you can tell me no?"

Jordan closed his arm around the woman's neck, pulled her back against his chest to subdue her struggles. The pretty little brunette's cornrowed ponytail tickled his chin, her smooth, dark throat soft as butter beneath his hand. "I said, get in the car."

"No!"

Her chin dipped into the inside curve of his elbow, forcing him to loosen his hold. And just like that, her hand shot behind her, aiming straight for his eyes. Her heel came down hard on his instep as the sharp point of her elbow rapped against his ribs.

When he fell back, she swiveled, snapped out a kick that caught him squarely in the solar plexus.

Applause broke out around the room.

"I did it." Tasha Van Sant, pretty little brunette, college junior and total sweetheart, bounced on the soles of her size six feet. Her dark eyes danced with pleasure. "You're, like, huge, and I just dropped you on your ass."

Jordan smiled from his prone position on the mat and accepted her outstretched hand. "And that's because…"

"Because the outcome of a confrontation isn't always about size, or strength."

Jordan climbed to his feet, looked at the other students. "And…?"

"It's about being aware of your surroundings," they chorused "and knowing your assailant's weak spots."

"SING," Tasha added, grinning. "Solar plexus, instep, nose, groin. Though I think I hit you more in the eye."

"Eyes work. And my groin appreciates the fact that you overlooked it."

"Who said I did?"

With a laugh, Jordan offered her a bow. "Well done, Tasha."

When he straightened, Jordan caught sight of Chip Coleman smirking in the doorway. "Okay ladies." Jordan nodded to acknowledge the detective, then turned toward his class. "That wraps things up for this evening. Next week we'll talk about techniques for breaking a wristlock, without breaking your own wrist."

After answering a couple last minute questions and deflecting one invitation to River Street for a drink, Jordan grabbed his towel and headed toward Coleman.

"And to think, these women actually pay to wrestle around with you on a sweaty mat."

"Well, they pay the Y. I'm just a lowly volunteer. But somebody has to do it."

"Jiu-jitsu?" Coleman rattled the change in his pocket.

"Some." Jordan wiped his neck. "Some Krav Maga. How to use your opponent's momentum against him. Situational awareness. Which, considering I'm talking to the detective in charge of my own assault, makes me sound like a giant ass-hat."

"Even the best of us can be caught unawares."

"Tell me about it." As the last of his students faded out the door, Jordan tossed the towel toward his duffel. "I'm assuming you didn't stop by because you wanted to watch me get poked in the eye."

"Well, that was a nice bonus, but no. We found Leslie Fitzsimmons' cell phone."

The words, the tone, struck Jordan like another kick. Found her phone, but not Leslie. "Maybe you'd better explain."

Coleman stepped into the room, and Jordan scanned the hall before closing the door. A couple of the women tended to linger, and this wasn't a conversation he cared to be overheard. He'd been honest about his own assault, using it as a – rather humbling – touchstone for that night's class, but saw no need for them to be privy to the gritty details.

"Ms. Fitzsimmons' mother has been adamant that her daughter wouldn't just take off without a word, and certainly wouldn't, and here I quote, 'allow some fool of a man to cause her to lose all sense.'"

"She never liked me. The old witch."

Chip's grin was wry. "I think that's more of a gender thing than a specific comment on your lack of attributes. But anyway, because she doesn't have to worry about little niceties like probable cause and convincing a judge to sign a warrant, she hired a company to track the GPS chip in her daughter's phone. Turns out it's in some house out on Tybee, so once again ignoring the finer points of the law, she drives out there and bangs on the door. A teenaged boy answers, accusations fly, the kid's mother calls the police, and what comes out is that he does indeed have the phone. Claims he found it behind a dumpster on River Street."

Because a nasty sort of bile wanted to rise in his throat, Jordan grabbed his water. "I'm assuming you checked her call record."

"Oh yeah." Chip's Mayberry face went grim. "Filter out the calls that the kid copped to, and it showed nothing outgoing between seven p.m. on the night in question and around one-thirty a.m., when our boy says he picked it up. But when one of the tech guys brought up the phone's internal call log, he discovered an aborted 911 originating from her cell in between the time of her last call and the time the kid started calling his friends. The numbers were punched, but never sent."

"Because someone got to her before she could." Jordan scrubbed both hands over his face, swore viciously as he pieced the timeline together. "Leslie witnessed my assault."

"Speculation." Chip rattled his change again. "But yeah, that's what I'm thinking at this point. You two argue, you exit through the stairwell toward your car. She waits maybe a minute or two before she decides to follow, get in one last word, and stumbles upon something she shouldn't. Like you getting your head cracked open."

"Hell." Feeling the weight of the uncharitable feelings he'd suffered toward Leslie that week, Jordan sank onto one of the plastic chairs lining the wall. Shock started to fill the space in his bones worn hollow from fatigue.

"On another happy note, Mrs. Fitzsimmons has demanded we look at you as a prime suspect in her daughter's disappearance."

If he wasn't so sick at heart Jordan might have laughed. "So I fabricated my assault, complete with concussion, to cover up the fact that I'd, what, killed Leslie to get her off my back?"

"Grief and worry don't leave much room for reason."

The detective had no idea how true that was. "Why spare me?" Jordan wondered aloud. "Why drop me off in front of the emergency room, for God's sake, and not Leslie. Unless... hell, what if Leslie was the target? But if that were the case, why not just leave me where I fell? What —"

"Jordan. We're pursuing all those avenues."

"I know. And I know that you know how to do your job. The, uh, list of license plates I gave you…"

"We're checking them out. And checking traffic cameras for the area near the hotel, see if we can place a car matching that description in the vicinity any time that night."

"She's dead, isn't she, Chip?"

"We don't have enough evidence to treat this as a homicide as of yet, but… okay, okay." Coleman held up his hands when Jordan's eyes went to slits. "My personal opinion? Yeah. The lady's probably done. I'm sorry, Jordan. I know this isn't how you hoped this would shake out."

AVA'S landlord stood on the porch under a circle of buttery light when Jordan pulled to the curb. The air had gone soft with twilight, but her white smock shone with smudges and bursts of color, like a toddler's finger painting gone awry. As he watched, she stabbed her brush toward an enormous canvas with the aggressive grace of a veteran fencer.

Then dunked the brush in what looked like iced tea.

When Jordan rolled down the window, Finn let out a greeting bark.

"Well, well." She looked up with a grin. "Look what the canine dragged in. Hello, lover. You come to pay me a visit?"

Jordan dug deep and came up with a smile. "You know I'm only using Ava to get to you."

Lou Ellen laughed, delighted.

"Finn, stay." Ignoring the dog's pitiful whine, Jordan grabbed his peace offering off the back seat. "And since she's not answering her phone and her car's not in the drive," he said as he climbed the brick steps to the porch "I'm deducing that she's not around, leaving me free to have my wicked way with you."

"Seems you're as clever as you are good lookin'. She's gone out of town for the night."

That stopped Jordan in his tracks. "Where?"

A moth danced in front of the spotlight she'd set up, and Lou Ellen batted it away. "I'm afraid that's for Ava to share, darlin'."

Recognizing a rock solid wall of loyalty when he hit it, Jordan glanced toward the carriage house. Its windows were dark, shuttered eyes that refused to look his way.

He'd sat outside for hours last night, and someone had broken in after he'd left.

He wondered if they'd seen him, and waited.

Not knowing what he was up against burned his ass.

"In case you're wondering about the window, I had it replaced today."

Having nearly forgotten the older woman's presence, Jordan drummed up another smile. But it fell flat after the first beat. "I could stand here, shoot the breeze, and pretend there's not an elephant sitting right on this porch between us, but I'm too tired for cajoling. Who's messing with her, Lou Ellen?"

To his surprise, she reached over the easel and patted his cheek. "I knew you weren't a pansy-ass." And before he could even begin to figure out how to respond, she picked up the glass, brush and all, and drank. "And look at you, too well-mannered to gawk at me like I'm crazy. I might be." She lifted the glass high. "But it speaks to your breeding that you didn't point it out. And just to calm your mind, I decided to paint with alcohol tonight, instead of the confounding contents of these tubes and jars." She gestured toward the paints scattered like discarded toys at her feet. "It makes the whole process more appealing."

"Lou Ellen –"

"Don't interrupt, lest I'm forced to retract my good opinion. You're not a pansy-ass," she continued, green eyes clearer than they should be. "And while I would sincerely love to be more forthcoming in regards to your question, I can only repeat, that's for Ava. But have a care how you handle her, darlin'. She's got a hard-ass shell, but inside, she's bruised. And her heart? It's gold. So you remember that, and this: things aren't always what they seem."

Feeling like he'd just been battered by a velvet-gloved fist, Jordan could only stare. "It's nice," he finally said "to hear what you didn't say. You love her."

"Like my own," she agreed. "Now, are you going to explain why you're carrying that big ole' stuffed whatever?"

"It's Donkey." He turned the animal around. "You know, from Shrek? Cute and lovable, despite the fact that he's an ass."

"Oh." She pressed a hand to her heart, then bent over and simply laughed. "Oh. That does it. Aren't you just the sweetest thing."

"Yeah, I'm pretty sure Ava doesn't think so right about now. I was frustrated with her this morning. I had a right to be," he said darkly "but probably could have handled it a little better. Not everyone's drawers are open. And wow, that didn't come out right."

Jordan shook his head as Lou Ellen broke up. "Since exhaustion has robbed me of the ability not to sound like an idiot, I'm going to bid you goodnight. Is it okay if I leave this here? Maybe you could sit it on Ava's doorstep, or whatever?"

"Darlin', I'd be happy to give Ava your ass."

"Saved by the bell," Jordan said as Finn started to howl. "I'm not even going to attempt a response. Thanks, Lou Ellen."

"Oh, child. It's my pleasure."

BECAUSE guilt and anxiety had tangled to form a nasty ball in his stomach, Jordan found himself driving toward his parents' house. And wondered that no matter how old a person got to be, when they were sick, were hurting, there was an almost primal yearning for home.

Turning Finn loose in the backyard, where he immediately streaked toward a squirrel that muttered irritably from a loblolly pine, Jordan let himself in through the back door. The heady scent of something baking – brownies. Hot damn. – made him doubly glad he'd stopped by. The smell, the sound of his mother humming in the kitchen brought childhood back in a flash of sensory memory. Here was continuity, and comfort.

The tangle in his stomach eased.

"Something sure smells good."

His mother, her blonde hair tied back in a red ribbon, beamed a smile as he dropped a kiss on her head. "Baby boy. What a nice surprise." And in an echo of Lou Ellen's gesture, Addison patted his cheek. But when he reached for one of the brownies arranged neatly on the plate, she deftly swatted his hand.

"Oh no, you don't. These are for a party tomorrow at Grace's preschool."

Jordan eyed the plate with avarice. Chocolate and caramel and fat. Oral gratification in a three-inch square. "There have to be two dozen brownies on that plate. Surely they won't miss just one."

Addison bumped him with her hip when he edged closer to the plate. "There are two and a half dozen, precisely, which is one for every child. And just in case you have any notion about cutting a couple in half so that I won't know one's missing, I'll just warn you that your father has already tried that particular trick. He paid for that by watching me eat the last of the Thin Mints he'd hidden. Imagine my surprise and delight to discover them in a package of whole wheat Triscuits." She blinked her big blue eyes.

Jordan leaned against the counter with a mock frown. "You're a cruel-hearted woman, Addison Wellington."

She licked chocolate from her finger, secured plastic wrap over the flute-edged plate. "Flattery isn't going to score you a brownie. And if you're looking for your father, he's in the study crying in his coffee while he does Justin's taxes. The boy's so overworked in that ER he didn't even realize it was April until we reminded him to come home for Easter. So your father's trying to make sense of Justin's dubious record keeping and illegible scrawl. I guess that's one physician stereotype he managed to succumb to."

"Well, he's not quite thirty. Give him a little time and I'm sure he'll develop an enormous ego and an eighteen handicap. Peddle some prescription drugs on the side. Probably find himself in a shaky marriage, start knocking down nurses like bowling pins."

His mother's fingers stilled on the plastic.

"Need I remind you, Jordan Nathaniel, you might be past thirty yourself, but you're never too old for a good swat."

"You wouldn't let me have a brownie," he grumbled. But when her eyes flashed, he pulled away from the counter. "Okay,

okay. I'll just go see Dad, since I'm not feeling the love in here."

He was almost to the door when his mother called him.

"Guilt won't get you a brownie, either. But you're my baby, and there's something more than fatigue in your eyes tonight." She pulled a single brownie from behind the toaster. "Here. I have my secret stashes, too."

"You're the best mom ever," Jordan smiled as he bit in, then strolled over to pull her into a hug. "Seriously, Mama. You set the standard."

"I lied." And she sniffled. "Flattery will get you everywhere. Go on now. And be sure to leave a few crumbs to torment your father."

Jordan found his father, bleary-eyed behind his glasses, holed up at his massive walnut desk.

And like coming upon his mother baking in the kitchen, found comfort in the familiar scene. How many times as a kid had he come in here, whether in excitement or shame, to talk things over with his father? To be praised, or scolded, in turn? To simply shoot the breeze?

Too many to remember.

Jordan stood in the hall and studied the room, in so many ways the typical southern gentleman's office. Richly paneled wood, window and floor coverings in shades of navy and green. Masculine paintings of shrimp boats adorning the walls. Heavy leather furniture.

And there, mixed in with the law books that had helped steer both he and Jack into their father's profession, a child's unskilled drawing, dozens of family photos. The baseball that Jordan had caught at his first Braves game. A clay pot – James' work, if he wasn't mistaken – that would leak like a sieve if it ever held water. Five bronzed pairs of baby shoes.

A faded photograph of Addison, on the day his parents met.

And there, on his father's desk, the razor sharp teeth of a four foot shark.

Tom told everyone who inquired that he caught the vicious beast off the coast of Key Largo.

What he kept to himself was the fact that it was Jesse – an avid fisherman – who had to reel it into the boat when their father realized what he'd caught.

"Well, hello Jordan." Tom looked up, noticed Jordan at the threshold. He gestured toward one of the chairs which flanked his desk. "Have a seat."

Jordan did, stretching his legs until his feet came to rest near his father's. They touched on all the usual topics. Sports, the weather, the pain of income tax season. The trials of training a dog.

The unimportant. The mundane.

"Something troubling you, son?"

Jordan crossed his arms over his stomach and looked out the double window. It was full dark now, but the landscape lighting showed small swarms of insects dancing about the azaleas lining the drive.

The tangle came back, and knotted.

"I think I may have been responsible for a woman's death."

"Well now." Tom pulled his glasses off and leaned across the desk. "That's a hell of a thing to say. You care to explain?"

Not really. What he wanted was to hit rewind. To speak pleasantly with Leslie. To agree he was a bastard, agree to another date, another chance. Agree to anything that would keep her from following him into that garage.

But because he couldn't, he looked at his father. And told him everything Coleman had learned.

"Jordan." His father sighed. Compassion and exasperation. "You can no more shoulder the blame for what may or may not have happened to that woman – you need to remember that there's no proof of foul play at this point – than someone who survives a plane crash can for the fates of the other passengers. You were a victim that night, too. And just because you survived and she – maybe – didn't, it in no way indicates that you did anything wrong."

"I realize that." In his head. His heart was another matter. "But I just feel... sick. Guilty, and tangled up."

"I think that's called 'survivor guilt.' And as much as I'm pleased that you came to my door – and you know it's always open – you know you could talk to Clay. He probably has experience with this kind of thing."

"I'm sure he does," Jordan agreed. "And maybe I will, when it's not so... immediate. But right now, I just... it feels like someone kicked me in the gut. Leslie was – and you don't need to remind me that I don't know for sure she's dead – she was a decent person. A little grasping, maybe, and certainly it ended badly between us. But I can't put it out of my mind that the last thing I felt that night was relief. Relief to be rid of her."

"People have a tendency, once someone is gone, to... paint a rosier picture of them. When you do that, it makes your own actions – at least the ones that put you at odds – seem questionable. Now, maybe in the heat of it you said something regrettable. But I know you Jordan. You're not the type of man to treat a woman callously."

"No." He hadn't been callous. Just annoyed. But how was that any better, if Leslie was still dead? "The whole thing just seems so random. Maybe if I knew where to point the finger in blame... violent crime is never easy, but it helps if we can fit it into at least some parameter of logic. The bank robber shoots the security guard because the guard draws his weapon. It's awful, it's a tragedy, but at least it makes sense. And the way this is turning out? There's just no logic that I can see."

TOM watched his son struggle, and considered how far he should wade into murky waters. "You know, Jordan, I've been thinking about that night myself." Kind of hard not to, when your son spends the night in the ER with a concussion. The thought of which still turned his blood cold. "What strikes me is the fact that the car you remember being abducted in, or that you at least remember waking up in, is not the car that dropped you at the hospital. I'm wondering if whoever dropped you there – I believe you said it was a woman that you recall pulling you out of the trunk– may not have been a party to the original assault."

Jordan angled his head. "So… what, like a bystander? She wasn't supposed to drop me off at the hospital? If she was a Good Samaritan who just happened along, why not call the police?"

"I don't know. Maybe she knew what they were up to, was part of it, and got cold feet at the last minute. Just a suggestion," he said at his son's baffled stare.

"You know what, Dad? That makes a sort of sense. I remember … I guess the best way to put it is a sense of urgency. From her. I can't recall what she said, really, but she kept digging into me with her nails. Physically trying to pull me toward her car. She seemed, uh, nervous almost."

"Well there you go," Tom said. "Maybe she wanted to get you out of there before the other, or others, knew what she was up to."

Tom could see Jordan's mind race as he looked at the situation from a new angle. "I'd considered the possibility that this was some sort of payback. Or even a kind of warning, though against what, I have no idea. But if you're right, maybe it wasn't intended to end like it did. Maybe it was an aborted murder attempt." With those words, the color leached from his son's face.

"Um…" Jordan boosted his hip and pulled out his cell phone. "There was this car. Last night. Could you excuse me a moment, Dad? I have to make a quick call."

Tom blatantly eavesdropped as Jordan stepped out into the hall.

After a brief pause, a muttered curse, his son ended his first call and made another.

"Hello, Lou Ellen? It's Jordan Wellington. That's right. Um, ha. Thank you. It's a relief to know you're watching my ass. But that's not why I called. Ava's cell phone seems to be set on ignore whenever my number pops up, so I thought I should pass this along to you. I want you to keep an eye out for this car." He described a dark blue domestic, Florida plates. "No, no, nothing like that, but I saw it parked out front the other night, and there's a chance the driver could be dangerous. If you see it near the house, I want you to call the police. Yes, you could ask for Detective Coleman. And if you wouldn't mind giving me a buzz, I'd appreciate it. Yeah. Here are my numbers." Jordan rattled them off. "And Lou Ellen? Thanks."

Tom tapped his fingers on the desk. He and Addison had heard rumblings about a dark-haired veterinarian from Caitlin, who'd apparently gotten the story from her friend who worked at the veterinary clinic. Jordan hadn't said boo so far, but Tom wondered at what he'd just heard in his son's voice.

"Sorry," Jordan said, as he walked back into the room. "All this talk of murder and mayhem made me nervous. I just needed to take steps to make sure the mother of your future grandchildren stays safe."

Tom blinked, and then the grin simply spread. And he marveled at the trick of genetics that allowed a younger version of himself to look back at him out of his wife's stunning eyes. "Sometimes I forget, Jordan, how very much alike we are."

"Two peas. First time I looked at her, it was like a lightening strike. Just… boom. All but blew me out of my sneakers. But she's not easy, Dad. She's got some baggage, and doesn't seem inclined to let me carry it for her."

"You'll bring her around."

"You're right." Jordan nodded. "I will."

CHAPTER EIGHTEEN

AVA eyed the animal with despair.

Gray fur covered a chunky body stuck on disproportionately short legs. Black fuzz stuck up between long ears. And the big, toothy grin on his cartoon character face made her feel like a reclusive ogre.

She'd managed to avoid Jordan for three days.

Jack sprang onto the bed, eyed the stuffed donkey with disdain, and flicked his tail before jumping to the windowsill.

"I know." Ava slid him a frown. "It's ridiculous. Adorable and ridiculous, and I just can't seem to get rid of it."

And the giver was much like the gift.

He'd seen the goon's car, was all she could think. Seen it, noted it. Had some reason to believe it might be dangerous. Did Jordan remember what happened that night?

Her stomach clutched at the thought.

She'd been waiting, half sick, for the police to show up at the clinic. Three days of jumping like a rabbit every time someone came through the door. And she'd spent three nights in a motel. The first night because she'd gone to see her father, and couldn't make the trip to Atlanta and back that fast. But then, she'd spoken with Lou Ellen.

And had hidden from Jordan ever since.

It was cowardly, and she hated to be cowardly, but she'd needed some time to consider her options.

At the sound of Jack's growl, her eyes jerked toward the bedroom window. Dusk had fallen, the first hint of dark a velvet shimmer on the air, and the curtains fluttered at the open window. Though they were drawn, the lace panels did little more than distort the view for anyone who cared to look in. Not that she'd worried about it overly, considering the huge live oak squatting outside the window. But she knew better than to think either it or the curtains would deter a determined peeper.

Casually as she could, Ava reached over and switched off her bedroom lamp.

And jerked as a shadow, deeper than the rest, shifted against the tree.

Maybe Spanish moss, she told herself reasonably. There was a good breeze kicking up outside, and Lord knew the stuff dripped and danced and generally made her feel like she was trapped in some gothic horror novel. But despite the reason, and despite – or maybe because of – the talk she'd had with her father, Ava pushed the window down and flipped the lock.

The goon wouldn't scare her again.

Stripping off her shirt, she tossed it aside, prepared to climb into her own bathtub for the first time in nearly a week. Lavender scented oil, she mused, pouring some in as she ran the water hot. That was supposed to be relaxing. Probably should have bought a bottle of wine, done it up right, but she settled for turning her music on low. And because Heartbreak Hotel seemed all too appropriate, resigned herself to thinking about Jordan.

The way she'd worked it out over the past few days, she figured she had three choices.

1.) She could continue to say nothing at all, ask him to run away with her to Tahiti and leave all her problems behind.

Ava bundled her hair on top of her head, and slipped into the steaming water. And thought, from the way Jordan talked about his close-knit family, that possibility highly unlikely.

She ran down her mental list, watched her skin pink up like a ripe berry.

2.) She could tell him a half-truth. Admit that she was related to the primary players in a major criminal cartel. Then conveniently leave out the part about his mistaken abduction by said cartel and – more importantly – how she'd pulled his ass out of that trunk.

Of course, clever as he was he'd probably figure it out on his own.

3.) She could tell him everything, and let the chips fall where they may.

Given the fact that those chips might involve charges of obstruction of justice, failure to report a crime, grounds for interrogation regarding her uncle's business, and either a quick, vicious death at the hands of her uncle's goons or a promising future in the cornfields of Nebraska as part of the witness protection program, she figured option three was pretty much out.

"Shit." Ava let her head fall back against the tub. Why, why, why did her life have to be so complicated? Why couldn't she have met a normal man, with no law enforcement proclivities whatsoever? Maybe settle down. Her cat, his dog. A house with a nice piece of land, so the animals would have room to roam.

Probably have a couple of kids.

Because she could see it, and see it clearly, shimmering like a mirage through the rising steam, Ava slapped her hand at the scented water. "Dammit, Papa. You never should have let Carlos drag you into that life." Now they were all paying for it.

And paying dearly.

When Elvis faded into Patsy Cline, Ava heard the noise. A scrape. A sort of groan. The creak that sounded like rusty hinges. Oh, God, she'd locked the front door, hadn't she? She'd been so distracted when she came in...

Hell. She might have left it open.

Heart banging like a drum, Ava thought about the shadow. Maybe it hadn't been moss, after all. Maybe her visit with her father had well and truly pissed her uncle off, and –

"Finn, no! Leave One-Eyed Jack alone!"

The sounds of a very playful dog meeting up with a very temperamental cat filled the apartment. First the barking, then a feral hiss. A thud, a shatter. A tightly voiced reprimand followed by a low canine whimper. The sound of the door again and then heavy footsteps on her wood floor.

Ava sat up, flipped off the music.

"Ava?"

She considered simply slipping beneath the water. Two minutes, three tops, and all her troubles would be over.

What the hell was Jordan doing in her apartment?

And while she'd like to be angry – would make sure to be, later – for the moment she was simply frozen. "In the bath," she finally admitted when he called her name again. No point in putting this off any longer. "If you'll just give me a minute to –"

Jordan pushed open the bathroom door.

"Sorry about that," he said as he stepped in. Like she'd issued an invitation. "I have Finn with me and I made the mistake of…"

His mouth was still open, but more words failed to come out.

"No, really," she said after an awkward moment of silence. "Feel free to barge right in."

"I knocked." He found his voice. And where it was cool, his eyes were hot. "You seem to be having some trouble answering things lately. Your car's in the drive; the door was unlocked. I'm not one to ignore opportunity."

He started loosening the buttons of his chambray shirt.

"What do you think you're doing?"

"It's customary to undress before getting into a bath."

Ava peeled her eyes away from the expanding swath of flesh, and reminded herself she had working brain cells.

"Pardon me, but you seem to have lost your grip on reality. This is my apartment, my bathtub. You're not getting in here with me."

"Oh yes," Jordan said, and dropped his shirt to the floor. "I am."

Honestly, the man was either stupid or had a will forged from steel. "Look, Jordan, I know I haven't been very accommodating the past few days, and I'll apologize for that. Of course, your blatant, bullheaded trespassing in my apartment – in my damn bathroom, for pity's sake – should pretty much cancel out any rudeness on my part. I agree there are some things we need to discuss, but this is not –"

His pants slid to the floor.

"Jesus."

"Jordan. Though there have been times I felt like I've seen God myself. I figure tonight's going to be one of them."

"You...you can't just..."

He raised a brow when she simply sputtered.

"I can't think."

"I can't say that I have a problem with that. But if you want me gone Ava, now's the time to say so."

And she knew without his saying so that it would be the last time she had to tell him. He wouldn't bother her again after this. It was what she wanted, or at least what she'd tried to convince him she wanted, since she'd seen him standing in her waiting room.

But now that the cards had been dealt, she just couldn't ante up.

"Just get in." She scooted forward to make room.

With a wordless nod, Jordan climbed in behind her, stretching his long legs out to the sides.

THE water was hot enough to boil shrimp, he thought. And slick and scented with one of those mysterious products women used. Lavender, he realized. He took a deep, bracing breath of it, and willed himself to settle. Damp tendrils of hair trailed down Ava's neck as she leaned back, and despite the emotion churning in his gut, he pressed a light kiss to her shoulder.

The past few days had been hell.

He'd been swamped at work, worried about Ava and angry with it.

She hadn't answered his calls, hadn't returned a single message. He'd driven by, pathetic fool that he was, and failed to find her car in the driveway.

But she'd been into work. He'd called there, too, and been informed that she was in surgery. Which meant that while she may have returned to town, she wasn't spending her nights at home.

It had been a knife to the heart, he thought as he grabbed one of those balls of mesh women used in the bath. Hot, sharp and lethal. To think that maybe she'd gone back with the ex.

And he'd considered saying screw it, throwing in the proverbial towel, and leaving her to her dubious decision. Until he thought about his conversation with Lou Ellen. Not a pansy-ass, she'd said. And that things weren't always what they seemed.

So he'd swallowed an extra thick serving of pride, and come over, ready to fight for her.

And simply melted, lust and tenderness, at the picture she made sitting in the old claw foot tub.

The little jumps in his gut that had been worry, had been anger, dissolved with the steam. This wasn't the time for battle. Whatever problems lay between them, he figured they'd work them out later.

Now was the time to show her what was in his heart.

With a squeeze of some bath gel on the mesh, he started rubbing it into her skin.

"Jordan. I... oh God, that feels good. But I don't know–"

"Shh." He brushed a stray lock of hair aside, kissed her neck. Gently. "It's okay. I do."

THE warmth of the water, the slick slide of soap across her skin, the feel of his body – big and hard – had Ava lulling in a kind of stupor.

Gone was the frenzied, uncontrolled heat she'd come to expect from him. In its place was restrained sensuality. Tenderness, even. She didn't entirely understand the change, given the fact that she knew he'd been angry, but it didn't seem to matter. She responded to him either way.

He slid the sponge down her arm, across her quivering stomach. Circled her aching breasts. When he cupped one, tested its weight, drew her nipple between thumb and finger, Ava felt the moan spill from her slow and sweet as honey. As she drifted there, in that pleasured warmth, his hand drifted up her thigh.

So slow, so soft, that Ava thought the anticipation would kill her. And just when she was on the verge of begging, he allowed his fingers to find her.

Nibbling along her jaw line, his breath warm and smelling of something sweet – peppermint, she thought vaguely – Jordan moved his long fingers in slow and torturous circles. Ava stiffened, half inclined to jerk away from the intensity of the pleasure, but he locked his arm around her stomach and held tight.

"No. Don't hold back." It was a hot whisper, and it shivered through her blood when his fingers plunged. "Ava. I want to watch you go up."

And she climbed, step by silky step, until she was desperate in his arms.

"Now." Body throbbing, mind spinning, Ava pushed away and turned so that she could take him into her. "For God's sake, Jordan. I want you inside me now."

"Easy," Jordan murmured. And getting a good, solid grip on her slippery waist, lifted her as he stood up. "Not yet."

"What do you mean, not yet?" Flummoxed, Ava goggled at him as he reached for one of her deep red towels. "You drop by unannounced, invite yourself into my bath, get me all stirred up and then…." she waved her arm around "have the nerve to tell me not yet?"

He also had the nerve to grin as he snagged her arm. "Careful sweetheart. You're gonna poke your eye out." When she growled, he wrapped them both in the bath sheet, damp skin to damp skin. Then he lowered his mouth to hers.

And kissed her breathless.

"I just realized," he said after he eased back, and Ava's blood was pumping madly. "That the cot in your clinic, or your kitchen counter – even that charming bathtub – aren't what I want for our first time. So though it nearly killed me to wait, I'm glad it didn't happen before." He lifted a hand, and laid it like another kiss against Ava's cheek. "I want soft. Slow and sweet. I want to savor you, Ava."

The towel fell into a crumpled heap at his feet, and Ava figured her heart landed right along with it. And when he lifted her into his arms, carried her to that big, brass bed, the space where her heart had been filled.

"Jordan." His name drifted out on a sigh.

"Ava." He laid her down. "Let me look at you."

SHE was... lush, he thought would be the right word. Dark hair spilled haphazardly from some sort of clip to fall across rounded shoulders. Her breasts, rosy-tipped from the bath, curved round and plump above a tiny waist. Full hips – and his hands itched to grip them – gave way to slim, pretty legs.

Her eyes, that deep, deep Spanish brown, flickered with a hint of impatience.

But he didn't want to rush this.

He'd spoken the pure truth. Jordan didn't want the first time they made love – the first time of many, if he had his way in the matter – to be done in simple heat, or haste. So he called up every ounce of his control to ensure that didn't happen. This was something he wanted her to remember for the rest of her life.

For the rest of their lives. Together.

The corners of his lips tugged into a smile as he brought his weight down next to her. The mattress sagged, and he took the opportunity to roll her beneath him. Then he kissed her again, with tenderness and possession.

AVA felt it, felt the blatant ownership with which his mouth claimed hers. And while some rational part of her brain continued to flash *mistake!* like a neon sign, the purely romantic, feminine side of her sighed, and reveled. His body was huge and so utterly male, his lips hard, his tongue hot. And his hands – those magic hands – deft and sure as they traveled her body.

"Ava." The murmur was reverent as he reached down to capture her breast. He gently cupped her tender flesh, traced lazy circles around her nipple. And then lowered his lips to her skin.

More, was all she could think as he opened his mouth, suckled. The heat of that wet space blasted through her and left her trembling. Teeth nipped at her collarbone, fingers trailed along her belly.

Then he found her thighs, pushed them wide, and proceeded to destroy her.

Hot and sweet, utterly carnal, the orgasm rocketed through her. Blew her apart, body and mind, until she broke into a million pieces. And as she gripped the sheets, coasted down, Jordan pressed a kiss to her inner thigh.

Reeling, she could do no more than breathe when he stroked her calf.

"That's my girl." He dipped his tongue into her navel.

"Right now? You bet."

And his chuckle was just a little smug as he worked his way back up. "We're just getting started."

"Considering I've turned into a human puddle, it's possible I'm already done."

"A puddle, huh? Guess I better take a dip."

He plunged.

Blue eyes hot, and fiercely triumphant, he caught her gasp between his lips. The small sound of shock vibrated there and had Jordan clenching his teeth. He gave her body another moment to adjust, then trapped her with his gaze.

"LOOK at me, Ava. Look at me and know. This isn't just sex."

It was everything.

The rhythm built, stroke by deep stroke, as Jordan slowly, thoroughly showed her. Skin, already coated in bath oil, slicked as they slid together. The air in the room went fragrant, and hummed with pleasured sighs.

Jordan struggled for control like a man drowning.

When her nails sank into his back, and her gasps became his name, he lost his grip on the line, dragging her legs to his shoulders.

"Ava." And with his hands linked to hers, he plundered.

OPEN now, no barriers left, Ava rode out the fierce possession. Those hot eyes bored into hers in a silent message of conquest.

She was his. And for this moment, by God, he was hers. As their bodies raced over that final edge, he emptied himself inside her.

"Oh. God."

Jordan turned his head, kissed her neck. And after a moment spent gathering his breath, said "Told you we'd see Him."

The laugh just bubbled up. "If there was any feeling left in my legs, I'd feel obliged to kick your arrogant ass."

"If there was any feeling left in my ass, I'd feel obliged to comment on the scratches you put there. I…"

"What?" she said when he trailed off.

"NOTHING. It's not important." Jordan shook off the weird sense of déjà vu. And dredging up some energy, brushed a thumb across her cheek. "You're beautiful."

Ava curled around him like a contented cat. "It's a little late for sweet talk. You already got me into bed."

"I did, didn't I?" He dropped a kiss onto her lips. "It just occurred to me that I might need to apologize."

"For getting me into bed?"

"Not a chance. For letting Finn in. He whined when I tried to leave him in the car, and… well, to be honest, I planned to use his sad puppy-dog eyes to help get me in your door. Which I'm going to scold you for leaving unlocked, even though it worked to my advantage. But anyway, I'm pretty sure he cracked your lamp."

"AH. That explains the crash." Although at the moment she couldn't care less. Her head felt fizzy, like she'd bathed in champagne instead of lavender. "Where is he, anyway?"

"Shut up in the kitchen. We've probably got about ten more minutes before he decides to launch a vocal protest." Jordan rolled to the side, and let out a short yell of his own.

"Okay." He scrubbed a hand over his face. "I'm not sure what's more disconcerting. Finding myself face-to-face with

Donkey, or realizing One-Eyed Jack just watched us have sex."
The cat twitched his tail from his position on the windowsill.

"Well, he's missing an eye. He couldn't have seen that much."

Jordan laughed, then leaned over to set the stuffed animal on the floor. "Um, Ava. About the other morning –"

"Don't." Suddenly desperate, Ava reared up to touch a finger to his lips. Not yet. She wasn't ready to talk about it yet. "Please. Can we just... be, a little while first?"

His eyes were intense as he searched her face, but he pressed a kiss to the palm of her hand. "Sure. No place I'd rather."

When he opened his arms, she cuddled in, but inside her something quivered.

"You know." Jordan stroked a hand down her back. "I think that may be the first time I've ever forgotten to suit up for the party."

"Suit up for the...." And what quivered stilled as she put it together. "Well, hmmm." He hadn't worn a condom.

She hadn't even given it a thought, and that was incredibly uncharacteristic. After some rapid mental calculations, the quiver shimmied again. Her last period had ended about ten days ago.

Noticing her silence, Jordan gave her shoulder a little squeeze. "If it will ease your mind I can assure you that I have a clean bill of health."

"What? Oh. That's… good. And same goes." She'd always been selective, and very careful, even when she'd been with Michael.

But aside from disease control, condoms provided another very important function.

As if he'd read her mind Jordan's hand stilled on her back. "So I'm guessing that since you were engaged and all," And wasn't his tone extra casual? "You're probably on the pill."

"I can't take the pill," she explained, equally breezy. "It makes me violently ill. And anyway, my engagement has been broken for nearly two years. The, um, issue of birth control hasn't really been a factor since."

"Ah," Jordan said, and gave her a little squeeze. "I can't tell you how happy I am to hear that. Not about the pill. But about the fact that you haven't needed it."

Ava leaned up on her forearm to get a look at his face. Aside from the obvious – and what she liked to think of as purely masculine – satisfaction that she hadn't been interested enough to sleep with any other men in recent memory, she detected a reasonable level of concern. But he hadn't lost his color or gone cross-eyed or broken out in hives at the idea that they'd been completely unprotected, so she had to give him credit. "If it will make you feel any better, I don't think I'm ovulating."

Jordan stared at her for a moment. "Just out of curiosity, you know this… how? Your ovaries put up a little sign that says eggs for sale when you are?"

"Actually, some women claim that they can feel the egg travel down the fallopian tube into the uterus when ovulation occurs. I don't happen to be one of them, but boy, wouldn't that be handy? However, the egg is typically put up for sale fourteen days before the start of a woman's menstrual period. Also –"

"Ava. Ava." Jordan held up a frantic hand. "Christ, never ask a veterinarian about reproduction, I guess. Lesson learned."

When Ava started to grin at him, he gave her a pained look. "I'm a guy, okay? And I grew up with four brothers. Female… cycles have never exactly been a hot topic of conversation for me."

"You are so damn cute, you know that? All flustered by the birds and the bees."

"Ha." Jordan sat up. "As fascinating as this topic is, I'll save us both the embarrassment and get the condoms out of my wallet."

"I'm a scientist." Ava decided she was thoroughly enjoying herself now. "Nothing embarrasses me. If you'd like me to explain how the stringier vaginal secretions during ovulation allow the sperm to –"

"No!" Jordan covered her face with the pillow. "No, I really wouldn't like you to do that."

Ava laughed so hard that her shoulders shook.

"It's really not funny," he complained as he lifted the pillow to frown at her.

"Yes," she disagreed. "Yes it is." Then she rolled on top of him and planted a kiss on his lips. "Now. Why don't you check on Finn and get those condoms? And when you come back, I'll teach you a thing or two about reproduction."

The look in his eyes this time was pure male appreciation. "You know, I've always wanted to play Doctor."

"Oh, honey, I'll do you one better." She brushed her tongue over his lips. "You stick with me, and I'll show you how to play Vet."

FROM his position in the tree, Bobby Lee Bender looked through the bedroom window with a kind of giddy disbelief.

It was that prosecutor. The one who'd taken over Elijah Fuller's trial.

What were the chances?

He'd seen the man on TV, caught glimpses of him coming and going around the courthouse from time to time. And after the other attorney had keeled over with the bad pumper, Bobby Lee had followed this one around the park.

He liked knowing who the players were on the chessboard he'd set up.

Of course, he hadn't anticipated the little queen in there.

Foul-mouthed bitch.

Bobby Lee wasn't sure just what to do about that. He'd already tied things up so neatly.

It excited him to remember.

The first one, well, the woman had badgered him, cursed at him. Threatened to call his boss because he'd stepped in her stupid flower bed and accidentally trampled some stupid plant. He'd been doing his job, hadn't he? And he'd had to shut her up. He just hadn't expected it to be so… satisfying. He'd made a few mistakes, sure he had. It was his first murder, after all. And he'd waited, sweating a little, a little nervous, a little sick, for the cops to figure it out.

Couldn't they see it when they looked at him? See the power he had?

But they hadn't seen it. No one did. They just saw good ole Bobby Lee.

Only he knew what he was capable of.

So the second… yes, the second had been a sort of practice. A way to hone his skill.

How long could he draw it out? How loud could he make her scream? How well could he clean up after?

Pretty darn well, it turned out. But he hadn't expected the full impact it would have on the city. What were a couple dead women, in the scheme of things? But he'd heard the talk, heard the term serial killer being discussed in worried tones and nervous whispers.

It had given him a thrill, that was for sure.

But Bobby Lee wasn't stupid. Contrary to what he'd always been told, Bobby Lee knew he was smart as a whip.

And being as he was whip-smart, Bobby Lee had waited months for the right opportunity.

So the third, well the third had just about dropped into his lap, hadn't she? Elijah Fuller was a sick, sick puppy, and he'd made the perfect fall guy. So the third, yes the third had been a pure pleasure.

He'd intended to stop at that.

But the woman inside the bedroom… Bobby Lee studied the lace-covered window. He couldn't see more than shadows, the occasional movement, and the freaky one-eyed cat on the sill. But he knew she was in there. The foul-mouthed bitch. And the assistant district attorney. It was a tricky situation, to be sure.

Chewing on that, Bobby Lee wiggled down the tree. And figuring he had some thinking to do, headed toward Bay Street.

Because being as he was whip-smart, and thirsty with it, he decided he might as well do his thinking over a beer.

CHAPTER NINETEEN

JORDAN awakened with a tongue in his ear.

"If you don't stop that," he warned, voice husky with the remnants of sleep and the fresh stirrings of desire. "You're going to have to make an emergency run to the drug store. We used all the condoms I had last night."

The licking continued unabated, and Jordan snapped open his eyes. He was rewarded with a sloppy doggy kiss.

"Ugh. Get off me, Finn." As much as he'd enjoyed playing Vet with Ava last night, he thought that might be taking things too far. He gave the dog a playful scrub between the ears, then rolled over to find the bed empty beside him. He heard the shower, peeked at the clock, and realized Ava must be getting ready for work. Despite the whole condom issue, he decided not to fight the urge to join her.

There were other ways of pleasing each other.

He stumbled toward the bathroom, knocking this time before stepping in.

"Hey. You're up." Ava pushed her dripping mass of hair aside and took stock of his long, naked body. "Literally." And the grin was fast and flirty.

"Pretend it isn't there." He grimaced as he joined her in the shower, slid his hand over her naked hip. "A perfectly good party to go to, but it seems I've nothing to wear."

"Ah, that's too bad. You know the rule. No shirt, no shoes, no service."

Jordan laughed, and pulled her close enough for wet skin to rub against wet skin. "I could try wearing a shoe, sweetheart, but I'm pretty sure that might hurt." Then he captured her mouth, torturing them both by spinning out the kiss.

Blood simmered, and his muscles tightened over it. He felt her pulse flutter against his and reminded himself of the situation.

"Well." Ava ran her hands over his chest when he stepped back. "I, um, guess I need to start stocking condoms. And dog treats."

Gripping her chin between his fingers, Jordan lifted it so he could see her eyes. When she saw the seriousness in his, that laughing brown flickered into hesitation. "Is that what you want, Ava?"

"If I didn't want you, you wouldn't be here. And we certainly wouldn't have done what we did last night."

"You know what I'm talking about. I meant it when I said it was more than sex."

Flustered, Ava turned to fiddle with the shower fixtures. "Water's getting cold."

"Ava —"

She jerked the knob toward hot. "You don't even know me, Jordan, not really. How can you know it's more? Let's just agree that we enjoy each other, and see where that takes us for now."

"Because I'm trying to be upfront about my intentions. I'm not above herding you, Ava. We've already established that. But I'd prefer to just point out the direction I'm headed and see how you feel about heading there with me. Maybe you need a nudge or two to get going, and I might be willing to adjust my pace. But the point is, we're going to end up there all the same."

"YOU'RE unbelievable, you know that?" Ava stepped out of the shower and grabbed a towel. Rubbed it viciously over her skin. Why did this have to be so complicated? "I finally have sex with you, and you have to talk the thing to death. We've known each other a couple of weeks. What man in his right mind hears I enjoy you, I'd like to keep enjoying you and starts bringing out maps and life plans? For God's sake, I –"

"I'm in love with you."

Ava lowered the towel from her face, slowly. "What?" She met his reflected gaze in the mirror. "What? Are you crazy? Are you nuts?"

"There's a better than middling chance." He wrapped his own towel around his waist. And his eyes, heartbreakingly blue, softened as he came up behind her.

"I don't know what you're afraid of. I can't know, if you won't tell me." He pressed his lips to the top of her head. "Maybe your ex-fiancé hurt you a lot worse than you're willing to admit. Maybe you've got some other kind of trouble. But I'm not going anywhere, Ava. All this hiding, circling and stomping around you've been doing, seems to me you're just wearing yourself out."

The towel slid out of her numb fingers.

"Jordan –"

"It's okay, Ava." He took her shoulders, turned her into his chest. "I know you've got to get into work, and fact is, so do I. This isn't the best time to discuss this, and I let you put it off last night. But I want you to understand," he cupped her chin again, tilted it up. "Want you to understand that I'm here for you. Whether you think you need me or not."

His cell phone rang, and Jordan dropped a quick kiss on her lips. "I need to get that."

Ava stood, rooted, and watched him stroll easily from the room.

And felt herself tumble helplessly, hopelessly into love.

He thought he was in love with her. And to give the man credit, well, maybe he was. She knew her heart, didn't she? He could just be the rare kind of man who knew his as well, without having to be beaten over the head with it.

But how would he feel about her when he realized what she actually was?

The daughter, the niece of violent criminals. And a woman who'd known about his own brush with violence, but neglected to come forward.

She had a feeling Jordan just might change his stance when that particular fact came to light.

"Shit." She sat down on the edge of the bathtub.

Despite the hiding, the circling, and the damn stomping around, Ava realized that she still didn't have a clue what to tell him.

JORDAN grabbed his pants off the bedroom floor and dug his cell phone out of the pocket. The number on the screen showed his boss's personal cell. Irritation flared. Despite Jordan's misgivings, he'd been pushing forward with the Fuller trial. He'd honed Daniel Hatcher's testimony until it shone like polished stone, stone that would withstand the inevitable chipping away from the defense. He'd strategized with Clay to apply the salient points of the profile to Elijah Fuller, had poured over the implications and applications of what physical evidence they had.

He'd set aside his own doubts.

But the rest of his team couldn't quite forgive Jordan for having the temerity to express those doubts in the first place.

Prepared to take whatever licks the master was doling out for the day, Jordan reluctantly answered the call.

"Good morning, Joel."

"Not from where I'm sitting. I need you down at the jail, ASAP. We're about to have a media circus on our hands, and it looks like it's your turn to play ringmaster. I don't know how that damn viper Ashby sniffed it out already, but she's broadcasting live."

"With all due respect, sir, what the hell are you talking about?"

"Cripes, turn on the news. Elijah Fuller's dead, Jordan. He hanged himself in his cell."

AS Jordan approached the door to the Chatham County jail, the media descended like locusts.

He knew a few reporters on a personal level, and tried not to think of the entire profession as a plague, but when they were coming at him with cameras and microphones he couldn't help but feel like Moses facing the Red Sea.

"Mr. Wellington! Is it true that Elijah Fuller hanged himself with his own pants?"

"Sources from inside the jail indicate that he left a suicide note. Can you tell us what it said?"

"Does the DA's office consider this an admission of guilt? Will the investigation into the murders of the three women be closed?"

"No comment," Jordan said as he muscled through the buzzing swarm.

An aggressively perky blonde pushed in front of the others and shoved a microphone in Jordan's face. "Lauren Ashby, WSAV. My sources indicate that there has been some dissension over your ability to obtain a conviction against Elijah Fuller. Do you feel that his alleged suicide this morning has saved you from facing an acquittal at trial?"

That one stopped Jordan in his tracks. "As I believe we are still operating under a system that deems a person innocent until proven guilty, I can only be sorry that Mr. Fuller has been denied his day in court."

"Is it true that due to your recent medical problems, District Attorney Feinstein was considering replacing you as lead prosecutor? That the head trauma you suffered impaired your ability to handle a case of this magnitude?"

So now he was not only incompetent, but brain damaged?

Jordan smelled a rat. But until he had a chance to sniff it out, the smart thing was to keep his mouth shut. "There will be a press conference forthcoming shortly," he told the bottle-blonde insect, and then the gathering at large. "You'll have an opportunity to ask your questions then. Until that time neither the members of the police department nor anyone from the district attorney's office will be able to offer further comment."

Steaming, Jordan turned his back on the reporters, and welcomed the blast of air conditioning that greeted him inside the jail. He produced ID, made the expected small talk, and stalked toward the cell where Elijah Fuller had been held without bond.

And stepped into controlled chaos. The assistant coroner conferred with an investigator from the medical examiner's office, crime scene analysts dusted and plucked and sealed evidence up in bags, the flash of a camera bounced off the concrete walls and stung the eyes. Fuller's public defender poked a finger toward Joel Feinstein's chest. Detectives Simpson and Dawson questioned a guard, because any suicide – but particularly this one – would be treated as an open investigation until fact substantiated theory.

And in the center of it all, the small, crumpled body of Elijah Franklin Fuller. Naked, because as the reporter outside had suggested, he'd apparently fashioned a rope out of his own pants. Jordan saw remnants of the fabric looped through an air vent, the rest still knotted beneath Fuller's swollen and purple face.

Scrawled on the wall, in what appeared to be blood, were the simple words: *forgive me.*

"Jordan." Six feet of strain in a pinstriped suit, Joel Feinstein called out when he noticed Jordan's appearance. And using it as an excuse to evade the other attorney's poking finger, strode over with a gathering frown. "It's about time you got here. We've got a hell of a mess."

"I apologize for my tardiness. I had to stop home, get some appropriate clothes. How did this happen, Joel?"

"The kid made a noose out of his pants."

"Yeah," he said drolly. "I got that. I'm talking about the fact that he was supposed to be supervised. A walk-by every fifteen minutes to prevent just this sort of thing. His attorney warned us Fuller was struggling with depression."

"And as I just reminded his defense counsel, there will be an investigation. Just like the investigation to make certain Mr. Fuller didn't have any help getting that noose around his neck.

Given his notoriety, the situation, you can be sure the police will cross their Ts and dot every I."

Jordan glanced down the hall, caught Simpson's eyes on him. "If they'd dotted every I to begin with, the man likely wouldn't be dead."

Feinstein's frown darkened. "That may be true, but that kind of comment is best kept to yourself. At least there's no family on record, waiting to sue for negligence."

Somehow, that made it more depressing.

Jordan looked at the bloody message on the wall. Fuller had begged forgiveness. For taking his own life? For stalking Sonya Kuosman? For killing three women in cold blood?

It could mean any damn thing.

But Jordan just couldn't reconcile the pathetic figure on the floor with what he'd learned about the killer.

"He wouldn't have expressed remorse," Jordan said quietly.

"What?"

Jordan glanced back at his boss. "From what Agent Copeland described in his profile, the man who killed those three women is a sociopath. He's incapable of feeling guilt over their deaths. To his mind, they deserved what they got, at best. And at worst, he didn't even see them as people. More a means to his own end. I can't imagine," he nodded to the wall "that this would be in keeping with his behavior."

"Jordan." And the tone was ice. "Exactly whose side are you on?"

"I like to think I'm on the side of justice. Barring that, at least truth. I know you were disappointed with me at last week's meeting, but I can't quite be sorry for it just now. If we'd gone to trial the evidence, such as it is, would have had a chance to speak for itself. And Fuller would have had a chance to defend himself against it. Now," he looked back at the figure on the floor. "Nobody gets the chance to talk. Those three dead women, least of all."

"You don't believe Fuller killed them."

"I had doubts. You know I had doubts. And after this?" Jordan shook his head. "I can't say that I do. But I get the feeling that opinion will be even more unpopular now than it was at last week's meeting. After all, this wraps things up. A little messily, but certainly more easily than a trial. Serial killer dead by own hand. Savannah streets safe once again. Makes a nice headline, doesn't it?"

"Jordan –"

He waved his hand in the air. "I know what you're going to say, so just spare us both the lecture. I know better than to air my misgivings to anyone outside this team. Unlike some people." He narrowed his gaze at Simpson. "But sir." And he turned a cool gaze on his boss. "I'm not going to stand in front of a camera and lie to the people of this city, politics be damned. Fuller might be dead, but we didn't prove him guilty of a crime. There was sufficient evidence to indict him, that's fact. And I'll happily lay out the facts as we have them. But beyond that, I'm not going to just brush this thing under the rug. Because if I am right, and Fuller wasn't our man, and another woman dies? I don't want her blood on my hands."

THE bar was old, another of those Savannah institutions. Handmade brick, pressed tin, the wooden floors scarred and stained. Chairs and stools were worn smooth from generations of asses. Whiskey spiced the air, and the sound of rough laughter salted it. Music pumped in a happy beat that simmered under them both.

Jordan noted the photographs lined like dutiful soldiers along the walls.

Samuel Bryson, R.E. Read, the first Savannah police officers to be killed in the line of duty. A timeline of police vehicles, from horse and buggy, to motorcycles, to the ubiquitous black and white. The Original Nine, the first courageous black men to overstep racial boundaries and take up the Chatham County badge.

It was a cop hangout.

Many a glass had been raised in triumph, in anger. To honor a fallen comrade, toast a fellow's retirement. To mourn the losses, celebrate the victories, and ease the stress of the day-to-day. Jordan respected the institution, and more, much more, the men and women who found their way through the doors. He'd joined them himself on several memorable occasions.

But this time, this time he was here with blood in his eye.

Jeff Simpson had taken a swipe at him one time too many.

"Hey Jordan," one of the female officers he knew called out to him from her stool at the bar. "Looking good on TV this afternoon."

"I don't know." The bartender, a portly ex-cop named Big Jim shook his head as he filled a pilsner. "That thing they say about the camera's true. Those pants made you look fat."

"Maybe you could spare me the name of your dietician."

"That's easy. Mick Donalds."

As laughter rolled over the music, the crowd, Jordan scanned the back of the room.

"Can I get you something, Counselor?"

He spotted Simpson in a booth, laughing with a detective from Special Victims and a blond man Jordan didn't recognize. And felt everything inside him tighten. "Ah, not tonight, Jim." He was feeling volatile enough without adding an accelerant.

"Somebody's in for it," he heard Jim murmur when Jordan began to push his way through the crowd.

Yes, Jordan thought, and felt the simmering frustration of the day click to boil beneath his skin. Somebody is. But he tried to remember to keep it cool, keep it civil, as he made his way to Simpson's table.

The laughter that bounced around the booth like a silver pinball died as Jordan stepped up.

"Miller." Jordan greeted the man from SVU and nodded to the blond, who looked barely old enough for his beer. "Sorry to interrupt." Social niceties aside, he shifted his gaze toward Simpson. "Detective. I'd like a word with you."

The surprised annoyance that had flashed over the other man's face slid into an amused mask. "Imagine that," he said to the table at large. "A lawyer who claims he can get a point across in just one word. I thought y'all needed a press conference for that. But come to think of it, you didn't say much more than no comment this afternoon. I guess the fact that the sick fuck that murdered Sonya Kuosman and two other women hanged himself in his cell was too complicated for you to get out."

So Simpson didn't want to play nice. That was fine, more than fine with Jordan. "Unlike you, I prefer to have my facts straight before I start flapping my mouth to the press."

"I have no idea what you're talking –"

Jordan slapped his hands on the table. "Yes you do." Leaned in. "I'm talking about the fact that you tried to discredit me by leaking rumors about my health. And Lauren Ashby, Simpson? Makes you wonder which one of us is brain damaged."

"Hey, I'm not the one who started spouting all kinds of behavioral voodoo after getting clobbered on the head. Hell, Fuller asked for forgiveness, the sonofabitch, before stringing himself up. What more do you want?"

"Um, gentleman…" Detective Miller began when several heads turned their way, the tables near them falling silent. "I don't think this is the place –"

"Oh, but Jeff has made it the place, haven't you, Detective? Just like you made the jail the place this morning by tipping off the press before I got there." Jordan angled his head. "Why the smear campaign, I wonder? Why make that preemptive strike?"

"I told you, I don't know –"

"If you're going to stab someone in the back, Simpson, at least have the balls to admit it was your hand on the knife. I think you're afraid. You read that profile. And you realized, when you saw Fuller's message, that it was one more piece that didn't fit. You knew I'd see it, too. And because you were afraid to lose face in front of your colleagues, maybe even in front of the city, you tried an end run around me. Discredit me, so that if I happened to point out that we have more questions than solid evidence, it would come off as… what? Post-traumatic stress? The incompetent ramblings of a damaged brain? It was a concussion, Detective. And while I may have suffered double vision for a couple days, I still recognize an asshole when I see one."

"Uncle Jeff," the blond kid said nervously as Simpson pushed to his feet, and Miller jumped up to get between Jordan and the other detective.

"You're going to want to take it down, both of you."

"It's okay." Jordan was already stepping back. And met the fury on Simpson's face with equanimity. "I've said everything I needed to say."

JORDAN lobbed the tennis ball as hard as he could and watched it soar toward the velvet black. Stars, like glitter spilled from a jar, winked against the night sky. The ball seemed to hang among them before arcing down toward a racing Finn.

From the dark came the solitary heartache of a street musician's sax.

The game, the dog, the lonely concert in the park soothed the little licks of temper that still wanted to bubble. Until he had it under control, Jordan figured he wasn't fit company for man or beast.

Well, for man anyway, he amended as Finn trotted back and dropped the ball at his feet. The beast, he was stuck with.

"Slobber face." Jordan scooped the ball up and felt it drip. "At least it keeps you quiet. Maybe I should get one of these for Simpson the next time he runs his mouth."

The image of the detective, his bull-dog face full of tennis ball, amused Jordan momentarily. Smiling, he threw the ball again, and indulged himself in the visual. Until instead of the ball, it was the man's own tongue Jordan pictured choking him, his mouth red and gasping as he drowned in his own blood.

Not a big leap, he supposed even as he felt his amusement fade into disquiet. To superimpose the image of the detective in charge of the investigation with the way the three women had died.

But because he had, and because it disturbed him, Jordan's mind clicked over to the murders.

The women's tongues hadn't been recovered. Trophies, Clay said, to feed the killer's fantasy. Help him relive the kill. To remind him of the power he had over those women. Clay considered it the killer's signature, and possibly indicative of verbal abuse as a child.

What, Jordan mused, if that was more important than they'd realized. If the three dead women – whom the police had been unable to link in any tangible way – were selected because of something they'd said. An argument, a putdown. Something controversial, something mean. Maybe they'd threatened the killer somehow.

Or maybe they'd sung nursery rhymes in public. How could he guess what made a psychopath tick?

Not that it did him much good to wonder over it in any case, Jordan admitted. In all likelihood the case would be officially closed. But he would call Clay later, run it by him for the hell of it.

And because those three women deserved as much.

Finn dropped the mangled ball again, but Jordan's cell phone rang before he could lob it.

"Wellington."

"I guess that concussion wasn't enough for you, so now you're picking fights in bars."

"Ah, Evan." Jordan winced as he recognized the private investigator's voice. "How the hell did you... no, no don't answer that. Your freakish ability to ferret out information is the reason I called you in the first place."

"And here I thought you wanted to ask me for a date."

"Only if you wear the dress." Jordan hesitated, because several things had changed between the time he'd left the message for Evan and now. His schedule had lightened, rather unexpectedly, with Fuller's death that morning. And he and Ava had made love.

He'd like to think that meant they'd reached a new level of trust in their relationship, and she would simply tell him what he wanted to know. But because he remembered the nerves she'd tried to hide when she'd seen that smiley face carved into the electrical box, and the way she'd all but leaped out of her skin when he'd told her he loved her, he decided to go with his original plan. If Michael Sheppard was behind Ava's troubles, Jordan would find out soon enough.

"I've got somebody I'd like you to look into." Jordan threw the ball, dropped onto a bench while he gave Evan the rundown on Ava's ex. "I've covered the basics – address, employer, criminal record – but I need to get an idea of what this guy's like. Any suspicious behavior, especially. He's got a white Acura registered to him, but I want to know if he has access to a black, late model T-bird. Maybe a friend's, relative's, whatever."

There was a pause as Evan considered. "I'd be remiss if I didn't ask you what this is about. I know it's not for the office, since I'm persona non grata there."

Evan had been a member of the SCMPD's counter narcotics team before an injury sent him into the private sector, but because he did so much work for Jordan's brother Jack – the defense attorney – a lot of people on the other side of the courtroom held Evan in contempt.

"I've got a friend who's been having a little trouble lately." Jordan watched his dog race across the grass, flashed back to the first time he'd taken him to Ava's clinic. One small stone tossed in the pond, he thought. So many ripples from it. "She won't say who, but this Sheppard guy's her ex. Maybe it's him, maybe it's not, but I want to know either way."

"So you know whose ass to kick. Got it. This... friend. Would she happen to be short, dark-haired, curvy? Likes to play with animals?"

Jordan managed a half laugh and dropped his head back against the bench. "Pulling a card from my lawyer deck, I'll have to say no comment."

"Speaking of cards, I hope we'll see you next week. Now that Copeland's gone I need another sheep to fleece. Give me a few days on this, Jordan. I've got a couple things coming to a head, but should be able to clear some time by the middle of the week."

"Thanks, Evan."

"Never a chore to do business with a friend."

Jordan pocketed his phone and took advantage of his seat to watch the oak leaves above him shudder in the stingy breeze.

Clouds crept over the stars, and the air took on the sort of weight that suggested a storm would roll in before long. Finn came over, but when he dropped the ball this time he growled.

Jordan felt it. That sly prickle across the skin that came from a different sort of weight in the air. The kind that came from another's presence. From someone watching.

Because the concussion – and what had followed – was an experience he didn't care to have repeated, Jordan reached down for the ball Finn dropped.

Fool him once, he thought. And slid the pistol from its holster on his ankle. The next time he wasn't going down so easy.

"Stay," Jordan said to Finn. He didn't want his dog haring off after whoever he'd sensed lurking in the bushes. Jordan couldn't know if their visitor was armed. And because he couldn't, he very casually eased off the bench, then did a quick roll until his back was against the tree. Finn whined, but Jordan had a moment to feel thankful that he'd followed the command. Then getting himself into the strongest defensive position he could manage, scanned the edges of the park.

Shadows danced. The crescent moon cast its waning light. Near the path the streetlights glowed artificial white, but nothing moved near them that Jordan could see. At the far end of the park something shifted, walked away, but from the movement of the figure, of the dark shape it carried, Jordan took it to be the man with the sax.

Packing up for the night. Heading home.

A car drove past, and Jordan looked at the make, looked at the license plate, but it was neither domestic nor had a chain link holder. Nor was it blue, for that matter. Not that the perp couldn't have switched cars, but he figured he had to draw the line of paranoia somewhere.

And was he being paranoid, he wondered?

Shifting, he noted another car – silver Taurus – and a van parked along the street. Some kind of service vehicle, though he couldn't quite make out the signage. He moved a little, trying to get a better look, when the sudden explosion of sound had him whipping around.

A crash, and Finn barking like a mad thing as he flung himself toward the hedge of azaleas. Jordan heard footsteps, running footsteps, heading in the opposite direction, and gained his feet to follow after the little coward.

But the yelp of pain from his dog had him swearing and turning back.

Crouched low, weapon aimed, he jumped behind the azaleas.

"Aw, Finn. You've got to be kidding." The animal sat shamefaced, his nose lodged inside a can. And squatting down, Jordan studied the label. "Vienna sausages, huh? Glad to know where I rate in the scheme of things." With one last scan over his shoulder, he holstered the pistol, worked the can away from his dogs snout.

And after ruffling the animal's fur, thought things over.

Whoever'd been watching realized he'd – or she'd – been made. That seemed clear enough, Jordan thought as he looked around. Maybe saw the gun, wasn't prepared for it. So had cooked up a little distraction by tossing the empty can into the bush.

Jordan walked over to a clump of what looked to be Chinese Photinia, saw the overflowing trash can on the other side. And squatting again, looked at the imprint of a shoe in the soft dirt. Boot, he thought. And judging by the size, probably a man's.

Straightening, Jordan frowned toward the direction he'd heard the footsteps as the man ran off. Could have been nothing, he admitted. A kid messing around, who'd gotten scared by Jordan's behavior. A vagrant. A would-be mugger. Nearly anyone. But Jordan had gotten that prickle along the skin, and he'd learned not to take any chances. So he dug his cell phone out of his pocket.

Then grabbed Finn's collar before he could nose in the dirt.

"No. Sit." He didn't want the dog to mess with any evidence.

Jordan dialed Chip Coleman's number. "Detective," he said when the man answered. "If you're not too busy, I've got something I'd like you to see."

CHAPTER TWENTY

"HELLO, gorgeous."

Ava blinked when Jordan slid into the pew next to her. Candlelight flickered across his face as he inclined his head toward the burning votives. "Any of those yours?"

"Uh…" she glanced at the cabinet beneath the statue of the Blessed Virgin. "One of them is for my mother." She'd lit one for her father, too, in the hope that he might find the strength to seek penance. To stand against his brother at trial. And one for herself, as well, asking for guidance through her current mess.

But given that a big part of her mess had just plopped down beside her, that wasn't something she was going to mention.

"I'm sorry." Jordan's hand slid over hers. "Sorry that you lost her. I never asked how she died."

"She, uh…" unsettled by the question, by his presence, Ava turned to meet his eyes. "Look, I don't mean to be rude, Jordan. But what are you doing here?"

"I wanted to see you."

"This is a church."

He angled his head to the side. "And because I'm not Catholic I'm not welcome?"

"What? It… no. Don't be ridiculous."

"Okay." And now he nodded. "I won't if you won't. This is a church, Ava, and one that appears to be part of your life. In case you misconstrued our conversation the other day, I'm interested in spending time with you outside the bedroom."

"Jesus." Chagrinned, Ava squeezed her eyes shut. "I mean jeez. Sorry," she said in the direction of the altar. "Um, how about if we go outside if you want to talk? I stay in here any longer and I'm bound to get myself in trouble."

The evening air was a balm, soothing the sting of embarrassment that wanted to stain her cheeks. Which was ridiculous. It wasn't like they'd been caught groping each other in the nave. But because she could still see Sister Mary Katherine's disapproving scowl as clearly as if she'd been suffering through parochial school just yesterday, Ava walked an arm's length away from Jordan.

Until he slipped one of those arms around her waist. "Pretty night," he commented, and guided her toward the Lafayette Square fountain. The water sparkled, pure against the lights, and his hand slid warm down her back. He smelled good – soap and man – and embarrassment was shoved aside by simple pleasure. Giving into it, into him, she leaned her head against his chest. His arms came around her and tightened.

"I've missed you the past couple days." He pressed his lips to her hair.

Guilt took a greedy bite out of her pleasure. She'd seen the press conference he'd given, knew he'd been upset that morning when he left, but had been too cowardly to reach out to him and offer an ear. Not that she expected him to tell her anything, she admitted. Because deep down, he'd been right in his assessment.

Despite his words, despite everything he'd shown her, a small, nasty part of her didn't believe it was more than sex.

That a man like him could care enough about her to really stick.

But that was the thing, wasn't it? She'd never known a man like him.

"I saw you on TV," she managed.

"Ah." And the arms around her stiffened. "Not my favorite part of the job."

"You were upset when you left that morning, and I figured…" Ava took a deep breath. "I figured out later that you must have gotten word about that man's suicide. I won't ask you for any details, but I just wanted to say that I'm sorry for whatever part of that disturbed you. Another death, or the fact that you weren't really able to do your part to give those women justice."

Easing back, Jordan framed her face in his hands. "Have I told you that I'm crazy about you?"

"You might have mentioned something like that."

He touched his lips to hers, then sank in, until Ava's head was spinning. "Both of those things disturbed me. There's a lot about this case that disturbs me." He brushed a thumb over her cheek. "Most people would have just said that I should be glad the bastard's dead."

Because she knew too much about what most people would say, Ava turned, strolled over to the fountain. And watched her reflection shimmer in the water. "If he killed those women, and it was like the papers said, there's no question society is better off without him. But…" she cast a glance over her shoulder. "That reporter said he wrote forgive me, in blood."

"He did."

"Maybe he was sick." Ava thought of her father. Of the grief that had caused him to snap. "There's a difference, I think, between sick and evil. Not that I'm a bleeding heart, or in any way excuse what he may have done, but I think people don't see the gray. It's either black or its white, and sometimes that's true. But there are a lot of shades in between. If you take the time to look."

Jordan raised a brow. "That's a very… well, I guess you could call it a very liberal viewpoint, though it so happens that I agree. For a prosecutor, I tend to hover closer to the center than some would like. But you're right. I think that Elijah Fuller was sick. However, whoever killed those women was evil."

"What?" Puzzled, Ava sat on the fountain wall. "I thought –"

"Could you hold that one for a second?" Jordan asked as his phone shrilled in his pocket. "Damn phone. It's been ringing off the hook all day. Excuse me." He strode a few paces away before he answered.

And though she'd intended to respect his privacy, couldn't help overhearing his violent curse.

"Where?" His voice had taken on the density of lead. He stood perfectly still, as if the slightest movement might cause him to break. "I'll be there. No. No, Chip, I do think it's necessary. Okay. Give me thirty minutes."

Letting his phone hand fall to his side, Jordan rubbed the other one over his face. When he turned, his eyes showed the kind of emptiness that could only come from devastation.

"Jordan?" Ava found her legs like rubber as she stood.

"What?" He looked down at his phone, seemed surprised to see it in his hand. "I'm sorry. I…" he shook his head, slid the phone into his pocket. "I'm afraid that was really bad news. Really, really bad news. I have to go."

"Is there anything I can do?"

Truly looking at her for the first time since he took the call, Jordan stepped closer, lifted a hand to her cheek. Then took her mouth with his in a kiss that was hard and desperate. Some dark emotion surged through him in a quiet storm, leaving them both battered when he finally came up for air.

"I'm sorry, I –"

"No. No." She laid her own hand over his. "Don't apologize."

"It's just, uh…" He stabbed his fingers through his hair, looked away. "The night I got the head injury, I was attacked. Pistol whipped, it looked like. Abducted, driven somewhere."

When he saw her hand tremble up to her mouth, he turned it over, kissed her palm. "I'm okay. I know it sounds frightening, but I'm okay."

Ava closed her eyes against the tears that threatened.

Was this it? Dear God, had they somehow traced Jordan's assault to her uncle?

"I'm okay," he repeated softly. "But there's a woman I know. A woman I dated. And that night we bumped into each other after a symposium. We argued. She still wasn't over the fact that we were no longer together. And…"

He trailed off, and Ava saw his throat work. And felt her own gorge start to rise.

"She must have followed me to my car, stumbled upon what was happening."

No. No. Please don't let him say it…

"She's been missing since that night. But that was the detective. On the phone. The detective in charge of the investigation. It seems a construction crew just broke ground for a new development across the river. They, um, dug up a body that they've tentatively identified as Leslie. That was her name. Leslie Fitzsimmons."

Stunned, heartsick, Ava lowered herself to the wall.

Her uncle's men had killed that poor woman. Of that, she had no doubt. Which meant that she no longer just had firsthand knowledge of Jordan's assault, but now of a murder as well. She had to tell him. Somehow, she had to tell him.

"They're expecting me at the scene."

"Jordan." She lifted her eyes, felt the film of tears she had no right to. Why hadn't she spoken up before now? For all her talk of backbone, she was a coward. "I'm so sorry –"

"Shh." Squatting down, Jordan brushed at the tear that spilled over. "Don't cry for me, sweetheart. But... I do have a favor to ask. Two favors, actually."

"Sure." She'd do anything. Anything to take away this guilt.

"It's likely to be a long night, and I was wondering if you'd be willing to check on Finn. Clay's gone back to Virginia, so I'm short an extra dog walker."

"Of course."

"Thanks. And more importantly, can you promise me to be careful? I'm not going to press, just now, but we both know there's more happening than what you're telling me. This thing with Leslie – it's tearing me up, Ava, and she hadn't really meant anything to me for a while. If something happened to you –"

"I'll be careful." She couldn't let him finish that thought. He was right. There was so much he didn't know, so much she needed to tell him. But she was afraid that once she had, she wouldn't mean anything to him, either.

"Good." He slipped a key off his ring, passed it over. "My front door. You can just leave it under the big pot of Easter lilies when you're finished."

With a final kiss, Ava watched him walk off into the gathering darkness.

And sat there for long minutes after, listening to her heart break.

THE billboard for Pine Bluff advertised it, in a nutshell, as unspoiled Lowcountry beauty meets upscale human development. Of course, in Jordan's experience, humans tended to spoil things no matter how upscale they might be.

He looked at the artist's rendering of a smiling father pushing a smiling young boy on a tire swing, overlooking pristine marshland and ancient maritime forest, while a smiling mother stood drinking a glass of lemonade – fresh squeezed, no doubt – on the wide, covered veranda of an enormous wood frame house.

In reality, the would-be development was a stretch of old cow pasture shaded by water oaks and loblolly pines, and dotted with giant earthmovers instead of houses. The marsh was back there somewhere, he was sure. Though this particular stretch tended to be smelly due to the nearly defunct paper mill across the river.

Package it right, Jordan mused, and people would buy any damn thing.

Turning into the gravel lane, he noted the billboard was faded, as the downturn in the housing industry had put the whole thing on the skids for the past couple years. But apparently the company had found some new backing, and started making tentative moves toward clearing the land a couple days ago.

Of course, all that activity had ground to a halt with the discovery of Leslie's remains.

And the others. It seemed Leslie wasn't the only one to have been buried there.

Sick at heart, Jordan parked in front of the construction trailer, and then picked his way over the carnage of churned earth and fallen trees left in the bulldozer's wake. Roots speared up, dirty fingers, and ruts deep as a grave threatened to swallow a man who wasn't careful.

Jordan fought off the vertigo that threatened to pitch him into the nearest one.

The air hung still and heavy, as if too shocked by the scene to move. But in the stillness, other things walked, and droned.

Jordan swatted at the insect biting his neck and followed the sound of human activity.

The smell of freshly turned earth mingled with the odor of diesel, the punch of brine drifting in from the marsh. And as he drew closer to the scene, the unmistakable insult of decay.

Taking a moment – just one more – to steady himself, Jordan pushed down the guilt, the rage that wanted to empty his stomach. And walked toward the klieg lights and crime scene tape, knowing that he owed Leslie at least that much.

A uniformed patrolman stopped his progress, but waved him on after he showed his ID. Jordan spotted Chip Coleman, round face grim, along with a contingent of county deputies, some South Carolina state boys and what looked to be two different crime scene teams. Jordan didn't even have to hear any of the conversation to know what was taking place.

There was a disagreement over jurisdiction.

As Coleman was otherwise occupied, Jordan approached one of the crime scene techs whom he recognized from SCMPD. "Denise." He greeted the woman. "What do we have?"

"What we have is a bona fide mess. That guy over there," she pointed to a short, pot-bellied man in mud-stained work boots and a John Deere hat, "is the one who uncovered the remains. Mass grave sort of deal, and the bulldozer really screwed things up by scattering bones like pickup sticks. But judging by the skull count, there appears to be four, all basically skeletal except for the one that's causing most of the fuss. No positive ID on any of them as of yet, but there's a tag from the symposium where that councilwoman was last seen still attached to the jacket on the…"

Jordan saw the moment it sank in. Color stained her cheeks even as she rolled her dark eyes. "Give me an F for sensitivity. I'm sorry, Jordan. I'd forgotten you were… involved."

"It's okay." He squeezed her shoulder.

"Anyhoo." She sucked in an embarrassed breath and gestured with a gloved hand. "John Deere over there, after upchucking all over his Timberlands, dialed nine-one-one like a good, responsible citizen should. County deputy responded, realized something of this magnitude might call for state resources, so in comes SLED. But then our good, responsible citizen decided to stand on the shoulders of the capitalism that's made our country great, and called the eight hundred number Ms. Fitzsimmons mother set up so that he could be sure to claim the reward."

Jordan's own tricky stomach heaved. "Don't tell me –"

"Oh yeah." Knowing where he was going with that, Denise nodded toward a patrol car parked at the edge of the trees. "Eugenia Fitzsimmons, present, accounted for, and currently detained. She was, well, I'll just try for sensitive this time and say she wasn't doin' anyone any good with her presence."

"Shit." He rubbed a hand over his face. Leslie's mother had been quite vocal in her opinions of him recently, none of which had been good.

"She don't like you much, seems like."

Regardless, Jordan resolved to express his condolences to the woman in person, as soon as the storm died down. "This sucks even worse than I imagined."

"'Bout to get worse." Denise whistled low as a pair of figures emerged from the shadows behind the lights. "The councilwoman was transported across state lines, and that means the feds. Unless my eyesight is playing tricks on me, I believe that's your brother."

Jordan turned to see Jesse, followed closely by fellow agent Brian Parker. Spying Jordan, Jesse waved Brian off to intercede in the growing battle between Detective Coleman and the South Carolinians, while he himself picked his way across the uneven ground.

"Denise, if you'll excuse me." Jordan caught the look on his brother's face, and figured they'd both be happier without an audience. "I need to speak with my brother."

He stepped around the bright yellow tape, raised a hand in greeting. And then stuffed it into his pocket, because he was desperately afraid it might shake. "Jesse. Fancy meeting you here."

But his brother wasn't buying the casual tone. "You shouldn't be. You shouldn't be here, Jordan."

Feeling the impact of that like an uppercut, Jordan's head snapped to the side. And he fought the urge to slap back at his brother, knowing Jesse had his best interests at heart.

"I had to come."

"It's not your fault. I don't care what that old bat's been saying, you know you did not cause this."

"I know. Jesse, look at me," he said when his brother turned to scowl. "She lost her daughter. She's been worried sick, now she's grieving, and I've been the easiest target for both. It's normal, it's expected, and I'm not going to hold it against her. And I had to come. For myself as much as for Leslie. You know me. You know I couldn't stay away."

"Yeah, yeah." But affection softened the words. "Yeah, I know you." Jesse pushed his glasses up and sighed. "Since I do, and since you're here, I might as well pump you for information. I understand they've uncovered four separate sets of remains?"

"That's the way it looks." Jordan scanned the raw and ragged patch of ground, eyes helplessly drawn toward a snatch of dirty red hair. "Apparently this is somebody's own personal burial ground."

And if things had gone another way, Jordan realized that he might have been interred there. "What do you think we have here, Jesse? I mean Christ, another serial killer?"

"Either that, or a professional dumping ground."

"Professional, as in, hit man?"

"Could be." And the implication of that stained the already fetid air. "We'll get a forensic anthropologist in here to see if we can identify the other bodies. If we know who's buried here we might get a better handle on why they're here, who we need to be looking for in connection to their deaths. It…"

When his brother's voice broke Jordan's gaze flashed to him in surprise.

"Okay, I'm sorry, but I have to get this out. It could have been you," Jesse said. "I know you realize that, too, and it goes without saying. But I just can't get past the fact that I could have been called to this scene, and stood by as other people argued over who had the right to dig up your grave."

"Jesse –"

"Give me a second. Give me a second so I don't embarrass us both. Okay," he said after he pinched the bridge of his nose.

"Okay." And the look he turned on Jordan was fierce. "I want you to be careful. I know you have a license to carry concealed, and I realize you know most of the self-defense tricks in the book. But you have to be vigilant, damn it. They already took you down once." He glanced away, laid a hand on the butt of his weapon. "If you want, I can see about arranging some protection."

Jordan snorted, more to cover the sting of emotion than from offense. "What? A body guard? Give me a break, Jesse."

Jesse's lips quirked. "You could always move back in with Mom and Dad until this is resolved."

"Mom is pretty damn scary."

The smile faded as fast as it had come. "All jokes aside, Jordan, I've got a bad feeling about this." He looked, as Jordan had, at that snarl of red hair. "Just promise me you'll keep your eyes open."

"Believe me," Jordan assured his older brother. "I've had my eyes open since I woke up in that hospital bed."

The night stretched out, interminably at times, but more productively now that the Bureau had stepped in to iron out the dispute over jurisdiction. Leslie's mother was escorted home, to everyone's quiet relief. Evidence was collected. Hair, fibers, soil samples. A beer bottle and a couple of cigarette butts. There were no useable tire tread marks or footprints because first the heavy equipment and then the workers had compromised the scene.

Jordan was able to identify the clothing that Leslie was wearing the night of the symposium.

Other than that, other than the red hair, the nametag, positive identification would have to wait on dental records for comparison.

Cause of death was undetermined pending the autopsy results. But judging from the amount of blood staining the top of her silk blouse, the delicate pink of her fitted jacket, Jordan concluded for himself that her throat had been cut.

And his own throat squeezed shut with the knowledge.

There were few clues to the identity of the other victims. But when a cut-crystal rosary was unearthed amidst the delicate bones that comprised a hand, Jordan's disgust was overwhelming.

The woman – for surely it had been a woman – must have been praying, maybe for mercy, when she'd been killed.

By the time dawn stretched its fingers of pink across the sky, he was gritty-eyed with exhaustion. Wired from too much convenience store coffee, disillusioned with the world, Jordan sweated out his frustration by taking Finn for a beach run.

Seagulls swooped and shrieked as the dog gave chase with delighted barks, and Jordan pushed himself, punished himself, until he doubled over on the Tybee sand. He dropped to his knees, not coincidentally, in front of the hotel where he'd spent a weekend with Leslie.

It seemed right to have to struggle to breathe.

He'd seen plenty of crime scenes, prosecuted some heinous cases. The darker side of human nature was nearly as familiar as his own hand.

But this was the first time a violent crime had struck quite so close to home.

Things may not have ended well between them, but he'd cared about Leslie once. Spent time with her. Shared meals, conversations, a bed.

And they'd nearly shared the same fate.

Jordan started giving more credence to his father's theory. Anyone who could so brutally murder an innocent woman would have no reason to spare him. A third party surely had to be responsible for intervening.

But why hadn't they stepped in to help Leslie?

Wrapping his arm around Finn's neck, Jordan watched the sun rise over the water. Daybreak, he thought. A new start.

He'd get justice for her, he promised himself, in a way he hadn't been able to for the three murdered women.

It may not be enough to ease all the guilt, but it was the best he could do with what he had.

"SO handsome." Ava stroked her fingers along his spine. "Yes, you are. Jack's a handsome boy. Now shoo."

Ava nudged the cat aside and picked up her coffee. Gripped it with hands that shook. Too much caffeine, too much what the hell am I going to do?

It had been all over the news, she thought as she stared blindly at the paperwork before her. Dead bodies, a mass grave. The speculation that Savannah had another serial killer on their hands, or that Elijah Fuller had worked with a partner.

Theories, gossip, paranoia ran thicker than pine sap.

She hadn't seen Jordan. Nearly two days, she thought, as she sipped coffee she didn't want, didn't need. Nearly two days since they'd sat at the edge of a fountain, talking of gray areas in matters of law.

Ava snorted. She was in one hell of a gray area, wasn't she?

She could continue to go on, go along as she had been, compromising not only her own integrity but Jordan's.

She could tell him what she knew. And in all likelihood sacrifice her freedom, certainly her livelihood, maybe her life.

But a woman – people, she corrected. There'd been more than one in that grave. – were dead.

Was she to stand by, say nothing? What kind of coward did that make her?

And the man she was involved with, in love with, maybe. A good man had nearly been killed.

She couldn't let it slide any longer, Ava decided, and sat her mug aside to rub her tired eyes. Whatever the cost. She picked up her pen, frowned down at the paperwork. Whatever the cost, she would do the right thing.

The cat bumped his head against her hand as Ava signed her name on a check. "Cut it out." She nudged him again. "If I don't get these bills paid, we'll be operating out of a cardboard box in the alley."

"You always did have trouble managing money."

The pen slipped out of her hand.

Later, she would curse herself for that little slip in her composure, but for now she simply picked it back up, placed it carefully in its holder.

And looked into the eyes of her uncle.

Her eyes, she admitted, and the thought of it left her cold. She had Carlos's eyes. But she used the chill to her advantage.

"Actually, I'm very capable. It's just more challenging to handle funds when you have to acquire and disperse them through legal means."

He laughed, low and smooth. And the sound of it scraped her nerves.

He was so handsome, she thought. Slim, well-dressed. Just a touch of gray to distinguish his temples. He'd shaved the mustache he'd always worn since the last time she'd seen him, and the cleanness of it suited his face.

The deadliest snakes were often beautiful.

Thank God, she could only think. Thank God Katie had gone home for the evening.

"Nice place you have," he commented as he reached into the inside pocket of his jacket, pulled out one of the black clove cigarettes Ava knew he hadn't purchased legally.

"I don't allow smoking in the building."

"Nice," he continued, eyeing her over the flare of the match he struck despite her warning. "Ambitious of you, to set up your own practice. You always had your ambitions." He gestured to the framed diplomas on the wall. "College, veterinary school. The kinds of things that take lots of funds. Your father, he worried he couldn't support you well enough to indulge those ambitions. It's why he came to work for me, you know."

She wanted to scream. She wanted to rage, to throw things at him, to hurt him as he liked to hurt her. It wasn't true. Her father had gotten caught in Carlos's web before Ava had taken her first step. Long before she'd had a notion of where she wanted to go, what she wanted to be. But it didn't stop the little thread of guilt that wanted to tangle her up with him.

"Cat got your tongue?" he asked as the smoke from his cigarette caused Jack to skulk into the corner and hiss.

"What do you want, Carlos?"

"Want?" He leaned against the doorframe, insolent, lethal. "You're my only niece. I wanted to see how you were doing."

"Why didn't you just ask one of your goons?"

"Ah." He strolled closer, tapped his ash into her coffee mug. "You wound me, querida. Visiting your father, claiming you've been harassed." When his gaze flicked up to hers, Ava's heart tripped like a hammer. "My men were supposed to watch out for you. You could have let me know one of them became... overly enthusiastic."

She hadn't seen the goon in the T-bird since she'd come back from Atlanta. There was that night, the night she and Jordan... she'd suspected someone was outside, she remembered. But apart from that, she'd been left alone.

And she'd been feeling relieved, maybe even smug.

But now all she felt was sickened. "What did you do?"

"It's of no matter." He tapped his finger to her nose. "The problem has been taken care of. He won't be bothering you again."

Slowly, because she wasn't entirely sure her legs would hold her, Ava raised herself from the chair. "Out. I want you out of here, you bastard. I won't let you put his blood on my hands."

"Who said anything about blood?"

When she bared her teeth, he merely grinned. "There's the Martinez spirit. I've always enjoyed you, Ava, contrary to what you might think. You and me, we're more alike than you realize."

"Guess I better schedule that exorcism, ASAP."

He laughed, delighted, and stuck the cigarette between his lips. But as he took a final drag, his easy expression hardened. "Pleasant as this has been, I think it's time I showed myself out." The butt plunked down in her coffee. "Take care of yourself, little Ava. And take care of your new boyfriend. I would hate to think that your relationship with me would cause you to... lose another man."

He slithered down the hall, and Ava listened for the sound of the back door before allowing herself to crumple.

He knew. Carlos knew about Jordan. Almost certainly knew what he did for a living. Maybe – probably – knew that he was the man his men had mistakenly abducted.

There were medical records, surely a police report – it was certainly an open case. Assistant district attorney assaulted. Oh yeah, that would heat the cops up.

And Carlos likely had a snitch on the force.

Money – its lure, its lies – corrupted even the best intentioned.

And if he knew about Jordan, knew the details of the case, he'd know Jordan had been dropped off at the ER that night. And, of course, he'd know from Ricardo that the man they'd abducted had disappeared from the club's parking lot.

The same night she'd been called there for a meeting.

Shit, shit, why hadn't she thought, why hadn't she realized it was really a simple puzzle? Take a few pieces, fit them together, and que pasada, you've got the big picture.

"Ava?"

Jordan filled the doorway her uncle had vacated only minutes ago, and all the blood rushed out of her head.

"Whoa, what the hell?"

Hands, she felt his hands on her. Strong, steady. Lifting her. Settling her back into the chair. One of them tapped her cheek, just a little tap – pat, pat – and gray dots swam across his face as she tried to focus.

"There you are. There's my girl."

"Jordan." Her vision cleared. Seeing the concern on his face, realizing how she must have looked folding like an accordion onto the floor, Ava fluttered her hand shakily. "I…" She had to think fast. "I guess I got a little light-headed."

"No kidding."

SHE was white as a corpse, Jordan thought angrily. And he'd seen enough of them lately to know. Pale, pasty, limp beneath his hands.

What she looked, he concluded, was terrified.

He sniffed, noted the stench of cigarette smoke in the air. But this stench had the kick of something spicy, like those things the Goths had smoked before the FDA had them banned.

Ava didn't smoke. One-eyed Jack, who glared at him from on top of the filing cabinet in the corner, sure as hell didn't smoke either. The sign out front indicated the clinic was a smoke-free building.

So someone else had been in the office, quite recently if he was any judge.

Someone who'd scared the hell out of Ava.

His lips thinned, but he kept his tone light. "Got some bills here, I see. I always get a little sick when I pay mine, too."

"What?" She blinked at the desk. "Oh, right."

"How about we get you some water?" He glanced at the mug on her desk, saw the black cigarette butt sticking out of it.

It rankled, that after everything they'd talked about, everything he'd said, she still seemed to be holding out on him. He wanted to shake some sense into her, demand that she just trust him, for God's sake, but he'd tried that approach before and all it had gotten him was her cold shoulder. He reminded himself that he had Evan looking into Sheppard. He figured he'd know all about the ex soon enough.

Well, maybe not soon enough, he amended as she seemed to struggle to pull herself together. Because Ava was hurting right now.

"I'll be right back."

"What? Oh. Water." She grabbed his hand as he straightened. "Jordan. Don't bother. I'm feeling much better now."

He could see that she was. Her color had come back – a little high, in his opinion – but it was better than the death-warmed-over look of a moment ago.

"Ah…" Ava brushed at an ink stain on her scrubs. "Wow. Let me just say, how embarrassing." Her eyes lifted to his, chagrinned. "Not the way you care to be greeted, I'm sure." And the chagrin shifted to sympathetic. "I'm sorry. I didn't even ask… your friend?"

"Positive identification was made this morning."

"I'm so sorry, Jordan."

So was he. And having just come from talking to Leslie's mother, was feeling bruised. And admitted he'd come by because he needed, simply needed, to see Ava. "You know, I've spent the past several days dealing with blow after blow. I'm... beaten, just at the moment. So I was wondering," he squatted in front of her chair, brushed a loose strand of that dark hair from her face. "I was wondering if we could go back to my place – or your place. Or a park bench. I don't care – and just sleep together. Or if you wouldn't mind lying with me while I sleep. I'm exhausted, Ava. But I have this overwhelming need to feel you next to me."

If she hadn't already done so, Ava thought she would have fallen for him right then. She studied his tired – wounded – eyes, and felt her heart turn over.

It would be best for both of them if she cut him loose. Safer for them, anyhow.

But not yet. Not when he'd just handed her a piece of himself and asked her to take care of it. "Let me close up," she murmured and leaned forward to kiss his head. "Then we can go – my place, your place, whatever. I'll give you whatever it is you need."

JORDAN took her face between his hands, kissed her. Then stood so that she could get past him to the door.

And after she'd gone, stood several moments longer, staring at the cigarette butt in her coffee.

CHAPTER TWENTY-ONE

JORDAN woke to the dark, and to tiny needles pricking his foot. Hoping to restore circulation, he tried to wiggle his toes but found them pinned to Ava's mattress. He opened one groggy eye to locate the source of the problem.

He and Ava weren't alone on the bed.

"What is this, Dr. Doolittle?" he mumbled and gave Finn a reproachful look. Sleeping on the bed was one of the few lines Jordan had drawn between himself and his dog, and from the sheepish way the animal glanced at him and then quickly looked away, Finn knew exactly what he was doing.

If he had to guess, Jordan would say Ava invited the dog up after Jordan had fallen to sleep.

So much for his authority.

"Yeah, you know which side your bread's buttered on, don't you, you little traitor?" Looking around, Jordan noted One-Eyed Jack glaring at him again from his outpost on the windowsill.

He guessed the menagerie was the price one paid for sleeping with a veterinarian.

Taking care not to disturb Ava, Jordan swung his legs off the bed and made a grab for his boxers, carelessly discarded along with the rest of his clothes when Ava had tucked him in with a bedtime story.

He was pretty sure he'd never heard that particular take on Sleeping Beauty when he was a kid. Her suggestion for how the prince should wake the snoozing maiden was a hell of a lot more entertaining than the Disney version.

Glancing at her, huddled under both comforter and dog, he felt the tightening in his chest that had come to be so familiar in the short time he'd known her.

She'd brought the light, when so much of the past weeks had been dark. And Finn, in a roundabout way, had brought her. Serendipity, he mused, and ruffled the fur between the animal's ears. Yes, that was the perfect word for it. He'd been looking for a veterinarian, and had found his heart instead.

For that alone, he'd let his sleeping dog lie.

Heeding the call of his stomach, Jordan padded toward the kitchen. Food had been more of an afterthought than a priority over the past week – certainly the past couple days – and suddenly he was starving. Pitiful, he decided, after checking the contents of the fridge. Food obviously hadn't been a priority for Ava recently, either. Maybe they could make a run after work tomorrow, stock up for the weekend.

He'd enjoy that, he realized. Sharing that sort of homey, domestic chore. Handy, he thought, as he unearthed a jar of peanut butter, a box of crackers. Since he hoped to work his way around to cohabitation in the not so distant future.

He peered out the window, scanned the street, saw nothing he deemed suspicious. A light came on in the big house, and Jordan gathered Lou Ellen was up for the day. He thought of the log she'd created for him, detailing most of the street's vehicular traffic – and pithy observations regarding the same – over the course of the past week, and wondered if she slept in the first place.

The woman loved Ava. That was obvious. It was also obvious he'd earned her stamp of approval. Seeing as she was the closest thing to family Ava seemed to have – he still wasn't clear on what had happened to her parents, other than that her mother had died – Jordan guessed that was another plus in his column.

He remembered how wistful Ava had seemed, how sad, the night they'd sat in her clinic and talked of family.

He needed to get her over to his parents', let her meet his. Maybe Sunday dinner. He'd talk it over with his mom.

Once he had, once he'd nudged Ava into that big, messy tangle of family ties, he figured she didn't stand a chance.

Grabbing a glass of water, Jordan balanced the rest of his booty in his arm and made his way back toward the living room. Popping naked crackers for a hold-me-over, he sank onto the sofa and considered turning the TV on low. But it wasn't yet six a.m. Not only did he not care to disturb Ava, but figured his late night viewing choices to be infomercials and eighties sitcoms.

Dumping his armload onto the coffee table, he spotted the photo album.

Ah, blackmail time, he thought and dragged the album onto his lap. Naked babies, prom dates from hell, really embarrassing fashion statements.

Good stuff.

It was full of Ava, as he'd hoped. As a squished looking newborn, a messy one-year-old shoving her mouth full of Barbie cake. Missed the boat there, he thought. Ava was more… well, Dr. Doolittle than Barbie. He smiled at her as a toddler, long brown pigtails blown into a sea swept tangle, constructing a castle out of sand – complete with a hermit crab sentry.

Jordan slathered peanut butter on a cracker and turned the page.

Ava, resplendent in the white lace of a first communion, posed with a woman who had to be her mother. The resemblance was strong, hair, build, smile – though Ava's looked a little pained. Jordan decided he wouldn't be too happy either with that tiara on his head.

And there she was as a teen, surrounded by a litter of pups, laughing as they licked her face.

"Jordan?"

He looked up to find Ava – fully grown – mussed and owlish in the doorway. She was wearing his shirt, he noted, and felt the trickle of heat beneath his skin. White against her dusky legs. One lonely button holding it together. The trickle turned into a flow.

Her big, brown eyes blinked heavily as she joined him on the couch.

"What are you doing?"

"Fuel." He held the box of crackers up and waggled it back and forth. "I guess I should have crunched a little more quietly. I didn't mean to wake you."

"That's okay." She shoved her hand into the box and rooted around until she produced a cracker. "If you hadn't gotten up, I probably would have, anyway. We skipped dinner."

"I'm not going to complain."

She smiled, sleepy and smug, and pressed her lips to his. "Me neither." Her smile faltered as she looked at the album on his lap.

Following the direction of her gaze, Jordan sat the crackers aside and flipped back to the picture from the day she was born. "For someone who started life looking like a raisin, you turned out pretty well."

"HA ha." Ava made an attempt to grab it from him, just playfully enough to keep him from guessing the panic he'd lit in her heart.

There were photographs of her father in there. She doubted Jordan had cause to recognize Luis Martinez – currently under federal indictment on murder and racketeering charges – but it wasn't a chance she wanted to take.

Jordan, whose reach was considerably longer than hers, held the album over his head. "Come on now, sweetheart. No need to be embarrassed." His dimples flashed in a teasing smile as he found a photo of her in a baby bathtub. "I've already seen you taking a bath in your birthday suit. Although I have to admit you've improved a bit in the past twenty-eight odd years."

"Very funny." Ava feinted high, and when he dodged low, managed to get hold of the album. She shoved it under the sofa. "Next time we stay at your place so that I can rummage through your drawers."

"Next time," he agreed, kissing her head as she settled against him.

And Ava's heart kicked, one hard beat, because she doubted there'd be a next time.

She had to cut him loose.

She'd lain awake for long hours after he'd fallen to sleep, trying to figure out a way out of the mess she'd inadvertently gotten herself into. She owed Jordan the truth. And it was becoming increasingly difficult to hide everything from him, the photo album being a case in point.

But if she told him the truth, she risked not only her life, but his.

Carlos's little visit had made that clear.

So the smartest thing, the safest thing, was to discourage him. Or not only discourage him, she realized, but hurt him. If she merely wounded his pride, he had enough tenacity to lick the wound, then take up the battle from a different angle.

She had to do her best to break his heart.

If he cared about her as he said he did, she figured she might just be able to do it. Lord knew the thought of hurting him was enough to break her own.

But all things considered, it was better than one or both of them winding up dead.

Of course, knowing what she had to do, and finding the fortitude to do it were two different things entirely. Here, in the dark, with his hand stroking over her hair as he fed them both crackers, she just wanted to sink in. To take this little slice of time, this small window of happiness, for herself, and for him.

"Morning's coming."

Ava glanced out the window beside them, saw the first gray light that presaged dawn. And thought, not yet. Please, just a little longer.

Fighting the urge to close the blinds, to burrow in like a bear in hibernation, Ava laid her head on Jordan's chest.

"I heard we might be in for some wicked weather late this afternoon," he continued. "But I've always liked a good storm."

Until just recently, so had she.

Ava decided she'd write down everything she knew. About her uncle's business, about Jordan's abduction – every detail she could come up with, however small. She'd leave it in a safe deposit box and tell Carlos that if Jordan – or Lou Ellen and Katie, for that matter – were to meet with any accidents, if he ever had any unaccounted for bad luck, if any of the goons were so much as to sneeze in Jordan's direction, she'd turn the information over to the DEA, the FBI, and anyone else who was willing to listen.

She'd spell it out in a will, leave the key with her father if something were to happen to her.

But for now, she was going to steal this time before the day came.

"How do you feel about taking those crackers and getting crumbs all over my bed?"

Jordan leaned forward to sit the box on the table. And turning, slid those long fingers along her collarbone to brush her shirt – his shirt – aside.

As it fell, she watched his eyes heat, and pleasure speared through the pain.

"How about," he slowly rolled her beneath him on the sofa "we skip the crackers and skip the bed, and enjoy the crumbs we have right here."

HE had to take out the lawyer, too, Bobby Lee thought as he lowered his night vision goggles, and ran the back of his hand over his mouth. Actually, the lawyer had become the main target.

Stupid. Bobby Lee had been so stupid in the park that night. Getting close enough to let the dog sense him, touching that can with his bare fingers, leaving his van parked on the street while he ran away like a goddamn girl.

But he hadn't been expecting the gun. The gun, or the way Wellington had just… crouched and rolled like some kind of ninja. He was a lawyer, for chrissakes.

Turned out the guy was some kind of black belt. Taught self-defense to a bunch of prissy bitches down at the Y.

But black belt or not, he'd gotten himself clobbered good, hadn't he? Yeah, Bobby Lee had done his research, and knew somebody else besides himself had a reason to want the assistant district attorney gone.

The man was a menace. All that work Bobby Lee had gone to, to set up Elijah Fuller – who'd been nice enough to write what amounted to a confession on the wall of his cell, tying the whole thing up with a big, fat bow – and the stupid prosecutor… didn't believe him.

What the hell?

Bobby Lee tucked the goggles back into his duffle, shaking his head over the situation.

At least Wellington had compromised the scene at the park by touching the sausage can to get it off his dog's nose. Bobby Lee had been relieved to learn the fingerprints weren't useable. And he had a good excuse for his van being there – he left it there a lot – because there just wasn't enough parking at his uncle's.

But Bobby Lee knew they'd taken an impression of his boot print.

Those boots might be housing some fish at the bottom of the river right about now, but the whole thing had still cut too close for comfort.

So the prosecutor had to go. The cops would believe whoever'd gone after him before had finally made good on – what was it again? The implied threat against him. And the woman… well, they'd figure her for collateral damage, wouldn't they? He might not be able to take her in what you might call the way he'd become accustomed, but a smart man knew how to adapt.

A smart criminal knew how to improve.

And above the rest, a smart *serial* killer knew how to eliminate people without getting caught.

JORDAN wasn't exactly whistling when he strolled out of court, but his step was certainly lighter than it had been a day or two before. He'd just kicked the defense team's collective ass on a pre-trial motion, thank you very much. And as the defendant was an upstanding citizen, businessman – rotary club member and church deacon, for pity's sake – who just happened to knock his wife around on a regular basis, Jordan figured he was allowed the spring in his step. Maybe the man did shoulder most of the burden of caring for his seventy-six year old Alzheimer's-suffering mother, but using the woman as an alibi when he'd actually been fracturing his wife's skull wasn't going to fly.

Jordan had had it with lowlife scum who got their rocks off by hurting women.

So many did, he mused with the familiar sense of disgusted bafflement, and not nearly enough of them ended up behind bars.

As if to bring that point home, Jordan spotted Chip Coleman leaning against the wall in the hallway. His step slowed momentarily, as the image of Leslie as he'd last seen her pounded into his head like a dirty hammer.

No, not nearly enough of them.

"Chip." He forced his feet forward, resigned to the loss of his brief sense of euphoria. "How are you?"

"Overworked. Underpaid. Caught the tail end of that motion." He jangled his loose change, something that Jordan was coming to recognize as a habit. "Guy seriously expected the old lady to testify on his behalf?"

"The old lady would have testified that little green men play pinochle in her parlor if we would have allowed it. She can't remember who her son is half the time, let alone if he was with her on the night of September nineteenth."

"Damn defense lawyers," Coleman muttered, and then grimaced when Jordan smiled. "Yeah, yeah. Your brother. I always forget you've got a barracuda in the gene pool. No offense."

"It would take a hell of a lot worse than that. You know, Jack actually has a barracuda – the freshwater kind – in a tank in his office."

"No shit?"

"Absolutely none. And as much as I enjoy hearing people take potshots at the opposing counsel, I'm guessing you didn't come down here with that in mind."

Coleman reached inside his jacket, produced an envelope that he passed over. Jordan slid out prints depicting the burned-out shell of a car. "Let me guess. This was at one time a dark blue domestic with a chain-link holder around its Florida tag."

"There's a photo of it passing through a toll station on the Florida turnpike before Sumter County deputies found it like this. Got your brother to thank, I guess, for getting this as quickly as we did. He knows how to throw his weight around when he needs to. The, uh, plate numbers matched up with the partial you gave us – the same make, same plate we were able to place on Bay Street the night you were assaulted – but it looks like the tag was stolen. The woman who reported it checks out – no connection to you or to Ms. Fitzsimmons that we could see, and a rock solid alibi for the times in question. No reason to believe she was involved in any way. But the two bodies inside the trunk…"

Coleman pulled out another print, and this time Jordan grimaced. "It's circumstantial at best, which is unnecessary for me to point out because I'm talking to a lawyer. Circumstantial at best, but going purely on those circumstances, on my own instinct and speculation, I think you're looking at what's left of the men – and the ME down there confirmed they were males –

responsible for your concussion and for Ms. Fitzsimmons' murder."

"Shit." Jordan studied the grisly photos. "Were they able to get anything at all from the car? Because if my memory, your instincts, our speculation is correct, this is the trunk I was in, too." And wasn't that image enough to make him shudder.

"They're sorting out what's left of the blood evidence, and you know how long that can take after a fire. We'll need a buccal swab from you, in case, but the way that car burned…" he shrugged. "You know there're no guarantees."

"They're in the trunk," Jordan tapped the photos, looked at Coleman. "It's significant. I'm no psychologist, but I've spent enough time dealing with this stuff to figure whoever did this was making a statement. An eye for an eye kind of thing. Or like when the mob cuts out a snitch's tongue. These guys messed up when they took me. I don't believe I was supposed to make it out of that trunk alive."

The change jangled again. "This is the third party theory you were talking about."

"I think this is more support that the theory's correct. But this is a hell of a lot bigger than we expected, Chip. We've got six dead bodies – four at the Pine Bluff site and now these two. A serial killer doesn't have people working for him, people he punishes when they make a mistake. And a hell of a mistake it was, because now there's a multi-agency task force involved. This smacks of somebody significant covering his ass, not a petty criminal with a grudge. We're not looking for some disgruntled, small time ex-con. We're looking for a serious operator."

Chip sighed and rubbed a hand through his sandy hair. "We're going to need to go through all your files, see who might benefit from you being dead."

"Cheery thought," Jordan said lightly, just as thunder rocked the building. Others in the hallway jumped, raising their brows and looking around as people tended to do given the circumstance. A couple women scurried over to the window. Lightening speared like a cloud had simply gotten pissed off and hurled an electric pitchfork, and one of the women let out a scream.

He checked his watch, saw it was nearly five. He guessed the weatherman had been on target.

"Well, hell." Chip looked as nervous as the two women.

"Don't like storms?"

"Do tourists know how to drive?"

It felt good to grin, despite the conversation. "Oh, I meant to ask you if anything had come from the canvass of the park." He handed the envelope of photos back to Chip.

"You know how it goes, nobody saw nothin'. The boot print is solid, but until we have a suspect to match it against, isn't doing us much good. The thing is, we've got a timing conflict. The suspects' car was documented in Florida the night this happened."

"If whoever is behind this could hire two people, there's nothing stopping him – or her – from hiring another. Wait," he held up a hand when Chip started to speak. "I realize there's no evidence showing the two things are connected. It could have been anyone in the park that night. But just like you trust your instincts, your intuition to tell you those dead men are the same ones we were looking for, I can tell you that whoever was in the park that night was up to no good. Could be a completely separate matter, but given everything else that's happened I still believe it bears checking out."

"I'm not planning to shirk the job."

"And I'll apologize if it seems that's what I was implying. You're a good cop, Chip. I wouldn't want anyone else handling the case."

Mollified, the detective blew out a breath. And Jordan could see that underneath the gesture, he was pleased.

"The silver Taurus checked out clean, as did the van."

"The van had some kind of commercial writing…"

"Glass Doctor," Chip acknowledged, but Jordan saw something shift in his eyes.

"If what you're not telling me is none of my business, or not relevant to the investigation, just say so and I won't push. Your case, your discretion."

"You make it difficult to be a hard ass. Look," Chip glanced around, nodded Jordan toward a more secluded corner. "Turns out the van belongs to the relative of another detective. Kid lives in the basement apartment of the detective's house, couple blocks over, leaves the van at the park sometimes because he can't always get parking along the street."

Jordan started adding, found the two and two. "Simpson's nephew."

"Shit, Jordan."

"He was at the bar that night, sitting with Simpson and Miller. I didn't recognize him, but he addressed Simpson as Uncle Jeff, when it looked like we were about to get into it. You think it was him?"

"I don't know. It's a theory. Maybe." Chip looked pained. "Maybe the kid leaves the bar, parks his van, and just happens to see you and your dog in the park. Hey, it's the asshole ADA who just dressed down my uncle in front of the whole bar. Maybe he's pumped up, just a little buzzed, thinks he might confront you. Maybe stands behind some bushes to observe until he works up the nerve. Then hey, the ADA has a gun, and suddenly confronting you doesn't seem like such a good thing. Better to cause a distraction, get the hell out of Dodge."

It made sense. It pissed him off, but it made sense. "You're not going to question him."

"Jordan –"

"No, no. I get it. I do. There's already enough tension between me and Simpson. You haul his nephew in, interrogate him, it's just going to stir things up even further, with the added pain-in-the-ass factor of putting you in the middle. More tension, more trouble than it's worth for something that was basically harmless. There's no crime involved, unless you want to pop him for littering."

Jordan nearly smiled again when more thunder made Chip jump.

"Damn storm. And you pretty much summed it up."

"Well," Jordan blew out his own breath. "Here's to hoping I scared the kid out of trying anything that stupid again."

"If it was him…. he lied, and smoothly, when I talked to him about the van."

"Must be a family trait. Look, thanks Chip. I appreciate you looking into it."

"Doing my job." The man looked warily out the window. "I better get out of here before the sky opens up. You will too, if you have any sense. And we'll need that buccal swab, ASAP."

"I'll stop by the station tomorrow."

When the detective had darted out the door, Jordan stuffed his hand into his pocket, banged his briefcase against his leg. Jeff Simpson seemed to be a thorn that just wouldn't get out of his side.

With the idea of clearing up his desk before he left for the weekend, Jordan started toward the elevator, then swung around and headed to the stairs. He wouldn't be getting a run in, in this weather, so the six flights would have to do. He'd just gained the fifth landing when his phone began to vibrate in his pocket.

Juggling his briefcase to his left hand, he slipped the phone out and surveyed the number.

And felt a tingle along his spine that had little to do with the ozone in the air.

"Hello, Evan."

"Jordan." His voice was a hollow plop, like a penny dropped into a well, so Jordan took the last flight two steps at a time.

"Hold on a second. I'm in the stairwell at the courthouse and the reception's for shit."

"They have elevators there, you know."

"I'm masochistic." He pushed through the door to the suite of offices the DA occupied, a little winded but able to hear. "You have something for me on Sheppard?"

"He's clean, Jordan."

Jordan halted just outside the door to his office. "What do you mean by clean?"

"As in squeaky. Clean as a whistle. Zestfully clean. Pick your descriptive term."

Jordan edged his door open with his shoulder, and tossed his briefcase onto his desk. The sky had indeed opened up, and rain pounded against his window. "That can't be." He watched the water slide down in silver curtains.

"It can. It is. Aside from the fact that I could find nothing to indicate the man has had access to, or knows anyone who has access to, a black Ford Thunderbird, the real deal-killer is that he's been out of town for nearly a month. You know he's a photographer, right? That magazine he works for sent him out on an assignment in California. Some kind of piece about forest fires and their aftermath. I got confirmation of his flight, his credit card's been used regularly at numerous locations, and the thing is, he wasn't traveling alone. Seems the man has himself a serious girlfriend, and her parents are out there, so it was a two birds with one stone deal. The man just got engaged, Jordan. If someone's been harassing your girl, I think it's safe to say it's not him."

Jordan dropped into his chair. He'd been so ready to blame Sheppard that he'd gotten tunnel vision about the whole thing. He knew better – years of experience with the law, with criminal investigations had taught him at least that much – but then thinking with the heart tended to cloud the head.

"Okay. So Sheppard is clean." It was a bitter pill, but he'd swallow it. And he'd simply have to lay down the law with Ava when he saw her later. This had gone on long enough. "I appreciate you checking into it for me, Evan. Send me your bill. I'll just try to make it back from you next poker night."

"Sure." Evan hesitated, and Jordan got a funny feeling in his stomach. Evan never missed an opportunity to rub in the fact that he was their resident card shark. "Before I go…you remember that I used to be counter narcotics?"

"Of course."

"Well…"

When he paused again the funny feeling turned into a pitch and roll. "Whatever it is, just say it, Evan."

"Well, I was checking on this Sheppard, and of course your vet's name popped up as they lived together for a little while, and I got to thinking: Martinez, Martinez. Not an uncommon name, but why does it seem so familiar?"

Jordan watched a battered oak leaf get plastered to the window, felt everything else recede.

"Look, Jordan, if you're not already doing so, you might want to sit down."

"SHIT," Ava muttered as she waited on Katie to lock the clinic's front door.

Rain pounded the rooftops, the trees, the thirsty ground like angry fists, tearing leaves that the wind picked up in its bitter breath and blew angrily against the glass. Water ran in a filthy torrent, displacing pine straw, churning into mud, and the azaleas shivered as the last of their blossoms fell like bright drops of blood.

The lash of it – wind and rain – stung her skin and whipped her hair into a slick tangle. In his carrier, One-Eyed Jack howled indignantly as bullet-like drops pelted him through the vents.

"I know, I know. I should have brought an umbrella. At least you've got fur," she pointed out with some annoyance. "Cotton scrubs just don't cut it."

"I'm sorry." Katie, peeking out from a bright green rain slicker, hustled through the door. "Forgot my phone. Go ahead and lock it and get out of this mess. I'm going to go home, make a big pot of tea and pretend I'm in England, where at least you've got all those misty, windswept moors and broody romantic heroes if it's going to rain like this."

"There's a comfort."

"Easy for you to mock, you've got a hot lawyer waiting to keep you warm," she said as she dashed out into the rain.

Not for long, Ava thought darkly and waved her friend off.

Thunder rumbled, mean laughter, and the clouds overhead roiled. Already soaked to the skin, Ava hurried toward the parking lot. She could barely make out her car through the river of rain. "Mother Nature's feeling bitchy," she decided just as a bolt of lightening split the sky. When the air crackled, she basically threw herself into the car.

"What's next? Toads?" Peering warily out the windshield, she shivered and cranked the heat along with the motor. Their sunny, eighty degree day had probably dropped twenty degrees. "Guess I should have listened to Jordan this morning, huh?"

Jordan.

Just saying his name felt like a bruise on her heart. She'd managed to dodge his calls twice today – the first time because she'd been genuinely unavailable; the second because she simply couldn't find the strength to say what needed to be said.

How could she tell this man that she didn't want to see him anymore? See him, ever again? She'd worked it out in her head. And it had to be another man. That was the only excuse he would believe at this point, because it was more than clear that she found him attractive, that she enjoyed having him in her bed. But she hadn't admitted to anything beyond that, had been very careful to avoid telling him what was in her heart. So if she claimed to be in love with someone else, there was at least a chance he would believe it.

She'd considered using Sam Bailey, but that just didn't seem fair, and was extremely unprofessional to boot. Sam was an important client, a good friend, and she wouldn't feel right abusing either relationship. Plus, she thought as she released Jack from his carrier, watched him jump out of the thing like it was on fire, Jordan seemed to be hung up on Michael as the source of every ill.

And she'd feel much less guilty about using him toward her own end.

Jack glared at her from the passenger seat before he started licking the rain from his paws, and Ava glared right back before setting the climate control to defrost. Yes, it would have to be Michael. She'd never gotten over him, she was looking to reconcile – maybe actively in the process. Last she'd heard, Michael was seeing someone, but Jordan didn't have to know that – and was sorry for misleading Jordan in any way.

End of story, she thought as she turned her wipers on high, her lights on low, and crept out of the parking lot. End of relationship.

With that thought depressing the hell out of her, Ava eased into the traffic along Abercorn Street, which moved like sludge. Heavy rain was to the south what crippling blizzards were to regular, sane people, so everyone drove like their ninety year old grandpas or else they didn't drive at all. Vehicles sat off to the side of the road, hazards blinking like frantic eyes, and the occasional truly stupid individual stopped right in the middle of the damn street.

Impatient by nature and in a particularly foul mood due to both weather and circumstance, Ava wasn't shy about using her horn. And on one occasion, her middle finger. Ava decided Katie would have been mortified.

Katie was also going to be less than pleased when Ava told her she'd dumped Jordan, to say nothing of how Lou Ellen was going to react. Jordan had brought Lou Ellen flowers the other day, for pity's sake, something about her doing him a favor. Ava had pumped Lou Ellen for information, but her landlord, her friend, had simply said that it was between her and Jordan.

Exactly what was Ava supposed to make of that?

By the time she finally made it home, the storm was at full rage overhead. The evening had gone black as the mouth of hell, and water cascaded down the stairs to her apartment. Ava sloshed through, slipped once, and nearly sent Jack into a panic that had him clawing at her as she unlocked the door.

"Should have left you in the stupid carrier."

Lightening crashed in an electric burst that literally lifted the hairs on her neck.

"Holy shit." Dripping, swearing, and shaking from cold, Ava dropped the cat and reached inside to hit the switch for the lights.

Nothing happened.

"Just great," she muttered. And stepping into the dark living room, slammed the door closed behind her. That last lightening strike must have knocked out the power.

She pulled off her jacket, hung it on the hall tree. Toed off her wet sneakers and kicked them under the bench. She was trying to remember where she'd left the damn flashlight when another bolt of lightening temporarily illuminated the room.

The shadow behind her became a man, and the man's hand clamped over her mouth.

"Don't. Scream."

It backed up in her throat. But she caught the familiar scent, grabbed at the long fingers to yank them away, and whirled toward her uninvited guest.

"Jordan, what the hell do you think you're doing?" Pushing at her bedraggled hair, she gave him a basilisk glare. It was too dark to see his face, his expression – too dark for him to see hers either, for that matter – but she knew the smell of him, the feel of his hand nearly as well as she did her own. "You almost scared me to death. For a moment, I thought you were someone else."

"That makes two of us."

Ava fell back a step at the tone. She'd heard him angry before, felt the heat of it that morning he'd found the window smashed in, but never had she heard the sort of cold fury as she did now. The chill of it practically burned her.

"How did you get in here?" she thought to ask.

He held something up, though in the dark it was difficult to make out exactly what it was. "Spare key. Your landlord was kind enough to lend it to me."

"Something I'll be sure to discuss with her at the first opportunity." Keeping her own tone even as she could manage, Ava tried to control the wild thumping of her heart.

All sorts of thoughts flitted through her head, but she couldn't say any of them were good. But instead of addressing his obvious anger, she took the coward's way out. Again.

"I might not have been so startled if I'd seen your car in the drive." She wrapped her arms around herself against the chill. "I guess I was too focused on getting inside."

"My car's not in the drive. I parked a couple of streets over, and walked."

"In this weather?" Her laugh was brittle, chunks of ice that broke as they fell. Shaking, she moved farther into the shadowed room, wanting to put some space between them.

He knew. Knew something, though the question was, what? Not just what, but how much? And how was he going to use it against her?

Of course, she'd been kidding herself to think it wouldn't come to this. She'd expected it, hadn't she, from the moment he'd walked into her clinic. "Not exactly the best evening for a stroll," she pointed out.

"I didn't want to take a chance on your uncle's men following me."

Ava froze, muscle by muscle, bone by trembling bone. The memory of the final scene with Michael blew through her in a frigid gale. And because it did, because she'd been here before, in nearly the same position with a man she loved, she took the cold, embraced it, because it was so much better to be numb.

"How did you find out?" she asked over her shoulder, relieved that her voice didn't crack. How much worse, how much more painful, if he knew her heart lay quivering at his feet.

Although in reality, it couldn't have been better timing. She wouldn't have to use Michael to get rid of him now.

"I was worried about you." Ava didn't trust the softness, the deceptive tone. She'd already heard his disgust for what it was. "The car that followed us," he said. "The slashed tire. The broken window. The visitor at your clinic with the clove cigarette."

He'd eased back to within touching distance now, though he made no attempt at contact. "I hired someone to do some checking."

At that, Ava whirled around. "You… you hired someone to check up on me?" She was so fired up that the ice cracked. How dare he? How dare he? "You paid someone to dig into what I told you was none of your business?"

"Actually, I hired him to check up on your ex. Imagine my surprise when he turned up cleaner than you did."

At that, a storm built inside her to rival the one outside. "I see. So I'm guilty by association. I'm not the prosecutor here, but I'm pretty sure that charge doesn't stick."

"No." Jordan grabbed her arm. "But how about failure to report a crime, impeding an investigation. How about kidnapping and accessory to murder?"

Ava's sharp indrawn breath told Jordan everything he wanted to know. He grabbed her other arm and shook her, not bothering to be gentle. "Did you help them kill Leslie? Or simply stand by and watch while they did? Or what… you got squeamish at the last minute and decided to back out? The murder of an innocent woman might buy you some time, but maybe you realized that knocking off a prosecutor is a pretty damn serious offense."

She started shaking beneath his hands. "You…" She gulped in air. "You think I had anything to do with that?"

Where was her anger, Ava wondered again? She needed her anger to warm her up. To fight off the unbelievable hurt. "How…" Oh, she cursed the tremor in her voice. "How can you even think that after –"

"After sleeping with you?" Even in the dark, she could see the disgust plainly in his eyes. Whether for her or for himself she couldn't be sure. "Wasn't that part of the plan? Seduce the one guy that could put you away, so that when he figures everything out he'll be so compromised by his relationship with you that you'll wind up getting off?"

That did it. Ava found her anger in spades. "You ignorant son of a bitch." She shook his hands off and shoved him in the chest, hard enough that he actually stumbled back. "First of all, if you'll search your memory, you'll recall that you kept trying to seduce me. I wanted nothing to do with you." She threw her arms out to her sides. "You think you've put it all together, do you? Well you don't have a clue. You want to know what my impression of you was that night, when I happened upon you in that trunk? That you were a big, stupid fool. I spent ten minutes trying to get you to move, ruined my best pair of pants, broke at least three nails, got blood stains on my damn car, and… oh yeah… risked my freaking life to haul your ass out of there before they could kill you. You think I want to be related to him? You think I asked to be a part of this? I wasn't around to see what happened to your friend, and I'm pretty much regretting that I was around to see you. If I had it to do over, I would have closed the trunk and pretended I never laid eyes on you. You have been nothing – nothing, nothing, nothing – but a pain in my ass since I did." She emphasized her point by drilling her finger into his chest. "So unless you have some charges you're willing to press, some reason for being in my face, why don't you hand over my damn key and get the hell out of my life!"

Her anger seemed to burn the chill from the room, and her labored breath puffed out like steam. Lightening cracked, thunder rumbled, and that icy gaze sizzled where it touched her skin.

Until he hauled her up against his chest.

His mouth crushing hers in a firestorm, Jordan's arms were the ones that shook. Hot tears leaked out of Ava's eyes as she felt herself melt against him. So cold. She'd been so cold, and here was the warmth.

Jordan cupped her face, brushed at her cheeks, and pulled back just enough so she could see him. "I'm sorry. I love you, Ava, and I'm sorry. I didn't understand."

Ava started to sob. "Oh God, Jordan, I love you, too."

Scooping her up gently as if she were a china doll, he carried her to the sofa.

And held her, pressing his lips to her hair as her heart emptied itself of tears.

CHAPTER TWENTY-TWO

"DRINK this," Jordan coaxed as he handed Ava a cup of hot tea. He'd gotten her out of her wet clothes, wrapped her in a blanket on the corner of the couch, but now that the anger had left her she couldn't seem to shake the chill.

"I feel a little sick."

"The tea's chamomile. Lucky thing you had it." The power was still out, but he'd managed to ignite the pilot light on the stove and heat a kettle of water. "My mom always swore by it when one of us had an upset stomach." And he knew she needed the heat now, as she seemed to be suffering a kind of shock.

Hell, so was he.

He'd not only had the rug yanked out from under him, but it had been rolled up and used to beat him when he was down.

Thunder rumbled outside, but the worst of it had died to what he thought of as an old man's grumbling. "Thanks," Ava said as he joined her, glancing up out of red and swollen eyes. The candlelight flickered over her tear-ravaged cheeks, and Jordan felt like a big bully.

"I'm sorry." He sought out her feet under the blanket and tried to rub some heat into them with his hands. No matter how many times he said that, it wouldn't make up for putting that wounded look on her face.

"It's too bad this place doesn't have a fireplace," she said, shivering.

"I'll keep you warm." He tucked the blanket tighter around her. "Ava. Are you ready to talk a little more?"

"Might as well." She eyed him over the rim of the cup. "You've seen my trump card. Why not get the rest of them out on the table?"

He squeezed her foot, drew both of them into his lap. "Okay. I understand the whole chain of events which resulted in you dumping me at the hospital. But what I'm still not clear on is why your uncle would have gone after me in the first place. Most of the drug cases I've tried have been fairly small time, and I can't see how they would have affected his pipeline, his business. It's not like there's a shortage of pushers on the street. There've been some pretty big meth rings busted up in the past few years, but far as we could tell, they were strictly local. Unless somewhere along the line I inadvertently stepped on his toes."

Ava shook her head. "It wasn't supposed to be you. That's, well, I guess you could call it the irony of the whole situation. I overheard the men who took you, that night at the club. I don't know how, or why, but they got you by mistake." She hesitated, and he knew she was struggling against what had to be a knee-jerk instinct for self-preservation. Growing up as she had, who she had, she couldn't help but see him on some level as the enemy. And though that burned, and badly, he tried to set it aside so they could get past this.

"Ava." When she wouldn't look at him, he gently cupped her chin. "Ava. You can trust me. I won't lie and say you won't be hurt by this, because we both know some repercussions are inevitable. By I promise you, sweetheart. I'm on your side." He brushed her lips with his.

He drew back, searched those bruised-looking eyes, and nearly panicked when they watered up again. "Uh-oh. I'm –"

"No," she said, and blinking furiously, pushed them back. "Don't be sorry. Don't. I'm just... I guess I'm just so relieved to hear you say that. I was so afraid. So afraid to lose you, to have to push you away when I wanted you so much. But more, I was afraid for you to look at me as something less. A lot of people have, because of what my family is, or has done."

"I look at you. And I see more than I ever hoped for."

"Oh. Well, now that's done it." A tear spilled over and she flapped her hand, set the tea aside so she wouldn't spill it. "Maybe I could just go ahead and tell you the rest, before I start to blubber like a damn baby. It wasn't supposed to be you," she continued, drawing a steadying breath. "My uncle was after the federal prosecutor in charge of my father's trial."

"Ah." So things began to make sense. And if he hadn't been so blindsided by his conversation with Evan, he probably would have made the connection sooner. "Stephen Finch. He was supposed to be the key-note speaker at the symposium I told you about. He called me, last minute, and talked me into filling in. I guess your uncle's men knew they were supposed to tag the speaker, and assumed I was the one. Pretty big oops. And pretty damn ballsy," his brows drew together "for your uncle to go after Finch in the first place."

"He loves my father." Ava shrugged when he only stared at her. "In his own very twisted way. He manipulates him, needs to control him, and has pushed my father into doing things that he normally wouldn't have dreamed. Not that my father is blameless – like the saying goes, you can lead a horse to water but you can't make him drink, but my father drank, and drank deeply. But Carlos was truly upset when my father was arrested, even more so when the indictment stuck. Part of that is self-serving – my father could be, and was, offered leniency if he rolled on my uncle. I think Carlos was prepared to intimidate, threaten, bribe – even murder – to get my father acquitted. He's used similar tactics before."

"Except now he's got a hell of a mess on his hands." Hesitating, Jordan considered how much to tell her of what he'd learned. But she'd shown her cards, and he figured he owed her no less. "About the men who abducted me..." he told her of the bodies in the burned out car. "The evidence isn't all in yet, but I believe those are their remains."

"Yes." She closed her eyes. Wearily, he thought. "Yes, that would be his way. Clean up the mess, eliminate the complications. Make the punishment fit what he saw as the crime. He's very good at doling out punishment." And when she reached for the tea again, her hand trembled. "He told me.

Knowing I'd feel guilty for going to my father about the harassment, he told me that his men wouldn't be bothering me anymore. Clean up his mess, make my life more difficult. Two birds with one well-cast stone. Your friend," she added, as her hand shook and the rain hissed. "The place where she was found, the other remains there would have been my uncle's doing also."

The knife of that had already been in his gut. If he was abducted mistakenly, how much more senseless did that make Leslie's death? But that kind of thinking wasn't productive.

"My brother... he's FBI, Ava. They're investigating the site. The who and the why."

"They won't be able to tie anything to Carlos. He's too slick. Don't say it." She held up a hand, looked at him with eyes that broke his heart. "I know that my knowledge of events that night could give them what they need for a warrant. I know you'll ask me to talk to them. Tell them what I know."

He squeezed her foot between his hands. "Ava. The man is a threat, to you most of all. I don't think you have a choice."

Ava leaned her head back on the sofa, listened to the dying breath of wind rattle the eaves. "Do you realize what it would mean, if I did? I'd have to go into hiding. Change my name, give up my business. Everything I've worked for. And even if I could handle that," she watched the rain slide down the window "I'm not sure if I could handle leaving you."

"Ava –"

"Don't." Slightly panicked, she pushed at the hand he lifted to her face. "I knew it was coming. Knew, from the moment you walked into my clinic, that my life would never be the same. I fought it – fought you – but this is the way it has to be. I won't let Carlos get away with it anymore. He destroys lives, mine not least among them. He drove Michael away. Brought my father to ruin. And I hold him responsible for my mother's disappearance. She wouldn't have simply vanished from a church parking lot if it wasn't for him."

"Wait. I thought your mother passed away."

"No one has seen or heard from her in nearly two years. I'm sorry, it's another black mark on me, but was easier to let you think that than to explain the circumstances."

Something shifted in his eyes. "That photo album I was looking at the other night. Is it still under the sofa?"

"I think so." She leaned over to move the candle closer while he dug the album out. "Careful, the glass is hot." He tilted it closer, studied a picture of her first communion, and her heart began to thud. "What?" Her throat was dry, her stomach jumpy. "What is it?"

Jordan looked at the image of the woman beside the child, her hair a lush mass of curls, her smile so vivid and bright. She glowed, positively glowed, as she hugged her only daughter. She wore a rosary.

A beautiful, cut-crystal rosary.

Jordan sat the candle down, and studied Ava's face. So beautiful, so like the woman in the photo.

"What?"

"This rosary." He tapped his finger against the picture. "It's very distinct."

"It is. My great-grandmother had it handcrafted for her upon her confirmation."

"I've seen it before."

"That's impossible." Her tone was confused, her eyes wary. "She had it with her when she disappeared. She'd worn it to evening mass."

"I saw it." Jordan gripped her fingers tightly. "The night they found Leslie. I'm sorry, Ava. But I think your mother might be buried there, too."

"BETTER?" Jordan handed her a cool washcloth for her face.

To Ava's dismay, she'd just spent the past ten minutes being violently, horribly sick. Now she sprawled on the ugly tile in her darkened bathroom, feeling as if the bottom had just dropped out of her world. She'd thought she understood the level of her uncle's depravity, but this went beyond anything she would ever have guessed.

He'd killed his sister-in-law in order to keep his brother under his thumb.

"It's my fault," she said hoarsely.

"What?" Jordan pinched her chin, dragged her face around toward his. "How could you say something that foolish?"

"They – my parents – moved to Savannah to be near me. After I set up my practice. They sold their place in Atlanta. That's where my father's family is from, where my uncle lives most of the time." Her lip quivered, but she bit it. "I told my father that I wanted to start fresh, that I didn't want his… activities messing things up for me here. He was easing back. Easing away from his brother. Until my mother disappeared."

Jordan sat next to her on the tile, and when he took her hand she laced their fingers.

"Papa went out of his head with grief. Uncle Carlos convinced him it had been a…a hit from one of their rivals, and Papa shot the man. It turned out the man was an informant. I guess it was Uncle Carlos' way, again, of killing two birds with one stone. Keep his brother under his control, eliminate the competition. But it would never have happened if it hadn't been for me. My mother would still be alive."

"Ava." She heard, understood, the sympathy in his voice, but was a little taken aback by the exasperation. "I was just about to tell you, again," he explained as he glanced over at her "how foolish it is for you to feel that way. But considering I've been beating myself up over what happened to Leslie, I guess that's pretty much the pot condescending to the kettle. I'm sorry." He lifted her hand, brought her fingers to his lips. "I understand the need to shoulder some responsibility, even if it's wrong. It shows you're a good person. But I can almost guarantee your mother wouldn't want that from you, or for you. Especially when your uncle is at fault."

Of all the things he could have said, none could have resounded more. "You're right. And as terrible as all of this is, the one good thing to come from it is that Uncle Carlos has dug his own grave. My father loves his brother, but my mother was... everything. I have to tell him, Jordan. He has to know what my uncle has done."

"I feel duty bound to point out that the burden of proof hasn't yet been met."

"Such a lawyer." And wasn't it nice, to be able to feel that little glimmer of humor through the tears? "We both know what the tests will show, though – God – I can probably get my mother's dental records to expedite the process."

"We'll arrange it," Jordan assured her. "I'm going to give my brother a call right now. I know that it's small consolation at a time like this, but everything you just told me is going to make his night. It's going to make a lot of people's nights. You're like the goose that laid the golden law-enforcement egg."

"Glad I could help," she said dryly. "Hell, a family full of do-gooders. What have I gotten myself messed up in now?"

Jordan framed her face between his hands. "Get used to it, Ava. Because for better or worse, you're stuck with us."

He left her sitting on the floor, staring after him, while he went in search of his phone.

JORDAN looked out the living room window as he finished his call with Jesse. One storm had passed, he thought as rain dripped softly from the eaves and the sky softened to twilight. And another one was just beginning.

He didn't kid himself about exactly how difficult – how dangerous – this was going to be for Ava. But she'd risked her life for his before he even knew her. How much more would he risk for her now that he knew she was his life?

"Hey." He turned when he heard her behind him, then opened his arms, sighing a little as she settled in. She looked better, he thought, and stroked a hand down her hair. Strong, brave. She'd need to be both to get through this.

"We've set the ball rolling," he told her.

"It's a relief. Scary, but such a relief," she said. "I want some kind of protection for Lou Ellen and Katie, Jordan. When this gets out, he'll try to hurt me. If he can't get to me, he'll go after the people I love."

"I'll take care of it. I'd like to wave my magic wand and say that things are going to be all better now, but the truth of it is that there's going to be a lot of ugliness in front of us. Aside from all the legal issues, there's going to be a lot of publicity – some of it negative – that we won't be able to avoid. But I want you to know that I'm going to be with you every step of the way."

She was quiet for a moment against him. "Will this hurt you? Your reputation, your career? I don't want to damage everything you've worked for. I don't think I could stand it. I really don't."

He eased back enough to look her in the eye. "Don't compare yourself to him, Ava."

"I'm a Martinez." She lifted her shoulder. "As much as I've tried to distance myself, I can't escape the fact that we're blood. And I... knew things, Jordan. Things that could have helped to put him away. Things that –"

"Things that could have gotten you killed."

"But it's not right. You're a good man, a law-abiding citizen. A prosecutor, for pity's sake. It's not right that your relationship with me threatens all that when you didn't know. I should have just... come clean with you well before now, because I did. I knew. Maybe we could just, I don't know, put our personal relationship on hold or something until –"

"Ava." He reminded himself that she was distraught, that she'd had a bad shock. Several bad shocks, actually. "What kind of weenie do you take me for?"

"What?" She looked genuinely surprised. "I don't –"

"And if I'm supposedly such a good man," he said right over her "such a law-abiding citizen, why the hell would you expect me to lie? We have a relationship, and it's damn personal. I want you to marry me."

The surprise morphed into shock. "Did you just... propose?"

"It was more that I stated an intention. This, however," he slid out of her arms, eased onto one knee "is a proposal. Ava, will you marry me?"

"I… I think I need to sit down." She did, right there on the floor. "Are you crazy?"

"About you."

"I…" She pressed her fingers into her eyes. Flung them out dramatically. "We've known each other for, what? A month. Not even. Less than thirty days, Jordan."

"I knew the minute I saw you walk into the bar in that red dress. My heart stopped. And when it started again, it beat for you."

He had the pleasure of watching her mouth fall open. Close. Fall open again. "How am I even supposed to think after you say something like that? Let alone formulate a…a…"

"Response?"

"See?" She tapped her head. "You've fried my brain."

Fighting a laugh, Jordan pressed a kiss to her temple. "You saved my life, Ava. Let me spend the rest of it with you. And besides." He kissed the other side. "Think what an interesting story it will make for our children."

"Sitting doesn't seem to be working for me. Maybe I should just lie down."

He gave in to the laugh, pulled her into his arms. "Say yes."

"Yes," she said against his shoulder.

He rocked, simply rocked her back and forth, as happiness bloomed inside him. "I can't wait for you to meet my family."

"Oh, God." She pushed at his shoulder, panic in her eyes. "Your family. Jordan, what will they think?"

"That I'm the luckiest man alive."

"Right. Mom, Dad. I'd like you to meet Ava Martinez. Of the Leavenworth Prison Martinezes. More likely they'll think that head injury my uncle's men gave you rattled your brain."

Jordan's bloom lost a petal at that. "Who you are has absolutely nothing to do with your uncle. And the fact that you are who you are in spite of him speaks volumes about your character. You're beautiful, successful, intelligent and kind. So don't let me hear you disparage yourself again."

"You're serious about this, aren't you?"

"As I've ever been in my life. I… hold that thought," he said when his phone rang. "That might be Jesse calling back."

Jordan checked the readout, saw the local area code. Not his brother, but he figured with the bomb he'd just dropped on Jesse any number of federal agents might be wanting to speak with him. "Wellington."

"Jordan Wellington?"

"That's the one."

"I…" There was a pause, the muffled blast of a horn in the background, and the caller cleared his throat. "Maybe this wasn't such a good idea."

Confused – because if this was a federal agent on the other end of the line he sounded like a nervous kid – Jordan worked to keep the annoyance from his voice. "Unless you tell me who you are and why you're calling, we can't know that, can we?"

"I…" he started again. "This is Bobby Lee Fuller. Robert. Robert Fuller. I'm Jeff Simpson's nephew."

"Jeff Simpson's…" Jordan shook his head when it clicked. "Right." He didn't try to disguise his annoyance any longer. "Well, Robert, as flattered as I am that you would bother to track me down on my personal cell after that little dance we did in the park, I have to confess that I just don't have time for a two-step right now."

He cleared his throat again. "How did you know that was me?"

"Well I only suspected, but Robert, you just confirmed it. As an attorney, I should probably point out that you neglected to exercise your right to remain silent, but as a man, I'm just going to say back off. I'm sorry you had to witness the altercation I had with your uncle, but I can't imagine he would appreciate you jumping in to fight his battles any more then I appreciate being jumped. Goodbye, Robert. Let's not do this again."

"Wait! Please."

The plea, the desperation, caused Jordan to sigh even as he rolled his eyes at Ava. Snagging her hand, he kissed her fingers, linked them with his before settling his back against the couch. And dipped into his reserve of patience. "Look, Robert, if you're worried about the other night in the park, you can rest easy. You annoyed the hell out of me with that stunt you pulled, but nothing you did constituted criminal behavior. I'll forget about it if you will."

"It's not that." Jordan heard him swallow. "It's... man. This is hard."

The misery in the kid's voice pricked Jordan's curiosity. "Just spit it out, Robert."

"It's... it's about that man who hanged himself. The one who they said killed those women."

"Elijah Fuller?" Jordan's tone went razor sharp. He squeezed Ava's fingers before dropping them to pay more mind to his caller. "You know something about Fuller, Robert?"

"I... you don't think he did it, do you?"

Boggy ground, Jordan thought. Maybe this kid had something to say and was calling on his own, but for all Jordan knew his uncle had put him up to it. To what end, Jordan couldn't guess, but he wasn't about to discuss his personal beliefs with Simpson's nephew. "What I think is irrelevant in the face of the fact that Elijah Fuller hanged himself. He was indicted for the crimes, and he's dead. Without a defendant, there's no case for the state to prosecute."

"But what if there was some kind of evidence, or something, that he didn't do it? Some, like, proof that he couldn't have committed the murders? Would the case be open again?"

Jordan's brows drew together. "Much as I enjoy shooting the breeze about the finer points of the law in a criminal trial, why the hell are you calling me with this, Robert? I'm sure, if you have any questions, your uncle would be happy to explain things to you."

"No! No, I can't talk to Uncle Jeff. He's... I... I think he's hiding something. Evidence. I think he's hiding evidence that shows that Fuller guy might have been innocent."

As if the night hadn't been explosive enough. Jordan tried to align his own thoughts, motioned urgently to Ava for a pen and paper. As she grabbed a candle, headed to the kitchen, he watched her retreating back with a swell of love and possession. She'd agreed to be his wife.

One hell of an explosive night.

He shook his head, forced it back into the very startling conversation with Simpson's nephew. "That's a pretty serious accusation, Robert. You have a specific reason for this suspicion?"

"I overheard him. A couple of times, I overheard him talking to someone about the case. So I snooped around his home office and found..." He took a shaky breath, blew it out. "Let's just say there was something that didn't make it into evidence. Something that could clear Fuller."

"What?" Jordan prompted. "What didn't make it into evidence?"

"Um, look, can we maybe meet? I'd feel better going over this in person. Alone. I… I can't have anyone finding out that I talked to you."

"We can do that," Jordan decided, and smiled at Ava as she came over, handed him a pen. He scratched out Robert's name on the back of one of her business cards. "The next day or so will be really busy for me. How's Monday sound to you?"

"I was hoping we could do it sooner. Like now."

"Now doesn't work for me, Robert. As I said, I have a lot going on."

There was a pause, then an explosion of furious breath. "It has to be now! You think it was easy for me to call you? He's my uncle, for good Christ's sake. I can't… look, I can't spend the next couple days around him knowing, acting like everything is cool. I took something, okay? From his home office. He's going to notice it's gone, and then he'll figure out it was me. He will. And then he'll, he'll…"

"He'll what?" Jordan asked softly when the kid's labored pants took the place of words.

"He'll… I'm scared, okay? I want to do the right thing, that's why I called you. But I'm scared of what's going to happen if he finds out. Or whoever it was he was talking to. I don't know what they might do if they found out I overheard them, or that I talked to you about what I found. They're cops. I mean, how do you get around that? It's why I tracked you down in the park that night, after I realized you didn't believe Fuller did those things. I knew you were the one I needed to talk to. But I got scared, when I saw your gun, and I ran away. But it's not right, what he did. Please. You're the only one I can think of who can help me."

Shit.

Jordan looked over at Ava. The last thing he wanted to do was leave her, and he flat out refused to leave her unprotected. But he'd questioned, cross-examined enough witnesses during his career to know when one was ready to spill.

And if Simpson's nephew really did have knowledge of evidence tampering, it could be enough to get the case reopened.

Jordan thought of Daniel Hatcher's lingering grief, of the three brutalized women, and knew what he had to do.

"What?" Ava mouthed when Jordan's hand sought out hers and squeezed, but he just shook his head and pressed a quick kiss against her hair.

"Okay, Robert. I appreciate the difficulty of what you're trying to do, and want you to know that it's the right thing. But there are a few things I need to take care of here before I can meet you. Just give me about thirty minutes to –"

"I can't wait. I can't… shit, a cruiser just went past. What if they saw me? They all know me, what if one of them says something to my uncle? This wasn't a good idea. I can't. I have to go."

"Robert. Robert, calm down." The kid was rapidly sliding into panic. "Even if they did see you, all they would have seen is you talking on the phone. Obviously you're outside. Are you on your cell phone?"

"It's a disposable. In case someone looked at my records. They can do that kind of stuff, you know."

Jordan knew. "That was very smart of you."

"It's just that Uncle Jeff is a cop, you know? He knows how to do all this stuff that I don't even understand. I should never have called you. Look, just forget it."

"Robert, I'll tell you what. Can you make it to the Enmark on Abercorn?" The convenience store was basically right around the corner. And very public. Not that he didn't believe what Bender was saying, but he also wasn't taking any chances. "If you can bring me whatever it is you took, that should be enough for me to get started." He'd need to talk to the kid, in depth, but that would have to wait for later. For when he had Ava safely settled and Robert had a chance to get hold of his nerves.

"Okay." The kid blew out a breath. "I can do that."

"Good. I'll meet you in ten."

Jordan hit end call, and turned to Ava. "How about taking a little ride with me? I have an informant who wants to deliver some potentially explosive information. Seems to be that kind of night."

Ava still felt a little woozy. The idea of going farther than twenty feet from her bathroom didn't hold much appeal. "If it's all the same to you, I'd like to stay here."

"Sure." Jordan nodded once. "You're ill, the power is out and – oh yeah – you've just lowered the boom on your homicidal uncle. Why don't I just run out and leave you here by yourself?"

"Jordan, you just told your brother all of fifteen minutes ago. My uncle can't possibly know what's happening yet."

"Ava, this is the same man who had you followed for weeks. Who kidnapped – murdered – your mother. Who tried to do the same to a federal prosecutor because he was confident he wouldn't be caught. He knows you and I have a relationship. You think he's above bugging this place to see what you're up to?"

The chill of that ran down her spine. But she knew Carlos better than Jordan did. "It's not his style. He prefers intimidation to something as mundane as spying. Jordan," she said, when she saw the doubt. "You have to trust me. I've had nearly three decades of dealing with my uncle, and he's confident that little visit he paid me will have me falling in line. He can't know – yet – that you would have seen my mother's rosary at the gravesite. Or that you hired an investigator – which I'm still going to skin you for, when the time is right – and put everything together. So I'll be fine for the next few minutes. Just go do what you need to do and I'll take that time to pack some things. When you're finished, I'll be ready to go wherever it is you need to put me."

She grasped his hand when she saw his hesitation. "I'm not stupid, Jordan. I know how serious this is. Once the shit hits tomorrow, I'm going to be a poster child for circumspection and cooperation."

"Can you at least go sit with Lou Ellen until I get back?"

"Um." Ava pressed a hand to her temple and tried to think. Lou Ellen's car hadn't been in the drive when she'd pulled up. "It's her mahjong night. She must have left after she gave you the key. And believe me, she'll be gone 'til the wee hours."

"Okay." He stabbed a hand through his already disordered hair. "How do you feel about firearms?"

Full disclosure, Ava thought. "I have a twenty-two in my purse. Unregistered. My father gave it to me."

He didn't even blink. "You know how to shoot?"

"I wouldn't carry it if I didn't."

"Good. A twenty-two can deliver a fatal wound, but unless the other guy is pretty damn close you're probably just going to piss him off. Use it as a backup," he suggested, and pulled a sleek nine millimeter from a holster on his hip. "The Glock's light, so you should be able to handle it. Are you familiar with its safety?"

"Show me."

He did. "Aim for center mass. Biggest target, biggest chance of you dropping them and allowing yourself time to get away. But you don't answer the door, Ava. You don't get near it, I don't care who knocks. If someone manages to get in, you shoot first, ask questions later."

"Ironic advice, coming from a prosecutor."

"Good advice, coming from the man who loves you." He yanked her close for a brief, possessive kiss. "I'm going to head out." He stood, slipped on the shoes he'd left by the front door, not bothering with the laces. "Lock up behind me and get your stuff together. I'll be back in about twenty minutes, thirty tops, and then we're out of here."

"I'll be waiting."

"I'm counting on it." With one last glance over his shoulder, he walked out into the storm-darkened night.

CHAPTER TWENTY-THREE

JORDAN hustled down the steps, swearing when he remembered that he'd parked his car a couple streets over. He quickly bent down to tie his laces, and then took off at a full-out sprint, water splashing him as he ran. By his estimation, he only had about five minutes to get to the Enmark. Robert Bender was jittery as a June bug, and Jordan didn't want to risk having the kid go haring off with his evidence because Jordan was a few minutes late.

He could always track him down, Jordan mused, and cut between two houses, leapt a soggy flowerbed. Hurdled a fallen trash can like he was lettering in track. Though if Bender balked, Jordan had nothing more than hearsay at this point. He couldn't prove the kid had even called, let alone disclosed incriminating information about his uncle. Wasn't that the point of the disposable cell?

No, Jordan needed whatever it was Bender claimed to have taken from Simpson's office.

Mentally congratulating himself for not letting his cardiovascular fitness slide, Jordan made it to his car in damn good time. He pulled a downed palmetto frond from his windshield, slid into the driver's seat and cranked the engine. The street was still dark, and he wondered how long it would be before the power company fixed the line. Though he could see lights winking through leaves that dripped with crystal raindrops. Abercorn Street appeared to be up and running.

There would be lights, people at the Enmark. Hopefully that would work in his favor, and not scare his little rabbit of an informant away.

Water sprayed as his tires fought for traction on the flooded streets.

There were two cars under the overhang for the gas pumps, Jordan noted when he turned in. And one parked in the darkened lot off to the side. Jordan saw the shadow of a man in the driver's seat. Bender, he thought, relief smoothing the bump of nerves as he pulled around.

But the man who turned to scowl when he caught Jordan looking was black, probably forty. Obviously not the twenty-something blond he'd seen with Simpson.

"Should have asked him what kind of car he'd be driving," Jordan muttered as he looked away, checked out the two vehicles at the pumps. A young woman. A guy with purple hair and multiple piercings.

Hell, maybe Bender had walked. Ridden a bike. Maybe he was inside. When he saw someone moving around the aisles, Jordan climbed out of the car, decided to check it out. If it wasn't Bender, Jordan would call the number logged in his cell. If Robert had decided to play games, Jordan would have to introduce the kid to hardball.

He nodded to the clerk, headed toward the back of the store where a blond man was stooped over, peering at the selection of wine coolers in the refrigerated case. Right hair color, right build.

"Excuse me." Jordan figured it was prudent to approach with caution. But when the guy turned around with a slightly annoyed "Yeah?" Jordan noted the vintage Lennon glasses, the well-trimmed beard. "Sorry." He held up his palms. "Thought you were somebody else."

"Why? You looking for a date, handsome?"

"Uh...no. Thanks."

"Too bad."

And using the other man's chuckle as an exit score, Jordan checked out the other aisles.

"You have a public restroom?" he finally asked the clerk after he'd determined Bender wasn't in the store. The man merely stared at him, so Jordan snagged a bag of chips from the display rack near the register, tossed them on the counter and asked again.

"In the back," the man said as he rung up Jordan's purchase. "No cottaging."

It took Jordan a moment, but then he realized the man was referring to the practice of anonymous sex in public places. Apparently the clerk had seen him talking to the man by the cooler and had gotten some bright ideas. "I'll try to control myself," he said dryly.

"Believe me. You'd be surprised."

Jordan wondered if that particular misdemeanor was something with which the clerk had had previous problems. And reminded him, as he threw down a couple of bills and grabbed the chips, why he avoided public restrooms.

But when he checked out the restroom – two stalls, both thankfully empty – he still couldn't find Bender.

Pushing through the back door, Jordan scanned the lot one more time. Water dripped from the overhang and slid down the collar of his shirt.

"Screw this," he said under his breath.

He was just about to pull out his cell phone when a white van pulled up. That's right, Jordan remembered. Bender drove some kind of company van. Glass Doctor, he thought, playing back his conversation with Chip Coleman. But the van in front of him had no logo that Jordan could see. And when a nearly three hundred pound man got out, Jordan stabbed his hand into his pocket.

"Okay, you little bastard." He pulled up his last incoming call, hit send. And listened to it ring and ring as he circled the outside of the building. His shoes sloshed, his shirt stuck to his back, and his mood went from bad to worse. When the guy with the Lennon glasses eased his Prius out of a parking space, sent Jordan an amused wave, Jordan ended the call with a stab of his thumb.

Maybe Bender had been legitimately hung up, maybe he'd chickened out, maybe he was simply yanking Jordan's chain.

But whatever the kid's excuse, Jordan wasn't going to waste any more time waiting for him.

Not when he needed to get back to Ava.

Ava.

Sweet God, when she'd told him her version of the night he'd been abducted it had been enough to make his hair stand on end. If he hadn't thought her a hell of a woman beforehand, his admiration had taken a serious leap. She'd risked her life for a perfect stranger, when it would have been so much easier for her to walk away from him that night.

Easier, he mused, but not even a consideration for Ava. She didn't – couldn't – walk away from what she thought was right, any more than Jordan could have done. She'd grown up with the odds stacked against her, but had managed to beat the house. Whether she realized it or not, Ava was a more upstanding person than probably half the people he knew.

Needing to hear her voice, to let her know that he was on his way back, Jordan dialed her number as he slid wetly into his car.

And listened to it ring.

"Stupid," he admonished himself as he pulled back into the sluggish traffic, turned his wipers on to clear the spray from a passing truck. Her home phone was cordless. It wouldn't work during a power outage.

When the light ahead turned red, he brought up his contact list, found the number for her cell.

And listened to it ring.

Cursing in frustration when he got her voicemail, he didn't bother to leave a message but simply tried the call again. "Come on, Ava. Pick up the phone," he muttered when the light turned green, and a chill danced gleefully across his skin. He cranked the heat, snarled at traffic, and felt his heart give a painful bump.

Why the hell wasn't she answering?

When the bump became a skip, Jordan cut behind another truck, shot down an alley. And pushed harder on the accelerator as he listened to her recorded voice.

AVA folded another pair of jeans, tucked them into her suitcase with hands that weren't quite steady. One-eyed Jack glared at her from the windowsill, clearly realizing something was up.

She hoped she'd be able to keep him with her, wherever she was going. A safe house of some kind, she guessed. Complete with armed babysitters of the federal persuasion. What was she supposed to do all day? Watch TV? Paint her nails? Play gin with whoever happened to be on guard duty?

Hell, she was going to go insane.

She sat Jordan's gun aside, zipped up the bottom of her suitcase and grabbed the organza bag she used to pack her lingerie.

She'd have to call Katie, she thought as she grabbed underwear, bras. Have her send out some kind of a mass email to her clients. Refer them to another vet temporarily – or maybe not so temporarily, depending on how things turned out. Family emergency, she guessed she could say, and snorted at the idea. Her family sure qualified, she thought viciously, stuffing red lace on top of white cotton. Incarcerated father, murderous uncle. And her mother...

Ava squeezed a camisole in her fist, and closed her eyes.

It was devastating, she realized, to have that little bit of hope snuffed out. She'd known, of course she'd known, that her beautiful mother had met a violent end. People always said that not knowing was the hardest part, and one day she might be able to agree that those people were right. But right now, with the knowledge fresh, and the image she couldn't help but conjure of that mass grave stuck in her head, Ava could only think that to have that hope ripped away was the cruelest pain of all.

At least, she thought as she wiped a tear from her cheek and moved into the bathroom to start gathering toiletries, her father would finally know his brother for the monster he was. That it had come at such a price for both of them was more than she was willing to pay, but since that choice had been taken out of her hands by her uncle's hatred, his greed, she could only try to find the positive, and cling to it.

If things went well, she would be rid of the shadow he cast over her life once and for all.

If not, Ava realized that she, too, could end up paying with her life.

That obviously wasn't what she wanted, she thought as she picked up mascara, concealer. Would her babysitters expect her to wear lipstick when they played gin?

Not what she wanted, she mentally continued, and simply upended the entire contents of the drawer into her cosmetic bag. She had so much to live for, after all. But it was... an acceptable risk, she guessed. One she had no choice but to take. And acceptable only if Jordan didn't pay the price with his.

Jordan.

How had this happened? How had he come to mean... well, everything to her in such a short amount of time?

Ava's mind drifted back to a conversation she'd once had with her mother. An argument, really, because Ava had confronted her mother about her decision to willingly involve herself with Ava's father, when she had to have known all the trouble it was sure to bring. Ava had been fifteen, a typical, sullen brat, she thought now. Angry because the parents of a boy she liked had made noise when they realized he'd been hanging out at her house. The house of a known drug runner. Certain her parents' sole purpose of existence was to ruin Ava's life.

Her mother had taken Ava aside, explained things in her characteristically simple terms.

"Ava," she'd said. "As my grandmother used to tell me – if love falls on a cow flop, there it lies."

Ava chuckled at the memory. While Jordan was far from a cow flop, the point was still the same. Somehow, she'd fallen in love with a big, gorgeous, unconscious fool lying helpless in the trunk of a car. And she'd been just as helpless to fight her own feelings. For her, love had fallen on Jordan Wellington, and there it lie.

Ava pressed a hand to her stomach when it fluttered. But this time, this time it wasn't nausea.

Jordan had asked her to marry him.

And unlike Michael, he knew exactly what he was signing on for. And seemed to want her just the same.

Despite the less than ideal circumstances – she couldn't overlook the fact that she was currently stuffing tampons into a suitcase, after all, and might lose her practice before this thing was over – Ava figured she was pretty damn lucky.

"Hello."

She dropped the box as she spun around. It landed on her foot, the sharp corner hitting her big toe, but Ava couldn't feel anything but the knock of her heart against her ribcage.

He was blond. The man in her bathroom was blond, innocuous looking.

The knife he held in his hand was not.

JORDAN slammed on his brakes to avoid crashing into the car stopped directly in front of him. More brake lights shone like irritated red eyes, and he realized the one-way street he'd turned down was a parking lot. A man stood outside his car, leaning against the door and smoking a cigarette, and Jordan rolled down his own window to call out to him. "What's going on?"

"Tree limb down." The guy motioned to the enormous oak that shaded the street. "Must've been hit by lightening. Someone called it in. There should be a crew here with a chainsaw in a few minutes."

A few minutes that he didn't have. There could be a perfectly reasonable explanation as to why Ava wasn't answering her phone. Maybe her phone was turned to vibrate. Maybe it was buried in her purse. Maybe she'd popped into the shower.

But reasonable explanations took a back seat to the panic climbing up his throat.

He pushed the gearshift into reverse, but just as he started to move another car came up to block him. "Damn it." He slapped his palm on the steering wheel and looked for a way out. The sidewalk was too narrow. The median thick with vegetation. "Okay, let's do this." He shifted into park, turned off the ignition, and climbed out of his car.

"Hey buddy. You can't just leave your car parked there," the man with the cigarette called as Jordan started trotting up the sidewalk.

"Sue me." Dodging puddles, more debris from the storm, Jordan pulled out his phone again and tried Ava. When he still couldn't reach her, his uneasiness kicked up to fear.

Why the hell wasn't she answering? Jordan was furious with himself for leaving her. And vowed to tear Bender limb from limb if anything happened to Ava.

As that thought swirled, Jordan turned another corner at a fast jog, and was past the white van parked on the street before it registered. He slowed, jerking around. Glass Doctor. Jordan trotted back, peered into the passenger side window. No one inside, nothing to indicate who it belonged to. Could be any number of these in the city. But really, what were the chances?

Jordan moved to the front, spotted the sticker that proclaimed the driver had donated to the Fraternal Order of Police.

Bender. Had to be. What the hell was the kid up to? The van was less than a block from Ava's house. Was he planning to jump Jordan when he came back? But how the hell did he know where to find Jordan? Had the little prick been following him?

And as all of those questions coalesced into fury, one of the little doors in Jordan's mind creaked open, and he heard Daniel Hatcher saying some of the glass flew in and hit Sonya. He'd broken the window. When he'd hurled Elijah Fuller against it, he'd broken the window. Hatcher had said something about having it replaced – and a week later Sonya was dead.

And Mackenzie Wright's car window had been smashed in, her laptop stolen. A little over two weeks before she'd been killed. It was in the police reports. Tracy Buckler… she was the first. Jordan pinched his fingers to the bridge of his nose.

Hadn't there been something about a neighbor's kid's baseball breaking the kitchen window, and a dispute? They'd questioned the kid's father when she was murdered.

Shit. Shit. Why the hell hadn't they seen the pattern? Why the hell… Simpson's nephew. Had Simpson suspected? Was that why he'd been so damn adamant about Fuller's guilt?

And if the kid was guilty, why had he called claiming that his uncle had concealed evidence unless…

"Oh God. Oh no. Ava."

Ava's window had been broken.

Heart screaming in terrified rage, Jordan took off at a flat run. But he had the wherewithal to pull his phone out again, managed to call up the one person he knew he could trust.

"I don't have time to explain," he panted when Jesse answered. "But send the cavalry to Ava's apartment right now."

"W-WHO…" Ava cleared her throat. "Who are you?"

The man wasn't one of her uncle's typical goons. Military-short blond hair. He looked well kept. Young. Like any guy you'd pass on the street.

Harmless. Why was it so much worse that he looked harmless?

He smiled, and it twinkled in his eyes. Shouldn't he look cold? Ruthless? Like the goon with the T-bird?

"I'm your worst nightmare." When he laughed at her widened eyes, Ava jumped back. The bag of cosmetics fell off the counter, lipstick skittering across the tile toward his feet. "That's what my mama used to say," he told her, and kicked at the tube. "Bobby Lee," he continued in a sing-song voice that made her freeze while her nerves shivered. "You're a no good piece of shit, just like your sonofabitchin' father. The day you were born was my worst nightmare."

Confused as well as terrified, Ava tried to figure out how fast she could make it to the bedroom. The man had a knife, but Jordan's gun was on the bed.

"How did you get in?" she asked, mostly hoping to distract him. If she could keep him talking, he wasn't using the knife. If he wasn't using the knife, she had a chance to get the gun.

He smiled again, rocked back on his heels. Passed the knife from one gloved hand to the other, and had Ava biting back a whimper. She'd felt the prick of a blade before, and it wasn't an experience she cared to repeat.

"You don't recognize me, do you?"

She stared at his face, but it appeared blurry. And was horrified to realize it was because she was looking through her own tears. She blinked, determined to keep her head. She wouldn't let her uncle win after she'd come this far. "Should I?"

He looked a little disappointed at that. "The others figured it out, but I suppose that's because our previous interaction was more one on one. You and me, we only saw each other from what you could call a distance, I guess. But I sure did notice your mouth."

"My mouth?" Ava watched the knife pass back to the other hand.

"You've got a foul one. Funny thing about that. It tends to set me off."

"Sorry to have offended you," Ava said a little more dryly than she intended. The man might be weird, but he had the knife. Which put him firmly in charge for the moment.

He angled his head, as if considering. "You know, you don't seem all that scared."

"You want me to be?"

"Oh yes."

"How's this?" When she made a break for the door, he slapped it shut an instant before she reached it. And pushed her against it, pinning her in place with his body.

He was hard. God, God, he was hard.

She wanted to close her eyes, she wanted to curl into herself, to get away from the insistent press of his body. She tried to bring back what she knew about how to defend herself in this kind of situation, but the knife he pricked just under her eye held her rigid as stone.

"Scared yet?"

It was a whisper, silky. From a man completely certain of his dominance, of his control.

"Yes," Ava admitted, the word burning like acid as it scraped her throat.

He moved the knife and – no. Please no – pressed his lips to where the tip had been. "Thata girl." A hideous parody of a lover.

Was this her uncle's plan? The final insult of rape before his man killed her? Had her mother suffered this way as well?

When a tear spilled, unchecked, the man nearly hugged her with what seemed like happiness. Ava smelled the rain on his hair, the sweat on his skin, felt the awful heat from his erection.

"I wish we had more time," he said, almost sadly. "This could have been so good. But since lover-boy will probably be joining us soon, we'll have to cut our relationship short." When her phone rang, quite close by, Ava's heart jolted into her throat. Jordan.

He'd walk back in, unknowing and unarmed.

Why hadn't she kept the gun in her hand?

"This was in your purse," the man said as he moved back a step, eased her phone from his back pocket. "It was ringing when I came into the kitchen a couple minutes ago so I figured I'd better... well, yep," he said as he checked the readout. "It says right here: Jordan. Guess our good little public servant is getting tired of waiting for me down at the Enmark. Seems awfully anxious to get a hold of you. You two plannin' to go somewhere?" he asked, seeming to notice her travel cosmetic case for the first time.

"I..." confusion mixed with nerves. "It was you on the phone."

"Sure was. I thought about taking care of this drive-by style. Bam. Bam." He held the phone up like a gun, mimicked shooting. "But he took off and left you here, and well, who am I to overlook an opportunity to have some alone time with his special girl. It was like a gift, really. I didn't think I'd be able to use this at all." He laughed when she flinched as the knife flashed under her nose. "It makes it sweeter for me. Of course, I can't do all the things I've come to discover I'm really, really good at, but if I left your body raped and mutilated, it might bring some uncomfortable attention down on me. Whoa there," he said when her legs buckled. "Don't you go passing out on me. It's no fun when they pass out."

Nearly swimming in terror, Ava forced her mind to think through the waves. "But Jordan knows you. He knew who you were. Or who you said you were."

"Oh, he knows me, alright. Or at least he thinks he does. We met – sort of – once upon a time. You know, this might work out better if you're in the bedroom. Both of you in the bed," he said almost to himself. "Might be easier to believe someone was able to break in, shoot you both, if it's apparent you were distracted. You'll have to take off your clothes," he said conversationally.

"No."

He slid her phone back into his pocket, drew a mean-looking forty-five from his waistband. "Oh, I think you will. Me – gun, knife. You – pathetic little female. You'll take off your clothes, bitch, and anything else I tell you to do. Now, open the door behind you. That's it," he said when her hand went to the knob, nearly slid off of it. "Sweaty palms? Wipe it off on your pants. Good girl."

He herded her into the bedroom. Ava kept her body between him and the pile of her belongings on the bed. He didn't know about the gun. If she could just get her hands on it without him seeing, she'd blow the bastard away.

"Undress."

"There's… there's all this stuff on the bed. I'll have to move it if you expect me to lie down."

"Aren't we the helpful little woman? Undress. We'll get to your suitcase in a moment."

Ava's trembling fingers went to the button of her shirt.

"Now, now. Let's not be modest. Turn around so I can see. Mmm-mmm," he said when Ava gritted her teeth and turned. "You have quite a lush little body. It's disappointing I won't have the chance to better enjoy it."

"Did…" Ava had to know. "Did you kill my mother?"

The man's eyes shot up from the slowly-widening expanse of flesh beneath her parted shirt, clearly off guard. "What?"

"My mother," she repeated, and eased ever so slightly closer to the bed. "We know my uncle had her killed. Jordan saw the grave. Were you there? Did you do it?"

He blinked, and brought his knife hand up to scratch his head. "I have no idea what you're talking about. I wouldn't know your uncle if he bit me on the ass, and unless your mother was about one when she had you, I can't imagine we've been acquainted. I generally don't do old ladies. That first bitch wasn't past thirty, and hell, the little blonde with the laptop was only nineteen."

She felt the mattress against her thighs. And slipped another button free. "I didn't realize Carlos had so many women giving him trouble. What, he's knocking off the daughters and girlfriends of men who cross him now?"

He stared at her for a full five seconds. "I don't know who Carlos is, and I'm sick of hearing you talk. Take the shirt off. Now."

When he aimed the gun at her head, Ava dropped the shirt. But couldn't stop herself from asking. "Did..." God, this was hard. "Did Ricardo give you the order, then?"

"Bitch, if you don't stop tossing all these crazy names at me, I'm going to have to cut out your tongue anyway, and screw the repercussions. Your bra. I want to get a look at your tits."

Cut out her...

It dawned on her that the situation just might be even more dire than she'd suspected. "You're." No. Please, no. "You're him. The one who murdered those women." Jordan hadn't believed the man who'd killed himself in jail was guilty. She remembered that now.

The man smiled again, and she finally saw it in his eyes. Not the coldness of a contract killer. But the sadistic pleasure of a sociopath.

"Very good. You go to the head of the class. Bra," he said again, but Ava's hands had frozen. When she'd thought him to be her uncle's man, at least it was the kind of danger she understood.

But this… she whimpered before she could stop it.

He chuckled, and taking the tip of his knife, flicked her bra apart himself.

A noise sounded on the front stairs, and her eyes met his over the torn fabric. "Well damn. Looks like lover boy is home early."

JORDAN did his best to ease through the door from the garage without so much as a squeak of hinges.

And without letting panic propel him into a situation that could get both himself and Ava killed.

Ava. His mind swerved a little on her name, threatening to propel him after all, but he'd heard her voice just moments ago, knew she was still alive, and was determined to keep her that way.

So he'd crept through the same window Bender had come through – he'd cut the glass, the bastard. Jordan's mind threatened to swerve again – hating the seconds it took him to toss the brick on the stairs, but wanting to distract Bender.

If Bender thought Jordan was returning, he – please, God – would focus his attention on that, and not on Ava.

He didn't want to give him time to focus on Ava. He'd seen what Bender's focus could do.

He crept through the kitchen, feet bare, eyes seeking, and noted the spilled contents of Ava's purse on the table. Her phone, her twenty-two were both missing. So Bender was almost certainly armed.

Had he used the twenty-two to disarm Ava? Or did the bastard use his knife?

Dropping into a crouch, Jordan duck-walked toward the bedroom, using the living room furniture as cover.

Come on, you little prick, Jordan thought as he edged closer to the door. Come out where I can see you. But the bedroom remained silent.

Sweet God, he considered as his throat worked, as every muscle in his body tensed. Had he miscalculated, horribly? Had he simply pushed Bender into doing the unthinkable?

But then he heard it, that low murmur that made fear crescendo even as his heart sang. "I won't let you hurt him."

And the answering snort. "Like you have a choice."

When she let out a muffled scream, trying to warn him "Jordan, don't –" he burst into the room, coming in low, as a shot splintered the doorframe. Ava and Bender grappled for the gun. Keeping his movements short and tight, Jordan managed to grab the gun and pull until Bender stumbled toward him. With a twist of the wrist the gun fell to the ground, spinning out of sight.

But Bender was quick. He had Ava pulled tight against him, knife to her throat. "Don't think I won't do it." His voice was shaky, but his eyes were calm.

"I know you will." Jordan kept his eyes on Bender's, because looking at Ava would be a distraction he couldn't afford.

Her arms and stomach were bare, her bra torn.

If he thought about that, he'd go crazy.

So he focused in on Bender. He had a good five inches, probably thirty pounds on the younger man, but he knew better than to underestimate an opponent because of his size. Not to mention he wasn't sure where the twenty-two might be. He had to assume Bender had Ava's gun. And more importantly, he had Ava.

And nothing left to lose.

"What did you do?" Bender angled his head. "Throw a rock on the stairs so I'd think you were coming in the front?"

"Brick," Jordan said, moving a little closer. He needed Bender to focus on him.

"Ah." The kid nodded. "You take one more step, my knife might slip. What tipped you off?" he continued.

"Found your van." Jordan shifted. Put his weight on the balls of his feet. "Storm knocked a tree limb down, so I left my car on the street and cut through the alley. And I wondered, why would Bender be parked here? Then I remembered something Sonya Kuosman's fiancé said about their broken window, and how Mackenzie's Wright's car was vandalized. Basic deduction."

"Wow." Bender eased toward the corner, tightening his grip on Ava. "How's that for my bad luck? Or your good luck, depending on your viewpoint."

"Serendipity," Jordan agreed. The kid was going for the gun on the floor. Maybe he hadn't kept the twenty-two on him. "I seem to be having a streak."

"Well, I hate to break your run, but you do realize I can't let you and your girlfriend live."

"If you hurt her, I'll kill you."

Jordan could see that his matter-of-fact tone struck home. "I'm sure you could try." But the kid looked less sure of himself. Until he angled his head again. "You know what's missing here? Sirens. Surely you called the police."

"Thinking your uncle will save you?" Jordan moved forward as Bender moved back. "Or," he thought of what he'd learned about the killer from Clay's profile "maybe you want him here, so he can realize what a fool you've made of him. It would have been so much easier for you to pop me on the street. Or when I was running in the park. Anywhere, really. But you had to draw me out, prove how clever you were, didn't you? Had to set it up like a little game. Well guess what, Robert. Ava there?" He risked a glance. Was relieved to see what he needed to in her eyes. "She's a material witness for the FBI, so turns out I called the feds. And more than that, she's not the kind of woman who's just going to lie down when someone grabs her. Elbow."

When he called it out, Ava pulled Bender's arm down, swung her hip out, and rammed her elbow into his knee. Surprised by the attack, Bender lost his grip on the knife and she turned inward, kneeing him in the head.

Swelling with pride, Jordan used his body like a battering ram and plowed Bender into the nightstand.

Something shattered. Ava screamed and Jordan rolled so that she could scramble away from the tangle of limbs. The kid brought his knee up, catching Jordan in the groin. But he blinked through the pain and smashed his fist into Bender's face.

"You little son of a bitch." He heard more than felt the crunch of bone on bone. "I'm going to kill you with my bare hands."

"Don't call me that. Don't call me that." Enraged, his mouth bleeding, Bender stretched his arm out to reach for the knife.

"Think again." Ava kicked it away with her foot, and pointed Jordan's Glock at Bender's head.

When Jordan rammed his fist into Bender again, and again – because let's face it, it felt damn good – his arm was grabbed from behind, his brother's voice sounding in his ear. "Stop.

Jordan, stop. I know it's tempting, but you can't kill him. The nice officers behind me might object. And, um, Ava?"

Jordan looked up, met Ava's eyes before she shifted them toward Jesse. "I'm Agent Wellington. Jesse. Nice to meet you. And I'd really like it if you'd hand me your weapon. Butt first. That's the way. And I believe this shirt belongs to you."

Her hand started shaking after Jesse took the gun. And her eyes were wide when she looked at Jordan. "Elbow." She lifted it up.

And despite everything, Jordan laughed.

EPILOGUE

"LET me take that," Jordan cajoled, and grabbed the empty casserole dish in his wife's hands. "There are enough able bodied people here to help clear the table. You should be sitting down."

Ava frowned, and tugged on the dish. "I may look like a beached whale," she said testily. "But I'm perfectly capable of standing on my own two feet."

Jordan grinned. Was she ever. He'd never met a person so adept at taking whatever curves life pitched, and batting them back like a champ.

"I know that, honey." He shifted, cagily snagging the dish – a remnant from the New Year's dinner they'd just enjoyed with the rest of the growing Wellington family – and dropped his free hand to her rounded belly. "But there are two little people inside you almost ready to come out. No one's going to confuse you with Shamu if you let the rest of us clean up."

"You're lucky I can't see my feet, or I'd plant one on your ass."

"I'm lucky, period." He dropped a kiss on her lips.

"Nice save," she said against his mouth.

"I thought so." When she wound her arms around his neck, he slid deeper into the kiss than he'd intended.

"Get a room," Jordan's younger brother Justin suggested as he walked by with an armload of plates.

Still wrapped up in his wife, Jordan's free hand connected to his brother's biceps.

"Ouch!" Justin nearly bobbled the plates. "Hey, I'm back on call in a few hours. Don't mess with the arm that wields the scalpel."

Jordan smiled into Ava's eyes as his brother walked away. "Go sit down," he coaxed again, and she reluctantly acquiesced.

As he watched her waddle – walk, he corrected, somewhat desperately. She'd scalp him if she knew he'd even thought the other word – toward his parent's family room, he contemplated his incredible good fortune.

Last month they'd watched her father deliver testimony that had resulted in Carlos Martinez being sentenced to several life sentences. His empire had crumpled around him like a house of cards, brought down at the hands of the brother he'd betrayed. Ava's father's testimony had earned him a plea bargain that would considerably shorten his time in prison, giving him hope that with good behavior he'd be paroled in time to get to know his grandchildren.

Lorena Martinez's body had been positively identified, and buried with due respect and ceremony in the cemetery near the church where she'd been abducted. Ava had handled the entire thing with remarkable composure, clutching her mother's rosary in one hand, the other tucked into Jordan's. She'd been surrounded by her friends and his family – her family now – for the kind of support that still brought a tear to his wife's eye when she thought no one was looking.

Robert Bender sat in jail awaiting trial.

Jordan tried to feel sympathetic instead of vindicated whenever he came across Jeff Simpson – after all, the Internal Affairs investigation had shown that the man had neither tampered with evidence nor had any inkling what his nephew was up to – but really, he was only human, and Simpson had behaved like an ass.

"Are you going to stand there all night, son, or are you going to take that dish into the kitchen?"

Jordan snapped out of his reverie with a start, then smiled at his father, patiently waiting for Jordan to quit blocking the doorway. "Sorry. Just taking a moment to appreciate the scenery."

Tom followed his son's gaze toward the family room, where Ava sat near the fireplace, hands draped protectively over her abdomen. The fifty degree weather hardly warranted the crackling fire in the hearth, but she looked so beatific sitting there, smiling at little Grace, that Jordan felt warm all over. He'd build her a dozen fires if she wanted them.

"Are you ready?"

Jordan understood that his father was talking about his impending fatherhood, as opposed to making his way to the kitchen. He took a deep – and admittedly shaky – breath. "As

I'll ever be." He cast a questioning gaze toward his dad. "Were you scared when Mom was this close to her due date with Jack?"

"Shitless," Tom said succinctly.

Jordan laughed. It was exactly what he needed to hear.

His gaze drifted back toward Ava. While neither of them had expected their first joking discussion about fertility to have... well, already taken root, so to speak, they'd been ecstatic after the shock had finally worn off. They both wanted a family, the kind two people nurtured until it grew and blossomed, ripe with love.

They had a bumper crop of love.

And speaking of bumper crops, he mused, as his father clapped him on the shoulder and moved past him. He supposed it would be time soon to start thinking about that little garden he and Ava had talked about planting. On the little farm they seem to have bought. Fresh vegetables for lasagna, plenty of room for the animals to roam, and good, messy dirt for their children to dig in when they got a little older.

And three bathtubs to house frogs.

"Oh." Ava looked up, startled, and pressed a hand to her back.

The casserole dish slipped out of Jordan's hands and shattered. "It's time?"

"I think so."

She met his eyes as other members of his family rushed in to see what had happened, happy chaos erupting when everyone realized the babies had decided it was time to join the fun. And instead of the nerves he'd been expecting, Jordan discovered that what he felt was excitement.

"They're a little early," Ava said, almost apologetically as he quickly crossed the room.

He took her hands and helped ease her from the chair. A new year, a new start. Two new lives.

"That's okay." He leaned down and kissed his wife. "We're ready."

Thanks for reading! Connect with me online at:
www.lisaclarkoneill.com
Facebook: Lisa-Clark-ONeill-Novelist
Twitter: LisaClarkONeill

And here's a sneak peak at Forbidden, the next book in this series, featuring FBI Special Agent Clay Copeland...

CHAPTER ONE

July 15, Present

JANIE Collier was hot, tired, and mad at the world.

Running away from home wasn't supposed to be so hard, but getting out of Charleston on foot in ninety degree heat proved to be more of an undertaking than she'd initially guessed. The asphalt was so hot that her sneakers sank into it, and about every fifth step one or the other of them threatened to come off. They were too damn big, anyway, because they were hand-me-downs from her sister.

Her stupid older sister who'd had to go and get herself knocked up.

Why the hell hadn't she listened when Daddy had told her that the Lawrence boy was no good? Hell, anybody with eyes could see Danny was only slumming when he asked her to go out cruisin'. Her older sister had a body like one of them centerfolds Daddy was always looking at, and that's the only reason Danny Lawrence had shown the least bit of interest. Rich boys like him weren't in the habit of making girlfriends out of poor white trash. Danny didn't even come inside the trailer when he picked Joelle up. He just sat in his Mustang and beeped the horn, like he was too damn good to dirty his expensive Nikes by setting foot in their home.

And wouldn't you know it? Daddy's prophecy had come true.

Danny Lawrence had gotten in her sister's pants one time too many, but now that she was pregnant he was nowhere to be found. His parents had sent him off to visit some relative for the summer. His daddy, a lawyer, had threatened to sue Janie and Joelle's daddy if he ever laid a finger on his boy. Since Janie and Joelle's daddy was a drunk, he hadn't had the good sense to listen: he'd attacked Mr. Lawrence at his high-falutin' home one night, demanding that Danny own up to his bastard.

Consequently, Danny had left the state, her daddy was in jail, and the child welfare people had been swarming over her and Joelle like flies.

Joelle, who was six months gone, was in a home for unwed mothers, and she – Janie – had just run away from her third foster home.

Not like those idiots were going to miss her. The wife had been okay, but her lard-ass husband looked at her in a way that made her feel like she'd come down with chiggers.

So she'd hightailed it out of there before Fat Hubby had decided to take those gropes-disguised-as-hugs to the next level. She was experienced enough to know exactly what the bastard wanted, and while she was no virgin, she preferred to pick and choose her partners. And if she chose wisely, she might be able to earn enough money to take the bus.

Janie shivered despite the heat.

Sweat trickled off the back of her neck, running down into her cotton panties, where little bumps of heat rash popped up like chicken skin. Looking at the road sign she'd just passed, Janie saw that she'd traveled approximately ten miles out of the city. At this rate, she'd turn fifteen before she made it to Florida.

Janie sighed, blowing out a breath that ruffled her sweat-damp bangs. She needed some shade, she needed some water, she needed somebody with *wheels*.

Coming upon a massive live oak, Janie dragged herself to the side of the road and sagged against the trunk. There was a fruit stand maybe a mile or two down the highway, and if she could just make it there she could buy herself an apple and a nice, cold drink out of the cooler. She'd love to have one of their cherry sodas, but she figured she'd better stick to water so she didn't get dehydrated. They'd studied that in health class last year, so she knew all about things like blood sugar and hydration. For the most part, school seemed like a huge waste of time, but she had to admit she liked learning about the body.

Maybe she'd go to college one day, become a nurse.

But first she had to get to Florida.

Janie pushed away from the tree and tried to convince her rubbery legs to move. She'd just about talked them into it when a car pulled alongside her. Warily, she looked it over – a dark-colored foreign job, one of those BMWs, she thought – as the man driving it lowered the window.

"Sugar you're not out here walking in this heat, are you?"

He looked to be about thirty-something, maybe a little older. She really wasn't the best judge of age. He was jacked and kind of handsome for an old guy, but that didn't mean she could trust him. After all, Danny Lawrence was handsome, and look what a crock of shit he turned out to be.

He turned in his seat to pull a soda bottle from a bag beside him, then extended it through the open window. "You look like you could use something cool to drink."

Janie hesitated, because she didn't know this guy from Adam. Just because he didn't look like a perv didn't mean he wasn't. She took in the expensive-looking watch on his wrist, the glint of gold on his ring finger.

He seemed okay, but still…

"Just take the soda, sugar. I promise I'm not going to bite." When she still didn't move, he held up his cell phone. "Is there somebody I can call to come pick you up? I bet your parents wouldn't be too happy about you walking down the highway all alone. I know I sure wouldn't."

"You have kids?" she asked, cautiously inching closer. He really did seem okay, and she was so thirsty.

"Just one," he admitted with a proud smile. "A little boy. And his mama would have my hide if she thought I passed you by without offering to help." He waved first the bottle, then the cell phone. "Would you like a drink, or would you like me to make a call?"

"There's no one to call." Janie accepted the beverage. "I'm on my way to visit my cousin in Florida, and I'm afraid if I call first, she won't let me come." Unscrewing the cap from the bottle, she upended and nearly drained it.

"Well Florida's a bit farther than I intended to go. But if you'd like, I can give you a ride down to Beaufort. Although if you ask me, I still think you should call your cousin."

"No." She shook her head, trying to decide what to do. She was hot and sweaty and exhausted, and the air conditioning seeping out his open window made her want to dive in. Hitching a ride to Beaufort might not be such a bad idea. Swaying a little,

Janie thought the heat must really be getting to her, because when she looked down the deserted road the pavement seemed to move in waves.

Before she knew what was happening, the man was helping her into the backseat. "Easy, there. You look like you might be having a little trouble. Why don't you just lie down and rest, and I'll wake you when we get where we're going."

She was conscious of him tucking her feet into the car, tossing the small backpack she'd been carrying in beside her.

Then the door closed with a muffled thud, and she wasn't conscious of anything at all.

CPSIA information can be obtained at www.ICGtesting.com
Printed in the USA
LVOW10s1820200813

348821LV00019B/972/P